THE LIVING AND THE DEAD

Patrick White was born in England in 1912, when his parents were in Europe for two years; at six months he was taken back to Australia, where his father owned a sheep station. At the age of thirteen he was sent to school in England, to Cheltenham, 'where, it was understood, the climate would be temperate and a colonial acceptable'. Neither proved true, and after four rather miserable years there he went to King's College, Cambridge, where he specialized in languages. After leaving the university he settled in London, determined to become a writer. His first novel, *Happy Valley*, was published in 1939 and his second, *The Living and the Dead*, in 1941. During the war he was an RAF Intelligence Officer in the Middle East and Greece. After the war he returned to Australia.

His other novels are *The Aunt's Story* (1946), *The Tree of Man* (1956), *Voss* (1957), *Riders in the Chariot* (1961), *The Solid Mandala* (1966), *The Vivisector* (1970), *The Eye of the Storm* (1973), *A Fringe of Leaves* (1976) and *The Twyborn Affair* (1979). In addition he published two collections of short stories, *The Burnt Ones* (1964) and *The Cockatoos* (1974), which incorporates several short novels, the collection of novellas, *Three Uneasy Pieces* (1987), and his autobiography, *Flaws in the Glass* (1981). He also edited *Memoirs of Many in One* (1986). In 1973 he was awarded the Nobel Prize for Literature.

Patrick White died in September 1990. In a tribute to him *The Times* wrote, 'Patrick White did more than any other writer to put Australian literature on the international map . . . his tormented *oeuvre* is that of a great and essentially modern writer.'

Patrick White

The Living and the Dead

Penguin Books

PENGUIN BOOKS

Published by the Penguin Group
Penguin Books Ltd, 27 Wrights Lane, London W8 5TZ, England
Penguin Books USA Inc., 375 Hudson Street, New York, New York 10014, USA
Penguin Books Australia Ltd, Ringwood, Victoria, Australia
Penguin Books Canada Ltd, 10 Alcorn Avenue, Toronto, Ontario, Canada M4V 3B2
Penguin Books (NZ) Ltd, 182–190 Wairau Road, Auckland 10, New Zealand

Penguin Books Ltd, Registered Offices: Harmondsworth, Middlesex, England

First published in the United States of America by
The Viking Press 1941
First published in Canada by The Macmillan Company
of Canada Limited 1941
First published in Great Britain by
Routledge & Kegan Paul 1941
Published in Penguin Books 1967
10 9 8 7

Printed in England by Clays Ltd, St Ives plc
Set in Monotype Bembo

Je te mets sous la garde du plaisir et de la douleur; l'un et l'autre veilleront à tes pensées, à tes actions; engendreront tes passions, exciteront tes aversions, tes amitiés, tes tendresses, tes fureurs; allumeront tes désirs, tes craintes, tes espérances; te dévoileront des vérités, te plongeront dans des erreurs; et après t'avoir fait enfanter mille systèmes absurdes et différents de morale et de législation, te découvriront un jour les principes simples, au développement desquels sont attachés l'ordre et le bonheur du monde moral.

HELVÉTIUS

Part One

I

Outside the station, people settled down again to being emotionally commonplace. There was very little to distinguish the individual feature in the flow of faces. Certainly it was night, but even where a wave of neon washed across the human element, it uncovered no particular secret, just the uniform white, square or oblong, tinged for a moment with the feverish tones of red or violet. In the same way his ears took sound, but selected no predominant note out of the confused stream, taxis unsticking their tyres from the wet surface of the street, the rumbling of the buses. All this was so much prevalent, and yet irrelevant sound. Like the drifting faces, a dim, surrounding presence, almost dependent on his train of thought for its existence there in the darkness. It was better like this, he felt, escaped only a couple of minutes from the too intimate glimpses, the emotional sharps of the railway platform. It was better to swim in the confused sea that was anybody's London. The personal was eclipsed by Eden's face that last moment on the strip of receding train.

Elyot Standish bumped his way through the crowd outside Victoria. The light that touched him, the street lights that have no respect for the personal existence, shaved his face down to the bones, left it with the expression of the street faces. The sockets of his eyes were dark. Two empty saucers in the bone. He remembered the face of the German woman, moments earlier on the platform, resting on her husband's shoulder in a last unseeing embrace. Or rather, you were drawn beyond the eyes of the little German Jewess into a region where the present dissolved, its forms and purpose, became a shapeless, directionless well of fear.

I expect Julia will have gone, Eden said hurriedly.

He heard the quick gathering of her voice, the determined planting of her feet on the platform as she drew him with her into the world of trivial incident, and the things you talked about before the train moved out.

But I told her to leave some bread and cheese, she said. You'll find it in the kitchen. Some bread and cheese.

As if he didn't know. But railway stations were like that. The trivial came into its own. It assumed importance in a white light.

You'll send me a postcard from Paris, he said.

It was really his own voice, but flat and stupid, unbearably banal. From Paris they retreated. It was on the way to the reason for Eden's going. The retreat was a move they both accepted. She began to talk about the weather, what kind of Channel to expect. She remembered the winter she crossed with Adelaide, and Adelaide was sick in her own hat. That made him laugh. Then he grew ashamed. For it corresponded so distantly with what he felt, that shapeless abyss between his lungs and his stomach. He wondered if he should take her hand, but, wondering, decided not. Even if they were not Eden's hands, dressed up for the occasion in a pair of old black gloves. He supposed he would never understand the motive behind the wearing of the gloves, why Eden, with her hatred, her fear of convention, had dug up a pair of old black gloves to leave London in. His mouth moved towards a question. It took courage from a moment earlier that evening, when for the first time in his life he had approached his sister without explicit words. But even this, remembered, could not launch him in pursuit of the motive behind the gloves. He failed, deliberately. Because this was something he must not touch on. It was one of the secret places, of which Eden's life was full.

And then it was time to get into the train. Then it was that quick succession of last moments, and the smell of apples and a magazine, and the voices calling through the yawning of a train, and the faces, and the faces, and the faces. She stood at the window and waved. A short, nervous, jerky wave. Because they had always been a bit ashamed of any gesture they spent upon each other. He noticed that one of her fingers was showing white through the black glove, before this became a speck on the lost hands, before her white face was withdrawing down an infinite tunnel of yellow fog. The little Jewess stood with a purposeless handkerchief. She held it crumpled against her cheek. With the train, the man turned back into Europe on what errand?

Elyot wandered in the street, homeward in fact, but in a sense directionless, on his own train of thought. He would never know the nature of this Jewish errand, the importance of which had dwindled with Eden's face. He would never fit a motive to the black gloves. These were threads from the so many threads of the mystery you had to accept. And in the streets at night, with the interweaving of passionless faces, the passage of the stolid buses, the downward falling of a steady neon rain, it was easy enough to accept. The whole business was either a mystery, or else meaningless, and of the two, the meaningless is the more difficult to take.

The street he walked stood in anachronistic silence. He was going home. Near in space, it still wore the distant expression, presented the vague purpose of familiar places that have been jerked out of their setting by an emotional upheaval. Even if here stood the pub on the corner with one queasy drunk swaying at the kerb, even if your legs had turned this corner many times, the eyes rested on a series of identical queasy drunks, it was unconvincing, the present version with the past, something that your mind could only take for granted. Detail was soluble in rain. He might have been merged with the drunk, fumbling now in his pocket for the bus fare or else the price of another drink, wondering feebly at the back of those yellow eyeballs if he was really going to vomit, or fall, just fall, into a receptive gutter.

Elyot stood on the kerb. He had time, all time in a dissolved world to watch many deliberating drunks. But absorbed, he was still no closer to the grease-spotted macintosh and sagging hat. The night dissolved without bringing you closer. Either to Eden, in spite of a chance moment of illumination, or to the excess humanity spewed out of pub doors. It was a remoteness once alarming, then inevitably accepted. He closed himself to sentimental regret, and felt with satisfaction the drizzle on his face, because with it a sense of still being there, the bones and flesh, heading homeward to bricks and mortar, and bread and cheese in the kitchen.

The drunk had ventured out from the corner, following the line of some imaginary tightrope. He moaned a little, and looked at Elyot, conscious perhaps in the way of the drunk or mad, that some transient thought was resting on him. But there was no contact. He meandered into the street, not so much man as the clown upon his tightrope, a flapping of empty sleeve and hollow leg. And then just at this moment, the moment before, Elyot realized it would happen, he must move from this fixed spot, at once, quickly, associate himself with the anonymous figure, that it was for this purpose they had lingered close to each other on the pavement. Because he could see it, the bus, ballooning down by lamplight, very red and ominous. The whole side of the street came careening over into his close vicinity. I must do this, his mind shouted, tossed out into the screaming of the bus. The lights spun. The whole neighbourhood moved. Except his feet. He was anchored where he stood. He was the audience to a piece of distant pantomime.

They put the macintosh on the pavement. The legs protruded stupidly, the turned-up soles, round them a sudden flowering of pale, uneasy faces. First and foremost this was an accident, an additional throb to be felt over the fish and chips or the last glass of stout.

What do you know! the driver said.

He was shaken. Down on the pavement he began to bluster. Because he was afraid.

Walkin' with his eyes shut, said the driver. And soused, into the bargain.

His hands shook.

Walking with his eyes shut. This has some connexion, Elyot felt vaguely, I am responsible for this. His feet were still lead, fixed to the same spot. He must drag himself into the circle of faces, associate with just such another face, flat on the pavement, that circumstance had lifted up and given a temporary distinction. He must advance and say – what?

Would you ever! said the woman with the newspaper twist. It was three months, come Easter, she had seen the milkman killed in Pimlico Road.

But 'e ain't dead. Or is 'e? she wondered.

Her head twitched in an ague of excited surmise.

They began to babble. A mingling of sympathy and pity, of ashamed exaltation, of practical advice. Elyot, advancing to the fence, saw, between craning necks, the thin trickle of blood from the corner of a mouth. It trickled out thin and private. No one had any business looking at this stream of blood. But there it was. And the man moaned in a disjointed way, as he had in drink, it might have been this still, the same obliviousness, detachment.

Out of the commanding of official voices, the blue police, rang an ambulance bell. The lips of the man blew in and out. On the blood a glitter of whitish froth. And I am standing here for what, you asked, for the buried moment, for that second of connexion on the kerb that broke too easily. You stood there, half attentive to the far-off voices, hushed now that the man was tucked on the stretcher, about to be carried away. It would soon be over. A keen spasm to be added to the sum total of everybody's individual sensation.

It was truly over, in the clanging of a bell.

Elyot Standish continued homeward, through the landscape of his own mind, through the remoter geography of Ebury Street. He had failed, in one of those moments of arrested initiative, to step off the pavement and rescue a drunk from a bus. He felt exhausted, sick. Intermittently he tried to seize on the significance of this incident, while coming to the conclusion, in defeat, that it was unimportant. The whole business was unimportant. It would join the regiment of unimportant events, the anonymous face fading on the wet pavement, Eden closing the compartment door, Elyot walking homeward up Ebury Street. Try as his conscience might to raise the dead, the dead continued to lie with folded hands. It was quite remote. But he continued to feel sick. Something had lodged itself in his stomach, forced downwards by the mind. And it was a struggle to keep it there.

Coming to the house he let himself in. There was no change in the ritual of this, the glance at the doorpost to see what damage dogs had done, as he skirted the milk-bottles left by Julia for the morning. This was going home. The drunk putting his hand in his pocket, searching under a handkerchief for his fare, was also going home. But your mind rejected this. The man perhaps was already dead. On the first floor Elyot turned on the light. It helped him retrieve himself from an avenue of too obtrusive images. But there still remained the house, in a white and honest light, in the corrosive silence of deserted houses.

You will find it in the kitchen, she had said.

He went on out obediently. There was a peculiar dead feeling in the house. At the moment he hadn't the power to restore a pretence of life. This had ebbed with the people who had lived there, the positive people, Eden, his mother, Julia Fallon. Sometimes he decided, in moments of uncomfortable honesty, that he began and ended with these positive lives, their presence or flight, that he had no actual life of his own. And tonight he was convinced, there in the kitchen, beside the symbols of the positive life. This may have ceased till morning, withdrawn in nightly anaesthesia, but its symbols remained, the apron on a chair-back, the cup with its pool of reddish tea, the old pair of blue satin mules that Julia wore about the house. Tomorrow I shall speak to Julia, Mrs Standish used to say, I shall speak, I shall say, firmly, but kindly of course, I shall settle the question of the mules. He heard his mother's voice, the outdistanced voice, and the voice of Eden that said the bread and cheese. Here, he said, is why. The bread and cheese. There was something solid, soothing about the yellow wedge. Only to look at this. He was not hungry. Automatically he bit a piece he had broken off. There was a soapy flavour of cheap cheese. Because, said Julia, it's the end of the week. Her words, her hands were as stolid as yellow cheese.

Since she came to them before the War, Julia had woven her own theme in and out of their concerted lives. It was never obtrusive. Sometimes it lost itself, lapsed for sulky, sultry days, to recur in its inevitable undertone. She had all the intuition and lack of rational understanding of the attached servant. Events in other parts of the household elated or depressed her as a matter of course. As Mrs Standish once said, Julia is a thermometer of everything I wish I didn't feel.

At night when she left for Clerkenwell, where she boarded with an aunt, Julia lingered, perceptibly, in the objects she had touched. There was a correspondence between Julia and the form of the yellow table, more than an echo in the cheap alarm clock. In the ticking, creaking, groaning night-life of the deserted kitchen, the old depressed house shoes carried on a deputy generalship.

Elyot was glad of this. It had grown cold. But the presence of Julia Fallon had restored the circulation to the house, was already a suggestion of the morning, the clinking of the milk-bottles that he could hear from his own room. Only, to remember the morning was to remember many mornings, was to pause. He left the kitchen abruptly and started up. He heard his own footsteps muffled on the stairs. He would go upstairs and sleep. In the morning he would work. On many mornings. Elyot, are you working? his mother called, exasperating him to the point where he ground his ears with his hands, because she knew from the experience of years that he closed his door after breakfast for one purpose. But this was part of the scheme of his mother's morning, to stand on the first floor landing and call to the top of the house. Often he refused to hear. He left the voice to ramble, a voice without purpose on the stairs. Once he had seen her standing vaguely, hand to chin, the sleeve drooping downward from an arm, as if she were listening for a lost voice, or wondering, trying to trace her own purpose on the stairs.

Of all the mute voices in the deserted house, his mother's was the most persistent, he felt, going into the drawing-room. Perhaps because she had made it, an interior shaped and reshaped, the way a room can receive the imprint of its owner's life, even the first warning of death. The house, and particularly this room, had become almost the sole visible purpose of Mrs Standish's existence. And it continued to live in the inconclusive way of the houses of the dead, defying any of his own personal conclusions that he had brought in with him from the station, from the accident in the street. Already he was drifting in a half-resentful, half-reassured lethargy, with the many themes that the house offered; these had lapsed only on his first opening the door. So much bric-à-brac, he tried to say, to pacify a latent inclination for the functional. But it was also his mother, the pretty and mostly useless objects that she brought home with the passion of a bower bird. Mrs Standish making her room. Mrs Standish sitting in the Louis XV *bergère* she had picked up cheap in the King's Road, cutting a French novel that she probably wouldn't read. It was the sort of thing that Eden had deplored, a concentration on upholstery, but Eden slamming the door in fury, running upstairs with white lips, had never deterred Mrs Standish from putting one more coat of gilt between herself and the humdrum side of living. She went and bought the peacock's feathers, she bought the goblet with the silver penny, she bought the little jewelled box that still stood on a corner table, accumulating verdigris where amethysts had been.

I exasperate my children, said Mrs Standish, expectant as a martyr. The exasperation remained, and helplessness, even after her death, not lessened by loss. Critical, you despised yourself, while adopting the consolation that affection allows criticism, that criticism only exists in an interested relationship. Irritation renewed itself, even now, at sight of her photographs in her own room. There was the picture of the girl in the little sealskin cap and tippet, the hands hidden in a muff to match, a bright, button-eyed face, almost too eager for its frame. And there was the later and more sophisticated version, melancholy in draped chiffon. Defending these photographs with irony in her lifetime, Mrs Standish had secretly enjoyed the spectacle of herself. Dying, the irony had died with her. But the satisfaction remained, overflowing with their subjects from the frames.

It was bourgeois to put photographs in rooms, Eden had said, about the age one said that kind of thing. He remembered it, oddly, the occasion, they were sitting at lunch, they were eating hot corned beef and dumplings, he remembered also his mother's reply: No doubt it's bourgeois to eat corned beef and dumplings, they smell, but I like them, I think I even like the smell. It was the kind of remark that threw him for the moment into alliance with his mother, in an age of alliances, how long before the train door closed and he watched the waving of a black glove. This is my sister, he had once said of a child in a white dress at a country party. Then he looked at her sideways. He resented her, as a small but fierce searchlight on many moments that he wanted hidden. As a relationship, it was like that. It was full of sullen, unshared, misunderstood passions. Looking at the picture of Eden on the drawing-room wall, she became the surprised child of a period earlier than the party dress. He remembered coming into the room, seeing her reading a book, seeing her turn, close up the book, and blush. Nothing was said. There was seldom very much said. You continued on different paths in the same wood. In time she was the sulky flapper, who also stared, in the bourgeois convention, out of the drawing-room wall. In the evening she closed her door on a typewriter and cigarettes.

Giving himself to the past, he wanted to get away, it was suddenly too pungent, like the vase of week-old anemones that shrivelled beside the amethyst box. He listened to Eden break the stalks. She had bought them in the street, she said, off a barrow in Pimlico. Her hands coped with the angles of their stalks. She sat with her face in her hands at dusk. She sat beside anemones. These, still huddled in their brittle frills, were not quite dead. They rustled like a kind of *immortelle*. They wore the intense, the used-up expression of Eden's face, persistent in a struggle against conventional procedure.

I have bought some lilies, said Mrs Standish, we must have a party, lilies and people, and what shall we have to eat? The excitement of his mother's voice, refreshed by an inspiration, as it came in on a September evening. Eden's groan. He stood on the edge himself, fingering the leaf of an interceding lily, never able to participate with any degree of conviction, in the smoke, in the scent, in the composite voice of his mother's parties. These had their relics too, if not the substantial ones of bric-à-brac or photograph. His toe touched the patch of *crème de menthe* spilt by the nervous Connie Tiarks. It lay upon the carpet like a chart of all the anxious moments at all parties.

Outside in the street the sound of traffic pointed to a less familiar present, that the house, that his mother's voice rose up to deny, her: Elyot, Adelaide is here, or: Do come in for a moment, Elyot, this is Mr Collins, he plays in a band, isn't that interesting? Even Eden's train had rumbled into a lumber room of images, where Joe Barnett sat in a corner, looking at his cap, his hands, his knees, and Muriel Raphael in a Tissot boater leant against the mantelpiece. It was so easy to substitute the dead for the living, to build a cocoon of experience away from the noises in the street. Like the old women in private hotels, the old women in Bayswater, Kensington, and Holland Park. This is what I am doing, he said, deliberately killing the noises in the street. Or the man, the drunk with the grey face scored suddenly with blood.

A face returned, to insist, to make some contact in a foreign world, from which you had purposely excluded it, out of an unwilling mind. It filled the half-lit, fireless room. Very close, he could have touched a face. He waited for the words he would not speak, because these were the words you never spoke, there was never any means of communication with the faces in the street. He continued to sit on the edge. Or he closed his door in the morning, he began to work, there were also the visits to museum and to library, which amounted in time to so many reverent comments on the literary achievements of the dead, and as much correct approval from the Sunday press. The *devotion* of Mr Standish to letters was the devotion of a single mind, it had been said. A devotion to the dust. My son is a scholar, said Mrs Standish, with the tactlessness that only a mother can be guilty of. And now his mother was so much dust, along with the other objects of this time-absorbing reverence.

He stirred inside his lethargy. Somewhere on a slab perhaps they had laid the queasy legs. But the face drifted behind his own, its lips blowing outward on unshaped words, trying to resist the shapelessness. It was this after all that every one of them had tried to do, his mother building her bright room, Eden taking the train into Europe, the Connie Tiarkses and the Joe Barnetts, each with a nervous but convinced contribution towards the business of living. Putting up a structure in the face of shapelessness, building, if not in brick or stone, a resistance to annihilation. And it was on this justification that the remote face on the pavement asked for admission, his theme as urgent as the others that wove and interwove through the empty house. This was a receptacle. They were two receptacles, he felt, the one containing the material possessions of those who had lingered in its rooms, the other the aspirations of those he had come in contact with. Even that emotional life he had not experienced himself, but sensed, seemed somehow to have grown explicit. It was as if this emanated from the walls to find interpretation and shelter in his mind. So that the two receptacles were clearly united now. They were like two Chinese boxes, one inside the other, leading to an infinity of other boxes, to an infinity of purpose. Alone, he was yet not alone, uniting as he did the themes of so many other lives.

2

Kitty Goose stepped down into the street. She could not pull too hard at a hesitant door, almost jerking from its socket either knob or arm. It was the weal in the hall linoleum that made the eye water, the breath catch. She suspected a burst shoulder seam. This before the rush, the bang of released door, that cleared the mind of anxiety, and set the ship knocker from Yarmouth dancing on its sea of brass. There was frost in the street, a thin, white fur, on the puddles a coat of gelatinous ice that snapped too loudly underfoot. This all added to the tension, of course, the sharp, frosty air tautening her hands, rolled already inside the muff into a nervous ball. Back there, she knew, they were watching, would have seen, on turning the head, the forms of the two Miss Spaldings, stiff as the parlour furniture, black and upright as horsehair chairs, and about as charitable as these. It was too much, the emotional parsimony of the two Miss Spaldings, just when you were ready to give more than you possessed. At least you could have offered the breath that was bursting in your lungs, the words that were waiting for expression in your mouth. But the street was unappreciative, if not exactly blind. Over the way a Mrs Hicks slowly wiped at a dusty plant. Kitty Goose composed her face to meet the world's inquiring eye.

Kitty Goose, Kitty Goose, she repeated over and over again. This was a habit that she had when happy, finding some satisfaction in the abstraction of her own name, or else attaching to this a string of vague but stupendous future events. She shaped her name in a half-chant, not loud enough for windows. She walked down the street with all the emphasized carelessness that goes with a secret and important errand.

It is two, three hundred yards, she said, trying not to run. Two, three hundred yards beyond the shop, beyond the blacksmith's, to the open mouth of the lane and the one elm, with its crown of cold, deserted nests. She listened to her footsteps deepen in tone as they passed the biscuit-coloured church, from which came an echo of Sunday school. Behind the frosty window of the shop, the barley sugar and acid drops pooled their colour, became a blur. And then by some dispensation she was in the lane, where the wind blew cold but unfelt between thorns, and a cluster of scarlet bryony clung to its withered navel-string. Now her face could take its natural line, now her arms could take possession of their separate wills, one hand pulling at a blade of grass, the other non-existent in the swinging muff.

Kitty Goose marched with a definite purpose, even though it was before its time. Better to wait in the lane than smoothing your gloves on the edge of the bed, elation falling as you caught your face in the glass. Better too, as she said, and he agreed, to meet at the corner than in the street. Because, she said. And he agreed again. He could come at three with the dog-cart, where the lane met the main road. Now from the safety of her own mind, she received the dog-cart at the front door, kept it waiting for a moment or two after Miss Emmy Spalding's knock, then swept out arranging her furs. Why, Willy, she said, you're early, she said. And Mrs Hicks stopped dusting her plant, and the two Miss Spaldings stiffened, mahogany and horsehair, behind the parlour lace. A pity winter had eliminated the possibility of a boater. A pity also – There were a thousand pities, among them her lack of courage to receive Willy Standish in the main street. But her legs were water when she thought of this, except as a fantasy in her own mind.

Anyway, that sort of thing was silly, silly and unnecessary, but which she liked to indulge in from time to time. Like Turkish delight. She had made herself quite sick that Christmas, the queer, soft, pretty stuff in its wooden box, and the powdered sugar falling down her front. She sighed and pulled a blade of grass out of a brown hedge. It had the pleasing, dead, wet flavour of wet winter grass. She walked slower, chewing grass, her mind pitched back to the scent of summer and the first touching of hands in a greener grass. And now she was early, very early, she sighed. She stood at the corner and arranged her furs. The little imitation sealskin tippet and the muff to match that she had bought on an expedition to Oxford Street. She supposed, against her better nature, she was a creature of luxury, what with the sealskin tippet and the box of coloured Turkish delight. Red and yellow, like the lights of Oxford Street, these burned still, and the recollection of a visit, her first, with the play at the Lyceum, and a night in a hotel. It made you feel unsettled. It was all very well, the school, and the lectures, and the concerts and parties at the de Veres', all very well but – Against the hedge she tried positions, with muff, without. Because Elegance was a secret ambition. At night she lay with her hands above her head, so that her fingers, on waking, would look long, and interesting, and white.

This side of Kitty's nature was innate, not encouraged. Her mother was one of those women who accept the body more in theory than in practice, you supposed. Knowing Mrs Goose casually, you might have wondered in what abstract frame of mind she received the attentions of her husband. Nobody knew Mrs Goose very well, more than casually, in fact. She was seen in the background of her husband's shop, where the shop became back parlour, and finally developed into kitchen. Farther than this she seldom ventured, except to walk with her husband on Sundays near the Castle. You supposed that Mrs Goose led more than this rudimentary existence. But no clue ever encouraged you to guess. You sensed perhaps that there was something different, without just putting your finger on what this difference was.

Walking in the Sunday streets, it was the thickset, fiery Mr Goose who drew the public eye. The physical Mr Goose. Because he was one of the small, thick, muscular men who make a first impression that is almost purely physical. His back compelled you by its force. His voice rose from deep inside. But five minute's conversation with the face made you wonder how the body had withstood so long a contact with the mind. Some people thought Mr Goose was mad, others that he was a monster. Mrs Illingford-Greene, for one, who was told while buying a leash for her dog: To the privileged the poor are muck, to be scraped into heaps to hide their own. And his eyes, my dear, could have burnt me up. Mr Illingford-Greene, when told, turned to a different page in the paper and talked about these radicals, they weren't even worth the price of shot. But Goose continued in his own convictions, smouldering inside his shop, where the smell of fresh leather and the flash of buckles struck you, like the proprietor's eye, the moment you walked inside the door.

With his friends, or with his family, sitting in the yard on summer evenings, in the light through limes and a sound of ducks, the eyes of Mr Goose would dwindle to a pale distance at times. Thinking of her father, more often than not, Kitty thought of those distant eyes, very pale, and distant, and absorbed. They were the eyes of a mild man. The abstraction of a man. That was the trouble with Mr Goose. In spite of material evidence, he had almost ceased to exist. Except as a concentration of theory. Whipped into action by a sense of justice, he remained too selfless to exist as a man. His physical existence exhausted itself on rage at a social system and an economic lie.

Professionally, as a harness maker, they respected Mr Goose. In the dark shop below the Castle, there was a good display of harness, as well as the useless things you stocked to attract a Mrs Illingford-Greene. Mr Goose found satisfaction in his work. He liked to work with his hands. Because, he said, it relieved the mind. Working late, by lamplight, his stubbled head like a winter field, the more essential part of him would wander into fresh utopias, till his wife, or, if it were the end of the week, his daughter, would appear in the inner doorway, and say it was long past the time for him to come and eat.

His wife glanced often from the inner doorway or, when there was nobody there, came out to him in the shop. She would sit beside him, mending. Sometimes she would merely sit, to sit and offer the kind of remarks that fit no conversational pattern, the words of a deeply felt relationship. The dim, withdrawing Mrs Goose, handsome now, if you came to think, more individual too than the presence of her husband sometimes allowed, had an almost gothic line, sitting beside him in the shop. Her hair drooped from its knot into a gothic wave. Her hands were the shape of unbroken gothic stone. All the more incongruous beside the square, cracked hands, stained perpetually in the cracks by the dye and polish that he used, the mobile, muscular hands of Mr Goose. Perhaps her origin and childhood had shaped the hands of Mrs Goose. The Sundays sitting in a high pew listening to her father preach, when the mind, drifting, touched on a gothic shore, the more actual images in painted wood.

The daughter of an Anglican parson, sermons and rood screens made a background to her life. She did not question these. She was not the questioning sort. Meeting her husband by chance, in a farmyard where she had gone for eggs, and overhearing his remark that parsons were a perverse, prying, pillaging, hypocritical lot, she was at first decently shocked. And then, perhaps her own fallow moments during many sermons, perhaps the warm pissing of the milk against the metal buckets, as the farmer and his boys sat with their heads against the cows and milked, perhaps the hen-cluck and a scent of steaming nettles, made her accept the speaker's voice, if not the substance of his words.

Why, she said, coming forward, with surprising ease and a kind of timid conviction, there's as much good in parsons as, well, in anyone else.

This was the first and only critical remark Mrs Goose had thrown at her husband's system. Marrying out of her caste, and admittedly not the questioning sort, it was her habit to accept what her life had dealt her. She was also in love with her husband. There was no time over for any existence apart.

The closed circle of two people in love, people with whom you are intimately connected, in humdrum detail, the everyday routine, was one of the first mysteries that Kitty Goose had failed to solve. Suddenly coming into a room, to realize your own intrusion, that words couldn't deny. Sitting on the floor in the same room, playing with a doll, she would pause sometimes and sit up on her haunches, feel the distance that separated her from two present, yet oblivious beings. There was nothing you could do, say. There was no asking for an explanation of something you could only sense. You could only accept the diluted, even if real, affection that came to you from each of these absorbed beings. But separate, essentially apart. And it made her wonder sometimes, especially on wet days, humming and screwing her mouth into odd shapes against the shop-front glass.

Growing older, she accepted the situation and passed to more absorbing problems of her own. She began to read. She read poetry. She read the poetry of Swinburne, and William Morris, and Maurice Hewlett. She even wrote a little herself, especially on summer evenings when the ceiling of her low room felt lower, and the air sifting through the ivy leaves oppressed her with a sense of futility that was both delightful and sad. On these evenings she would come down late for supper, expecting to hear her mother say: Kitty, you look pale. She looked, she felt pale. She felt that somehow she must learn to suffer, the vague, indiscriminate, undetermined suffering of which there was indication in the verses that she read and almost understood. She was ready. She was waiting. If only there were some clue. Finding none, she began to express her discontent. She crammed her head with Swinburnian similes and wove them, on hot, passionate evenings, into verses of her own. Perhaps she was creative. She borrowed a life of Christina Rossetti out of the public library to study symptoms.

Treated with irony by her father, she pouted at first, then

slightly changed her tactics. Here, girl, he said, read these, you forget there's a belly as well as a soul. So she struggled, yawning, through works on socialism and economics, finding no immediate significance in her father's remark, but some pleasure in her martyrdom. And she was becoming, she suspected, an intellectual. She was *superior*. She walked down the shopping streets, and glanced sideways at the windows, at a reflection of herself with a play by Bernard Shaw beneath her arm. Altogether it made you feel free, emancipated, your foot firmer on the pavement, even if your voice faltered still talking to Mrs Illingford-Greene. And Saturday evenings with the S.A.L., which she joined as a matter of course, were an additional stimulus, if not the intended one.

If the Society for Art and Letters lived by intention rather than achievement, at least it was well patronized, a gathering of schoolmasters, older boys from the grammar school, and young bank clerks with Fabian ideals. They met in the houses of members, in parlours rarely used, in which an air of must and awkwardness prevailed for the first half-hour. The young men sat with their knees together, or their legs stuck out across the carpet. The girls arranged themselves, chin-on-hand, the earnest, muddy-skinned girls of the S.A.L. Existing nominally on conversation, coffee, and the exchanged book, it lasted in fact from the necessity for a group of people to unbend together in a room. The earnest conversation, the catchwords, the names, which Kitty Goose soon turned on as skilfully as any, all this was so much preliminary. But afterwards handing coffee, with the plates of biscuits, and the sponge fingers, standing in one of the long loose gowns that she had been wearing since she learnt to take an interest in herself, the young men gathered round her, the nervous schoolmasters, the awkward bank clerks, who jumped at the rattle of a spoon, who laughed before she finished a remark. And this was fun. Her laughter came in heady gusts. The moisture stood on the edges of her face, round her forehead, at the roots of her straying, reddish hair. She was a pretty girl. She had grace, a kind of self-critical dignity, and enough intelligence for strangers to credit her with more. But those who knew her disagreed over the capacity of this. When she grew older, when she had almost forgotten evenings in the front parlours with the S.A.L., the intellectual powers of Kitty Goose were always a subject for argument among those who called themselves her friends.

Not yet arrived at the age of dissection, she postured in imitation furs, in the lane from Little Swaffham, at the corner where the main road passed to Bulford, on a winter afternoon. She moved in a world of sense, the numb and grudging winter landscape that could not mould her to its cast of feature, on which her eye rested with pleasure, because beyond it she supplied details of her own. The tree with its sawing branches, the field with its conical mounds of dung dissolved gently in the mind of Kitty Goose. Beyond this, outline was a myth, gesture mechanical. She put up a hand to touch her hair, where it was combed up into its knot, straying in spite of this, into the air, against her hat, a strand advancing across her cheek as far as the corner of her mouth. I shall arrive, she felt, looking a fright. Her mouth tightened on this possibility. A sudden thudding of the heart, an enclosure of the winter landscape, the bark and stone. With her foot she kicked at a stone, lodged firmly in a patch of ice. Sunday, he said, they're not monsters, he said, and sooner or later – you must. Sooner or later he would come. If this was the Sunday. If she could hope that this was not the Sunday. If she could retreat behind the week. A small, bright bird offered a cynical eye from the hedge.

All the irritating details of her life conspired to meet her at just this moment. She felt very stupid, numb, extravagant in imitation furs. All her life, she had to admit, she had fumbled awkwardly, her mind groping in a maze of word and action. She heard her own giggle against the voices of parties. She felt her cheek blush for the arguments she had floundered in and lost. Kicking an unimpressed stone with her foot, she was above all a flounderer, this Kitty Goose, this irrelevant figure in a winter landscape. You're not unintelligent, Kitty;

it's time you thought to do something, Father said. He said it between mouthfuls of tea, giving it some thought, as if considering the possibilities of an individual. And she had accepted this, her potentialities as an individual, her intelligence, even pouting a little at what she thought was underestimation on her father's part. After all, she had read, or sat with many books. She had read Bernard Shaw. She knew what to say about Ibsen. Before an onslaught of November wind blew the hair adrift at the nape of her neck. Yes, it's time you thought to do something, he said. This again was before Little Swaffham. And now she had been there a year. Every morning she went to the school. She sat upright at her official table, she folded her hands among the copy-books, and smiled the kind of smile you smiled for small expectant village children whose noses ran. Humanity in the abstract was one thing. But the cold, running noses of small children, their stumpy hands, red and blue with the cold, and watering from chilblains, these froze the best intentions into the bright smile of condescending charity. Or sometimes it grew sweet, for she liked to win people, Kitty Goose, whether the eligible bank clerks of the S.A.L., or the small, snotty children of the elementary school at Little Swaffham. It gave her confidence.

Far from the schoolroom where she taught, in the channel between hedges, and a cold wind, a lack of confidence was what she regretted most. Regretted also the occasions when she had tossed her own momentary self-possession into the circle of pimply young men who jumped at the sound of a tea-spoon on its cup. The wind drove the spirit from her face, made the circulation dwindle in her toes. Willy, she said numbly. As if this would help. At three o'clock, she had said, if this was the Sunday, in the Swaffham lane. If she had stayed in her room, at least she could have cried, face down on the crocheted quilt made by Miss Emmy Spalding as a girl. It's a clean room, as you see, said Miss Emmy Spalding, showing her in that first day. We've had teachers before, said Miss Spalding, they was all very content. Miss Spalding then went out of the room leaving the teacher behind. She was a teacher, she told herself, with a little start of amazement, of fear, for she was no different in the glass, unchanged from the face that swept directionless on a wave of Swinburne in the room at home. And still directionless, the teacher in the lane, in spite of official mornings at a raised table watching her own superior hands underline in red ink, she was the blown grass in country lanes. On Sunday you'll come to tea, he said. Sooner or later. Father's all right, he said, it's Mother. Mrs Standish, she composed already in her head, Mrs Standish, I hope you won't mind, I hope you won't mind if Willy, you see it is like this, it is like this, it is like. If Willy could hold her hand. If you could write the necessary on a pad and offer it between smiles, avoid the pitfalls of a trembling voice. Kitty, he said, it's all right, we're as good as married, he said, this is one of those formalities, they mean nothing, but after all. But after all, she was a schoolteacher, she was the daughter of Edwin Goose, a free-thinking, socialist, Norwich harness maker, she was an object for condescension, in spite of the theories her father taught, which were all very well for the kitchen at home, for the intellectual talks of the S.A.L. But they offered no assistance in the practical business of social intercourse. I am a snob, she admitted dejectedly. I am a teacher and a snob. Altogether she felt dejected, standing there in her common furs, waiting for someone who did not come.

Then she heard, or thought she heard, through wind and tree, with a tightening of the hands, the first detached echo of a hoof. It came rattling, bouncing, the clop–clop, the scattered stone. The little brown mare, blowing out her pink nostrils, preceded by her own spray. And then a face, you focused, below a cap, worn a bit too much on one side, with the smile that always struck you like the unexpected and left you out of breath. Forgetting if her hair, if the hat were respectable, she dissolved in gratitude.

Well, he said.

Well.

She patted, with unconcern, the sweating neck of the strawberry roan.

I'm late, he said.

No, she said, quickly, gratefully. No. I've just this minute arrived.

Because it was like that, telescoped entirely, the whole quarter of an hour. For a long time it was like that with Willy Standish, for many quarter-hours.

Get in, he said.

She had.

You look ripping, said Willy Standish.

Receiving this, it was almost an original remark.

Willy! she gasped.

His cheek was cold, and beyond the cold, it was smelling of shaving soap.

Willy, she said, it's good. I nearly died leaving the house. And they know, of course. They know. Don't make her go so fast. Not in this wind. Please! Because my hat.

It was altogether exhilarating, the motion, and the wind, and the branch that scraped her cheek. She gave him one of those intimate glances that are more possessive than the clasped hand. Supporting herself on the leather of the dog-cart, on the side that was not his, her fingers strained with elation. They drove on under flying trees.

Never tired of remembering it was only last summer, she had to restrain herself now from making the remark. It was only last summer, in the lull between croquet and archery, that the rambling voice of Mrs de Vere said: Kitty, whom don't you know, let us see, this is Captain Standish, I think that everyone else, I think yes, Captain Standish is the only stranger in our midst, now where are the arrows, Eddie, surely they brought them out of the shed. You looked away from a new face, after the appropriate smile, into the placid, less disturbing one, of old Mrs de Vere. There were ripples in the lawn from a recent mowing, the decapitated daisies, chairs beneath the copper beeches, she saw, and Mrs de Vere in an unfortunate hat. Mrs de Vere was rich. She was kind. Floating up affably from the early life of Mrs Goose, and accepting the misalliance as a Christian, she sometimes asked Kitty to her house. She liked to have young people in her house, believing mistakenly that this was a pleasure for her son. Eddie embarrassed, embarrassed everyone else. And handing tea, offering a mallet, trundling largely with arrows from the shed, Eddie was perpetually embarrassed. Eddie made Kitty giggle. His large and spongy, priestly hands. He started up the uneasy suspicion he might be Going into the Church. Not that anyone minded, really. It was just the state of suspense that you deplored. If only Eddie would declare intentions, everyone would feel relieved. But the state of suspense, of speaking in a lowered voice. Even the indulgent Mrs de Vere felt herself compelled to tread softly, so as not to disturb what might be hatching in her offspring's mind. As a mother she would cheerfully have given him anything he had asked, the whole Church if he had wanted it, holding it out on the palm of her hand, like something from an allegorical group. But Eddie, remaining embarrassed, continued to read St Augustine, in a sun hat, in the shrubbery.

Kitty Goose on the lawn at Mrs de Vere's was thankful for Eddie's presence, for all the more familiar faces, against the intrusion that had taken place. She resented this. His look. Desperately she noticed by a distant elm the spread table and the lemonade. From India, he said, on leave, or more than leave; the Army, you could take it from him, was a pretty rotten show. She resented his idiom, to which she was unused. But more than this, the face, that made her hands tremble on a bow, pulling an arrow that fell too short, twanging an unaccomplished bow. Oh dear, wailed Mrs de Vere, this makes me feel like St Sebastian. In a strawberry hat, like a strawberry ice. Oh dear, it made you laugh in drawing a bow. It made. Then she noticed his teeth. They were very white, even, above the little cushion of his under lip, and this was full and red. In India you clapped your hands, said someone, and the lemonade came running. And you, Miss Goose, he asked. On his hands the veins were swollen from exertion. He was brown. He had the thick, black, curling hair that just avoided being too thick, too black. Altogether it upset her. And the cleft chin.

Altogether Willy Standish was an instance of how nature and breeding can avoid the fashion plate. He was at his best on lawns with a pair of spaniels. Or in a boater, in a punt, in a white shirt rolled at the elbows. If the physical convention were any indication, Willy Standish should have been a credit to his family. But there was also the streak of what his mother called morbidity, not knowing how to give it another name. Everything else she approved. It was right to use a mild slang, to exhaust your body in violent games, to shoot at pheasants, to spend a riotous evening with young women from the theatre. These were the pastimes and the privileges of the governing classes. But when Willy said: I'm going to leave the Army, why, because it makes me miserable, it also made no sense. This, decided his mother, was the strain of morbidity. The schoolroom water-colours that she still kept in a drawer in her writing desk were, well, the quaint relics of a precocity that had pleased her at the time. It was not queer to have a child who painted passably in water-colour. It was queer to have a son who left the Army to become a painter. One patronized art, sometimes, one didn't produce it. But even more nonsensical was Willy's later announcement: I'm engaged to a girl called Kitty Goose, who is she, she teaches in the school at Little Swaffham, she's the daughter of a Norwich harness maker. His mother took to her sofa with a pad soaked in eau-de-Cologne.

Everyone always worked themselves up, felt Willy Standish. He liked to enjoy himself. He liked to lie in a hot bath after tennis. He liked to dabble in paint, or not, just as he felt inclined. I shall be a painter, he said. Because you had to do something, and provided you did it pleasurably, this was the important consideration, provided you could wring the last drop of pleasure from living, it did not matter if you approached the problem with any specific ability. Though he did have a talent of a sort, a kind of sensuous ability with colour that made people exclaim, if they did not know already that Willy Standish aspired to paint.

But above all, Willy was the tilted hat on summer afternoons. From under a tilted hat he looked at her, this girl on the lawn at Mrs de Vere's that made him realize he wasn't bored, packed off to archery, if you please, stuck for a summer afternoon. Then this girl in a sailor hat and a veil, trying not to be freckled, she was the freckling sort, and giggly, through the bitten lip, and conscious of herself, the way she jumped when their hands touched picking up an arrow in the long grass. Already mentally you rehearsed the hand following the line of neck, the mouth pressed into the groove of mouth. The sudden violent desire to do, say something, in the absence of tail feathers, that would arrest this wandering glance. But she darted away in words, telling stories that made the others laugh, laughing herself, acting a little pantomime for almost everyone. Then he told the story of the rope trick, he had to tell something, and everybody listened, they asked questions, everybody interested. But she looked at the bottom of her glass. He followed the movement of her ankle, tossing gently from a deck chair. Her eyes were fixed intently on the bottom of the glass. Perhaps, said Mrs de Vere, when it was all over, when the hands were sticky with lemonade, when another arrow was a sight too many, and people were in the first mumble of departure, perhaps Captain Standish could make a detour and drop you, Kitty, said Mrs de Vere, an unconsciously amiable strawberry ice. Perhaps it would be out of Captain Standish's way, she said in a rush of breath, in a desperate manipulation of veils, looking at no one but Mrs de Vere.

But without escape, there remained the isolation of the dog-cart. His hands upon the reins. And then the slow, consoling silence. Sometimes, she said, on summer evenings she was reconciled to being herself. He agreed to the possibility of this. He had felt it himself, most memorably once at sea, passing a moonlit Crete, and again in the hills of India, where in the upper hills at sunset the snow became a copper pink. Then they drove a bit, and knew there would be a second meeting. He put her down in the lane, in the bend above Little Swaffham. She looked up at him, smiling, giving it right into his face.

So that in retrospect, as well as in the present moment, the dog-cart was a kind of link, linking them physically as they moved through the lanes of their relationship.

Willy, I'm terrified, she said now, and he could feel it in her hand as they passed beyond gates into the upward sweep of grassland that lay between the road and the first sight of gardens.

There were too many trees, she felt, larger than other trees, in this parkland, the unmoved oaks and labouring elms. The sky froze in the deepening afternoon. And then the house, which was already frozen, the steps her feet touched between stony columns. Her mind stripped ready for each impression, recoiled as it encountered them. I am part of this, she told herself without conviction, already speeding a guest from a terrace, hallmarked with the pearls she would wear, at home in pictures in the papers, perhaps talking to a duchess. But it was wrong. Wrong to walk into a waiting house, even with Willy who belonged in it, walking in like a thief, into its large rooms, with their fringe of insolent furniture. He left her a moment, and she stood, this thief, fingering her own furs, bludgeoned by a clock. Reminded by the furs, she knew she was a snob, rejected it at once, her breath rose, she wanted to possess this atmosphere, take it with brilliance, and make it her own. Should they go in, he asked, returning. Yes, she supposed, yes.

This, said Willy, is Kitty.

He offered it to the room, on to which the door gave, no more at first to the intruder than a suggestion of firelight and firelight reflected in a silver kettle. There was much silver. Candles in silver candlesticks behind their glass shades.

How do you do, Miss Goose?

It had the high, harsh tone of an Englishwoman defending

the formalities. They touched hands. Somewhere another voice, a man's, veering into welcome. She had ceased to exist for herself, for anybody, whether accepting a cup, or giving an answer when asked for one.

Mrs Standish spoke about her sons, of which she had three. They were not so much personalities as her sons. These she had given to the Army, the Navy, and the Law. The Law, who was present, stood with the smile of an elder brother for a younger's indiscretion, and she could feel his smile. It was indulgent, in-the-know.

Lord Stockbridge, said Mrs Standish, marshalling the conversation, is putting down a thousand partridges.

She offered this on a charger to Kitty Goose. Willy offered tea. His breath swept down from time to time, a breeze from a distant and more temperate zone. But nothing to oppose to the partridges, to any of the foreign idiom through which she picked, together with the fragments of cake.

They rattled like pebbles, the released words.

No, she said, no. Or: Yes, yes.

Out of the twilight and the glow off reddish curtains, chairbacks formed their scrolls. There was the portrait of an admiral. Additional faces added their features to the actual scene, the nameless Colonel, gathering crumbs from his waistcoat, the small, indeterminate man who was Willy's father, who spoke to her of shooting and of daffodils. He had warm, dry, apologetic hands, and suffered from knowing that he bored his sons.

Goose was a queer sort of name, the Colonel said. From what did it derive?

Mrs Standish uneasily supposed it was just another East Anglian name. An exasperated hand poured a saucer of tea for her little dog.

It was pretty much tenterhooks, with Willy swallowing too much cake too quickly. If you hadn't been nervous, you could have enjoyed the irony of comparison, this and the tea that would be starting soon at home, the cod balls and cold Sunday roast, and Father arranging his moustache in the cup, with an almost mystical concentration, his eyes distant in a steam of tea. But nervously she shrugged this off, trying to impress, if not in words, by her graceful silences or a well-timed smile.

Mrs Standish began to talk neighbours with the Colonel.

There was a continuous tension between Willy's mother and herself. The woman's face, her voice, gave her no loophole. Her breast rose steeply, unimpressionable, with an old Flemish brooch pinned to a slate-coloured dress. She was grey and distant, the flashing rings, the drooped lid. And her teeth seized a word and worried it. There was a perpetual killing of words, as if someone in particular might stoop to pick one up, and use it in desperate reply. One of the words peculiar to her own existence, or one of the names that must remain names.

The father leant forward to say something that didn't come. His hand opened and fastened. He was embarrassed by his sons. And she couldn't help him, Kitty knew, they were clinging to opposite shores, even though floating in the same sea. A sea of red damask, and silver, and dissolving firelight. She was suddenly appalled, as if she were going to scream. She almost wanted to scream, to see if a drooping and averted lid would fly upward, surprised, and uncover the hatred in a cold eye.

Clearing his throat, sighing, the Colonel prepared the moment for his disapproval.

Discipline, he was saying, is the mainspring of our educational system. The public school. Forget about discipline, said the Colonel, and you'll find yourself with socialism on your hands.

Mrs Standish felt, was it a draught, or the first shiver of approaching danger.

Oh Lord, sighed Willy.

What's that? asked the Colonel.

There's always the Army, said Willy.

An elder brother laughed down his nose.

Ignoring the remarks of renegades, the Colonel stroked his chest for an imaginary crumb.

The educational system, said the Colonel, stands or falls by discipline. Don't you agree, Miss Goose?

They were waiting, the whole room, pressing in, the wall, the face, the silence politely discouraging. And then she wanted, she had to throw the stone she had held so many hours in her muff, hidden in the clenched and anxious hand, the body rigid in its isolation.

I'm hardly in a position, she said, and she was surprised the way her voice took possession of the room, the way her eye caught, she hoped, the flicker of an eyelid: I can hardly say. The only experience I have comes from the elementary schools.

Oh, said the Colonel. The elementary schools.

Yes, she said. I teach, you know, in the school at Little Swaffham.

Oh, said the Colonel. That's interesting.

In focus, the room seemed smaller. But her throat was dry.

What a pity it's dark, Oliver, said Mrs Standish. You might have shown Miss Goose the daffodils.

Her husband moved his lips unhappily. It was months before daffodils. Rather than increase confusion, he preferred silence.

Any bulwark that conversation built now was threatened by destruction. The mood was silence. And soon it was time for the insincerities of leaving, these reduced to a formula by Mrs Standish, because she was not pleased, because she had no desire to repeat her experience of this girl, now gathering her cheap furs, and no doubt preening herself on the second bargain she had found in Willy. Mrs Standish, surrounded by her room, looked at the fragments on her tea table. She left it to her men to take unpleasantries off her hands. It was enough to cope with what she imagined was an assault upon her dignity. She stood in the firelight and contemplated a left-over slice of bread and butter.

Mr Standish came out as far as the steps. Willy was helping the girl to get into the dog-cart. Mr Standish hoped, diffidently, that he would soon see her again. But he did not sound as if he thought he would.

And now, Willy, she said, as they spun down the drive in the light from their two little lamps, past receding oaks, and a sudden salient elm. And now, you see, I've done it. It was awful, quite awful!

Laughing, she wanted to cry, in spite of the escape, and the relief of cold air, and Willy's hand. Her voice reeled out into the darkness, crazily and much too loud, like the hoofs of the mare on the hollow road.

It didn't matter, he said, because nothing mattered, and she was splendid, she was the most splendid girl. Slopping over a bit? he wondered, his voice unnatural from returning to the cold, he still had to say, to put an arm, touch the warmth of her body that became his. You shelved the tradition of suppression without giving it another thought.

You'll love me, Willy, she said, you'll love me, won't you, because, because I just couldn't think of anything without.

It was true. She could not press herself close enough. She could not assure herself too often. Because if assured, her life, it seemed, had reached its beginning and its end. She closed her eyes. She felt his mouth warming on her own. She died many times over in the rushing darkness.

Surviving somehow, Kitty Goose became Catherine Standish about the middle of the following spring. It happened very tastefully, quietly, with a minimum of Standishes. Now I am Catherine Standish, she said. She began to wear larger, droopy hats, because she felt changed with the changed name. She was conscious of her own impetus, entering a room. She was less dumpy, lumpy, anxious, in fact, she was more Catherine Standish and less Kitty Goose. This former tenant of her body remained behind in Norwich, though there was an amusing photograph, that Willy insisted he liked, and really it *was* amusing, of the sealskin tippet and the expression that used to go with this. For Willy, perhaps, she was still Kitty. But to most of Willy's friends, with the exception of Maudie Westmacott, she became Catherine Standish as a matter of course.

You must call me Catherine, she had said charmingly to Aubrey Silk, bringing him into her circle, because he was a friend of Willy's, making him an intimate friend of hers. Best of all she liked to hear the tradesmen call her Mrs Standish. Ringing up the stores or the wine merchant if anything had been overlooked. Yes, Mrs Standish, *certainly*, over the telephone. This established her position more securely than anything else. Sometimes she thrust back her head, pursed up her mouth carelessly, and thought about her mother-in-law.

Buying the house in Ebury Street, because it was still a respectable and at the same time not too stuffy address, and close to Chelsea for Willy, who had found and rented a studio, they settled down quite soon to the amusing business of marriage. As Willy remarked, it was so like an odd and unusually prolonged charade. Though often that year they surprised themselves. At transitory moments, over a dessert, or waking in bed, you became aware of a real and consequently strange face, which had to be fitted at once into the pattern of the travesty. You played the charade for all you were worth, ignoring the moments of uncertainty. You lost the stranger on the stage, the little amateur stage, like the stages at the end of the drawing-room. They laughed a lot, at themselves and at the audience. Independent of history, of time, of the business of being two ordinary people, they could afford to. Nothing belonged that reflected on their own importance.

The way things happened, you had to take everything for granted, Catherine felt, in her withdrawn moments. Like being Mrs Standish, like sables round your throat, like the clothes that more than fulfilled the primary function of being clothes, like the house with all the pretty things she had bought at Liberty's. All these were too far removed from what used to be the possible that you couldn't hope to adjust the mechanism of your mind. You had to import a brand-new mechanism to cope with the new person, the other values. And as she was both sufficiently intelligent and sufficiently naïve, she did this successfully. Later when she had children of her own, they were often surprised at her lack of surprise. If it were suddenly announced that the moon had landed on the earth, it would have been part of her legitimate reaction to say: well, now, let's put on coats, and go out and see, and as we might have to climb, perhaps we ought to take sticks. She was never surprised, she was seldom bored. It was fun, in a world of endless possibility, created when she married Willy.

Most delightful was the house, which was so very different from the concept of house, from what her father, for instance, would have considered necessary for the process of living. If she ever felt herself a traitor to a once professed creed, it was easy enough to argue that she did so much enjoy herself. And after all, who was this girl nosing into books she didn't understand, building an intellectual shell that she lived in with anxiety? She was a more shadowy, bogus version of the delightful Mrs Standish, who sat at home in her drawing-room, and smiled to herself when she heard the chiming of her French gilt clock. This had a golden tone. She surrounded herself with yellow gold, the brocaded curtains from Liberty's, and the flowered wallpaper, the neat, small, sprigged flowers which were just the thing at the moment. She was all day long going up and down stairs, just for the pleasure of going up and down stairs, for enjoying possession of her territory. Or she would run to the window, call to the maids in her excitement, to watch soldiers passing in the street. The scarlet, and the brass, and the brassy music moved into the receptive landscape of her mind, with all the other fascinating details recently collected there. And the moisture of excitement stood round the edges of her face, on her forehead, at the roots of her now more controlled hair.

She was quite happy by herself in the house. Willy stayed away a lot. He was painting. He had, of course, the studio in Chelsea. Sometimes she went down, and they had a picnic, and she held her head on one side and made the appropriate remarks for Willy's paintings. But it was still a game, and he knew it was, and he liked to encourage her to play a game. He came up behind her and kissed her on the neck, between the shoulder and the neck, which closed on his face in protest and in pleasure. They were very much in love. Physically in love. They broke off frequently in the middle of a conversation, because of the greater importance of a private obsession. They sat and looked at each other, and you could see the bones of their faces, as if the flesh had shrunk.

Later they began to adopt and recover friends. There was Aubrey Silk. Willy said he thought Aubrey was rather an owl, but a nice owl. Catherine said she thought probably a lizard, a yellow lizard, with an air of dated formality, like a Tenniel drawing. And discovering this, it drew her closer to Aubrey, whom she would have quite liked, ordinarily, but who promoted her wit, and for this reason was to be liked and patronized some more. Aubrey lived at Regent's Park. He had a fortune and a collection of Impressionist paintings. He hoped to wean Willy away from paint, said Aubrey, by asking him often to his house. Sometimes he went to the studio, sat looking carefully at his toe, and talked about romanesque churches and wine. But without looking at the paintings. He avoided these.

Maudie Westmacott was a different proposition. Willy might have thought twice about introducing Maudie to his wife, if Kitty hadn't been a good sort as well as being his wife. But this somehow made it right. And there was no reason why they shouldn't have fun together. Kitty said she thought so too. She kissed Maudie on the cheek. And Maudie kissed Kitty. She talked to her on the telephone and called her Kitty *darling*. She sent her a present of grouse when she had a present of too many from a peer. Because opening a show at the Gaiety with a song, the show was called *Thumbs Up*, at the time when Kitty and Maudie met, there was always plenty of grouse. Maudie told Kitty a great deal about her life, all the people she had met, she had met a great many, names that for Kitty had the lustre of possibly distinguished names, and she sang all the songs she had sung in all her shows, it was usually the opening song, after which Maudie lapsed into one of a dozen girls and a variety of dresses. But anonymity never worried Maudie. There was always the General. She had a little house in St John's Wood. And people in restaurants stared at the star sapphires that she wore.

Sometimes they made a party, Kitty and Willy, and Maudie and a friend of Maudie's. They went to the Grafton Galleries. Or they went to a restaurant after the show, one of the plushy, intimate places that make you sad or gay, according to the company you're in. But Kitty was usually gay. At supper her head was full of popular songs and the names of the people Maudie met, she harboured in fact no actively disturbing thought, frequently no thought at all, for it was difficult not to be influenced by that kind of environment. And Willy loved her. Maudie said it made her cry to see two people in love. She could cry at will. It was her most admired accomplishment. She sat there, in a pearl dog-collar that the General gave, and a hat with an aigrette. She sat and cried. Then when everybody clapped, she ordered a second bottle of fizz.

If she had misgivings at all, these came to Kitty when she was alone. Winter afternoons alone in the house, assuming the character of Mrs Standish, the possessor of an empty house and the intruding kind of nostalgic thoughts that are not un-known on winter afternoons before the curtains have been drawn. It was sometimes difficult then to believe in the sub-stance of things, whether the furniture, or events, the racketing with Maudie Westmacott, the conversation she made with Willy, even their whole relationship. It made her sit with her chin on her hand and wonder. This, she would persuade herself, is only the moment before snow, soon I shall watch it snow in the street, the greyness absorbed in so much lovely obscuring white. Before her marriage, on such occasions, she had read Swinburne in her room. Sometimes now she opened a book, sat with it open in her lap, half attentive to the phrases in a book, trying to fit words to the shape of her own nostalgia. But its shapelessness left her suspended in a sense of frustration, an uneasy suspicion of being alone. At dinner with Willy, she would shrug her shoulders frequently, or warm her hands at the fire and wonder if it had started to snow in the street.

There were moments of reflexion, transient as snow. She was quick to catch up again to her own pace. There was always the telephone. She was as closely dependent on the telephone as the soul on its confessional. Hearing her own voice, timing her own laugh. It was more soothing, this statement of your personality, than words at the other end.

Some time early that summer they drove down to Maidenhead. Willy and Catherine Standish, and Maudie, and a friend of Maudie's, a young man called Miles or Giles, Catherine never could remember which. It would be an awful rag, thought Maudie, to drive down and have supper on the river, and Miles or Giles, though dull, had a simply ripping car. So they drove down. They took a long time, in the high and temperamental car, in their trailing green gossamers. And Kitty had a little detachable parasol that became detached near Staines. Everyone talked and laughed a lot, everybody but Miles or Giles, he only contrived to laugh. Careering to the end of the world, felt Kitty, determined not to look backward into her mind.

Having dinner on the terrace, it was warm enough for that, the river quickly blotted out, tree and water, the almost stagnant green of summer grass, and the paler water, became a moving, liquid black, with long skeletons of yellow light. The restaurant was an open box with one side open to the darkness, spilling its contents on the terrace, the little, bright tables, the pink lights. All a bit careless and studied at the same time. Like the voices, like the voice of Kitty Standish, that she sometimes made deliberately precious, a kind of brittle monotone that she and Maudie talked.

They were eating lobster thermidor.

This is not a very brilliant thermidor, said Kitty.

In what was neither light nor darkness, she was a shimmer of phosphorescent green.

No, said Maudie. A quite unbrilliant thermidor.

Miles or Giles remarked that he had eaten an excellent thermidor at Gatti's. Nobody seemed to notice this.

It was unimportant, whether the lobster thermidor, or the remarks of Maudie's friend, who was one of the smooth, anonymous young men's faces. It was immaterial, whether you discussed the subtleties of lobster thermidor, or what. It was like this. Everything was becoming like this. You had become that detached shimmer of phosphorescent green on the surface of facts, of events. Some day perhaps would come the bang. Only it was difficult still to believe in bangs. Down to the water's edge they had spread a strip of soundless carpet.

Maudie was wearing diamonds. Released from gossamer, her head was rounded off into a golden turban.

Maudie shouldn't wear diamonds, said Willy.

Why? asked Maudie.

It only advertises the fact.

After a bottle of champagne it sounded immensely funny. The champagne pricking your nose, and Willy's joke.

It was going to be an evening.

If some old B leaves them on the mantelpiece, said Maudie, you don't expect me to put them behind the clock. They brighten a poor girl's life. She must have jools.

She deliberately pronounced it *jools*, which made it excruciatingly funny.

What jools will Willy leave on Maudie's mantelpiece? she asked.

Willy'll leave a good smack-bottom on Maudie's mantelpiece, said Willy.

Kitty, said Maudie, what haven't I missed!

It went click clack, a pinging of lights, that shivered and quivered against the background voices. The voice at a distant table referring to *that man*, either in disapproval or discovering a likeness, bore in on Kitty, it made her stationary. She was on the edge. Because *that man*, whatever the reference, continued to play the game she had ceased to play. She stood hesitating on the edge. The face that had been so intimately a part of hers, in thought, and darkness, existed by itself, apart. There was no denying this. It was the old *malaise* recurring. It was not confined to the drawing-room on winter afternoons. It was not an emotion that could be obscured by snow.

They had begun to eat a *bombe*. There were big, lush strawberries garnishing its edge. She pushed at a strawberry with her spoon.

Maudie, sing a song, said Willy.

His mouth hung open sometimes after drink, which made it seem over-lush. The moist, red, uncontrolled lips breathing over Maudie.

Maudie's got a frog, its owner gulped.

Please, Maudie. A bawdy Maudie.

Miles or Giles felt he had to laugh.

Willy put his hand on Maudie's arm. It seemed heavier, fleshier, paler from subjection to the months in London, than fumbling through summer grass.

A Maudie bawdie, Willy babbled.

Go on, Willy, said Maudie. There's still drink.

There was still time, much time, the time spent on terraces, and past time on plush. The time spent by Maudie and Kitty on the same sofa, but in opposite corners of the room. Watching each other. She had spent much time, she realized, watching Maudie. And now in the golden turban with its floating plumes, she was more than obvious, was over life-size. Like a great silky bird. And you recoiled from the touch of birds. That time the swallow fell exhausted on the carpet, and you shuddered to lay it on the windowsill, the smell of ivy in the room, and lying on the bed afterwards.

A fizz for Maudie's objections, mumbled Willy, and the glass slopped over on to his hands.

Suddenly she thought she was going to be sick. The voice that was her father's said, lie still, girl, you're not well, but lie still and it'll pass. If she had his conviction, about this and many things. His hands growing intent when he talked. Man is fundamentally good, it's circumstances that rots him, he said, he's not born with meanness and indifference, he's born for the expression of positive good. But when you were this phosphorescent presence, the lights passed through, the inconsequent voices that were part of the general inconsequence.

I think, said Kitty, I – shan't be – a moment. I –

Then she ran up across the terrace. She ran inside the restaurant between the shoulders and the pink lights. Her skirt hobbled her as she ran. So that she felt like some large, freakish, intruding bird that panted in a nightmare of pointing lights. It was in on the right, somebody said. It was in. It caught on the knob. Then the frizzed face rising from the table, beside the bowl and its powder puff, to administer extreme unction.

There, dearie, the cloakroom woman said.

She supported this head that lolled, objectiveless, on the basin-edge, the hair damp, sickly, that strayed along the face. Kitty Standish down on her knees took stock of the returning universe, of which the substance was cold and porcelain. She closed her eyes on a last gasp of nausea.

It looks to me as if somebody, the cloakroom woman said, as if somebody's going to 'ave a happy surprise.

I'm drunk, said Kitty.

Her head lolled.

Take it from me, the cloakroom woman said.

She looked prudently for a ring.

I've got a nose, she said. And I'm four times wise. There was that first time, she said. It wasn't all Ostend. Reachin'? You wouldn't know ! My hubby said it was the French cuisine. But I put two and two.

Put two and two, that made the probable the positive, that you didn't like to think, because unknown, it was something that other people, that you put right out of your head. Now for the first time, under the pressure of nature and advice, you felt you had to admit, to yourself as well as the world. It made you lift up your head and look at the shabby remains of a face, its expression frosted over with surprise. I look a fright, she said. She touched her cheek. She was actually going to have a child. It made her feel rather solemn. It invested her with dignity. She got up carefully from the floor and began to powder her nose.

The cloakroom woman was describing her accouchements, Numbers One to Four.

It'll be lovely, dear, she said.

Is all this happening to me, felt Catherine Standish, tired, this same face, that was always the same face, fitted to many moods. This ought to be important, she said, not taken for granted, like ordering half a dozen of hock. Then her mind stumbled with a little throb of pleasure on the prospect of finding names. Willy, William, William was out of the question, because Willy, because there were never two of anything. Three years earlier she might have called him Nigel. I shall always be futile and silly, she decided, and did not regret her complacency, because she was too tired.

The cloakroom woman stood in a haze of retrospect, her crumbling face, on which lay two little islands of hard, dry rouge.

Kitty! cried Maudie. You left us *delib*'ately. It wasn't nice of you, Kitty.

She spoke with great concentration, though without malice. It was too late for malice.

The lady hasn't been well, the cloakroom woman said.

Nobody's *well*! cried Maudie.

Kitty looked at her, or this Mrs Standish, with her freshly acquired importance, looked at all the Maudie Westmacotts, and decided in one swoop that she disliked her sex. All the artifices, telephone and otherwise, were only coatings to this dislike. Now she sat back. She could afford to. If only it had happened before, if only she had had the courage to admit. Courage was now less abstract, she felt.

I'm going to have a child, Maudie, she said.

She waited keenly for the reaction.

Christmas! said Maudie. It's too late for practical jokes.

Maudie drooped, the plumes sweeping in a tired arc in what

was now the wrong direction. Her face was full of shadows, bluish shadows, and between her breasts. She looked at Kitty, dully, out of a great distance, disliking her also perhaps, if it came to the truth.

Where is Willy? asked Mrs Standish. We must go.

Willy? Willy's blotto. Willy has passed out, said Maudie.

Going home, it was even a longer way, with Willy a collapsed body which breathed hard. There was dew in the air now, in a sleepy, distant countryside. Catherine Standish was exhausted but content, as she sat there in the importance of having a child. Whether Willy knew or not. It was more her business, anyway. She was glad of that. The child that she was making would remain hers, at least for a very long time. And she enjoyed this, her new possession. It was a safeguard, she felt unconsciously, against the expressionless *malaise*.

Willy was surprised and interested.

She sat up in bed sipping her tea that the maid had just brought.

Well, he said, and again: Well.

He could not accustom himself to the fact. He had the surprised, withdrawn look of a man persuading himself he was going to be a father. Sentimentally, it was momentous. This was something he had given her. It was his.

Kitty, he said, allowing his voice tenderness.

She offered him her cheek. She lay back in bed, enjoying the situation.

Of course, it'll be a long time, she said, sounding almost bored.

Yes, he said. Of course.

He went off into the bathroom, wondering still.

She began to have a great deal of time on her hands. The days when Willy, after the first burst of attentiveness, stayed down at the studio, he was painting hard, and then he was working at an art school, painting from the life, because he needed this, he said. He also engaged models. Sometimes he told her things they had said, the funny or stupid things. And she smiled indulgently, as if she were humouring a child. The child that she was carrying made her feel older than Willy, an adjustment she didn't altogether resent, because of the superiority it gave. And now the games they had played seemed more than childish. She even began to discuss their financial position. Because she realized, through some stirring of responsibility allied to her physical condition, that there was such a thing as a financial state. But investments bored Willy, and didn't interest her very much more. To the end of her life, she inclined to trust to the moment, to hold out her plate and trust that someone would fill it. So far it had worked.

That summer she went down to Brighton. Willy came to her at weekends. It was pleasant like that. She enjoyed the luxury of her own thoughts, even the most trivial, and then Willy at the weekend, to talk to her at table, and offer her his arm along the front. During the week she even lapsed back to some of her old preoccupation with the intellect. Because she was superior, carrying her child, she wanted to taste all the little attendant pleasures of an intellectual snobbery. That winter, perhaps, she would take lessons in French. She would read French. She had always enjoyed the sight of someone cutting the pages of one of the softbacked French books.

Aubrey Silk came down to see her. To hold her hand, he said, but only metaphorically, because Aubrey never did anything that was considered incorrect. Sometimes she thought him bloodless, passionless. Aubrey did not exist except as a number of intellectual enthusiasms, and even these were carefully damped by order of the conventions into which he had been bred. It irritated her sometimes. He made her feel vulgar, over-physical. He sat there and talked to her gently in the lounge, his foot moving in some more tasteful pattern on the over-patterned carpet, his voice losing itself in a rush of traffic along the front. But ultimately it soothed her to listen to Aubrey Silk. Even when the voice waited for some reply, and she had to go through a bungling strategy, some business to convince that she had listened, which didn't really convince, she still felt comforted, immeasurably soothed, just by the presence of Aubrey Silk. Just because he was passionless and removed. The Brighton Front dissolved in the voice of Aubrey Silk. She wandered contentedly in her own thoughts, picking her way through the coloured and fragmentary events that might or might not happen. There was no distinct, definite day on the calendar.

Catherine, he said, stopping, he had been talking of Théophile Gautier. Having a child improves you, Aubrey said.

That brought her with a bump of surprise into the existing scene. Because it still surprised her, this process of having a child. And Aubrey, it was strange, Aubrey's remark, just as a remark made by Aubrey.

Why, Aubrey? she laughed.

It made her put her hand to her hair. It made her compose her mouth as if she was at the photographer's.

One of these things, Aubrey shrugged, that border on the personal.

But she looked at him for some time afterwards as he talked, recovering his conversation, if not Théophile Gautier, wondering about Aubrey. He was remote also in time. His collars were always too high. Aubrey had been left behind somewhere in the late nineteenth century. And this was satisfying too, because it made you feel modish, nineteen-eight down to the heel.

Good-bye, Catherine, Aubrey said. It's time I thought about catching my train.

She realized he had come to see her. His dry, cool, bony hands.

Winter was full of fresh delights. Aubrey asked her to go with him to concerts. She could not take herself seriously at concerts, just as many of the books she read were a kind of self-conscious exercise. But there was always the anticipation in settling in your seat, there were always the programme notes, and the tuning of the violins excited. As a girl she had sometimes been to concerts, because this was part of the ritual, the

S.A.L., the chamber music in Norwich rooms, and the little concerts organized at home by Eddie de Vere, who played very beautifully on the flute. Sitting forward with her chin upon her fist, she knew that faces watched her. But she closed her eyes. Sometimes this was spontaneous. Listening to a phrase from Purcell, she succumbed to the lulling of flutes. They drowsed under her skin in an uncapturable lethargy. She did not want to seize the flutes. She sat very still with her eyes closed.

So all that was genuine enough, and moments beside Aubrey at the Queen's Hall. She sat, untouchable, in a grove of violins. The great horn drew a sigh of relief, because she was beyond its reach, very soft and warm and guarded inside her furs. She became critical too. This week it was the strings, the next the brass. And Aubrey encouraged her. All her life, men encouraged Mrs Standish. The fact that she accepted their encouragement contributed a lot towards her success.

Aubrey, she yawned, I am so tired.

She nodded gently on the way from concerts. She could feel her soft body, that grew weekly softer, more voluminous, more self-contained and mysteriously assured, rocking in the cab. Outside, rain or frost. The glitter of varnish on cold wet nights. Inside, the intimate leathery smell of the cab, the little box that they soon warmed with themselves. Sometimes she put her head on Aubrey's shoulder and almost slept.

Sometimes I think the happiest moments of my life are spent in cabs, she said. Going from place to place. There are no responsibilities. And the motion. You can sink down. It's even better than a hot bath.

He called her a sensual little beast.

She enjoyed that. She laughed. In Aubrey's dry voice to be called a sensual little beast, the way they always called her little, when really she was quite tall. Taller than Maudie Westmacott. That made her bite her lip and turn to Aubrey.

I always thought Willy would marry into the chorus, Aubrey said.

She resented this. She resented her own thoughts.

Oh, Willy has his sober moments, she said.

She did not want to think of Willy, of anything outside the little intimate box of the cab, where Aubrey still remained soothingly remote.

Aubrey, dear.

She took his hand. She liked to hold his just responsive hand. To wonder. She did not want anything more, oh dear no, not for a moment. But she enjoyed the sensation of not having to recoil, and at the same time wondering if there might be a possibility of this.

When they got home, and he stood by the door as she rummaged for her key, she could feel his presence.

Aubrey, dear, she said, I'm so tired –

Sometimes she let him put the key in the lock.

It's been the most beautiful evening, Aubrey, dear.

She stood inside, in the dark house, smiling because she was tired, she was content, wondering if Aubrey, if Willy. Soon she was too exhausted to wonder.

Nights when Willy came in late from his own errands, and she heard his feet counting every stair, very heavy and uncertain, she tried to hide her resentment in pretended sleep. She screwed up her eyes a bit too tight, her nose just over the sheet. It was hard to resist the temptation of a word thrown in the direction of the dressing-room, where recently Willy had begun to sleep. Sometimes she liked to feel he was sleeping in the smaller room that opened off her own. He was almost as close. On other occasions, not. The evenings when his trousers fell on the floor, and you heard the bump of money and keys, the sock torn off its unwilling suspender. Then she screwed her eyes up more tightly and frowned. When people took advantage of her she had that hot feeling behind the eyes.

On the whole, and by agreement, they had slipped into going different ways. It had begun with the pregnancy. This new development in Mrs Standish that was not entirely physical, but also a change in mind. She continually had to find excuses for not being the person she was in the first year of their marriage. He found her often looking at him, amused. That swinging motion of the crossed leg as she sat and looked at him across a room.

What's the matter? he frowned.

What? she said, absent. Oh, nothing.

He sat for a moment. She seemed to have muffled the whole house, through this absorption of hers, and the period of waiting. Then he went out. She heard the door downstairs. She sat, passive enough, except for sudden flickers of desire in remembering his face, a little coarser than a year ago, underlining what had once passed muster as a not too obvious handsomeness. If spasmodically she grew afraid of her own position in relationship to Willy . . . misgiving settled down again into the lethargy of waiting. Later on, she would say, I shall make the effort, but not now, this is not the time.

In the meantime she was taking desultory lessons in French. An occupation, she said. The butter from the muffins that she ate at five fell on the pages of her grammar. There were textbooks in every room in the house.

Talk of *entente cordiale*! said Willy.

I must have an occupation, she said.

She was sitting at the dressing-table, combing out her hair. On the table the crimping irons, on a little methylated spirit lamp.

You can't expect me to go to parties, she said, and this without a trace of malice.

No, he said.

But he suspected malice.

It helps to pass the time, she said.

So he went to another party, somewhere; the geography of London was growing vague. He had friends in Chelsea, the vague acquaintances who talked shop in the background of Willy's conversation. Sometimes she met them on the telephone. In the same way, by accident, Maudie Westmacott, on a day when, feeling out of sorts, she had cancelled her lesson for the afternoon.

Maudie's conversation was a blur and crackle of immediate solicitude. She had not seen her darling Kitty for how long an age, she was on her head, the rehearsals, and the dressmakers, and the General, who had left for Monte the morning before, and when should they meet, she couldn't wait, an intimate talk between girls was what she, Maudie, needed most. But somehow the meeting remained one of those still crystallizing projects common to the telephone. And her darling Kitty went into the drawing-room, wondered, very silent in her search for facts, in collecting the non-existent evidence, that she felt, somehow felt in the crackle of the telephone. If Willy were no inducement, Maudie was. The voice of Maudie Westmacott made Willy suddenly desirable.

Maudie rang, she said casually at dinner.

And what did little Maudie have to say?

He was as unconcerned as, well, soup. He went on smoothly drinking his soup. She found herself rolling pellets from a square of bread.

Maudie took her usual time to say nothing at all, she said.

Her fingers flattened out a pellet.

You don't like Maudie, Kitty, he said.

As if I – why, she said, why should I waste my time disliking Maudie Westmacott?

It was true. What she disliked was his unconcern, and her sudden concentration on his wrist below the cuff, that reminded her of all the small tyrannous ways of physical desire.

No, she said afterwards, long after the subject had lapsed, bending over him in his chair. Why should I dislike Maudie Westmacott?

She kissed him and thought she found on his mouth some cause for reassurance. I'm strong enough for any Maudie Westmacott, she felt.

And the child. Taking careful, leisurely walks, she was never tired of returning to the child. His face she had already formed from old family photographs, already she could even hear his voice. Walking in the leafless Park, withdrawn from its seasons, it seemed, at that time of year, she matched its apparent sterility with her own fruitfulness. She strolled warmly in her furs. Glances passed without encounter over the softening lines of her face, over the rounded line of her figure. There was no contact left between Mrs Standish and the faces in the Park. She was walking in her own landscape, ignoring the champed bit or the bowling hoop.

So that when voices, out of the anonymous voices in the Park, forced her back to a reckoning, she could not take this at first. She had to pause, touching bark beneath her glove, supporting herself against the first tree from the onslaught of approaching voices.

Oh no, Willy, said Maudie. You make me laugh.

She walked with that slight swagger that Maudie Westmacott brought from the joy plank into the Park. She was wearing violets. She was wearing a sable hat.

And for that reason I'm not to be taken seriously, said Willy. Perhaps.

Well, what's a man to do about that?

His cane stammered on the asphalt path.

Mrs Standish, rooted by her tree, was thankful at least for the passivity of trees. Because her hand trembled on unresponsive bark. Her thoughts were painfully her own, and her voice, congealed somewhere at the back of her throat. She could feel her face grow shapeless, her feet take the opposite direction from Willy and Maudie Westmacott. I must go home, she said, I must make a scene, or not make a scene, I must escape to something more familiar. Above all she wanted to open her own door, hoping perhaps to find behind it a solution, or some contradiction of what she had seen.

Willy, she said, oh, Willy, in the intimacy of a cab. Here in an enclosed space, her feelings crested over into indignation. It was not an unpleasant indulgence, a sense of injustice. Again if the evidence. She almost resented a possible contradiction. She took out her handkerchief. She held it in a tight, hard ball. Her eyes were hot, bright. Thinking of her child, her baby, it suddenly became her baby, it was too much, the eyes could not resist the additional pathos of motherhood. And she began to cry. It hurt her. The hard, jerky crying that came back at her in the cab, making it more dreadful, like the crying of another person.

It was too much, she felt, after many hours of waiting, after going to bed early, after many hours of reconstructing the possibilities of what Willy was to Maudie Westmacott. She lay in a hot torment of sheets and the dubious comfort of eau-de-Cologne. Her throat either choked with anger, or softened with a helpless tenderness. A bell, in the next square, ignoring her existence, tolled for people on another star.

Willy, she called, when she heard him in his room. Willy, come here a moment?

Prepared with strategies, these left her with Willy present in the room.

Willy, she said, I haven't been well.

She sounded fretful through eau-de-Cologne.

Why, darling, he said, and he was so solicitous he made her cry; you've been taking too many walks.

No, she said, through that hot throat. Just my usual, she said. I strolled a little in the Park.

She couldn't say it herself. It got itself said through that swollen throat. And the heavy darkness.

As long as you don't do too much, he said.

She could feel his hand on her arm. She wanted to return to the Park. She wanted to say, but the Park, and Maudie in the Park.

Have a good day, dear? she sighed.

She might have been almost asleep.

So-so, he said. Worked while I had the light. Anything I can get you? he asked.

Was there anything he could get, when she knew, when her hand, and touching her arm with his hand, and then her face, if he could put his hand through and touch the real state of her feelings, she longed for that, Willy withdrawing a burnt hand.

Because now it was more anger. Alone, she was furious. She put on the reading lamp when he had gone and lay there rigid in her impotent anger.

So it became a game of knowing and watching. She made him feel how remote and superior and all-informed she was, without either of them ever really còming to the nature of the information. But her smile suggested she saw through Willy Standish, his gestures and his motives. So Willy frowned frequently, as he always had at that swinging motion of the leg. His eyebrows met above the eyes in a dark, almost a perpetual frown.

Working? she sometimes asked in the evening.

Her voice, her smile transposed the word, giving it an accent of disbelief.

Yes, and no, he said.

It irritated him to hear her ask about his work as if it was a game, and it was, which was what made it hurt. Everything was a game. Especially this game played by Catherine and Willy Standish in the evening, before he could decently escape by going out. Willy's life was full of evasions. She told herself reassuringly that Willy was weak, but knowing it, that never helped matters a bit.

Catherine, he said one evening (he had never called her Catherine before). We've got to draw in our horns.

What do you mean? she said, with a not altogether deliberate surprise.

I've slipped up over an investment, he said. We'll have something less to live on.

How you lived, on what you lived, never made any great impression on Catherine Standish. She was in the habit of accepting circumstance. This inability to connect herself with an economic problem was replaced in her mind by a simple division of her life into phases when she was with servants, jewels, and furs, and phases when she was without. It was simpler and also more pleasing like this. But this was later. Now she connected Willy's announcement, whatever the mysterious behaviour of investments, which she did not pretend to understand, she connected it with something more ominous, more deeply personal than the stock market. She listened to a twanging in her ears. She was willing to spill out resentment on an opponent she could easily name.

But this is absurd, she said.

It happens, said Willy.

Yes, she said. I suppose.

She looked at him quietly, very closely.

Well? he asked.

He was annoyed.

Nothing, she said, tapping with her foot.

Call me a fool, he said, thickly.

No. I was wondering. I was just wondering if perhaps – if perhaps there wasn't – some *thing* –

Go on, he said. Say it.

They were both sitting too straight, in contrast to the padding of their voices, the careless gesture of a hand. And then she capitulated; she knew she would, as if she were a little afraid to penetrate any deeper, she made herself take the easier road. She preferred her own uncertainty.

What shall we have to do? she asked.

He looked at her. He was breathing slower.

Ease up the pace, he said. Get rid of a maid. I might give up the studio. We'll have considerably less.

He said all this rather pompously. He had won. He was reinstated. They both sat breathing more freely in the zone of uncertainty, where the shadow of a doubt was nameless.

Later when Mrs Standish discovered details of what she used to call, still later, Willy's financial debacle, she discovered that she was wrong. Whatever a certain person was to Willy, the present situation was simply due to some mysterious crisis in the City. But she had learnt, at least, to prefer uncertainty. And this is significant. She deliberately chose a cloud, which took possession in middle age, transferred its cloudiness to her, and helped her blur the too emphatic line. The only unpleasantness is what one makes, the maturer Mrs Standish used to say. It was one of the things that used to exasperate her son.

Mrs Standish had her son on a wet night in January. It got itself over somehow, just somehow, she felt. It was like that. In her exhaustion she could not credit herself with much. Recovering, she took a great deal of credit. She had given birth to a child. The event was very distant from any process of natural evolution. She decided to call her son Elyot, her mother-in-law's maiden name. To see what that will do, she said to Willy. Because the elder Mrs Standish had remained among her tea things, apparently unaware of Willy's wife.

If Elyot was a kind of peace offering to his grandmother, he played much the same part in relationship to his father. Fatherhood to Willy Standish was a state of pleasure and surprise. He walked in and out of the room where his wife lay, very languid, yet commanding in her bed, and looked often at the smaller object, mostly fist and topknot, that they told him was his son. And Kitty's son. She watched his change in attitude. Gauging it, she put out a sentimental feeler. Moments alone, she gave him her most encouraging smile, for which the present Willy fell. He bought her a handsome bead-embroidered bag, which was too much in fact for the recipient. She sounded hoarse thanking for the bag. Months later, going ironically to the same bag to write out a cheque to pay for it, the sentiment became reduced. But not now. It was *dear Willy*, his kindness, his thoughtfulness, which she had almost killed by indifference. Mrs Standish built up her own disgrace. She took quite a masochistic pleasure in ticking off the list of her more unfortunate qualities. Because she loved him. She was confident of this, recovering something of her physical passion. Those little rushes of desire that rose without regard for place or time. She shuddered now for what may have been her dispossession during pregnancy.

Since Willy's mistake the mere business of living was full of opportunities for sentimental *rapprochement*. They had withdrawn a story into their house. On the ground floor and in the basement a milliner, a Mme Adorée, was now installed. Mrs Standish persuaded herself it was Bohemian, living above a shop. At the same time she could regret what had been comparative magnificence. Now that we are living on top of each other, she would say, when Mme Adorée's shop bell became intrusive, we must simply learn to give and take. In this frame of mind she dismissed the two maids. She was all enthusiasm for simplicity, which she tried to impart to a dubious cook. She had to make it fun, fun to remember the way to do things for yourself, fun to open the door on the girl's day out. Because she had engaged a girl, a young girl, to see to the child, and the practical details of housework, which if allowed to emerge from the abstract might very well cease to be fun.

She is just over sixteen, she said to Willy. Her name is Julia. Julia Fallon. She comes from Northumberland.

At first hearing, the name did not fit its owner. Then on consideration it did. She had all the integrity, the dignity, the directness of a Flemish primitive. Watching her grave, slow movements with the child, there was an absorption in them that reassured. Julia Fallon and the objects that she touched were united by this strain of absorption. The basin she held in her red hands rounded into shape with those same hands. She breathed rather hard in her absorption, whether down on her knees scrubbing the floor, or sitting with the baby in her lap. Ungainly perhaps. But you overlooked ungainliness, as in the Flemish primitive, for the sake of economy and logic, and the effort that lends integrity. Julia took possession of the child. He became hers, in the way a child does. A child is always the possession, not of the mother, but of the nurse. Receiving him from Julia's arms, Mrs Standish sometimes almost realized this.

To Mrs Standish, her baby was sweet, amusing, pathetic, provoking, hers. When she could concentrate on motherhood, she did so with a passion that expended itself in kisses and in noises, and in holding the child's head against her cheek and watching their joint reflection in the glass. It was all genuine enough, after the manner of Catherine Standish. And the baby looked at her solemnly, sometimes too solemnly, she felt, as if she was a little idiotic in her efforts to express affection.

He understands. He understands too much, she said to Julia. in half-resentment at the precocity she was wishing on to her child.

But Julia only took him stolidly.

He's natural enough. He's only a baby, Julia said.

With Julia the baby became a small, interested human being. Sharing her solemnity, he listened to her monologues, delivered while stringing beans for the cook, or holding him propped on her lap in the Park. It was the kind of recitative that mingled the past and the present with the future. There were no barriers in time. The baby sucked his fist and listened to the flow of words, followed its swinging, changing course, felt on his fist the shape of words, closed with the first indications of form before the lids fell on his heavy eyes. He lived in a world of Julia Fallon's, with a scent of yellow soap and of shredding beans. And for Julia the child became part of her intimate history, in which the path from school was lined with nettles, in which the boys made stones skip across the frozen pond, in which there was the day our Emily fell and bumped her eye upon the mangle. Julia's whole existence, past and present, was very real and tangible. She had an unconscious respect for the substance of things. Wiping the dribble from the baby's mouth was a gesture of humility, and deep respect.

It's so nice, Willy, Mrs Standish said, I feel I can leave Baby with Julia. She's quite devoted to the child. If only she won't spoil him, she said. That's always the trouble, of course, with inexperienced girls.

Anyway, she felt they could leave the baby with Julia the weekend they decided to go to Dieppe.

It's so long, Willy said, since we've been away by ourselves.

And of course she was eager to agree. She was always too eager now to agree to anything that drew them closer.

So they decided on Dieppe. It was bright and cold, the grey, watery sky, with its patches of blue and streaks of black, and the sea that was a deeper, blackish blue. On the boat, it took your breath. And a veil blew in the wind. And Willy had to hold on to his cap. But they were both in high spirits, over everything they did, eating the cheerless cold roast beef in the saloon, or watching the approaching sickness of the passengers. She hung on his arm and they staggered up and down, struggled against the tilted deck. They were a handsome pair. And you felt they knew. But nobody really grudged them that.

Altogether it was an expedition. It had the spirit of this. You could feel it in the glossy atmosphere of the damp French watering place, in the palmy vestibule of the rather vulgar, ornate hotel. And so much taken for granted, almost a change in relationship signing your name at the reception desk. If this were Maudie Westmacott, felt Catherine Standish. She caught herself swaggering across the carpet when the porter left them alone in their room. The swagger of Maudie Westmacott.

There were moments, and this was one of them, when she thought she would have it out with Willy, just in a joking way, the question of Maudie Westmacott. Because since the baby she had begun to feel safe. But always she paused on second thought. And now. She wanted this to be, well, some kind of festival, she put it sentimentally, she wanted nothing to come between her and the expression of what, at moments like these, she felt that she felt for Willy. So she swallowed Maudie Westmacott.

It was a day of trudging and excitement in small, damp streets. There was always another corner to another street. She had to see. She had to look. She had to buy the chocolates and the macaroons. In her enthusiasm the stately Mrs Standish became once more Kitty Goose, the straying hair beneath the hat, and the bright, expectant look she had worn in winter lanes. If we had not been extravagant, felt Mrs Standish, this would be Paris. But in her present mood she did not resent the alternative. She could make it a touching second-best, full of intensified sensation, the sensation sometimes attached to making the best.

Willy entered in. Not without suggesting he had often been abroad, not without a trace of patronage, those travellers' tales that fitted themselves to every moment of the present as it happened, and practically obliterated this. There was the time in Naples, and the time in Smyrna, that *she* might like to share without completely grasping. But she even encouraged patronage, grateful to hang on his arm, or to sit with her hands in her lap. After all, what did it matter, provided she expressed by an attitude or word the tenderness she felt for Willy?

So he talked. They dined. And they sat at the Café des Tribunaux, where it was cold, it had begun to drizzle. Willy said what an advantage it was to be able to sit on the pavement in France. Yes, she said, shivering, wondering if her shoes, if the soles of her shoes. Willy said she must try a Pernod. *Garçon*, he said, *deux* Pernods. It wasn't the right time of day, he explained, she must remember that, but a first day in France without a Pernod, you just had to have a Pernod. So she tasted with some misgiving the pale and milky liquid that they brought her in a glass, that she wanted to enjoy, that she wanted to drink with the right air of drinking Pernods on French pavements. Because Willy said.

It's an acquired taste, said Willy, who had been abroad.

Yes, she said. It must. But it might be good if. In time, she said.

Her whole life was centred in that glass of nauseating yellow green. She had to drink it down to justify her life, with Willy waiting to intercept each indication of nausea.

You'll get used to it, he said.

He ordered himself another.

If she could say to him, Willy, let us go home, this is unimportant. If she could express half the things she wanted to express on this particular night, and which had lain dormant since their meeting, waiting for expression in damp French streets. But two glasses of yellow-green, quite motionless, imposed themselves, their opalescence. Willy's face grew cloudy with his second. She was slipping, slipping, away from what she liked to believe was a moment of tangible happiness.

You never begin till your third, said Willy, perpetually knowledgeable, ordering this.

She opened her bag and fiddled about with things inside. She had to put this gesture between herself and her inexpressible disappointment.

You're not giving in? he said.

No, she said, dipping her mouth.

He began to talk about India. It unfolded like a cloud, drenched with many colours, the forms that intermingled in the formless cloud of narrative. She watched him. You noticed the whites of his eyes when he was drunk. There was too much white to the eye. She remembered the eyes of her china doll, taking out the eyes when the head broke, and laying them on the washstand. The detached eyes, that were like Willy's after drink.

Let's go home now, Willy, she said.

Home's tomorrow, Willy said. It's too much water. Too far.

Yes, she said. But the hotel. Let's go back to the hotel.

The hotel? he said. Yes, he said, vaguely.

She looked at what was still her first unfinished drink, that was a kind of justification, that stood on the marble table. The whole day, many days seemed to fall with a malicious plop into the pool of yellow-green. All right, she said, it's like that. She was tired.

Later when she lay beside his breathing, surrounded by a distant chiming of dark bells, it was difficult not to review her failures. When she had been determined on this particular night to bury failure. There are the moments, the days perhaps, when you are given the inspiration to explain, not in words, which are always only the coded message, the days when your face is a mirror, and your hands illuminate a meaning. It was one of these days for Catherine Standish, realized through her intuition, if otherwise indistinct. And now the waste of any such dispensation, beside what was nothing more than a dark breathing, the passive ridge of a man she had married stretched beside her in the bed. It horrified her now to find that Willy could grow so impersonal. Just a man she had married, out of so many men, or less than this, the inanimate ridge. Switching on the lamp she could not believe that this face would ever grow personal. Just a movement of the too fleshy lips, the in and out of the lips in breathing, a twitching of the nostrils with their shadows of hair. Morning was a distant suggestion in the foreign room. She got out of bed and walked between its shiny furniture. The light from the lamp was too pink. Because it was what you could call a luxury hotel. It was what Willy had chosen from a guide. It was the setting for what should have been this moment of wordless explanation, too intimate, too private for furniture, transcending the vulgarity of French veneer. But possibilities slipped with the chiming of a clock, towards a distant morning and the rain on asphalt. She stood with her hair hanging helpless down her back.

Willy said over coffee he thought it was a miserable place. She wondered a little herself what had decided them to come. There were salty streaks on the windows of the room. They sat all the morning with English papers in their hands. Willy suggested at lunch that they catch the afternoon boat back. Yes, she agreed. Yes.

So Mrs Standish resumed the building of a protective cocoon inside the reduced body of her house. She believed that, technically, this was now what the agents would have called an Upper Part. But it was a term that did not take into account the subtle layers of its owner's cocoon, the mornings and the afternoons that wrapped it closer, the business of mere living in a house. She saw very few people now. She had the baby brought downstairs and left on the hearthrug, where she played with him. Soon he was walking across the room. It all happened logically enough, in what had become the smooth, dull, colourless passage of time. She did not expect events, or events themselves, in such environment, became eventless and accepted. It was with no great sense of discovery that she found she was going to have a second child. This was the inevitable outcome of a settled relationship. Whatever the discrepancies in taste, their separate ways, she was Willy's wife. There were the nights he spent beside her in her bed.

The second child was a girl. She was darker, smaller than the boy. Her small, intense face wrinkled often in emotional storms. You were conscious early of her watching eyes. In a moment of romantic stress, her mother decided on the name of Eden. There was no particular reason for this, which made it embarrassing for ever after when people asked you to explain. It was just that, lying in bed on a peaceful morning, Mrs Standish decided on the name. Behind it perhaps a sense of her own frustration. But she never pinned this down.

At three the little boy was a solemn, sturdy child. He wore knitted suits. And she dressed him also in a white outfit, with a full, stiff, linen skirt, and a pair of white kid boots. He stood in it stiffly, formally, like a biscuit figurine. And soon the girl too had discarded the white robe, the mystical, gothic skirts of the baby's robe. Emerging from her baby's abstraction, she began to assume a character with her clothes. And it was all both mysterious and transparent, the children growing, saying unexpected things, looking up at you over milk when you walked into the room. Sometimes you felt it was something you had watched, all this development, the actual process, as you watch the bean unfolding under water, publicly in the glass vase. But more often it was something that you felt was going on secretly, apart from you. To Mrs Standish, her children were already very often their own enclosed entities. Even though she felt their arms round her neck, the brushing of their cheeks, they had ceased to have any close connexion with her own body.

Everything happening so quickly, Mrs Standish hadn't time to feel surprised. Because surprise is not compatible with collapsing time. She worked at her French lessons. She went to the stores. And in between, she was now and again conscious of events, sometimes the past events, which had cut adrift from her life, their significance, whether Maudie Westmacott, or the loss of the ground floor of her house. Because now there was Mme Adorée's hat shop on the ground floor, and Mme Adorée herself, sleek and raucous, with a goitre. In the basement her two girls sat trimming and snipping at the hats. And just as in the case of the house, with its superimposed detail of other people's lives, it was the same with Maudie Westmacott. Any emotional twinge that Mrs Standish might have felt, was complicated, obliterated by the other moments of her life with Willy, the night at Dieppe, the silences, and the difficulties of language. Because Willy's life was a different tongue. She seldom crossed the border now. She left him to loiter on his own way. His days were a perpetual loitering, now that the indiscretion of paint had been admitted, now that the studio as a possible bolt hole had been removed. He sat a great deal in the Park, in summer beneath a tilted hat. He exchanged drinks with his friends. Sometimes he talked poverty and thought about getting a job.

If their friends were mutual, they were the kind, negative ones who are a bore. Like the Wilcoxes. These came to dinner and you felt yourself becoming the Catherine you were for Willy only when the Wilcoxes came, evenings when you listened to your own voice, and found you sat with a smile on your face after the justification was gone. But the Wilcoxes came regularly, at least about once every three months.

The Wilcoxes came the evening Mme Adorée called Mrs Standish into the shop. It was difficult for her, said Mme Adorée, she did not know, she was *agacée*, and Mme Standish was always so nice, but it was one of those things, and the warm-blooded young girls in her workshop, they were *gentilles*, the *jeunes filles bien élevées* that Mme Adorée employed, *mais on ne sait jamais*. Yes, Mme Adorée? asked Mrs Standish. It was not nice if Mr Standish come into the workshop with her girls, Mme Adorée said, if he bring bonbons to her girls, and there was the one young girl, *bien élevée mais*, she was turning her head, it was the age, she was thinking of only these things, and talking of the bonbons of Mr Standish, she was so excitable about men, she was talking of nothing but Mr Standish.

Mrs Standish hated for a moment, not Willy, but the sleek French face of the milliner who had shaken her equilibrium. The face was directly responsible. It was always this way for a moment with Mrs Standish, more the agent than the reported fact. The discreet, powdered face of the Frenchwoman, with the dark eyelids. She wanted to put up her hands against this face, knowing before the announcement, to say: Yes, yes, I know, but not yet. Instead she was visibly calmer, if under her skirts her knees shook. *Mon Dieu, les Anglaises*! Mme Adorée thought. But Catherine Standish was no longer existent physically. She flickered. Just a flicker of the breath, and the little emotional images that started into the foreground of her mind, Willy and the bag for which she had paid herself, Willy sitting in a cloud at the café in Dieppe.

Madame will realize it is not my fault if I tell what I think I ought, Mme Adorée said.

Because it was time she said something to the *Anglaise*, standing with her hand on the knob. She felt she had been cheated out of an emotional display.

Yes. You were quite right, Mrs Standish said. Quite right, Mme Adorée, she said, slowly.

Then she went upstairs. Her knees still shook.

This'll be a bore, she said to Willy, talking over her shoulder as she dressed. Malcolm will tell us about his boat.

It was unimportant what she said. She felt stiff. And the stiff words that slid ungainly along her tongue.

If we hang on long enough, it'll be over, Willy said. Even the Wilcoxes.

She could hear the rustle of his collar in the dressing-room next door. It was a strange, detached ritual, the taking off and putting on of clothes for the eating of meals. In the kitchen at Norwich they sat down to cod balls on Sunday. She remembered the grain of the kitchen table, the channels she had dug with the prong of a fork. Before the pantomime. She had acted herself into a series of parts, some of them verging on the Guignol. At home there was a cupboard under the stairs into which she had crept when frightened.

There, she said brightly. Do you like Mother in her new dress?

She stood smoothing it over her hips. In a corner of the room the little boy, his cot, where he sat turning a picture book, he had slept there since his bronchitis, when they moved him down. He sat looking at her gravely over the picture book.

Yes, he said softly, strangely attentive, yet removed, his face still pale from bronchitis. When will it be over? he asked, fretfully turning the pages of the book.

Soon, she said. You won't notice. You won't even notice Mother's been gone.

I wish it was over, he said. I wish it were morning.

She went across and put her hand on his forehead. She trembled a little, she couldn't stop it. And sensing this, he looked at her, wondering, he was half afraid.

Ten more minutes, she said. Then Julia will put out the light.

He looked at her going out of the room. She could feel his wondering eyes, that made her hold herself too straight, as protection against the child's eyes.

It was much as you expected, in the dining-room, in the drawing-room, the things you said to the Wilcoxes, and Eve's cure, and Malcolm's boat. But the ball flew, from custom, with mechanical agility. You almost had time to think, if you let yourself, if your mind abandoned the easy ball. Willy did this sort of thing with conviction. He made Malcolm Wilcox feel gauche, even while grateful for the attention, that arm round the shoulder, and the intimate flash of teeth. Malcolm had a boat on Southampton Water. He went there at week-ends, to return full of technical terms for his friends. The skin was stretched tightly over your face after an evening with Malcolm's boat.

And then, said Eve, you sit with your legs in Epsom salts. Right up to the knees.

Mrs Standish in her drawing-room felt that she had learnt by heart all the conversation she had ever made. She had learnt it on marrying Willy, something acquired with her attractive room, the Liberty curtains and the chiming clock. But soon it will all be over, she said. I shall go upstairs and take off my clothes, I shall lie in my bed, I. She cut herself short. She held herself rigid, as brittle as a conversational phrase. Yes, *yes*, YES, she said, through words, or sleep, or the chiming of a gilt clock. The French face on the mantelpiece had creamy eyes.

When they were alone again, she felt it very forcibly. Willy and herself alone in a house. Because this was what it amounted to, the children sleeping, and Julia Fallon. The little boy moved his head in his cot. A hot and sleepy protest came, from a long distance, out of his half-closed mouth. If I were asleep, she said, that sick pounding she became, her stomach. She slipped on a gown and went through into the dressing room.

Willy, she said.

He was standing in his shirt tails, scratching his head.

Willy, I want to talk, she said.

Mm? he said. At this time of night!

Yes, she said. Because, you see, because it's like this, she said.

Her clasped hands offered no assistance to the word, were lumped together ineffectually, except as a guard against trembling perhaps.

There's a lot we've got to decide, she said.

What *are* you talking about? he asked.

He had stopped scratching his head.

Mme Adorée says.

Her voice shouted.

Mme Adorée says. It's all so absurd, she faltered. And going into her workroom, Willy. And all that, she said.

His mouth had grown tighter.

I think you're getting hysterical, he said.

That focused the blurring line. She felt she was standing on the carpet, even if her breath caught still, and words escaped from her control.

I suppose I haven't an interest?

You don't often show it, he said.

It made her want to dramatize. It gave her movement. All the moments she had lived with Willy crested over in a wave of pity for herself.

No? she said, harshly. And the times I've been shown it wasn't wanted. What about those? Those don't count, I suppose?

All right, he said. We've made a mess. For God's sake, let's leave it at that.

But this was more than she could do, control the impetus of words that jostled for expression.

And Maudie Westmacott? We've got to ignore that. And shopgirls in the basement? And all the misery, she said, her voice keeling over here, all the *misery* of deceiving.

You make me tired. You're ludicrous, he said.

Which made it worse, because she was just that, blurting, blathering, she knew, so much that accumulated over the evening and the evenings of years. She felt her whole ludicrousness, physically, and the ludicrousness of badly spoken words.

But we shan't ignore it, she persisted.

She beat her hands on the dressing-table. She heard the bottles rattle.

If you think I'm going to stand, he said.

Go on then, she said. Go on!

He had begun to put on his trousers again.

That's just what I'm doing, he said.

His voice was over-high.

The world's big enough for the two of us, shouted Willy Standish, or it seemed like that.

I'm sure, she cried, matching his voice. Go on, she said. We'll see.

We'll see? I know? he shouted.

Ssh! she cried. You'll wake the child.

Damn the child, Willy said.

That was too much, too much bitterness, together with her

ludicrous face that watched her in the glass. She felt the hot approach of tears. Through the door the child had begun to cry. She went back into the other room. The child turned in his bed and cried. She held his head too tightly against her.

Darling! she cried, crying with him. Poor darling. My poor, poor darling. You mustn't be unhappy, she said.

But she could not control the spasms of her crying, as she held the child against her body, and this translated itself to the body of her child. He cried with her, but with the desperation of a child, for there was no reason for any of this.

Poor darling, she kept on moaning.

She listened to her own voice.

3

Ssh! She cried. You'll wake the child.

He watched the little thread of light stretched underneath the door. It cut across the darkness separating him from all that. The other room was all sound and light. You thought it was going to burst.

Damn the child! the room shouted.

His jaw faltered. He was alone in darkness, in the dark tunnel, pushed there, held there by the voice. And at the other end was the sound of milk, and Julia stroking the light on beans. He had that hot moistening of the throat. And the hot fever of sheets that was more than the fever of bronchitis. He could not get his legs out of the plaster of sheets. He could not run back to where Julia switched off the light, her kiss. He was lost between darkness and the frightening separate noises in the other room. So he began to cry. It consumed him. He was his own crying. He groped towards morning with his hot hands.

Then the door opened and she came in. She held him, and this was frightening too. Because she was crying. She was crying for the lost morning.

Poor darling, she kept crying.

He could not move against wet silk.

You mustn't be unhappy, she said.

But her voice didn't convince. He wasn't sure that she was any farther from being afraid. He wished it was Julia, both because he wanted to know if Julia had escaped the night, and because Julia never cried, except she said her tooth was bad, then Julia cried.

Julia, he sobbed, against silk.

That made her smooth his hair. Quieter too. As if she was thinking. The little yellow thread of light had whisked away from under the door.

Would you like to get into Mother's bed? she asked slowly, speaking as much to darkness, and still thinking, her voice. Would Elyot like to sleep with Mother?

He nodded his head against her side, feeling on his cheek the rub of silk.

Very well. Wait a minute, darling, she said.

She turned on a light. She went and looked out on the landing, listening. Then she slammed the door. Her face was still listening when she spoke.

Elyot will keep Mother company, she said.

Even though her voice touched on him, her face was distant, even as she picked him up and put him in the cold, fresh bed. She sighed a lot. It made him wonder again about the noises in the next room, that was now silent, it was flat like rooms at night, they only opened out in the morning. And now in the fresh bed, morning itself was not beyond reach. He sighed too, imitating her.

We'll soon be asleep, shan't we? she said with determination.

Yes, he sighed.

And he almost was. He was the silky sigh of darkness that her breast was. He curled his fists against her breast and slept.

Poor darling, she said, a long way back, or in sleep. Once he woke to feel a kind of choppy sobbing, that made him wonder, not afraid. He drifted in the warm scenty smell back to his own unconsciousness.

It slipped away easily into odd moments, the night that Mother cried. This was a moment you took out to wonder at, sometimes secretly by yourself, you did not even ask Julia why. But most often you did not think. Because it was mostly walks, and wet days against the windowpane, and Eden screaming, and the doses of syrup of figs, muddy at the bottom of the bottle. Sometimes Julia's tooth ached. He walked softly, not to hurt the ache.

Is it better, now Julia? he asked.

It's right up me face, said Julia through a hand.

You ought to have it out, Mother said.

Oh no, mum, said Julia. We'll give it another try yet.

It puzzled him why she called her mum, as if she was Julia's mother.

Why do you call her mum? he asked.

Because, said Julia.

She isn't your mother.

What do you think!

Then why do you call her mum? he asked.

You're just a silly boy, she said.

She began to put on her hat, that had a bird, like a swallow with a white eye.

It's time we went for that walk, she said.

Once in the Park, he had pulled off the bird on Julia's hat. It was like a swallow in front, but at the back it was a yellow, gummy card. He bit his lip when she smacked his legs. He hated Julia and her flat bird. He hated the walks on asphalt. He hated the South Kensington Museum. He hated Eden, who was his sister, they said, pushed by Julia in her shiny pram, which was Eden's own intimate world. It was not much fun having a sister in a pram. They seldom met on equal ground, except to prepare for skirmishes to come. He trailed by himself round the edge of ponds, the water that was yellow in summer, in winter grey. This was a vaguely consoling sea. He sat on the edge and thought. That is, he let his mind wander, shapelessly, out of reach of the irksome details that forced it into a certain shape, away from the people who did Everything for His Own Good.

Julia elbowed him and said:

Come on, mister, where've you got to?

He frowned.

I'm having a think, he frowned.

And what are you thinking of? she asked.

Nothing, he said, carefully.

Which was truer than it sounded, he knew. There was not much connexion between the blur of *things* that eddied and jostled in his mind, not much meaning, that you could explain to people, anyway.

Eden looked at him out of her small, wondering face. It was not the wonder of a face impressed. It was more the wonder of contempt. Sometimes he could feel the small, wondering contempt, which was the contempt of sisters in prams. And it exasperated him. Sometimes he put his hand on the back of her neck, to feel how small and frail it was, to measure the smallness with his hand, and to see, if he squeezed, just a little, and then a little, to see exactly what. When Eden screamed.

I'll take the brush to you, said Julia. A big boy, five years old, and a torment to his sister.

Yes, he was five. On his fifth birthday, he had a pink cake, like a rainbow inside, and a lot of children he did not like who came to help him eat it. They stood about in the rooms of the house that was no longer his. The strange, resentful children. They resented each other because they were strangers. There were very few children that he ever knew. Eden, and possibly Connie Tiarks, and there it just about ended. But then it is usually like that. And on his fifth birthday he was no different from any other children. Even though Mme Adorée said: *Il est énormément intelligent, ce petit, je vous félicite, Madame.* Mme

73

Adorée gave him a little book of French songs. It had '*Savez-vous planter des choux?*' and '*Sur le pont d' Avignon*', which he learned to rattle off with Mother, run together in a movement of sound, from which he could not detach the words, let alone their meanings.

Ell-yott, Ell-yott, cried Mme Adorée, when he passed the shop. *Tu vas chanter? Une seule petite chanson?*

So that he dared not look inside the shop. He was afraid to encounter in this gauzy cave the face of Mme Adorée as it peered out. She had a funny, swollen neck and protruding eyes. When Mme Adorée spoke to him, he felt embarrassed and looked at his toes. And the two workgirls came up from the basement, smiling, and laughing, and stuck with pins. They bent down over him and made a fuss. They kissed him and he felt hot.

Julia said they was saucy girls.

Why is Mme Adorée called Mme Adorée, Julia? he asked.

That's her name, said Julia. It's French for Adored.

Oh, he said. How do you know?

I'm not stupid.

She pulled the hatpins out of her hat.

It sounds silly, he said.

No, she said. It's only French.

Mme Adored! Mme Adored! he sang, till he began to laugh.

It's so silly, he laughed.

You're the silly one, said Julia.

She sat on the chair to change her shoes.

And those girls, he asked, what are their names?

Blessed if I know, Julia said.

He loved Julia.

Julia, he said, will you marry me?

She sat in her stockings, on her flat feet.

It'll be a bit of a wait, said Julia.

I'm five, he said. And two months.

Once he went with her to Oxford Street and saw a suite of furniture. He said that they would have that. It was shiny and smart, upholstered in what looked like crumpled velvet, with buttons pinning it down.

Mother began to say she was poor. She didn't know what she was going to do.

I shall have to sell my furs, she sighed. And what shall I do without my pretty furs?

She had a habit, when you were brought in most evenings, before it was bedtime, and she was alone with books, she had a habit of asking for advice. Or at least she spoke out into the room, sitting carelessly in her chair, with one hand drooping over the side. It fascinated him to watch this hand, while pretending not, while sitting on the floor with a picture book. And the hand was pale, if they had not turned on the light, or it hung golden in the firelight with a glittering of rings. She got up and moved vaguely to touch a flower in a vase. He felt that she was not there. In spite of her asking voice, she was not there. He watched the hand as it moved a lily. It was white, and it smelt as white as lilies.

What shall we do? asked the absent voice.

Julia saw a fur in Oxford Street. She's going to save up and buy it, he said.

She laughed.

Yes, she said. Of course there's always Oxford Street.

It hurt him that she laughed. He turned the pages of the picture book. But people were mostly like that. The voices that asked the questions and seemed to know the answers, and you wondered why they asked, why they remained a long way off in a world of hidden answers. Even Julia was like that. But in Mother's face there was something particularly mysterious, connected, he felt, with the noises in the room that you didn't mention, or only once, and then not really, you were afraid to lift up the curtain on Mother's face.

Where is Father? he once asked.

He heard the scraping of a turned page, and the bumping of

his heart, that was a bumping also in the dressing-room. Then there was silence and a chiming clock.

Father, she said, has gone away.

Somehow he did not want to ask why.

There was a boy in the Park, he said, who can turn a double somersault. He lives in Eccleston Square.

He did not look up at Mother's face. He was a bit uncomfortable, almost afraid.

Come here, darling, she said.

Why?

Come and sit on Mother's lap, she said.

He did so unwillingly, sat there stiffly, allowed her to stroke his hair. It was too close, too close to the scent of darkness, and the slamming of a door.

But the moments of unexplained, awkward intimacy were rare. Sometimes there were other people, the men who smelt of cigars, and whose faces talked above your head as you looked at their watch chains. Mostly for the men you weren't there. But the ladies held out their hands, and asked you your name, the ladies smelt fresher than flowers, a mingling of many flowers at once. There was the lady also that Eden bit, because she did not want to be kissed. Julia said Eden made her ashamed. He did not much like being kissed, not any more than Eden did, but without protesting, he let himself be drawn in, up against a strange sensation of flowers.

Most of these people wore new clothes. But there were some who wore funny clothes and came on quieter afternoons. They sat in their old, careful clothes and called Mother Kitty, and thanked her a lot. They were sometimes rather stupid, he felt, to thank for what was only tea and cake. Not like the others, whose kisses smelt of wine and flowers, for whom Mother talked and laughed a lot. For the funny ones, she was sometimes silent. She let them tell about the places they came from, and often in the middle, would go out to the telephone.

Grandpa and Grandmother Goose came once. Grandpa Goose had cracks in his hands, and talked in a funny way. Julia said you must be nice to Grandpa, because, she said, of his cataract, because Grandpa Goose would soon be blind. He sat quietly in the drawing-room, without saying very much, his hands on the knees of his tight black suit. Grandpa was very tight in his suit. When he spoke, the words exploded into the room. It made you surprised to hear anything so loud bursting into the drawing-room. But you liked Grandpa Goose, in spite of the first strangeness of a voice. Leaning on his knees you soon felt very close, explaining the book that he couldn't see, that you had just begun to read, the *Castles and Palaces of England*, that Julia gave.

I want to live in a castle, you said.

That's lots of people's complaint, laughed Grandpa Goose, just as if it was measles.

Mother, dear, said Mother, it was funny to think she was her mother. Mother, she said, and she sounded annoyed, wouldn't you like to take off your hat?

No, dear, Grandmother said. We must go in a minute. To catch our train.

And soon they had gone, and the strange sensation of your hand in Grandpa Goose's hand was a rough tingling in the memory.

Good-bye, Elyot Standish, Grandpa said.

It sounded almost as if you were nothing to do with him. There was a difference in Grandpa Goose, in his hands. He was going back to this difference, which Mother said was Norwich.

Elyot Standish went upstairs. He was conscious of a difference in his name. He hadn't thought about his name. It was as if he had received this from his grandfather on the doorstep, and there it sat for the first time. He hung about disconsolate in the drawing-room.

I wish my name was Goose, he said.

You mightn't if it were, said Mother.

She still sounded angry, and a little sad, as she moved about tidying things in the room.

Why doesn't Grandma Standish come?

Because I don't care to have her, said Mother.

And that was that.

Time went slowly. He wished he could have had two birth-days a year. But soon he was six, and it wasn't much different from being five, except that the presents were different, and he didn't feel well after eating too much cake. Of the presents, he liked the books best, there was one about Indians, and one about the wild flowers of Great Britain, both of which he was learning to read with Mother, when she wasn't busy. But Mother went to meetings, she said the Kaiser made her blood boil, and if it wasn't for the Entente Cordiale. That was some-thing to do with Mme Adorée. Once, coming in from a walk, he had stuck his head through the shop door and shouted: Mme Adorée is the Entente Cordiale. It gave her great pleasure. She screamed like a bird, and you knew that Mme Adorée was pleased. But often Mme Adorée said that her blood was boiling too. Before it was hot, before the children in the Park were leaving for the sea, and the water in the ponds had grown yellow, and you trailed over asphalt in a heavy shadow. Mother said she was too poor that summer. They could not afford to go away. And everything grew yellow, the faces of the houses, the grass in the parks, the sky very often was a yellow glare. Sometimes you could not sleep at night. You opened the window wide and listened to people sitting in their gardens.

It was about this time there began to be a numb feeling in the streets. Mother was pale and excited. Her face had drained away from the stuff she put on her cheeks. Julia said the boys would be going to the War. And soon there were bands and flags, and crying and laughing and kissing in the streets. Whole mornings people did not answer you, because they were talk-ing about the War. It began to frighten, the half-knowing what it was about, all the half-knowing, whether at the War or in the next room, which nobody ever explained. Julia said: Say your prayers. But it didn't help, after the saying, the rattle of words against the darkness, the darkness was not impressed by prayers. And you began to feel it was you that mattered, it was only you, not prayers or Julia, that paved the way to morning. Which made it more frightening than before. It was more than being alone in darkness.

Night hung heavy the curtain hung thick and sticky behind you could not lift know *savez-vous* was what Mme Adorée the bunch of shiny cherries that she picked and then she said *les Boches* it was all up with *les petits enfants* was the Kaiser from the *Illustrated London News* walking in the field the shells flowered soundlessly to run the mud clung the feet the mud Ell-yott can no longer run your feet are mud and the bump at the bottom it will burst flow like candlelight behind the hatbox that the cherry trimmed must reach must shout the sewn mouth so many stitches did not move sewn to the carpet like the feet.

He was standing at the bottom of the stairs.

You've been walking in your sleep, Mother said.

Above him the candlelight she held. She floated. Her nightgown and her hair were streaming out by candlelight. She wore the dressing-gown with mignonette, a field of greeny yellow sprigs.

But the Germans, he said.

Give me your hand, said Mother. It's a dream.

As if it wasn't still, standing near the stairs, your eyes swelled, were no longer yours.

We'll soon be asleep, she said, walking.

It was too much trouble to explain, to explain what. He let her lead him up the stairs, a long way back.

It was in the basement, you said, shivered. And Mme Adorée.

Yes, she said. Here we are. Jump into bed. There.

It was a dream.

Of course, she said.

You looked at a field of mignonette, the eyes closed, behind the eyes, under your chin the sheet felt safe.

The War depended largely on Mother, she read the battles out of the papers, or she made it recede, she came upstairs while you were having tea, and said you would leave for the country in a few days' time.

You will go to Somerset with Julia, Mother said.

Will there be cows? you asked.

Yes, I expect there'll be cows, she sighed.

Then she told Julia in another voice about the tickets, about the Macarthys. You were going to live with the Macarthys, she said.

So the War gave way to the currant bushes in the Macarthys' back garden, there was one currant bush that had strayed round in front, was in with the marigolds and phlox, and the delphiniums, the butterfly delphiniums, Mrs Macarthy said, it made her spit through a gap in her teeth. Currant bushes in leaf had a green glare that was always afternoon. You walked down the brick step, hollowed by feet, into the green glare, and the big white patches of the cloths they laid on the currant bushes, like big white cotton flowers. At the corner of the house there was a smell of kitchen water. It lay against the red brick. But farther, you came to the smell of grass, and in late summer, pears that the wasps had opened. The back garden was a continual humming, your own, or the girls' voices from the kitchen, or the wasps and bees, if you lay with your face amongst the grass the whole world was a world of humming, in a green, afternoon glare.

In front the light was sharper, clearer, you could see the Bristol Channel in the distance, across the fence, from the room where you did the lessons that Mr Macarthy set. All the morning you sat in the room. Morning was sums, and history, and the first Latin declensions. And outside in the sharp light everything looked very orderly. You could not wander in the front garden as you did among the currant bushes. The front was as ordered as a Latin declension. The beds were lined with flints.

The garden belonged to Mrs Macarthy. Mr Macarthy sat in his room, even when he wasn't giving lessons, he sat there just from habit perhaps, he had once been a schoolmaster all the time, now he had arthritis. Mr Macarthy was a mild man, he did everything slowly, partly because of the arthritis, partly because of his gentleness. He was a good man, Julia said. Though he wasn't a parson, he sometimes preached in church on Sundays, and he went and preached in the almshouse to the old men. Mr Macarthy got up with difficulty into the pulpit. In his surplice he looked like the figure off a tomb, the long straight lines of stone. In the winter he wore mittens on his stiff hands. His fingers stuck out from the knitting with its big holes, like the fingers of a knight from his chain mail. Altogether Mr Macarthy was like one of the knights you saw on tombs.

If Mr Macarthy was quiet and gentle, Mrs Macarthy talked a great deal, spitting always through the gaps in her teeth, rushing at things and pushing them over, or she opened a drawer and the drawer came out. Mrs Macarthy was made of plush, several cushions fastened together, and these were a kind of darkish plush. She also had a soft, black moustache that tickled mysteriously when she kissed. You dreaded Mrs Macarthy's kiss. Just as you dreaded her voice calling, asking you to come and lace up her boots. There's a good boy, said Mrs Macarthy, sitting blowing in her chair. Your hands caught in the tangle of boots. The black, flopping tongues, and the snapping laces. On frosty mornings in the dining-room, the boots crackled round your cold hands. You almost cried for hatred of Mrs Macarthy's boots.

Time went both slowly and quickly in the Macarthys' house, sometimes you thought one way and sometimes the other, or perhaps it was really like that, a quickening, then a slowing of time. The house was full of clocks. Some of these had stopped, like the old, wooden German clock with two pinecones hanging on chains, the clock that Mrs Macarthy refused to wind. He looked at the German clock on the landing, it became a queer thrill to walk past, because of the Germans, and the German spies, and the corpses of prisoners they boiled down for tallow.

Sometimes he broke into a sweat, watching for a movement of the still hands, imagining he saw them move.

But there was not much movement in any of the house. It was full of things that people had stopped using, or the things that Mrs Macarthy had collected as a girl, the glass slippers, and china lambs, and the certificates for choral singing with their signatures in yellow ink. Parts of the house were particularly still. The place at the end of the landing where potplants stood on a bamboo table, and where there were usually bodies of flies. It was breathless by the table of begonias, and the one rambling aspidistra that Mrs Macarthy made you sponge. Breathless, and hateful, like Mrs Macarthy's kiss.

In the attic it was also still, but pleasant, under the stillness a sound of life, the creaking of heat or cold, the murmuring of insects that flew or built there. In the attic there were rows of apples and pears, that you ate occasionally, the ones from the back. It was good to sit and wonder the things that you wondered, and about the War, the killing, the people in the village whose men had been killed, the drained faces and the reddish eyes. Mrs Delbridge has lost a son, Mrs Macarthy said. Then everybody kept silent. Mrs Delbridge was different. Because her son, you did not say it, was dead. Mrs Standish has a dead son. It made you wonder, till your hands were sweat, if the sparrow lying stiff in the frost, if Elyot Standish could become this, or the graves of the dead people that you did not, *could not* have any connexion with. As if death. I don't want to die, he said. He heard his voice, that was the voice of Elyot Standish, who would perhaps die. But there was some comfort in the buzzing of insects, in the smell of apples. He hung on to these to make sure, even if the echo of his own voice was a wondering still, a wondering if death.

The thought of death that is constantly with us, said Mr Macarthy in one of the sermons he once preached. But this was not altogether true. On the cliff path, for instance, against a mackerel sky, with the people gathering driftwood down below. Or racing Eden down the summer hill, when you fell panting on the bed of docks. Because Eden had begun to take part in things, no longer sitting in a pram, was part of this same being alive. She sat and listened to the sermons of Mr Macarthy. She sat picking at the pew. She lowered her head at the *thought of death that is constantly with us*, letting it pass over her, like the meaningless parts in older people's conversation. There were many dead parts that you let pass. It was sometimes dull.

I want to be an airman, Eden said.

It made him snort. As if Eden. Well, he had to laugh.

You couldn't be an airman, he said.

Yes, I shall.

She hated him.

You couldn't even be an airwoman, he laughed.

I shall be an airman, she scowled. I'll fly to France. I'll fly to America. I'll show you, she said.

You'll fall in the sea, he said.

Well. Even if i fall in the sea.

That began to annoy him, the absurdity of girls who are also sisters, and her face that grew purple in a rage, her lips became slate blue. Eden had a temper that he had to provoke. It filled him with both contempt and rage. He was a small core of disgust for so much frailty. He was also a little concerned by what he had released.

I'll do anything I like! she screamed.

You're only a girl, he said quietly.

He was white with hatred and contempt. Then she threw the paperweight that hit him in the chest, its thud, and the pain that was more surprise.

There, she said, quietening.

They looked at each other across the room. The thought of death that is constantly with us, Mr Macarthy preached. It was immanent, not in the fields of France, which were unimportant, because distant, except in Mrs Delbridge's eyes, it had found a sudden interpretation in Mrs Macarthy's sitting-room.

I'll give you something, he said, with the quietness that follows after surprise.

I hope that bursts your ear drum, he said.

His hand released the scream that almost split the house. The pointed screams that were without respect for walls. He waited for what, in the absence of collapsing brick, would be more personal punishment.

Julia was red and angry when she came.

I'm ashamed, she said. Downright ashamed. You'll have the stick, my lad. You'll be sorry, Julia said.

And he was, for a little, in his room, running his finger along the quilt. He felt dry and empty after crying, after the exhaustion of so much passion. He ran his finger over the quilt and picked through past exasperation, Eden in tears, and the absurdity of girls. You could never share things with girls. Or with anyone perhaps. It made the finger pause. You were shut up in a box, in a room, in the sound of roosting birds, and the distant sounds of sea, and farther, soundless, the shells in France. It was darker now, and cold. His cheeks had dried.

Elyot, called Eden. You can come to tea.

He went out into the passage. She looked communicative, but shy.

There's fish, she said.

He did not answer at first. But he was not resentful. As if she could not help herself. As if she was not aware of the discovery he had made. He walked along, apathetic, in the first stages of renewed contact. He was dignified, but still a little miserable.

Oh, he said. Fish.

Yes, she said. Herrings. And there's someone else coming tomorrow. A girl called Connie Tiarks. She's about as old as me.

That made him resentful again. Even if herrings. Connie Tiarks.

Marching with the authority of a Greek messenger, with more than his share of information, Eden launched on the next announcement.

And Mrs Macarthy's heard from Mother. She's gone to France to be a nurse. I wish I could be a nurse, she said.

Then she stopped, remembering.

4

Waiting in the restaurants was a return to yesterday, the resentments, the bursts of superiority, the silences, the irrelevance and stupidity of the conversation overheard from other tables, today or then, almost but not quite, like the one-armed man in the uniform. There were many uniforms, of course. That clothed it with a difference. But deeper than the outer skin, you found the little pieces of debris from many emotional moods that would never quite fit together again. Even the annoyance at being kept waiting was unconvincing, something built on the pattern of habit. Or else it may be, she felt, that irritation is more intense for the unpunctuality of the people we know well than for those we know vaguely.

Catherine Standish sat looking at the bread a waiter brought. It was French bread, full of holes, the kind that looks as if bubbles have burst inside the baking dough. Remembering the strangeness of her first French bread, she regretted that it could become just bread. It was familiar, like the voices of the officers, that rippled in French or sauntered in English across the Paris restaurant. Because Paris had evolved from abstraction in the mind, a city of contemplated pilgrimage, into one of the places you passed through, getting somewhere, somewhere else. She was on her way with Rhoda Swansey from the hospital at Rémy to spend a fortnight at home. Paris was incidental. A night and a couple of railway stations. This is terrible, she felt. She wished he would come and buy her a drink.

But at least there was a flicker that October morning looking in the window of the little cheap jewellery shop, finding it registered still, the potency of paste bracelets and the rows of detached, *diamanté* heels. She had found at the back of her own reflexion the old sensations, half buried. She had gone right back and rooted in the heap of still unsatisfied, innocent desires,

till her body slackened to another line, and her face grew unprotected in its self-confessed nostalgia. Any intrusion from
the present, from the honking of the traffic or the pavement
noises, would have been pointless, if achieved. Only the voice
rang a bell. It came up out of the blue and gritty Paris morning,
it fitted itself into her ear, it made itself part of the first personal
intimate moment she had experienced in so many months.

If it isn't Kitty Standish! she heard.

It was too close, too intimate, for a moment a nerve in her
body that she wanted badly to suppress. It was too much like
so many of your own failures compressed into the accents of
another voice.

Well, she said, Willy!

She began to laugh. Because it was relief. They stood and
laughed on the pavement. Their laughter bounded in the faces
of the French with too insistent a *bonhomie*. She could feel that
her cheeks were red. But she continued to laugh. It absolved
her from the next move.

Kitty, he said, come and sit down. There's so much we've
got to talk about.

Yes, she said, doubtfully. Yes, but there's Rhoda, Rhoda
Swansey, we're travelling home together from Rémy. I promised I'd be at the hotel at twelve.

Yes, on second thought, Rhoda Swansey was imperative. If
unconvincing. Their words blew about them in little furtive
gusts. Looking sideways at each other, there was still too much
comment, too much surmise in the half-glance. Willy was
thinner, greyer. She was beginning to let herself go. But however speculative the individual mind, they dealt publicly in the
kind of words that are used for conveying information. The
calm, friendly unembellished words of letters written after the
recovered temper, to settle things with dignity, to discuss the
details of separation. Or you wrote from time to time, again
informative, inquiring or telling about the children, spilling a
platitude on war, stating the degree in which you personally
had been involved, but not emotionally, of course, commis-

sions and nursing and that sort of thing. So that conversation, once started, once you had chosen your definite line, was easy enough, up to a point. Then it began to get difficult again.

It's nice, she began, trusting to a lame inspiration, it's nice to have seen you again, Willy, and know that you're safe and – well, *safe*.

It petered out. It left her standing in a cold wind, in a hostile Rue de Rivoli, talking to an English officer.

Kitty, we've got to have dinner tonight. Get rid of this woman. Somehow. Lock her in her room. I insist.

It was Willy talking in a uniform, his hand that her arm felt through the sleeve, which was more than an encounter of flesh and bone. She found herself regretting his smile. It was so deliberate, but like a convention, you accepted it.

This one evening. After all.

Then it began to seem stupid, and complicated, the whole business of two people with their over-complications, their immense capacity for entanglement. It was too much, in the middle of the street, to make the fumbling approach to your own or anyone else's motive, to correct anyone's mistakes. Feeling on her face the lean October wind, and looking not exactly in Willy's eyes, she said slowly:

All right then. Where shall we meet?

Now she was sitting, had been sitting in the restaurant Willy named, she had been sitting there twenty minutes past the time that Willy had decided on. None of this matters, she said, and yet I shall want to kill Willy. Restraining her hands from bread, she thought up the things that perhaps she would say. Nowadays there was little to say. The War. Even if this was not Willy, it made a limited alternative, there was only the War, and personal emotions, and shop. At Rémy all these were closely and inevitably interwoven. She read a chapter from a book to a group that sat in the summer shade or winter sun. But books had become disconnected from life. They were mostly written before. The present was composed of maps and lint, rumour, and the opinions of a surgeon, of the frequent encounter with feverish hands, of the many soldiers who lay in Mme de Bonneville's house, and who sat or strolled in her gardens, in the different stages of recovery. There was no way out into another world. Even sentimental engagements, or the bleaker adventures of the body, described an additional circle inside the existing one. That made her wonder again about Willy Standish's emotional life, if and how he had become involved. Maudie Westmacott sang still, the same song though they changed the name. They called it 'You Can't Say No to a Soldier', probably with relevance. However you deplore a popular song, it usually has relevance. Catherine Standish bit her cheek. This will never do, she felt, pouring water out of the carafe.

Sorry, Kitty, he said, with just that accent of sincerity which always stopped your rage.

Willy's charm always cheated. It was so close to the border line. You couldn't argue out of your defeat. She looked at what had been Willy Standish, safely now that he was ordering the dinner, at what he had become, this separate existence. The bald details she had got in letters were as informative as a *Who's Who*. If you could lean forward, as the innocent sometimes did, and say: Now tell me about yourself – have it arrive on a plate with the soup. If you wanted to. And she was not sure that she wanted, exactly, that she wanted to become involved again in any but the official biography of Willy Standish. She tried the hotness of her soup.

Do you remember? he said.

It was going to be like that. It was also without malice. Because for Willy Standish it could afford to be, looking with the detachment of a stranger at this woman who had been his wife. It was his distinctness that he enjoyed. Emerging out of the vague, possessive years of marriage, to find you were yourself, distinct, your own thoughts and inclinations, no longer the fumbling composite of your own and another person's desires. So he could afford to be jovial. He could deal kindly with his own mistakes, and the supreme mistake, which was Kitty, sitting in front of him now in her unbecoming uniform. Garish, with her head of uncompromising hair, she didn't fit inside the uniform. Without it, she would have tried to Express Herself, you felt. With it, she merely looked a little odd.

Willy made her self-conscious, his eyes. Switching from the particular to the general, she began to say something about the tonal differences of French and English. She could feel the accent of affectation creeping upward into her voice. In a moment she would be talking books.

Remember the Pernods? he asked. The Pernods at Dieppe? If ever you hated me, Kitty, it was then.

Oh yes, I hated you! she said, with that over-arch conviction, in a too high voice.

But she needed protection. Either books or war. Not the emotions. With Willy Standish, at any rate. Walking beneath the *charmille* at the bottom of Mme de Bonneville's terrace, there was the young English lieutenant, he had the crisp, clipped, terrier look of so many healthy young Englishmen, who have also the bewilderment of dogs. You talked to the young English lieutenant as you would to a nice bewildered dog, firmly, reassuringly, with your mind on something else. Allowing him to talk about home, you heard your foot slur along the gravel in the stillness of a green evening, heard the breath catch on the desperate approach, the hand felt, and the texture of strange clothes. It was not exactly physical. You were too detached. Like stroking a dog.

After the War, Willy was saying, as if it would end, ever, he was thinking about Australia, he said.

Willy telling her his plans. She struggled with a piece of meat that was strange, dark, unpleasant, almost anything that the imagination cared to name. She hated that piece of recalcitrant meat.

Australia, she said, in jerks. Well, I suppose there are always apples.

Because she just couldn't take it out on the meat. Because she also wanted to see in Willy just one little trace of bitterness.

89

But he sat talking about Australia, ignoring a would-be clever remark, reminding her of her clumsiness. Willy, she realized, was dependent on himself. She could not tear through the envelope. Just as the young lieutenant at the time, his clumsy, touching hands, had made no impression on her own distinctness, in spite of her consent. She had been a bit afraid at first, sleeping with a strange man, who amounted to so many conversations, the encounter under the *charmille*, before the pretence of intimacy. She lay there listening to his breath, to his voice. She felt the clumsiness of hands. In two more days he would go, he said. Lying in the darkness, he had gone already. It was something more emphatic than time or space.

You've changed, Kitty, she heard.

It was Willy growing sentimental, Burgundy having its way.

None of us stand still, she said.

Sharper than she meant, when she did not mean, she wanted to lean across the table, she had the courage of Burgundy. Forms melting, the gold and the plush, had a tenderness of line for Catherine Standish after just that extra glass.

We'll have to meet again, he said. You can't talk in restaurants. Or letters. It can't be done.

Yes, she agreed, warily.

She had leant a little far perhaps. If you could think clearly, know how much you wanted to give or take. She was getting fuddled, she thought. She looked in the mirror and straightened her hat.

It was too late, too blurred, the voices at tables, the songs in the street. The evening was a white tablecloth with the little map of Burgundy. She watched her hand pouring salt.

Funny pouring salt, she said. I've never quite believed.

She watched her finger rubbing salt into the map of Burgundy. They were leaving from the next table. They were catching trains.

Walking back to the hotel, she could feel his arm. Silent mostly, they waited for words. They could feel the pressure of unreleased words. Dark and cold, with a cat mewing down a cul-de-sac. More urgent, more personal than Europe, the mewing of a formless cat. That was the trouble, she felt, behind a mastered hiccup, if you strayed aside from the open path of bare official events. That was why you talked war. To resist the pressure of the personal that you wanted and at the same time feared.

The night porter's face was yellow with sleep. He waited, bleary and indifferent.

To say now, she felt, to say Willy, or no.

Good night, Kitty, he said.

He was waiting perhaps, she was waiting, they were waiting for this ultimate overflow of words.

The night porter began to cough. A weary rumble of censure and phlegm.

Good night, Willy, she said, brightly. You'll write to me sometimes. Tell me you're safe.

It echoed too loudly down the street, the interplay of formalities, that no one really listened to, only to say, say, to fire the last shot in a friendly battle.

But it was over, and the keys, and the rack of postcards, the dusty postcards that nobody wrote. The lift was out of order, said the porter, she would have to walk. Bumping up the stairs in darkness, she was not particularly there, or anywhere. Drink made her miserable, she decided, not for the first time. It was only drink.

5

It was clear that the girl called Connie Tiarks did not fit into the old pattern. So that a new pattern had to be made. And everyone was annoyed at first, whether Mrs Macarthy, who couldn't decide which of her rooms she ought to prepare, or Julia, harassed with washing and sewing, or Elyot and Eden, who resented at once the inquiry of a third mind. Elyot and Eden, most of all, resented the intrusion of this watching face. Even though it amounted to no more than the pale, timid, lumpy face of the girl called Connie Tiarks.

This is Constance, said Mrs Macarthy on the first evening.

Three points of silence, they stood about in the sitting-room, listening to their own silences, Elyot, Eden, and Connie Tiarks. Elyot felt very close to Eden. He could feel it across the room. The foreign element of Connie Tiarks threw them together like attracted poles. And mostly it remained like this. You ignored each other's weaknesses.

Mrs Macarthy began to talk. She was speaking to the mother of Connie Tiarks. The mother would leave in less than an hour, so that they hadn't unharnessed the horse, because she was going away so soon. There was a great deal for Mrs Macarthy to say, for which everybody was glad, thankful for the shelter of a talking voice. You could take shelter with your own thoughts and watch the Tiarks girl standing by. In spite of being Eden's age, she was larger, she was lumpier, and she wore her pale, fine hair gathered in two white bows on either side of her face. Connie was as fair as Eden was dark. Even Eden's face was dark, not exactly in colour, except through temper, but it gave you the feeling of a dark face, especially when she talked. It made the fair, pale Connie Tiarks afraid.

You remember me, Elyot? asked the voice of Connie's mother, between mention of diet and laxatives.

You remembered the flat Mrs Tiarks, it was Sunday dinner, and the gravy splashed on her arm from Father's carving.

Yes, you said, stupidly.

There was nothing else to say.

We knew Captain Standish in India. My husband's regiment, Mrs Tiarks explained.

So Mrs Standish said, Mrs Macarthy replied.

Colonel Tiarks was long and thin. He made jokes that Mother said were puns. He made a joke that you thought funny at the time, until you thought it over a bit, and really it wasn't funny at all. But at the time, with Father carving the roast beef, you were propped up high in the dining-room, it was exciting, the strange faces, there were chocolates in little dishes on the table. Colonel Tiarks looked at the beef, which Father carved with a bending knife, the Colonel drew in his moustache and said: Big bones for the big dogs, little bones for the little dogs, and gristle for the cats. And you laughed. Mother was laughing. You looked at her and laughed. You could not stop. *Gristle for the cats*. Afterwards Mother and Father said Colonel Tiarks was a bore. Mother said she thought Mrs Tiarks was the biggest bore of all. But Father said, no, he stuck to the Colonel. Until they agreed they were about equal. And in time the joke wasn't funny any more.

Mrs Tiarks said she heard that Captain Standish was doing some very distinguished things. In the War, of course. Mrs Macarthy agreed, in a rush of spit. But there the matter ended at once. Mrs Macarthy looked at Mrs Tiarks. Mrs Tiarks looked at Eden. The air became very meaningful.

Yes, yes, Mrs Macarthy sighed.

Soon after that Mrs Tiarks left, and Mrs Macarthy took Connie up to her own bedroom so that she could have a cry. Downstairs you listened for the crying of Connie Tiarks. Your ears strained towards the ceiling.

Listen, you said.

You could just hear.

Let's go and listen on the landing, said Eden.

You stood on the landing, and the crying of Connie Tiarks was a thin mewing through the door. After a bit it began to get dull. You simply went away.

I don't like her much, said Eden.

No, you said. Not much.

Eden thought she was silly, that she wouldn't like her at all.

Because Connie Tiarks was the third face, tagging down the passage behind, drinking milk opposite at tea, her hand touched the cup that yours had touched, and like your hand, the cup was yours.

Why are your bows white? asked Eden.

I don't know, Connie said.

She looked as if she was going to cry.

I don't like them white, said Eden.

Eat up your tea, Julia said. It's none of your business, anyway.

But Julia didn't understand what it was about the bows of Connie Tiarks. She gathered up the plates afterwards, rumbling and thoughtful after tea. And Connie watched her sweep the crumbs. Connie was afraid.

Bedtime was like this too, but worse. She was placeless, and sleeping in a strange bed, she began to shiver long before there was any question of cold sheets. If she had a bed. But Mrs Macarthy had still to make up her mind. It was her neuralgia, she said, holding the hot water bottle. Tomorrow we shall see, Mrs Macarthy said, but tonight you shall sleep in Eden's bed, she said. That made the lights quiver, the linoleum cold. But getting undressed, watching, at least you kept to opposite corners, unlike sharing a strange bed, or having a stranger in your bed.

Where are you going to sleep? asked Eden.

As if she didn't know, sitting up already in bed.

Mrs Macarthy said, began Connie.

Her knees shook inside her nightdress, which was as cold as sheets. She was standing alone in a linoleum desert. She could not move towards the bed.

Once last summer, when it was hot, we had our mattresses out in the orchard, Eden said agreeably.

But she was watching, there was no move made of which she approved, if this were a move towards the bed. She resisted with her eyes.

Now then, Connie, Julia said, coming briskly into the room. It's time you thought of getting into bed. Make way for Connie, Julia said.

I thought, said Eden, I thought so! No one's coming into my bed.

We'll see about that, Julia said.

I'm not sleeping with her! cried Eden.

It was an indignity to be resisted, the lumpy face of Connie
Tiarks that lurked there frightened by the door, the fluffed-out
hair released from bows. Eden screamed. They would not
touch her. It was a resistance of passion, like everything she
did, the dark, emphatic face that failed to contain its own emotions. She sat there screaming with passion in bed.

I don't want, wailed Connie thinly, I don't want to get into
her bed.

The doorway that was no protection, half-way between two
strange rooms, was still kinder, even its draught. There was
less hostility in air.

I don't want to sleep anywhere, she whimpered.

It was a soft, uncertain crying next to Eden's screams.

What's all this? asked Mrs Macarthy.

She stood in the doorway, the plushy contours, and the
hand that held the hot water bottle to her face.

It's about the bed, Julia said, as much as to say she knew
from the start.

Mrs Macarthy stood looking uncertain whether to be annoyed or pained. Her lips began to munch on words. You were
warned by the working of her black moustache.

You're an abominable child, Eden, she said, and you heard
the water rumble loosely inside the half-filled rubber bottle. As
if I don't do all I can to make you children comfortable.

Mrs Macarthy often said this, not so much to make it known
as to reassure herself. Like her frequent reminder that she loved
children. She could never remind herself enough.

This is most provoking, she said. Nobody thinks I might be
in pain. And the beds aren't aired, she said. I owe it to the
child's mother not to put her in an unaired bed.

She's not coming in mine, said Eden.

She sat clutching a handful of sheet.

Nobody asked you, said Julia. I tell you what I'll do, mum,
if you like. I'll make up the sofa in the dining-room. Connie
can sleep there just for tonight.

It was just about settled, in spite of Mrs Macarthy's expression of debate.

Yes, she said. That is an idea. Yes, Julia. We shall do that!

Her hand was a plump hot water bottle. She was a series of water bottles, in plush. Tonight she was all vagueness. She was not herself. She was enjoying the luxury of neuralgia and the sympathy that nobody gave.

Yes, said Mrs Macarthy, giving it a broody emphasis. In the dining-room. Come along, Constance. We shall leave this ungrateful little girl at once.

Then they all went out. Upright in bed, Eden listened, heard the slipperless pattering of the girl called Connie Tiarks. Perhaps she would catch cold. Perhaps she would die. Eden fastened her mouth. She deliberately disposed of Connie Tiarks. It was a simple, unemotional act. She performed this frequently in her mind over the people she disliked. Death was the clicking of the catch.

Julia came presently to turn out the light. She did not look towards the bed. She turned out the light on an empty room, whisked herself away into darkness, the harassed hair and the red face. Julia got red in the face when angry, Eden pondered in the formless room. Alone, her shoulders began to wilt. She wanted the reassurance of a face. As if victory in itself were an unsatisfactory end.

Julia's an old stuffpot, she said.

But there was the raspberry jam, and buttering the pikelet, it was Friday afternoon in the kitchen, and don't tell Mrs Mac, said Julia, her hand was red with raspberry jam. Sitting in the darkness Eden felt the worm of misery raise its head. It rose and swayed its head in her stomach, as if her whole affection for Julia were rooted in that part of her body. All her misery and love came definitely from the pit of her stomach.

She got out of bed. She went across the passage. She wanted to hear her own voice.

Elyot? she whispered, pushing the door.

Yes? he asked across the darkness.

I did it, she said.

That made her feel better.

I wouldn't have her in my bed, I wouldn't sleep with that Connie Tiarks.

Yes, he murmured. I heard.

He could feel her sitting on the end of his bed. Again they felt very close, in the darkness, their whispers, their breath.

She's pretty feeble, Eden said.

She had begun to shiver. It translated itself openly to her voice. But she had to listen to this, to her reassurance. It was also good to touch the eiderdown on Elyot's bed.

You'd better go back, he said.

Yes, she shivered. I suppose.

He could hear her feet.

Isn't it awful! she said.

What? he asked, drowsily.

That girl. And those white bows. We shall have her about for ages, she said.

Her voice clung on, lapsed across the passage, drifted into darkness.

The house had been tensed ever since the arrival of Connie Tiarks. It got right under your skin, a feeling of hostility and expectation. So you waited. You appreciated the climax in Eden's room, the sounds across the passage that you sat up to hear better, propped on an arm. It made you restless. It was like the War. This had become the faces of Mr and Mrs Macarthy at the breakfast table, after the morning papers. You watched and you felt it coming on, the restlessness, you went outside and wandered up and down among the currant bushes in the back garden, till Mr Macarthy called round the corner and it was time to do arithmetic. Above the back garden the sky was either blue and oppressive, the heavy, blue and white summer sky like bulged washing over your head, or the thin, grey, untouchable sky of winter, each of them equally disturbing. You just had to walk up and down, while your breath came out in a hum of exasperation, and the palms of your hands were feverish.

He told himself he was Elyot Standish. It was unconvincing at such times. Or lying in the dark house, waiting for the unexpected to happen, that never did, that never would. But he lay and listened. He heard a mouse squeak, then the long, unfurling sound of somebody's snore. He wondered a bit about Connie Tiarks, who would look pale and grublike, no doubt, undressed in the dining-room. His mind slid over this, like the nude female statues in the book on Greek sculpture that Mr Macarthy had. Eden laughed, standing naked in the bath, or running across the hot linoleum in summer. She was either unconscious of herself without clothes, or else unashamedly interested. But his body had begun to make him ashamed. He was determined to hide himself, from Julia, from Eden, though to himself he became an object of passing and furtive contemplation.

It was an uneasy feeling. There were many uneasy feelings in the house, in the first stages of falling asleep. You changed your side again and again. The sighs were white as moonlight that the wardrobe released. The footfall lay on the carpet black as velvet. And downstairs Connie Tiarks crumbled into marble atoms on the sofa.

Downstairs Connie Tiarks curled, frightened, catlike, in a fixed line. She dared not uncurl a hand, move a leg, now that she had finished crying. The clock had pillars before they turned out the light. She had fixed her eyes on the familiar face, because any clock is the same face, and remembered the little leather travelling clock of her mother's that was a wedding present, she said. Thinking of her mother made her whimper past her pillow, into the plush arm of the sofa that Mrs Macarthy had pushed back. There were also the travelling photographs of her father, one in uniform, and one in a knickerbocker suit. The warmth and familiarity of her own possessions made her shudder again, remembering the scene in the bedroom. Her life, as she waited for sleep, seemed to open into an avenue of unfamiliar misery, that sleep itself protracted in a fretful journeying from place to place. She was afraid. She was uncomfortable. She was dissolving in a rain of hot, pervading misery.

It was the dining-room sofa that became the unshakable cross of Connie Tiarks. Even after they moved her to the room with the pincushion bulging from the china shoe, and where it was some comfort to wake against the trellis of puce roses. Eden could always remember the sofa, when others forgot. At breakfast or at dinner, even with her back to this memorial, Connie was reminded in Eden's eyes. Mrs Macarthy had said it was most provoking, and such a big girl. But Eden pursed up her mouth and looked. Or at times she said coldly, when she wanted her way: Who wet the sofa, Connie, I wonder who it could have been? This made you hot and sticky. It made you almost do it again. There was no escaping what was almost a lily, flowering in a field of plush.

Connie Tiarks was the weak sort. She would always be the weak sort. Soon she learned to bear this. And there were the sheltered moments too, the moments of placid sensation, sucking a chocolate bar, the sun on bricks, waking and drowsing, waking and drowsing before anyone took command.

Let's play at war, Eden said.

It made Connie quail.

I'll be the English, Elyot said.

No, said Eden. I'll be the English.

All right, he said. I'll be the French.

Wasps were heavy in the trees. A breeze ran in a light shiver over the crest of grass.

Who'll be the Germans? Eden asked.

As if she didn't already know. Her voice hung lazily inquiring. A wasp dug into a yellow pear.

I'll be the Germans, Connie sighed.

Her hands became green, twisting grass.

Will you, Connie? Eden said. All right, then, Connie's the

Germans. Now you must run away and hide. Before the French and English attack.

Connie went slowly up the hillside to where the elder bushes began. She felt almost gratefully the scratches coming on her legs, the touch of twigs, the cool-warm of concealing leaves. She lay against leaves, her heart beating, or the ground, it was difficult to tell, the thumping which swelled around you, the beating in the ears. She was lumpy, she was ugly, even if Mrs Macarthy, she heard through the door, had tried to call it plain.

The English and French began to advance. You could hear the firing of a French gun. There was a swishing in the undergrowth. And soon it was over.

You're our prisoner, Elyot said.

Am I? she answered, doubtfully. Then we can begin something else?

Not until after the War, said Eden.

You're our prisoner for the duration of war, said Elyot, in the voice of Mr Macarthy reading from the paper over marmalade.

It was true enough. She believed this.

We're going to put you in prison, said Eden.

Eden's eyes were bright. She talked very quickly as they marched down the hill, and the blood came jerking into her cheeks. She could never control her excitement. Sometimes Elyot was surprised. But he also admired her, unadmittedly, at moments like these, beside the frightened placidity of Connie Tiarks. You marched down the hill, and you were getting somewhere, in the warm, dusty afternoon, either Somerset or Flanders, you were marching towards some something which it was difficult to describe.

This is the prison, Elyot said.

Connie groped in darkness past the rakes and hoes, and what must be the mowing machine. The light outside sawed out the shape of door. Voices came to her fitfully. Soon it would be tea, she said. She stood quite placidly, waiting for time to bring her release. She could stand very long like this. It was easy.

There were no words. These were what frightened her, the quick, flashing words of Eden, and Elyot's calmer, commanding ones.

Outside the light grew purple on the Channel. Julia walked among the currant bushes. Julia often sighed now. She said it was the War.

I wish it was over, Elyot said.

What? asked Eden.

Why, the War.

Oh, she said. The War.

They trailed through the cooling grass. As if the house had fallen back, and the tool shed containing Connie Tiarks, and they were alone in a sudden and fearful intimacy. He did not like to be with Eden then. It was difficult enough to cope with the beating of his own heart. He could scarcely understand his own fears, without the additional dependency of hers.

Sometimes he went off alone by himself. It was a relief on stuffy afternoons, when words were tied to the root of your tongue, to find yourself in the seaward lane. His thoughts rambled directionless, between the hawthorns, branching, solitary, and instinctive. He walked with his head hung down, his lips pushed forward, watching the movement of his own feet. Sometimes a cart grated in the lane, staggered above and past the hawthorns, with an old man calling out from on top of a load. He liked to pass the old men on carts in lanes, because they were not disturbing. It was still being alone. It was still being yourself, in the presence of cowparsley or nettles. Just the grunt of an old man and the smell of hay or seaweed drifting past. You walked on. You walked round and against the hill, where the wind had combed out the trees into peculiar shapes. And just beyond that was the bay that they called Ard's Bay, though nobody could tell you why.

It was an almost enclosed, almost a circular bay. He spent many hours looking into pools. There were crabs. There were red, blunt anemones, and the paler, trailing kind. He took up the smooth stones in his hand, the red and the mauve stones, that shone when you took them out of the water. And standing on the rim of the bay, holding the rounded stones in his hand, everything felt secure and solid, the gentle, enclosed basin of water, the sturdy trees that sprouted from the sides, his own legs planted in the moist sand. At Ard's Bay everything was plain sailing. You looked into water and saw the shape of things.

Where have you been, Elyot? Mrs Macarthy asked when he got back.

Because Mrs Macarthy had to know everything.

Nowhere, he said. Nowhere much.

Because Mrs Macarthy and Ard's Bay were quite separate. They had to stay like that.

The bay was his special property. Later he found the cave, going inward through the wall of rock, and he could sit and watch from the ledge of rock any outer activities, and listen to the sea as it nosed the shore. He gathered pieces of wood. He gathered the coloured stones. And on the wall of the cave he scratched with a crumbling finger of stone, no particular design, but he liked to draw, he liked to sing to himself as the line became more and more intricate on the surface of the rock. It gave him great pleasure to feel he was doing this, secretly, unknown to the Macarthys, or Julia, or Eden. He very much needed this secret life. Something that he didn't have to explain, and which he had chosen for himself.

Once he had taken home a handful of the mauve and reddish stones. He put them on the windowsill.

What are those? asked Mrs Macarthy.

Those are just stones, he said.

I don't see why you should bring home stones, Mrs Macarthy said. You might start making a collection of stamps. Stamps are educational, she said.

He did not answer this. When she had gone, he looked at the stones. He wondered a little himself. They were dull and colourless, unlike the glistening stones he had picked up out of pools. These belonged to the bay. Soon it was dusk, and he picked up the stones one by one, slowly threw them out of the window, heard their heavy landing in the undergrowth.

Mr Macarthy asked what he was going to be. Even if kindly, for Mr Macarthy was always gentle, this was the sort of thing you found upsetting.

I don't know, you said.

And suddenly it became difficult again, the knowing what, as if he could choose what. He was in a jumble, shifting from leg to leg. He wanted to be left alone. Outside the sky changed, it was always changing, he watched it, and time swelling into leaf and egg, but by degrees, and it swept you with it, gradually, and this was right. He did not know what he would become. But he would be swept round the corner surely enough.

Mr Macarthy didn't press the point. He sat in his study, doing acrostics, and making nets with arthritic hands. Netting and acrostics left Mr Macarthy in a continual maze that he chose deliberately. Like his own silences. At meals he was mostly silent, over against Mrs Macarthy's talk. He smacked his lips rather as he ate. Absently. He sat a long way behind the smacking of his lips. You heard him walking about the house, the distant, muffled thumping of his rubber-guarded stick.

Mr Macarthy knew a great deal. He knew Latin constructions and French verbs, he knew also compound fractions, and understood the Bible. But it did not bother him much. It flowed out of him and away, as if it were no longer of much importance. Because nothing bothered him, that was why you liked sometimes to go and sit in the room with Mr Macarthy, to look at the book full of Greek sculpture, or to read in the encyclopedia about the Nile. Mr Macarthy never pounced down unawares on your thoughts. He sat and netted, and you heard his breathing, and it gave you that warm feeling of just not being alone. It seemed to annoy Mrs Macarthy. She said he was indifferent. There was the afternoon the chimney caught fire, with the girls and Mrs Macarthy helter skelter about the house. The house could have burned, snapped Mrs

Macarthy at supper. But Mr Macarthy said he had never known a chimney fire that wasn't more emotional than actual, and helped himself to cold roast beef.

After a time it seemed unlikely you would ever leave the Macarthy's house. In Bridgton you knew the people in the streets. The shop people learnt to call you by your name. And Dr Willis filled your teeth. Eden went often to Dr Willis. She drove in with Mrs Macarthy and Julia, and the house felt empty after they had gone, after the wheels of the dog-cart had grated into distance outside. The whole house was surrounded by distance. Your voice sounded hollow and funny on the stairs.

Let's play at something, said Connie Tiarks.

Mm, he said.

It made him sick.

I'll play anything you like, she said.

It was dull about the house. He went outside.

I've made a house in the orchard, she said.

She wouldn't stop following him about.

Let's play at murders, he said.

Oh, she said. Murders. How?

I'll be your murderer, he said. I'll tie you up in rope and strangle you.

Can't I just be with you? she asked.

It made him feel sheepish then. It was the voice that Connie Tiarks put on, using an unfair advantage, and that lumpy face.

There's nothing to stop you, he said, trying to make it casual.

She followed him up the garden path. Her feet sounded grateful, her breath. So he became resigned, unwillingly, to the presence of Connie Tiarks.

Ever climbed the mulberry tree? he asked.

No, she said.

She sounded afraid.

I've climbed to the top, he said. You can put out your head through the leaves and see the Channel.

He began to climb the mulberry tree.

Wait for me, Elyot, she said.

So they both began to climb. She was determined. The light failing inside the tree, inside its thick foliage, she looked up desperately not to lose sight completely of his heels. His panting, higher, was discordant with her own. Their shoes laboured over bark. It was a long way up, in a desperation that was very close to exhilaration, even when she tore her knee.

I'm at the top, he called. I can see, I can see as far as Wales.

When she pushed up her scratched face, he did not resent it. They were both close against the sky. Their silence was mutual. So that Connie was afraid to speak, and breathless, she clung on afraid and a little giddy to the bending bough, tried to obliterate herself in Elyot's silence. She was quite content, because she was Connie Tiarks, with the mere privilege of existence. He allowed her to keep this, largely, with the generosity of his sex. Afterwards, on the way down, he even thought of suggesting to Eden that Connie was not a bad sort.

That was before she began, it happened at first slowly, her fingers slipping as surely as a fruit off its twig, her dress the downward flare that brushed his face, he saw, the rushing was the white dress, the head that tumbled with the sickness of a fruit, her voice stretched out in air. For half an hour or more, and at once, in two seconds, he knew that Connie was falling out of the mulberry tree. He shouted at her. Through his anxiety he felt annoyed. Because this was just the sort of thing that Connie Tiarks would do. Connie was a girl. She was sent to exasperate him.

Connie lay on the ground, on her back. Out of her purple face, not much paler than the mulberries that she crushed, came a muffled and protracted kind of screaming.

Connie ! he called, as he slithered from the tree.

Now he was very much afraid. He wanted very much to run away, from what had ceased to be the known Connie, from this uncontrolled and frightening object screaming purple in the face.

Bending down, he began to shake her.

Shut up, Connie! he shouted roughly. Listen, Connie! he almost screamed.

Because you had to scream, to make an impression on that purple face.

I've broken my back, Connie moaned.

It came pumping through her lips. It hit him sickly. He could have cried. But not for Connie, for himself. It had happened somehow to himself. He had to do, do, he had to do something, he felt.

I'll give you my knife, Connie, he said. If only you'll get up.

If only he could escape this painful sensation of being exposed to the unexpected.

She continued to moan, as he sat and watched her, though her face paler, her lips quieter, she had become reduced to a quiet gasping. Then perhaps she would really die after all. Vaguely he saw them dressed in black. In the cemetery the soil smelt new when they dug it up for funerals.

Oh dear, Connie said. I felt so awful, she said.

That began to annoy him again, feeling his heart subside, and his courage return. There was also the question of the knife.

You were only winded, he said.

Yes, she said. I felt awful.

He looked at her, daring her, expecting her to talk about the knife.

I'm sorry, Elyot, she said.

There's no need to be sorry, he said.

But he got up and turned to hide his relief.

You needn't give me the knife, she said.

Oh, he said. I didn't mean to. You needn't worry about that.

He went off by himself into the house. He felt ashamed. It was Connie Tiarks, and being like that to Connie Tiarks, and hating himself for being like that, it made him turn a corner in his mind. He went now to the bathroom and washed his face. He felt fresher now. Free from the face of Connie Tiarks. But looking at his own face, beneath the still damp hair on the

forehead, he had the uneasy feeling of wanting to say something that he would not say.

Oh well, he said.

He consoled himself like that. He slouched a bit when he
walked, as he saw the boys in the village do. He fortified himself unblushingly behind his superior age and sex.

Later in the year Connie left. She was going to join her
mother in London. Because Mrs Tiarks was in reduced circumstances, Julia said.

I'll write you letters, Eden, said Connie.

All right, said Eden. I haven't your address.

But I'll send you it, said Connie, undeterred.

She also said she would write to Elyot. That embarrassed
him considerably. He could feel himself blushing behind the
knees.

We'll all write to each other, Connie said.

Her face glowed with gratitude for the letters she hadn't yet
received. She clung to the possibility of this. She wanted badly
to be friends.

It'll be funny when you've gone, Connie, said Eden.

It made Elyot look at her in surprise. But her face was pursed
up seriously. He really couldn't understand Eden.

Connie looked as if she might cry. She was wearing a pair of
grey cotton gloves. The narrow piece of grey fur round her
collar was fastened up tightly under her chin, cutting her head
from her body; it emphasized her rather lumpy face.

Mrs Macarthy came into the hall.

Now say good-bye, Connie, she said.

So there were the good-byes, to Julia, to Eden, to Mr Macarthy. Connie kissed everybody, making it a sort of deliberate
mission. So that Elyot was afraid for a moment she might be
meaning to kiss him.

Good-bye, Elyot, she said.

She shook hands gravely. Remembering now her purple
face as she lay among crushed mulberries, this that they still
had as a secret between them, they had never told, because

somehow they were both involved, he found himself regretting many things. The things you didn't say. Or that only Mother said. Mother always knew what to say.

We shall have to hurry, sputtered Mrs Macarthy. Anyone would think that we had all day.

She was already settling under her plaid, smoothing her gloves, gathering the reins. Connie began to climb in beside her. The horse swayed uneasily.

Good-bye, Connie, Eden screamed. Send me some postcards as well as the letters.

Because parting changes everything. At parting there is sometimes a conscience, there is sometimes none. Eden even felt a sense of loss, watching the receding face of Connie lose its features down the lane. As if some known possession had been taken from her, as if she would no longer be able to keep up a familiar custom. It was like that.

Yes, it was dull when Connie left. Something had been rubbed out of the familiar pattern. A new pattern had to be made.

Going for walks there are always the flat stretches between the corners and the hills, they are pretty well endless, they are like the weeks between events, the cloudy, anonymous weeks that connect phases. Nothing is done that is not tentative, depending on the wind for its direction. In the evening you hang over the gate. You listen to the voices in the lane. The path you take knots itself fretfully, pointlessly, in the orchard grass. You get left outside the body of events, like the stone on the antipodal cherry. And not everyone is a Mr Macarthy, sometimes this exasperates, even without knowing why, there is not the substitute of nets.

Elyot, said Mrs Macarthy, Julia will have to give you a dose.

But it was not that. That was the trouble. It was not really anything.

Then Mother came suddenly. It was a surprise. After rain all the morning, the smudge of clouds, the muddy Channel, the gusts of rain blowing up through the trees, and drops hitting the windowpane, you looked out to see the gate open in the hedge. She had only come for a little, she said, then she was going back to France. But as it was, it was exciting enough, when you ran outside to be kissed, to kiss, the rain getting in between your faces, and the scent that came back; you had almost forgotten so many warm moments between sheets.

There, she said, straightening up. Oh dear, she said. I can smell the rain. In the West you can always smell the rain. But I shall be glad to warm my hands. Run along, Elyot. It's cold.

She sounded tired. She was the same, and at the same time different, and it was not altogether the stuff that she put on her face. Mother had a habit of talking to you as if you were hardly there, it was this now, it was this and more, she looked from side to side in the garden, as if she had forgotten. As if she had forgotten also the officer she brought. This officer was called Charles. He had a clipped moustache, and could make a noise with his finger joints. In a way it was a good thing that Mother had brought the officer along, he could make the noise with his finger joints, he let Eden touch his moustache, and everyone, he said, must call him Charles. But Mother was quiet. She sat sideways in her chair, with one hand hanging over the side.

Later when it was beginning to get dark, and everyone else had gone out of the room, she said that she had something to tell.

Come here, Eden, Mother said.

And Eden went. She had been trying on Mother's hat. Mother looked over, and you knew that this was, well, something that you knew you did not want to know, to go any closer, when she looked at you, and it was better before when she did not notice than to have her looking like that with her eyes.

Elyot, she said.

Yes, Mother?

Your voice sounded feeble, a kind of bleat, because

something was coming you did not want to hear, to stay or walk your legs didn't know. But you went, all prickly under your clothes, you went and she touched you with her hand.

Children, she said, you don't know, something very sad, that you don't realize, has happened, she said.

She was holding your head against, you could feel something going on under her dress, and your own hands that were hot and tight. You were too close to her breath. It came out sharply from down in her dress, it was this you could feel, and in your hair.

You remember your father, Elyot? she asked.

Yes, he said, uncertainly.

He was trying quietly to free his head. His body was stiff, like the night the door flew open on the other room, and the voices in the other room, my poor darling, she said, with footsteps on the stairs. This was Father. It was more Father than the other glimpses, faint now, such as carving beef for Colonel Tiarks. Father was the slammed door. He wanted more than ever to resist.

Well, Father, she said slowly, Father is dead, Father has been killed in France.

That made Eden cry. She could not remember Father, but she cried, it came tumbling out, and Mother cried, as if it was Eden that had started her.

He stood there stiffly. He looked out of the window, at the garden that was growing grey, at the drops that shuddered cold and clear on a rose bush by the window. He could see everything very distinctly. He had never seen anything so clearly, the red, curved thorn on the bush, the pattern of a spider's web. He had no part in this crying. He could not cry. He had no part in anything. It frightened him a little. He could feel himself tremble. Even when he found himself alone, after Mother had picked up Eden and carried her out, after their voices had left the room, he continued to stand there, shivering, dry. When Julia came to call him to tea he was still standing stiffly in the darkness, in which both room and garden had disappeared.

It began to occupy him more and more, his not being part of anything. When they all drew together round the fire, Eden sitting on Charles's knee, and the stories Mother told of the hospital in France, of Mme de Bonneville, she was a countess, and at the same time a sort of saint in whalebone, Mother said, she made them laugh, she always did, but you had to force yourself to laugh, pull yourself in from a long way off. So that on the whole, because you had only just discovered this, you were sorry that Mother had come from France. Sometimes she laughed and it did not sound like laughing. Just as the crying, from which you had escaped, did not feel or sound like crying. And this made it more difficult still. Like finding you were dreaming, early, and half asleep, the water jug that Julia left you might or might not have seen in sleep or waking, it was not quite real, the sort of daylight real, and then you knew it was, it was, you were awake, you had been awake, the jug stood there as plain as an enamel jug. But it still belonged in a way to sleep. And Mother belonged in a way to sleep. Everything she did was not quite real, like sleep, only there was no waking. He stood a long way off and watched. He began to develop a perpetual frown. There was a great deal that puzzled him.

Sometimes I think you're a bad-tempered little boy, said Mother. Sometimes I think you don't love me any more.

She pulled the head off a dead flower. Her dress spread out round her, copper-coloured, as she stooped, it caught on the spikes of winter flowers, it shook and caught the beads of dew. She was so beautiful that he would have liked to touch her. But he did not know what to do, or say. He stood kicking at the frosted ground.

And after three days she went away again. The last evening they stayed up late. It was particularly gay and sad. Mr Macarthy talked. He talked a great deal, for him. He talked about death. But it was not death on the tombstone, it was not Father, or Mrs Delbridge's son, it was sort of grey and colourless, it packed itself round you like cotton wool, the words that Mr

Macarthy used, till Charles said weren't we being highbrow, and Mother said, well, perhaps abstract was the word. Then for a moment everyone was quiet, except for breathing. Mother said this time tomorrow they would be in London, they would catch the boat to France, they would start being herded like cattle again, but it was better like that, you didn't have time to think. Yes, she sighed, through her cigarette.

You found yourself looking at each other. She had little wrinkles round her eyes. There was so much that you must tell quickly, that you knew, that Mother knew, she was looking at you for the first time there in the room, she was not at a distance. But suddenly she blinked her eyes, and said:

I know who's getting sleepy. Julia, it's time they went upstairs.

In the morning a car came to take them to Bridgton.

Good-bye, darlings, Mother said, just before her veil dropped. We'll hope, we'll hope it'll soon be over.

It had begun to rain again.

Soon it will be over, she said, you said, or the wind from the Atlantic, or the wind from the coast of Wales, or Sunday bells, or the frozen, frilled mouth of the speaking shell. It began to happen like this, in spite of newspapers. It began to be a ticking in the house. Julia cried. She was crying for the Boys. But it went on quietly, the ticking in the house, a pressure in the bay, a seeping in the earth when the sun got through.

It was nothing and everything to do with Elyot Standish. Doing the things they told him to, it was a matter of overcoats and dynasties, of toothpaste and broccoli. This was what he amounted to, a recipient of food or learning or the rules of hygiene. But this did not account for the sensations that went on inside him apart from the Macarthys and Julia. There was something that fumbled out of his own body, as he walked against the sky, becoming as much wind as body, or when he lay on the shore, and the sound of the water lapped across the chest, a blaze of sun shone between the bones. Later he began to wonder about this. Now he only accepted it in surprise. At night he would wake for a moment, to wonder, before he found it was too late, he was sinking in the sea of turned faces, just before or after the event.

Soon it will be over, she said.

It happened driving into Bridgton. Blossom had a little star on her rump that you watched, through the voice of Mrs Macarthy, you could get quite dizzy at times if you stared both long and hard enough at the star on Blossom's rump. The journey to Bridgton was a long blur. There were the hedges and the same cottages, it was always the same, nothing ever happened on the road to Bridgton. Not before the old man ran out, his beard blowing in the wind, that old man looked a little bit mad.

He's most certainly off his head, Mrs Macarthy said.

She clucked at the horse to get her past. But the old man shouted, he stood in the road, till Mrs Macarthy grew quite red.

There's been an Armistice! the old man shouted.

An Armistice? said Mrs Macarthy, going now from red to pale.

I been heard it in Bridgton, the old man said. Yes. The Huns are beat. There's no more fightin'.

What's an Armistice? Eden asked.

Mrs Macarthy was very quiet. She sat with the whip upright in her hand. Her black moustache had begun to quiver.

You'll remember this, young man, the old man said.

His trousers were gathered at the knees with cord.

Oh dear, oh dear, Julia cried, beginning to look for her handkerchief.

What *is* an Armistice? asked Eden.

The War is over, said Mrs Macarthy.

The War is over! you shouted. You sang it all the way to Bridgton. You called to strangers in the street. Because it did not seem as if there were any strangers any more. In Bridgton you bought the flags, and sang. You bought the bag of liquorice all-sorts. And Mrs Macarthy talked about the Hand of God, and kissed Julia outside the post-office.

Eden said she was going mad. At tea she blew in her milk and nobody minded. She said she was going to stay up all night, because nobody seemed to mind.

When you got home, Mr Macarthy came out to the gate. Because Mrs Macarthy called.

Fred! she called. Fred!

The spit bounded into Julia's face.

Fred! she called. We're saved! God has saved us. I knew He would.

But Mr Macarthy was very quiet. As if there was too much that was too difficult to say, and laughing and crying and singing and speaking, none of these could help very much. He just stood at the gate and said: The War is over – to himself, almost as if he did not believe.

Mrs Macarthy got the bottle of port. You had the glass of port watered down. And Julia had a glass of port, she held it with her finger crooked, her hands were mottled red. Mrs Macarthy said she would propose some toasts. She said, slowly, one by one: To Peace, To the Soldiers, To our brave Allies, and each time everybody took a sip.

Eden said she was feeling drunk.

What nonsense! said Mrs Macarthy, turning the colour of port and water. Really, what things you say, Eden! Really. On a spoonful of port.

Mr Macarthy cleared his throat.

I expect it's the Armistice, Eliza, he said.

That made Mrs Macarthy calm. But Eden kept on screaming, over and over again, I'm drunk, I'm drunk! she screamed, kicking up her heels, and burying her head in a cushion, so that you could see the seat of her drawers.

Drunk is not a nice word for a little girl, Mrs Macarthy said. She always used *tipsy* herself.

Julia giggled. Her glass shook. Everyone laughed, except Mrs Macarthy, even after Eden had stopped being funny.

Because the War was over. Because there was to be no more killing. It was good. Everything was good now. Only you felt a little sick. It was too many liquorice all-sorts, perhaps.

6

Leading him down a passage that smelt of boiling potatoes, Frau Fiesel opened a door at the end and said that this would be his room. The chatter of Frau Fiesel, it had a breathy, ingratiating lilt, rose and fell, leaving an occasional familiar word clinging in his head. But the journey in the train, but the close, potatoey atmosphere of the apartment stood between him and the moment of interpretation. The words remained, in fact, occasional and familiar. He could make no headway in this foreign sea. And all the time Frau Fiesel smiled, her voice retreated and advanced, she was at once both amiable and remote.

Hoffentlich werden Sie sich sofort zu Hause finden, Frau Fiesel said.

His mind scrabbled after phrases in exasperation. He felt that without assistance Frau Fiesel's smile might break. But out of his always inadequate vocabulary, that had collapsed somewhere on the frontier, all he could salvage now were the words *Brötchen* and *ja.*

You will soon be at home here, I hope, Frau Fiesel said helpfully. You would like to wash perhaps, and rest a little before we eat. You will find hot water in the basin. It is sometimes red at first, but afterwards you will have no trouble.

Her smile drew back still wider, to console.

Ja, he said, and again: *Ja.*

Then he was alone.

Across his forehead and his forelock his hat had left a band of sweat. Rooting in the suitcase he unearthed his brush and began, in a surge of voluptuous exhaustion, brushing slowly at his matted hair. His face was undistinguished in the glass, shadowy, apologetic, and smudged by the plains of Germany. It swam up out of a green sea that was half the shimmer of reflected trees and half the blur of physical exhaustion. But none of the radiance of light, the melting of colour in the sea of glass, concealed from the swimmer his own dejection. There are moments when the human mind admits its own shadowiness. And it was one of these.

Leaving behind all sense of geographical ties at Aachen, Elyot Standish found himself floating, placeless, timeless, there was no end to his present or past fluidity, there was no connexion between himself and any of the intervening years. There were even few significant points, forming out of this void. An afternoon standing on the edge of an almost circular bay, fingering a smooth and reddish stone. The bay had dimension, the stone a certain solidity. Then the years flattened out into a general monotony of time, broken by a few twinges of pain, the transitory and intensely personal hells of school.

Well, Elyot, said Mrs Standish, you'll always have to thank your Uncle Stephen for your education, if it weren't for your uncle's allowance, I don't know what we should do.

At the time it was a rather dubious gift. And Uncle Stephen, well, practising the law and a sense of duty had given him a tinge of unctuousness. Looking down from a considerable height he stirred the money in his trouser pockets, he asked you to lunch and gave you sherry, an impression of Uncle Stephen inevitably became a bluish chin behind a glass of dry Amontillado sherry. You sat on the edge of the chair and made the suitable, the grateful remarks. You felt like the little, frilled trick dog in the circus, sitting on his tail and waiting for the biscuit. On the whole, it was Uncle Stephen who was the ringmaster of the school years.

I don't want to sound a snob, said Mrs Standish, remembering perhaps the drawing-room in Norfolk, I don't want to sound a snob, but I'm glad you're going to a *good* school.

He didn't say anything to that. It was a statement, anyway.

And he had grown more silent. He felt happiest behind a closed door. There was no luxury so great as the privacy of an empty room. Round these rare islands flowed the school years. *The formative years*, said Uncle Stephen. The years of sports, and intricate, passionate snobberies, and physical violence, and mental barricades. It took a long time, a very long time. He found himself beginning to hate. When it was all over, Uncle Stephen decided on a year in Germany before Cambridge. It was a further fit of generosity that left you doubting your own capacity for gratitude. Events developed beyond your own will. You drifted on the wave of someone else's decision. And behind it all there was still a suspicion that all this might be directionless. Was there a sudden and self-decisive, an undoubted moment of clarity?

In the meantime, he waited. He was always waiting. And the other people, the people he had known, drifting also in the wash of time, sometimes twitched feebly out of the past, pulling on the line of their relationship. There was the letter from Connie Tiarks, for instance.

Dear Elyot, [Connie wrote]
I expect you will have forgotten all about me. It is such a long time since I fell out of the mulberry tree!!! But I often wonder about you and Eden. I am now at school in Gloucestershire. I shall be fifteen at the beginning of May, so am feeling terribly old!! There are a number of girls I rather like, and several of the mistresses are sports. I usually manage to get home for the weekends, Mother is living in Cheltenham now, since Father died you know, or didn't you hear? He had an attack of angina. Of course we miss him very much.

Last summer I went to Brittany with the people of a girl called Pamela Withers, who are awfully good to me. We went to St Malo, Rennes, Vannes, Quimper, Tréboul, Lannion, Dinan. It is really a quaint part of the world, and so full of historical interest. I have a piece of pottery that I bought in Quimper. I think I would like to collect pottery from all over the world, because I think it's a good thing to collect *something*, don't you?!

Do you like reading? I have just read *Wuthering Heights*, which is perhaps a little morbid!! I like Sir Walter Scott. We also go for walks.

The country is very pretty, especially in the spring, and autumn tints.
    Hope you won't mind my writing to you like this!!
                        Love from
                                    Connie (Tiarks)

Receiving this at school, it was the term he had been made a prefect, the large hand of Connie Tiarks, read furtively in the passage, then hidden in the pocket-book, was a constant source of embarrassment. More so the prospect of replying. As if he could write to Connie Tiarks, or what to write to Connie Tiarks. He composed letters in his head, the insipid statements that remained unwritten. The notepaper of Connie Tiarks smelt of some kind of innocent soap. It made him feel a pig, but at the same time he was unable to rid himself of this sensation. Finally he tore the letter, carefully, into little bits, and threw it down the lavatory. This relieved him of the source of embarrassment, if not the sense of shame. He continued to have this long after he had pulled the chain.

Less easily disposed of or assessed was his relationship with Eden. On the whole, he didn't know her any more. Drawn out into an awkward shape, her wrists too long, her ankles, she sat sullenly withdrawn under an ugly schoolgirl hat. As if a lowering velour cloud had settled on the known face, masking its spontaneity. There were days when he hated Eden with all the intensity of this freshly developed emotion. Ignoring his own aptitude for silence, he hated her because she sat apart. She wore an aura of secrecy. She wrote letters, endless letters. She made mysterious visits to the chest of drawers, which she insisted was hers, emphatically, not in words, but by a soft approach. He hated all this, but perhaps he hated her most because she was his sister, because in this intimate relationship he failed to understand the paradox of distance.

Crossing a room she was less communicative than furniture.

Where are you going? he asked.

To post a letter, she said.

Evening made it whiten in her hand. There was no more significant object in the room. He felt himself resenting this.

Who've you been writing to? he asked.

Someone, she answered.

She held her chin up, white also, and sharp. She moved quietly in her flat shoes. He looked at the rest of her face, but it was shadow, under the ugly velour hat.

If I wanted to know who it was, he said, I'd ask.

But already she was gone, the door banged, already in his mind across the street, the stilted progress of the black stockings, passing between the taxi-cabs, on their secret errand to the pillar box. He got up and fiddled with the gramophone. The needle grated on the first bars. Then there opened out the little cheep cheep, the pointed, insinuating notes of the violin, too knowing, too cocky, with a sarcastic quiver borrowed from his own voice.

Soon it will be over, he said, soon we shall be going back to school.

Loathing turned to relief, and relief to loathing.

Later they sat with books, watching each other over books.

Why are you looking at me? she asked.

She could not read. He would not let her read. He sat lumped up across the room, and all the time she could feel his eyes.

Why should I look at you? he said.

Turning the page she almost tore, he could hear the sudden tear of breath.

Just because you're older, just because you're almost seventeen, you think you're pretty clever, she said.

All right then, I'm a fool.

You needn't tell me that, she said.

Oh, he said. Girls are generally obtuse.

But he felt pretty foolish, lumpish. He even had no pleasure from a vocabulary that might or might not impress. She sat with that over-virtuous expression on her face, protecting herself, forcing him out of the room with his own shame. Then the simultaneous turning of a page. The air was tense with futility.

If he had wanted to resist the violence Eden roused, but there was a half-craving for its stimulus, as if, taken away, nothing would exist, the empty room, the stuffy streets, Eden herself was agreed on this, silently, unwilling to withdraw. She hated him with equal passion. Sometimes she went to her room and cried, the luxurious tears of self-pity, pausing a moment for a footstep that might prolong the reason for dissatisfaction. Time, she felt, age would reduce the tyranny. This is the usual panacea. She looked forward, out of the wilderness of fifteen, to a state of emotional independence. The cold, untouchable look of older people always made her envy them.

Time instead made you wonder, brushing your hair in the mirror, or was it distance, made you wonder at the comparative simplicity of things a year ago. It seemed like this at any rate to Elyot Standish. The mind clung gratefully to the known detail, to Eden in a black velour hat, while the feet ventured into foreign worlds, on the worn, German bedroom carpet. Outside, he could hear, they were preparing what Frau Fiesel had described abstractly as *Essen*. Outside, across the street, in the late afternoon shade of limes, the German voices of German children. He shivered under his hot clothes, just for the strangeness of it all, and his own isolation.

Frau Fiesel said he would soon get used to the German food, it was good and plain, it was good and plain because Germany had lost the War.

Then came a peculiar, sighing silence, through which he reached for a kind of sausage that his tongue tasted gratefully, the rough, raw, meaty texture, with the flavour of garlic. There was nothing equivocal about this. Eating it he felt safe, consoled, he could withdraw from his embarrassment. But embarrassment persisted fitfully.

First meals in strange houses are full of this embarrassment, the unexplained histories that start up with strange faces above the napkin, the arbitrary ritual of other people's tables. There were the eyes, the eyes of Hildegard, the face, the attitude, that became, you gathered, Frau Fiesel's daughter. The eyes of Hildegard were pale and inquiring. She hoped he would enjoy

Germany. The pale eyes of Hildegard would watch for a lapse in taste. He said, between mouthfuls, he was sure he would. Because it seemed the only thing to do, apart from the limitations of vocabulary.

The Germans were a wonderful, a misunderstood people forced out into the wilderness, said Herr Richter, who became by deduction Frau Fiesel's brother.

Herr Richter liked to use the word *Volk*. It bristled from his small, intense mouth like the greyish stubble from his shaven head. He moved in a perpetual cloud of exasperation, at everything, or nothing. Herr Richter had been a prisoner of war, Frau Fiesel explained in the living-room. He had suffered very much. Frau Fiesel seized on her brother's suffering as a source of steely virtue. She was for ever discovering virtues, whether in her brother, or in the good plain food of Germany. We have so little, Frau Fiesel often sighed. So little of what, you felt it better not to inquire, fearing to encourage across the border the abstract glitter in Frau Fiesel's eye.

Frau Fiesel was kind. It was the sort of kindness that made you feel you were on the verge of trespassing. It made Elyot choose his words carefully, a wadding to what he wanted to express, out of pure respect for Frau Fiesel's sensibility. Both physically and mentally she was soft. You felt if you touched her she would sink in, the outer, unresisting flesh, it would sink and never come out again, remain like the dip in an eiderdown. So it made you go warily. He wanted to avoid all unpleasantness, like mention of her husband, the late Professor, or economics, or *Vaterland*. The words of Schiller drew from her voice a volume of quivering platitude.

Fitting himself in, locating and skirting the danger zones, was a tentative, if not unpleasant process. His mind began to pursue and catch the foreign idiom. He could nearly always express himself. Or almost. His argument lumbered in a German way. As if his ideas meandered in a world of featherbeds, recognizable, but a little inflated, changed. He was changing in himself, mentally. He found that he had become a person.

Other people, Herr Richter at lunch, asked him his opinion. He had, he was permitted, he was expected to have a mind, an opinion of his own. This was suddenly awfully important.

Walking in the old town, that had remained untouched by recent passions or present uncertainty and discontent, Elyot Standish enjoyed this important discovery. There was a balance and proportion in the blue and golden renascence town that went well with his frame of mind. He walked firmly down the streets. He was very receptive. He wanted to absorb, there was no chimney, no façade too distant to possess, to assimilate. He stood at the street corners and smelt with pleasure a gust of baking bread, or heard the dray rattle over cobblestones. All this had come to his senses for the first time.

Meeting Hildegard Fiesel in the street, just by chance, out of other faces, they walked homeward. It was about lunchtime. Hildegard was secretary to a dentist. She came in to lunch, she ate quickly, resentfully, then she rushed off to her work again. He was still upset by Hildegard. He was sorry the morning he met her in the street. She clashed. She was a discordant note in his freshly acquired complacency. And she talked, a great deal, some of which he couldn't understand, she pointed out things of interest, she pointed out the palace, which he must see, she said, it was a place of great historical importance. Hildegard made him feel inconsequential, that he had all time on his hands, while she was a superior being, a breadwinner, of economic significance. He had discovered also that she was four years older than himself. And this gave her a surplus of superiority. He was still young enough to stand in awe of age.

They must see something of each other, they must go walking at weekends, because she was free then of course, she said, as they climbed the stairs together.

She smiled at him, and for the first time her words, her smile had any direction. For the first time, in addition to the pale eyes, the colour of mackerel freshly caught, he noticed the rest of Hildegard's face. She had the golden, shining face of the young German girls. She had the sleek, shining hair. Walking upstairs her voice became excited, breathless, mounting with the climb. On her chin the delicate traces of sweat. She was very firm, a golden brown. It was as if her whole body had suddenly formed emphatically and irrevocably out of the hitherto vague impressions of Hildegard drinking soup in the evening, Hildegard bending over a book, soothing her mother, scolding her uncle.

Thank you, he said. At the weekend.

It would be good also for his conversation, she said.

Walking through beech trees her voice glistened. There was a green and gold of beech trees, and the expectation of a late Saturday morning. He listened to her voice, without interpreting the words, choosing to enjoy the tone. That was the benefit of half grasping a foreign tongue, you could reject the implication of words for their shape and cadence. Just as the trees, in walking, bathed by the stream of Hildegard's voice, stood less for tree than for a suggestion of light, of colour, into which his own thought intruded, confusing the trajectory of a word with the bright, boughward leaping of a squirrel.

He wanted to speak to Hildegard of this, if he could, in so many words. But you couldn't. It was not so much the barrier of words. He looked at her pale, unseeing eyes, as she pointed to objects of interest, interspersed between the more subjective details of her own life. She moved as firmly as her voice. She had changed for Saturday into one of the harsh blue Prussian dresses worn by the little girls for school. It brought her closer, physically, the contact of arm, an encounter of warm breath, the swaying of a blue skirt. But she remained a creature of words and decisions, turning him to shadow at her side.

She was glad he had come, she said, because he was someone she could talk to, she had need of a friend, she had a great many difficulties to face. Her arm on the back of his hand brushed him back to consciousness. Her skin was as warm as a flint. If he were to take the arm in his hand, if he were to hold it against his face, he felt sure that the arm of Hildegard Fiesel would have the warm, pungent smell of a struck flint. But she went on walking quickly, swinging her arm. Their feet shuffled through the dead leaves. There was her mother, she said, she was fond of *Mutti*, but *Mutti* did not understand, *Mutti* lived still in the pre-difficulty age, before the War. She would not understand that to work was a necessity, something to be borne for this reason, even when a Dr Rosenheim. Her words began to come too quickly. Growing excited, her nostrils twitched, filling him with a misgiving that was both a physical uneasiness and distaste for someone else's problem. Rosenheim employed her, Rosenheim was filthy, she said, a Jew, no one but a Jew would take advantage of situations. Her breasts struggled with emotion under the tight blue dress. They would change the conversation, she said, anyone who was not a German, anyone who had not suffered in the War, would not, after all, understand.

But he wanted, he wanted very much to understand, and failing to say as much in words, he wanted more definitely to take up Hildegard's arm in his hands. He wanted to touch her. Perhaps he was in love. He wanted, in an agony of discomfort, to explore this new sensation with his hands. Her silence left him in a state of painful expectation and desire.

Perhaps I understand, he said awkwardly. Better than you think.

She smiled at him doubtfully, though warmly, looking through him with her pale eyes.

Nobody understands, she sighed.

He tried not to hear her satisfaction. He wanted her to remain physical. His eyes rested, diffidently, on her breasts.

I expect you think I'm quite an ordinary person, she said. Like Onkel Rudi. Onkel Rudi is against me. Perhaps you'll have noticed that. Onkel Rudi is bitter and middle-aged. He hates me because I am young.

Drawing him into a world of her own, making him acknowledge this, he began to doubt the reality of trees, the stones their feet touched in fording a stream, all these were unreal, undergoing some form of reconstruction in Hildegard's voice.

But I'm a match for Rudi, she said. Rudi is dead. But you can't kill ideals.

The remnant of a now almost non-existent Elyot Standish told him this was the place to laugh. But undergoing the change, he had begun to settle into a sort of surprised solemnity. They had sat down in a clearing and begun to eat the little, meagre packages of bread and cheese put up by Frau Fiesel earlier that morning. He sat and watched Hildegard eat bread and cheese. The impatient, sensual movements of her mouth. He wished she would stay like this, quiet, let him explore the painful feeling in his stomach.

All that late afternoon, wandering, sitting, in the forest Hildegard made with her voice, out of her own opinions and obsessions, he knew that he was not himself. He was a strange person, subscribing to arguments in which, soberly, he could not believe. But he watched, he listened to her, he was obsessed himself, with the form of Hildegard. He was becoming what she wanted him to become. His hands took the glass beer mug when they sat in the little forest beer garden, his mouth went through the business of drinking beer, his feet followed her along the path, past the cascade that fell into a basin of acid moss.

Everything in Germany was too green. There was a hectic, feverish tone about the undergrowth, from which you could detach a smell, strange and repellent, of rotting leaves. Passing a cemetery at dusk, the urns wept white draperies.

Ach, sighed Hildegard. She sometimes wished she were dead.

This did not sound ridiculous, as it might still by daylight, with some traces of judgement left. He no longer questioned the emotional crises with which Hildegard's life seemed swept. Dusk and his own feelings, the scent of ivy on a wall and the pulse in his own throat, announced a rightness in her sentiments. He was overflowing with a sentimental devotion, that he wanted to, had somehow to express. Remembering Werther, he had a suspicion that this was probably a Great Love.

Hildegard, he said thickly.

He took her hand.

He was very sweet, kind, young, she said, walking, squeezing a hot hand. It was because of his sweetness, kindness, youth, that she loved him, she thought, and because as a contrast, she could not forget, it kept coming into her mind, because he was the complete antithesis of Dr Rosenheim. The name vibrated in her voice. Dr Rosenheim was present, if not his face, as an idea that took possession. You could touch the warm, puffy air. It was something that Hildegard both resented and encouraged.

Suddenly she began to cry. A stormy, breathless kind of crying, as much an outburst from the darkened undergrowth as a protest from Hildegard. And it swept in little heady gusts, he was as much a part of this emotion, that he kissed, awkwardly, baldly at first, feeling his way to a collapsing mouth, almost toppling them over, they were spinning, spinning in a darkness of sweeping leaves and locked arms. Out of the darkness he spoke to her in borrowed words. They were not his, he knew, without shame. After the first impact there was no shame, surprise, except vaguely perhaps for the firmness of her now expectant body, and a sudden strand of hair that he found across her mouth.

She spoke in little frenetic phrases, the German words, or less coherently, an intimation of desire. She clung to him with her mouth. If you could touch a fever it would be this, the insistent body, the fierce mouth. He was relieved at last to touch above her shoulder the cool, the passive leaf mould, the first contact made by the returning senses.

Walking through the darkness afterwards, the hands returned small pressure. So much taken for granted, there is no reason for this, for the pressure in the darkness. The body is essentially possessive. It announces its prerogative, it refuses to acknowledge other possible worlds. Possessing, allowing himself to be possessed, Elyot followed his own feet, threading apparently with purpose the outer details. They passed children who were singing, their faces lit by paper lanterns. They were caught up distantly in the singing of the children. Their eyes followed without conviction the swaying of the paper lanterns on their beansticks, the small, intent children's faces. They were crossing tramlines, he knew. There was a shower of sparks.

Back at the apartment, Frau Fiesel said there was beer and potato salad in the kitchen. She appeared cloudy in a grey shawl.

No, said Hildegard, she was tired, they had walked very far, she was exhausted, she said.

Frau Fiesel began to murmur about *die Jugend*.

He listened to the closing of Hildegard's door, listless on its hinges, the sighing of a door. You felt either repudiated or taken for granted, it was difficult to decide which, if you were not too tired to decide, if you were not too tired to drag the feet towards extinction in a featherbed, the welcome stupor of eiderdown.

Hildegard, because she had ideals, liked to talk about the dignity of *die Ehe*. He felt a suspicion of disquiet meander under his skin. Because Hildegard had also entered into a different phase. They sat about a lot. They sat on the balcony in the evening, stiffly, officially, deserted. Or they read together. They read *Hermann and Dorothea*, and Count Keyserling. Frau Fiesel began to treat him very solicitously, almost as if he were ill, pushing a spiritual pillow under his head. Only Onkel Rudi was sceptical, because he was bitter, Hildegard said, because he hated and misunderstood her, he resented her personal happiness.

Listening to Hildegard, or sitting in the neighbourhood of one of Frau Fiesel's monologues, he sometimes felt he would suffocate. The mind swam feebly in the close, stovey atmosphere that increased with autumn. Faces came and looked at them. There was Fräulein Nusz, and Frau Geheimrat Behrens. There were the solicitous voices that matched Frau Fiesel's own. For him and Hildegard. Were they yet *verlobt*? inquired Frau

Behrens. He listened beyond, to Onkel Rudi's gramophone, where Onkel Rudi himself sat inside a palisade of Bach. Hildegard's voice among the coffee cups, with her *nicht, Elyot, wie, Elyot, was sagst du dann*, asked for perpetual reassurance that he found himself unwilling to give. He clung to a saving phrase of Bach.

Out of a few weeks had formed this situation, netwise, without his knowing, out of his own vanity. Hildegard's body, the moment in the forest, the still exciting embraces in corners of the living-room, were a projection of this vanity. He began to feel gauche again, humiliated by the women's voices, and jealous, he wanted to possess more than Hildegard, himself. So that he excused himself very often, slipped out into the cooler air, beyond the dark and faceless houses, sometimes walked for several miles along the outskirts of the forest, alone with the sound of stirring bracken and already a smell of frost.

Hildegard pouted. She looked angry. Walking alone at night, she said, was a sign of eccentricity.

He thought that she sounded stupid. He looked straight in her pale eyes.

Perhaps, he said, equably, content enough to leave it at that.

Onkel Rudi went walking at night. And look at Onkel Rudi, she said.

Onkel Rudi went walking at night in the rather high-crowned velour hat with the bow that fluttered at the back. His coat was thin and greasy at the elbows. He was retired, an engineer. Onkel Rudi, unconsciously, became a zone of reassurance. Passing him near the tollgate, it was evening, the moon on oaks, you realized it was Onkel Rudi who stood against the tree, you listened to him making water, quietly, you listened to him belch, you heard him laugh, either in relief, or, as Hildegard had said, in madness. But it reassured, the laughter, the private attitude. Like the phrase of Bach. Because Onkel Rudi was at once so very personal and complete. Elyot listened to his own departing footsteps, that became a clearer footnote on himself than any fumbled reasoning.

More tangible than mental defences was the letter from his mother, round about Christmas, that came in resinous with *Tannenbaum*, that penetrated oilily, the warm, confiding oilness of melting candles. Dearest Elyot, wrote Mrs Standish, I have heard from Uncle Stephen that your grandmother is dead. Grandmothers, even mothers, especially dead grandmothers, intruded oddly into the relationless existence he now led. It is very sad, wrote Mrs Standish, naïvely, through some pricking of the conscience, that did not begin to deceive. He smiled. At a distance his mother made him smile. He thought about Grandmother Standish, seen occasionally in holidays under the guidance of Uncle Stephen, the cold, boring, or the hot and equally boring, tennisy weekends in Norfolk. Touching Grandmother Standish's hands you were touching rings, her face beneath an official kiss was a stratum of firm bone. So that there was little death could do, you felt, there was no action sufficiently corrosive, nothing that Grandmother Standish could not withstand. However, she lay in a coffin, she was dead. In the street they were singing a hymn, a tenuous German Christmas hymn, that he tried to receive suitably, to call to his aid in reacting dutifully to Grandmother Standish's death. But his eyes were as dry as hers above the tea things on the lawn.

Ashamed for his own materialism, he felt he was at least one degree more sincere than his mother, recalling her *very sad*. Or perhaps there was sincerity in this, there was some ultimate well from which she drew. Sitting by the fire with the evening paper, her eyes grew moist for accidents to strangers. How *appalling*, Elyot, she said. *But*, resumed Mrs Standish, with a jerk, coming down to brass tacks, all news is not bad news, your Uncle Stephen tells me that your grandmother has remembered you, he says it will amount perhaps to £400 a year, from the age of twenty-one. Unashamedly, he calculated quickly in his head. This will be a great help, Elyot, dear, wrote Mrs Standish, you don't realize what a scrape it's been, your father's extravagance, and the rates, and the and and and.

He sat contemplating £400. Because it has been a scrape, she said, more than you'd suppose, because I *won't be sordid*, I must have a few beautiful things. His jealousy dissolved before the gold dress. Aubrey's taking me to dinner, she said, it feels so beautiful, Elyot, darling, because I can't afford it for a moment, there's some chicken if you're hungry, and do be careful of your eyes. He folded the letter. He was somehow, inextricably, an accomplice of his mother's. After all these months, she stood there in the gold dress that time had tarnished, but that left its mark still upon the stairs, ebbing molten as she mounted.

Elyot, was machst du? called Hildegard. *Wir warten.*

At least she did not come beyond the door.

She was going to sing a *Weihnachtslied*, she said.

He put the letter in a drawer. In the passage the scent of pine boughs, above the pervading stuffiness of stoves. Voices rose in the living-room, ventured out on the *Weihnachtslied*, that he must face, go in, to the clear, expressionless soprano of Hildegard, to the undertonal drone and crackle of Frau Fiesel, Frau Behrens, and Fräulein Nusz. But he preferred the silence of pines. There was a freedom in the brush, the scent of pines non-existent in the living-room. But he went in to where the tree stood in the alcove, in the unctuous atmosphere of melting wax that had almost drowned the freshness of the pine. He stood there feeling he must look foxy and suspect, in the midst of this gaggle of old geese, that he could not help despising, he had to, he wanted to sing out above the cackle of old voices, because he was free, he was free, he said, more remote in this than the climbing, self-contained soprano voice of Hildegard.

Hildegard sat stiffly at the piano, in a position self-conscious, maidenly. She sat with her eyes lowered over the keys, on the nape of her taut neck a glitter of golden hair, scraped up too quickly, stiffly, into the little braids. The *Weihnachtslied* was an official act that she performed yearly. But inwardly she quivered with private emotion that translated itself hollowly once into one of the high, clear notes.

Aber sing'. Sing' mal, Elyot, Hildegard said, turning on him a slow, sweet, bitter smile.

From the tree he could almost hear the pinging of artificial frost. The tree was bright with coloured balls, green and scarlet, and a silver star that shone among the candle flames, a scent of resinous burning. He smiled back at her brazenly.

Then it broke off, the song, with the smashing of the piano lid, leaving the older voices raised on an accent of surprise. Frau Fiesel looked like an old, amazed, and injured squirrel when Hildegard slammed the piano lid.

Ach, Hildegard! Frau Fiesel said.

She could not play, said Hildegard, he sat alone in his room, or stood there by the Christmas tree, looking, smiling as if, he was altogether hateful, she said.

She went out of the living-room, leaving behind her a trail of half-suppressed emotion.

Sehen Sie, Frau Fiesel said.

That was repeated in glance, if not in word, by Frau Geheimrat Behrens and Fräulein Nusz. Round him their reproach struck silently, or by implication, as he nipped the flame from a candle that had burnt too low.

Frau Fiesel sighed. She picked at imaginary cottons on her skirt. She said that Christmas was not what it was, the Christmases before the War, there was plenty then, everything was different, changed by the War. For which he was responsible, he felt. He became an immediate object for her reproach.

Many winter days Elyot heard Frau Fiesel's voice protesting against snow, he heard the slamming of the front door as Hildegard came from or went to her work, the rubbery thud of the snowboots that Hildegard threw off in the hall. Many little acts on the part of both endeavoured to retrieve lost ground. But the bird wasn't caught that still had a wing, said Onkel Rudi, irrelevantly, over the soup. Elyot pretended not to understand. But there was a secret tie, an understanding between Onkel Rudi and himself. The soup was good and nourishing, said Frau Fiesel. She always said this when the soup got thin. It was her way of pacifying her conscience in the face of material circumstance.

The conscience has a habit of rousing in the thaw. You listen to the rain on cobbles after the anaesthesia of snow. I should go to Hildegard, said Elyot, I should try to explain away this pantomime of two people in opposite corners. But he resented even her appearance now. The golden, sealed surface of her face that would blur in a gust of hysteria. There was a falseness in Hildegard that he could not quite bridge. He felt his emotions had been enlisted in an illegitimate cause. So that he held back continually. He tried not to think of the gauche physical encounter in the forest. Because this pointed to an Elyot Standish as false as Hildegard.

Once she came to him, it was springtime, you could hear the drip of melting snow, and the sound of thawing wood, she bent and held her face against his cheek.

Elyot, she said, her voice thick with bitterness and passion.

He did not look up, move, went on reading the book, his breath held in, withdrawing inside himself, away from Hildegard. So that she went and stood by the window, her fingers jerking at the little acorn that dangled from the blind.

She could kill herself, she said, and nobody would care.

Springtime also, Eastertime, when the edge of the forest was sown with black overcoats, very *bürgerlich* on holiday or Sunday afternoons, sitting on the municipal seats, or admiring the groups of formal sculpture. Frau Fiesel announced that the Rosenheims would take coffee on Saturday.

Mutti, nein, said Hildegard, red. How could she make her sit with her employer, her Jewish employer at that? No. it was bad enough, the necessity to work, but *am Kaffeetisch*, with Rosenheim!

Frau Fiesel said it was a *Pflicht*, and Herr Rosenheim was an upright man. And very soon it was Saturday.

Herr Rosenheim was a small, bright, apologetic Jew. He had shaved too close, his skin shone, altogether he was shining bright, as if to make the best of things. And he smiled, he smiled too much, to put you at your ease, out of his own un-easiness, his whole body quivered with an eagerness to please. His smile smelt of some kind of antiseptic wash with which he had gargled before setting out. Now he hovered on the carpet edge, and sidestepped in doorways to let other people pass.

Frau Fiesel was overjoyed. She said so several times. She ran, or she sailed like a balloon on a gust of gratitude, she sailed in a swish of skirts to fetch a vase for the flowers Frau Dr Rosen-heim had brought.

Frau Dr Rosenheim said that already she had forgotten the winter. She patted the golden ball of cowslips she was holding in her other hand. She fluffed them up with a little, light, ner-vous motion of the fingers.

Cowslips made her ready to forgive. Perhaps she was senti-mental, she said.

Her husband laughed. She was sentimental, she was some-times quite stupid, lightheaded, in fact. He could not heap up too much derogatory praise. My wife, he explained, is a Vien-nese.

For six mornings now, the Frau Doktor said, something had made her sing as she stirred her bath.

She asked Elyot had he ever been affected in·the same way.

He said yes, though he couldn't remember if he ever had. But Frau Dr Rosenheim was like that.

Here Dr Rosenheim explained his wife was a *Künstlerin*, in temperament at least. He blushed with pleasure. He hovered over her with his eyes.

The Frau Doktor sighed. She said he always made excuses. Then she laughed, and everybody else.

Kaffee, Frau Doktor? asked Hildegard.

The cup descending firmly rounded a definite period. Hilde-gard was silence. She took possession of the room, picking at crumbs, or looking at her shoe. Sometimes she blushed too. She slopped the coffee in the saucer when she gave it to Herr Rosenheim. Hildegard sat with her eyes cast down. Her eyes watered when she bit her tongue.

Hildegard is quiet, the Frau Doktor said.

It was the spring weather, Hildegard said, that sometimes depressed her. The moist, steamy atmosphere. Sometimes she felt she could not breathe.

She went to the window and jerked it up.

It was air, *air* that she needed, she said.

Frau Fiesel shivered. She said that draughts.

It was nonsense. It was fresh air, Hildegard said.

Her voice caught.

Herr Dr Rosenheim said that on Friday they had heard *Tiefland* at the Opera. His wife was a lover of music. As if this were an additional virtue in her favour, he could not stop loading her with these. His eyes lingered appreciatively on the small, pink lobe of her ear. Mentally he touched it.

Hildegard cleared the coffee things. A sharp, discordant rattle of cups.

Elyot, she said, you will bring the plates.

In the kitchen he looked at her back. He could look right through Hildegard now.

Well, she said, turned still. Now you will think I have lied.

Why? he asked. How?

About Dr Rosenheim. But it's true, she said. It's mortifying. I feel I can't look him in the eyes.

As if you have the opportunity. You forget the Frau Doktor, he said.

But this was no special victory, suspecting some time now that Hildegard lied, whether eyes or voice. She had looked beyond him at someone else. He had stood proxy for a second person. It was too far back to the moment when he might have been hurt. Time had left him detached.

What was he trying to suggest, she asked.

Once as a child he had stuck a caterpillar with a pin, watched the writhing, and a green liquid. Disgusted, he had felt sick.

We must go back, he said. We're forgetting Dr Rosenheim.

Only now he didn't feel sick. He gave an additional twist to the pin. He left her and went out into the passage.

Frau Rosenheim's laughter reassured. Her voice in speaking had a little, warm *glissando*. Banishing winter, stirring the golden ball of cowslips, ruffling them with her fingers, her voice had come spontaneously, with a sensuous conviction. He envied Frau Dr Rosenheim, or her husband, they were the same, and interchangeable. He remembered his mother in the copper coloured dress, spread out on the winter path so that it touched the spikes of flowers. He remembered the edge of Ard's Bay, where you looked down into pools, into the mouths of anemones. Because there is a kind of connexion between all positive moments. These are also interchangeable.

Through the living-room door Frau Rosenheim was telling of a walk they had gone near Goslar. It was a story of no particular point. But it disturbed him. More likely than not, he would never see the Rosenheims again.

Probably it was mostly like this. He would always regret the flutter of flown pigeons. You stood with a few feathers in your hand, afterwards, in the empty turret. In the same way, he regretted luggage labels. You will catch such and such a train, wrote Uncle Stephen, the term at Cambridge starts on such and such a day.

Elyot Standish sat about writing labels on the evening before departure. The ink dried greenish-yellow on his pen. He looked at the bundle of little red tags, at the dust on the luggage, and the fragments of scrapped paper lying in the corners of what had been his room. Silence split the full year in retrospect. It lay there in the still, disordered room, summer outside again, deeper than the first afternoon. At times he felt very thin, almost substanceless, in spite of the moments of positive experience that bring conviction. Even these, strung together, pointed to another person. They did not explain the shadow in the glass. There is that general conspiracy on last evenings to reduce the body. There is the water dripping from the tap. There are the gaping voices behind the wall.

Frau Fiesel had begun to snivel. She wrote his name in a

birthday book. She talked about *das Leben*. It was altogether *traurig*, she said.

Outside, the steamy scent of limes became the gas flame behind trees, that wavered, he could feel his stomach, like the yellow flickering of gas. His hands hung by his sides, no longer self-assertive, balled in his pockets. He was going soft. He was dissolving in the warm air. He.

Nun, Elyot, said Onkel Rudi, appearing soundless in the passage.

He poked his head in at the door.

Fresh starts, fresh troubles. *Schön*, said Onkel Rudi. *Schön*. Then he laughed and went away.

The voice swelled into the phrase of Bach. You could hear it behind the closed door. It opened out in Onkel Rudi's room. And you suddenly felt firm again, behind the little picket fence planted by the voice, by the phrase of Bach. There was a purpose, a stability in Bach that translated itself to your hands as you tied pyjama strings, as you opened the bed. There was a purpose, caught from the music, even in the personal mistake. He did not regret these. Lying in bed, there was perhaps even an ultimate pattern, woven partly from mistakes.

Elyot, she said.

He heard the creaking of the door. He lay there, neither surprised nor resisting, but confident, listening to the music.

She had come, even if *Mutti* heard, and suspected she was immoral, which she wasn't, she had to, she said. Because he had been unjust, even though she had lied, he might call it that, about Dr Rosenheim.

She came and sat upon the edge of the bed. He could hear her quick breathing. But unconvincingly. And who was Dr Rosenheim, and the scarcely more palpable figure of Hildegard beside him on the bed? Behind the music there were many dim faces peering from the dead year.

She began to resent his silence again.

He was hateful, she said. He was unreal, detestable. He roused emotions that he couldn't return.

She was very eager, was Hildegard, to pin the blame on someone, perhaps with some truth, he did not know. There was very little he knew, least of all himself.

She was only telling him, she said. That was all she had come for. He had tortured her enough.

But she sat there waiting, he could feel her waiting, the direction that was Hildegard, oppressive even in the darkness.

Yes, Hildegard, he said, wearily. I'm all of that, if you like. You're right.

Because beside sleep it was immaterial, and the meandering of flutes, that traced a thin, purposeful line across the face of personal bewilderment. He scarcely listened to her going. He walked down an avenue towards the beckoning of flutes.

7

Après moi le déluge, Mrs Standish was fond of saying, not quite knowing if this had been heard or read, or if it were one of those vague but sometimes pregnant phrases that she found floating in her head. Anyway, it pleased her, its melancholy, prophetic tone, it was something to turn on the tongue, alone on winter afternoons, reviewing all time in what had become a slightly shabby drawing-room. Noticing the dimmer colours, the encrustations of virtu in her once pretty room, Mrs Standish decided the effect was less shabby than *interesting*. Her mind was nimble with saving phrases. Because this, she had realized, was the only way. If she was no longer pretty, witty Kitty, she was the *interesting* Mrs Standish, a label that stuck to her with all the dignity of middle age. She moved well. She had explored the ultimate possibility of her own setting. She listened sympathetically to men, and gave them the impression she enjoyed it, the yawn caught somewhere in her handsome throat. It was a technique taught her by economic necessity. She could be very gracious at a supper table. And afterwards.

She would accept a cheque, after protest, in which she never went too far.

These principles, like the telephone, stood firmly in the jumble of an otherwise untidy life. She liked to lie late in bed. She liked to spend a cosy afternoon in her Louis XV *bergère*, half conscious of the novel that she read. She liked to wander casually through her house, or what the agent more brutally referred to as an Upper Part, crumble the petals of a flower upon the landing, open a drawer on its untidiness, or even go to the kitchen and nose vaguely into bins.

Dear me, madam, Julia said, you don't half clart about.

Because this was Julia, you accepted it. Because Julia had become a liaison officer with a world of meat and vegetables, and other depressing material things. The children grown, and incomes such as they were, she had developed logically into this. Or more. Time and intuitions had formed her into another sense. Julia handled many awkward moments on the doorstep or the telephone. Julia knew how much the children ought to know.

Mrs Standish's children were her passion, she remarked, in some truth, but more from habit. Darlings, she sighed, complacently, alone, those mornings half asleep in bed. Though sometimes her own voice made her open her eyes and wonder. Her children. Such an abstract concept frightened her a little. Because she didn't know them. She had never known them. Even the child in the womb, so personal, tangible, in its way, still remained an abstraction. Months, even days after birth, sealed the envelope, wrapped it in the strangeness, the aloofness of a foreign personality, resentful of possession.

Children are essentially resentful, whether of love or of indifference, she decided in more bitter moments. There was Elyot. Or there were several Elyots, the one created out of correspondence, the boy mooning in his own room, the polite, impersonal creature who answered questions on the Cambridge Backs. Elyot was a shadow that fell across the substance of her friends, the men who brought her presents, who filled her drawing-room with conversation and cigar smoke. Elyot standing sideways. His manner was perpetually sideways. Smoothing his hair, she could sense withdrawal. Or they sat in untidy silences. She could feel his disapproval of mentioned names.

If you could pull the veil away from your children's faces. If you could touch their faces. Or if you could achieve contact through the humble, factual detail. As Julia did. Take off your socks, they're wet, said Julia. He sat in the kitchen and took off his socks. He talked baldly in bald words, received or not by Julia, it did not matter, the kitchen held an occasion that was somehow or other complete.

It's no good, Aubrey, said Mrs Standish. I try.

Aubrey Silk remained a changeless detail in the face of change, embalmed in an epoch he had touched on briefly in person, if more frequently in spirit. Dove-grey, she thought of him, or in black, with the pale veins making of the backs of his hands almost identical maps. He looked at her critically above his high collar. His head rested on his collar, or on the tea-plate held to his chin to catch crumbs, then he looked like a St John the Baptist lolling gravely on his charger. The criticism of Aubrey Silk was not too positive to hurt. She believed that Aubrey actually was kind – kind enough, on lifting the flap, to let it fall into place again.

Yes, he said, Catherine, yes, you try. Why not give it a rest?

Then he asked her to marry him. It was how many times, she counted, the rite of a proposal from Aubrey Silk, that discovered in her no fresh excitement, only the mild, warming pleasure of sentimental retrospect. This was one of the absurdities, felt Mrs Standish, her regular, illogical, highly stupid refusal of Aubrey Silk. Almost as if she relished her own stupidity. She could feel the shape of her refusing smile. She deliberately composed it on her face.

Thank you, Aubrey, said Mrs Standish. I expect I'm really masochistic.

She enjoyed the use of words, the more adventurous ones,

of which she only half grasped the significance. These represented a tribute to the intellectual life, on the brink of which she hovered longingly.

Marriage doesn't dispose of the children. I can't foist my own children. No, Aubrey, she said.

That made him protest.

No, she said, not unwistfully.

It formed those two nostalgic wrinkles on either side of her mouth, pursed up in just the way that made her acquaintances remark that Catherine Standish was a *brave woman*.

No, she said. I enjoy my children, Aubrey. I enjoy their difficulties. They're an adventure!

She was pleased with that. It almost made her feel she was creative.

So Aubrey didn't persist.

You mustn't have any regrets, she said, touching with a hand. There's always friendship. I like to look at you in that light. Yes, Aubrey, it suits us.

Though there were regrets, for Mrs Standish, the glance backward at the house in Regent's Park, the feel of the house in Regent's Park, for the things in Aubrey's house were smooth to touch, they had the rich discreet texture of Aubrey's hands. I am really very stupid, sighed Mrs Standish, and why? She tried to find some solution in the coffee stain on the hem of her dress. Spilling things, she mopped at them with her handkerchief and hoped that they would work in. They did, if not into the stuff, into Mrs Standish's accommodating mind. Because it was easier to accept. If not the Aubrey Silks. She laughed. Oh dear, no. She liked to stretch in bed at eleven o'clock, her body distinct inside the nightgown, she liked to hold up her arms welcoming nothing but her own unseizable well-being, till the sleeves tumbled back from her arms down to the little tufts of reddish hair. The mere existing inside your own sensual envelope was good. Something more permanent than the shared sensation. So Mrs Standish sheltered behind her children. And Eden, she said, was just at the difficult age.

Dear Mother, [Eden wrote]

I mean to do something when I get home, I don't know what – yet – but something useful. I was never any good at sitting. This place is hell, the last terms. Do you ever feel you will suffocate, just from being cooped up with so many useless women? I've *been thinking* and I've got to do *something*. Oh God, why does time go so slowly! Do you know I've been ticking off the days on a piece of paper? Now that it's warm we can get outside. Sometimes I can get away on my own. If I'm careful. And damn what happens, anyway. If you go about a mile along the Charlesford Road, over the fields, you can see the sea. There are primroses now. Yesterday I went into a cottage and a woman gave me milk. She had just lost her baby from meningitis. And two others stillborn. Her husband works for one of the Nobs in the neighbourhood. Well, we had quite a talk. She showed me a postcard from her brother, who's at sea, written from Galveston, Texas. You couldn't keep me on here, darling, even if it wasn't last terms. Because it's time I *began* – not just sit round hearing about people's fathers buying hunters and people's mothers being at Cannes. Do you know the woman I talked to in the cottage went into service when she was a girl for £9 a year. And she wasn't *bitter!* –

Mrs Standish was disturbed by Eden's letter. It pointed to a conscience, to an independent mind. Not that she hadn't a conscience herself. In a rush of conscience, she often gave half-crowns to beggars, and the thought of accidents made her sick. There were also the days, remembered dimly, when she had listened to her father in the Norwich kitchen talking of William Morris, and evenings with the S.A.L., the discussions of socialism and readings from Bernard Shaw, which sent her home excited, sleepless, turning in her mind an argument or the expression in a glance. *Or* the expression in a glance. Perhaps this. She preened herself amusingly in words and the young men stammered when she handed them sponge fingers. Because she was bright, stimulating, like the ideas she stole from books. Often she had worn – now a hideous thought – an amber necklace that was bright, distinct, like the bright distinct thread of unapplied ideas. Her father brought passion to ideas that somehow died in spite of him. But Eden, it was a sign, she felt, the letter, of passion inherited or revived, and it troubled her intimately, through her own conscience, that she had neglected the possibility of disinterested passion for so long.

That's over! said Eden, the first day.

She had gone upstairs to settle her things.

At least I have my freedom, she said.

Discarded, the black velour hat fell with an unprotesting flop on to the counterpane. The years, the school years, the dead age of surrendered personality, seemed irrelevant, more obtrusively negative in the falling of a hat.

My poor darling, was it so terrible? said Mrs Standish. Women, I agree, are impossible *en masse*. However. We're having scallops for lunch.

Her daughter this first day made her breathless, uncertain of herself, full of considerations, almost as if it were a first maid, certainly not her daughter. And the hair, the heavy, black fringe, drenching the shore of the white face, was new, done in this different way. It was strange how intimidating the mere physical changes could be.

Good – you heard her, brushing the hair, the voice of Eden in the aired room. Even the food, she said, at school they manage to kill the food.

I expect you'll have an appetite, said Mrs Standish weakly.

She could feel herself making flabby remarks. She knew she would be happier going downstairs, anticipating the approach of Eden, this warm but not yet assimilated idea. And perhaps, in between, somewhere on the staircase or in her own mind, the relationship would have resolved itself.

I think I'll go down, she said. I'll tell Julia you're coming.

In the street a tin piano, the cracked strips, playing a popular tune. It drifted into the upstairs room, a frail, distant, and slightly inebriating tune. There is always this about pianos in the street. It made Mrs Standish pause, her glance on the shore of foreign hair.

Mother, said the voice that became Eden's. It *is* good.

Then the collision of the backs of brushes.

Yes, said Mrs Standish. I know.

Sometimes it was good to kiss, in just this way, that was out of the question with men, a lover, or even a son, that was absent also in the gesture of other women officially rubbing cheeks. Mrs Standish realized that she loved her daughter physically, the arms, the cheek, touched now, and that she derived a comfort from this. Even when the ultimate separateness of soul frightened her, she returned gratefully to the sympathy of touch. She wanted to close her eyes.

Yes, she said.

It was quieter in the street, the tune withdrawn. We are standing here like a group of statuary, probably looking stupid, she thought.

You've grown quite thin, Eden, she said.

It was the moment of implied release. Because, after all, the mystic must return to his original structure of flesh and bone.

Oh, said Eden. I didn't think.

She frowned. It reminded Mrs Standish that this, this foreign country under the black fringe, was still delicate ground.

Well, perhaps not. I'll tell Julia you'll be down in a minute, she said.

The first days, which succeed the last days of school, are unhurried enough to wear a look of permanency. There are no more compartments, there are no days, there is just time, and this has a purely personal tinge, it is yours, it is at the same time infinite and governable. Treacherous also, Eden found. Because you have time to look at yourself. It was almost the first time Eden Standish had looked at herself critically, from all sides at once, which is quite different from sensing a mere self in a desperate, groping manner, between pauses in older people's conversation, or after the lights are out. She had spent a great deal of time in darkness, subjected to this by a hand that reached for the light. Really this is a very subtle form of tyranny, she felt.

The forms of tyranny. Sometimes she thought along these lines in the bus, shut in by the flat, dimensionless faces you find in buses. She thought about the face of the woman in the cottage, that had emancipated itself somehow into a shape of its own; it was very clear and salient in her memory, and at the same time distance had given it a larger significance. It seemed as if the woman in the cottage had become the one live, permeating experience of the last few years, a flash of intuition beside the years of conventionally acquired knowledge.

Perhaps the important things only happened in a flash. In the space of a day, almost in the falling of a velour hat, you became a different person. You forgot the intermediate process, the chrysalis schoolgirl, out of which bursts the white, mysterious moth. She was very white, incalculable, under her dark hair. She had time to notice this too, could take an interest in her sharp face, in which the cheeks burnt red, in anger or excitement. She went about, and she began to paint her lips as she saw the others do, timidly at first, then forcing the lipstick down on her mouth, in a movement suggestive of both resentment and desire. In glance candid, she looked at the people that she saw. She was curious. She did not give much thought to the impression that she made, because she was not conscious of herself, except alone, when the mind, turning on itself, begins to ask, to criticize. Then she was a white, waiting body, standing in a mirror, in a distant striking of clocks.

Mostly, though, she avoided these, the mentally or not so mentally voluptuous moments. She had a kind of austerity that found them suspect. Just as she began to question leisure. Because it had become pointless, her own movements, the cups of tea, the cigarettes, the movies after lunch. She was being seduced by the permanency of leisure, her own infinite time to spend. And this was hard to resist, the voluptuous stroking of empty days. She could feel her mind settle into a state of numb and helpless discontent.

You'll have the nap off the carpet, Julia said.

Julia went shopping with a string bag. She planted her feet firmly on the ground. You heard her coming up the stairs. You heard the door at seven-thirty, out of the half-sleep, the darkness that she pulled back with the curtains. Her hands were a mottled, bluish red, as cold as the early morning air encountered in the bus from Clerkenwell. She lodged there with her aunt, now that the house was full. She arrived with a ticket in her glove. She left with pieces of stale loaves, or the remnants of a pudding in a basin. Everything she did was logical, aloof, the whole pattern that Julia made, it continued, this life of Julia's, because of and yet apart from the lives of the others in the house.

I'm altogether futile, Eden felt.

She sat in the kitchen, by the kneading of dough, she sat there watching Julia's hands.

You'll yawn your head off, hinny, said Julia.

Yes, she said. I know.

She went upstairs. She read, the books that she half finished, the way her mind skipped from argument to argument, disappointed by the first promise. Or she walked, as a release, long walks that took her into places that had no bearing on herself, the long, listless, eyeless streets, from Camberwell to Bethnal Green. She walked along the Mile End Road, its wide and windy pavement, where she was ignored quietly, nobody looked at her. She was altogether pointless, rootless. She failed to fit into the pattern of the streets, she played no part in the emotional pattern of the groups at windows or standing in doorways. It even seemed as if her own emotional, sentient life had ceased.

I can't understand you, her mother said. When there's so much you might do.

It slipped out, thoughtless, through the smoke from her cigarette, forgetful of a letter, I *mean to do*, that had disturbed the complacency of Mrs Standish, sensing unapproved activities.

I mean, she hurried, you might, for instance, go up to Elyot for the weekend.

Even if it weren't the season for punts, Mrs Standish approved the air of Cambridge, felt it might settle the mind discreetly.

No, said Eden.

She did not want, could not think, she had forgotten Elyot, except as a vague presence appearing at certain seasons of the year. She did not want to take her own into the presence of an equal vagueness. The thought of silences in Elyot's room.

I think, said Eden, I'll get a job.

A job! said Mrs Standish. But what?

It hit the nail abjectly on the head.

That is the question, said Mrs Standish.

It was a discovery that made her go on looking, just a little too long, the eyebrows raised as if she enjoyed the tension in their arch. It made you want to kill her quietly. Instead of it, you slammed the door, and went upstairs and cried.

It made you sick, the business of being Eden Standish, the books skipped beside a midnight fire, the futility of walking winter streets. Promising yourself that soon – And then against the iron fence, the man in the macintosh, the voice half frozen, half liquid with the words of the Welsh singing, that she heard, not so much her ear, as right inside her, she was listening to it with her whole body, that became the contorted body of the man, sick inside the greenish macintosh. Feeling a scurry of grit on her face, she told herself she was sentimental. She was listening to the singing of a Welsh cripple. She was moved by the sick pallor of the face, the bones of a singing face, and the red, inflamed boss that grew from the side of the nose. She would walk, was already walking away. But she felt a tightening in her mouth. She was older, she felt older. She would go inside and look in the glass and find that this was true, that she was actually several years older. And it went on inside her, the singing, the voices of faces in the street, that flowed past her, melting with her own face. She had seen something for the first time. Her legs trembled when she closed the door, afraid to move from this discovery, a singing and revulsion in her own body.

Compassion is oddly physical. Without opportunity, she wanted to give expression to this fresh sensation, or not altogether fresh, traceable perhaps to the woman in the cottage. Instead, she continued to read, but with more direction. She discovered and read the *Capital* of Marx. She forced her way through a shell of words, finding a momentary satisfaction in her own endeavour, but also the disappointment that lies behind the passionless word. She staggered beneath the volume of these, their weight and aridity. Good Lord, but I was sentimental, she said, I fairly reeked. And she closed her door, she made notes, on a second-hand typewriter just acquired.

Finding a book, noticing a title page, Mrs Standish scented trouble again. Though smiling at the same time. A little quirk of pleasure for the intellectual enterprise of her young. Marx impressed her, his dullness. She had immense respect for intellectual exercises that were also dull, lacking the courage to embark on them herself. But misgiving now hammered at respect. 'Communism – a Contemporary Neurosis,' she had read somewhere. A quarterly, no doubt. She took in two or three of these, to glance through opening paragraphs and increase her conversational stock. Eden and neurosis, Eden in her room, the hard, bright look in Eden's eye. Mrs Standish handled possibilities. But she spent a morning with the dictionary before getting on the telephone.

What would you say, asked Mrs Standish, if Aubrey were to offer you a job?

Casually enough, it fell like wadding into the saucer of her coffee cup. It was one of those indulgent moments after lunch best suited to diplomacy.

Aubrey wants a secretary, said Mrs Standish. There are the collections. He's cataloguing the collections. And he's offered you the job of secretary, she said.

The coffee after lunch, the black coffee in little cups, is an inadequate, irrelevant and slightly insipid drink, felt Eden. And the afternoons, or the job that Aubrey Silk, the house in Regent's Park, in which the floors are very shiny where the carpets finish, because it gives the *servants something to do*, polishing the floors. This is the logical outcome of the irrelevance of

147

Eden Standish, something for Eden Standish to do, if not exactly floors.

Well? asked Mrs Standish.

I suppose it's about my mark, she said.

For Eden Standish, multiplied, there were always the Aubrey Silks. Sometimes she could not lift a hand. She felt she would go to her grave like this, the hand unlifted. Yes, she was altogether futile after lunch. And bourgeois. There was painful satisfaction in knowing this. A newly discovered and impressive label, she plastered it on everything.

You're such a *difficult* girl, her mother sighed, with a certain amount of satisfaction.

Relieved also. Mrs Standish complacently held her finger in a metaphoric dike.

There were difficulties for Mrs Standish, the difficulties of children, the difficulties of money and love, Humphrey Butler, for instance, making a scene at Rule's, because she said she was out of sorts, no, Humphrey, she said, no, and then the scene, of course he was drunk, and Christmas soon, without a warning the tinsel in the shops, and Elyot's luggage, and Elyot's voice. But it was intoxicating also, the way they spun around her, the so many faces, as if she were the centre of the universe, she liked to think, as if she were a copper-coloured sun, which was a fascinating thought, sometimes she really was, and it had always been like this, so many subsidiary planets revolving on intricate paths round the orb of Catherine Standish's sun. It was like this then. And they brought her things. Elyot brought her home a Japanese print, because he was at this stage, the stage of moustaches and Japanese prints, discreet, shadowy enthusiasms from Cambridge colleges. She bought presents herself, a great many presents, with the cheque that Humphrey gave. And she bought lilies and put them about her room.

There, said Mrs Standish. We could almost have a party.

Yes, Mother, Elyot said.

Her enthusiasms often embarrassed him. He preferred to read. He was making notes on the *Dramatic Works* of Büchner.

On the whole people bothered him, the effort, the having to commit yourself, and most of all emotionally. He sometimes shuddered now over the episode of Hildegard. Because this was something over which he had no control. His relationship with Hildegard presented a picture of himself jigging wildly on the end of an invisible rope.

It was about this time that Connie Tiarks appeared, out of the blue, as she put it, with a cheerful aptitude for cliché. He went into the drawing-room to a face that he dragged up, almost out of the past, it would not quite fit itself to Connie Tiarks, in spite of her protesting that it did, producing the evidence of past events.

I expect this will be a surprise, said Connie, her hand held out stiffly, her voice a mingling of cheerfulness and doubt.

Connie passed you a remark, and it always limped upward, somehow questioning itself at the end. She laughed much too much, startling a silence, protecting her own inadequate remarks. She looked up at you hopefully out of a large and lumpy face.

When he asked her what she was doing, she said that she was passing through, which was not altogether surprising in Connie Tiarks. He remembered her chiefly as a creature of transit, an incident on a sofa, another under a mulberry tree. Connie Tiarks would always be this. Her hands were always on the verge of reaching for gloves.

Yes, she said. I'm on my way to Cheltenham.

Which struck a note that he recognized, the rushing of water from a cistern, that made him blush.

Of course, he said. Cheltenham. Yes.

We've lived there since, she said.

Yes, he said. Yes. I remember.

It's nice for Mother, said Connie Tiarks, without explaining, except that with Connie most things were *nice* out of pure gratitude.

Mrs Tiarks lived in a boarding-house in Cheltenham. She had her annuity, which she supplemented by making bridge- and dressing-jackets for the less distressed gentlewomen she knew. Her anaemic fingers wandered mechanically over the surface of the stuffs she worked, fortunately without appreciating the inherent ugliness of these. She drew a certain mental comfort from her occupation. Surrounded by snippets of silk and brocade, she sat at her window, flat and bloodless, beside a pot of maidenhair.

Cheltenham was altogether pleasant, Connie said.

Elyot found it difficult to talk to her. He found himself looking at her face, it sat roundly on her large head, in a kind of scallop arrangement of hair.

There were lectures, she said, uneasily. And concerts. And archery in one of the parks.

But it was not so much Connie, it was all people, the words that came from mouths, people trying to communicate in words.

Had he read any good books? she asked, her voice growing brighter with desperation.

At sixteen she had begun to take an interest in literature and art. She had begun to expose the Dutch masters on her mantelpiece, and to copy passages from Whitman and Tagore into a leather notebook. Her mother wondered a little. But as it seemed a harmless and ladylike pursuit, Connie was allowed to persevere.

Isn't it funny, our sitting here together after all this time? Connie was saying, Elyot heard.

A great deal was *funny* to Connie Tiarks, again perhaps from making the best, from continually supplying surprises to an otherwise unsurprising life.

Why, he said, why funny, why not for instance inevitable?

Regretting at once, because it was a remark he would not ordinarily make, and these would sometimes fit themselves to his mouth, he was left to face the discrepancy between himself and the remarks he made. Words were so seldom a literal translation.

Connie Tiarks had mottled over.

Well, she said, touching a flower, a large amorphous flower in the pattern of her dress, touching it as if she hadn't noticed it before. I like to think things are inevitable, Elyot, she said. The *nice* things, of course.

They listened to the fire. He felt uncomfortable behind the legs. Because Connie was searching for a thought, something pregnant, apposite, he could scent it, that she had probably copied out of a book.

That's all very well, he said dryly. But does it guard against monotony?

That again was clumsy, and this time cruel. He had no control, it seemed, over his own intentions.

No, she said. No. I want to be *comfortable*. That's the main thing.

It came with a kind of desperation that he quite believed, behind it the crumpets and the gas fire in a boarding-house in Cheltenham. And she clung desperately to her assertion. Her face was guarding it.

I want to feel I *know*, she almost sighed.

Poor Connie, as she became in time, in the voice of Mrs Standish, there was no end to the poverty of certainty in the life of Connie Tiarks, she was inevitably always reaching for her gloves. Looking at her, Elyot detested himself. Or looking at the face of Connie Tiarks many times repeated, in many places, that he did not know how to touch, either in the fumbling of words or the more consoling silences. Elyot is a scholar, his mother said. He retreated into books. A second-hand existence.

Hello, you two, Eden said.

They looked round, as if protecting an unguarded moment. Because Eden did not belong, standing with a cigarette in her mouth, destroying a moment from the doorway, not wishing to inquire, but purely destructive, just her presence.

We're having a talk, Connie said.

As if it mattered, you felt, to Eden, to her drooping, thoughtful cigarette. Connie remembered she had been afraid of

Eden. That is not uncommon in children, she told herself, to reassure. But she remained uneasy now.

Oh, said Eden.

She went away. She could not think, Connie or Elyot, who did not belong, or for that matter Eden herself. She had to go back over and over again, to her voice making promises. She had met him that afternoon in Lyons.

There was a potency about cheap music that wasn't to be despised, he said.

She heard the sugar cannon off the cup, closer than music, like his hand.

If you wanted to drug yourself, she said.

She explored warily, not the hand, rejecting this ambassador of the face, her eyes wandered over marble. There were also many Jewesses.

And didn't she, sometime? After all –

She summoned up her collapsing breath, collapsing for no reason, but collapsed.

Sometimes, she agreed.

She smiled even at a face. They were two people meeting in the marble wasteland. She began to catch up to her disappointment, the banality of just a face that she had not even chosen, it had sat there, but perhaps after all there was not much selection in these matters, the face, the moment presented itself with a dictatorial flourish.

She heard his breath, gathered for the next remark.

Did she listen also to good music? he asked.

You can't always cope with the obvious. It wins. Even when you know, it wins. Like the voice of Maynard. Eden Standish knew this, even before he had become Maynard, or Norman Maynard, that she could never say, she called him Maynard, it kept the right accent on the whole business, she wanted to keep this between herself and Maynard's face. She told herself this, afterwards, after the first spasm of being afraid. And she *was* afraid, the hand trembling on a tea cup, in a rain of Grieg.

Music, he said, was a kind of divine reparation for human weakness.

She floated repugnantly, but surprised, but listening, she floated in a sea of Jewesses, their faces upturned to a marble sky.

He began to tell her about his wife, who was no longer his wife, she lived at Putney, he was an architect, he said. Sympathy and understanding were very rare qualities. He wanted to live in the country, together with sympathy and understanding. That was why he appreciated this sudden, well, he had found himself, they had found themselves, by some strange coincidence, together, she had been good enough to listen.

Eden looked at him. He took it. She could not get away from her repugnance. She wanted to, she wanted to kill it, her humiliation. He looked at her with the bland, unseeing expression of someone obsessed by his own emotions. Or not quite. Someone wanting to share his own emotions. He handed them to her, like a tepid cup of tea.

Afterwards, becoming Maynard, he remained unchanged. Very quickly you knew everything about Maynard. He was very grateful, he said. It made her want to turn away. It made her hesitate before answering the telephone. Because he rang her up, because he had to see her, because she was the only person with whom he could discuss the prevailing problem of himself.

Sitting in Maynard's rooms she smoked too much. She was uncertain. She did not know, not quite, what she wanted, if she was really listening to a voice.

Once he put his head in her lap.

No, she said.

She went away soon, inventing an excuse.

She would stay away, half waiting, would invent the ultimate excuse, say no, Maynard, I shall not come again. After all, as an individual you ought to be able to do this. If there were an individual. There was a business of sex, a business of being men and women. This was what made her afraid. And she did not want to be naïve. I am old enough, if not in experience, she said.

Maynard sat, his knees turned in against each other, his hands held back to back between the knees. Pretending not to look, she said that this time she would tell him. There was something about his abjectness that she could not bear.

Eden, he said, sometimes you're very cruel.

Why? she asked, hoarsely.

She wanted to push away his words. They were something to resist.

Because, he said, you hold yourself back. Half the time you're holding back.

She heard, looked, with a kind of fascination. He took his hands from between his knees. She watched the knuckles of his hands.

Anyway, it was perhaps impossible, he said, the perfect relationship between a man and a woman without the recognition of sex.

Then he touched her. Physically taut, she still quivered.

Well? she asked.

It was poor defence. In the late light, that she was glad of, it flattened and reduced the unequivocal forms, the spire only just clung to the window, a last moment of corroded elegance. She listened to her heart, that took no account of time, the chiming of clocks in the square outside.

Eden, he said.

She felt him down against her knees. On his neck, she saw the little whorl of hair, against the white neck, very close, and somehow more abject than the whole of Maynard. If she could summon pity. But it was not this.

All right, she said, her other voice, speaking for someone who would walk in perhaps through the closed door.

She took off her clothes. It was stupid to be naïve, she felt. But she trembled, the so many flags of flesh, the uncontrolled flapping of the body. If she could ignore what she felt, in his body the gratitude of Maynard. Even when she closed her eyes on the visible Maynard there was still this, that she must offset with something of her own, something more than the chafing of the flesh, the mouth on mouth. But it froze upon her mouth. She reached out through years, upon her back, through the leaves of trees, and the sound of still, basking water, to the state of physical perfection. Then her hands touched sheets. This then was sex, the rumpled bed, the sense of aching nausea, the dead weight.

Let me, let me go now, Maynard. Please.

She reached towards her clothes, a lighter pool upon the chair.

But she must come again, she mustn't let him down, he said.

Yes, she said. Yes. Only now, she had to go.

Her feet said, and the pulses in her body, a leaden clapping that was mercifully very far distant from the mind.

She came to him always in the late afternoon. Her life had divided into three distinct and unrelated zones, the sterile but frenzied area of Maynard's room at dusk, the house in Ebury Street, with its undertones of safe, familiar voices, and the window over Regent's Park, at which she sat alone, or beside the voice of Aubrey Silk. She had gone to Aubrey in the New Year. She sat there, mornings, the house silent about her, muted by the many attentions of too many servants. Sound was altogether muffled, the passage of a duster, the passing of feet. Your own breathing had an unreal, fragile quality, like the Bavarian music box on the table in the drawing-room. As if it had transferred to you, out of its own gilt throat, a solemn, anachronistic tinkle.

She began to be, ironically, a sort of high priestess to Aubrey Silk's collections. In a way she was grateful, as you are for the lucid moments. She knew by detail the Monets and the Renoirs. She was learning to judge Chinese jade. At appropriate times she poured tea from Lowestoft, diffidently, her mouth pursed a little at her own gesture, at the unreality of Eden Standish in this connexion, pouring tea or handing corn-flour cakes. Five p.m. is perhaps the most unconvincing hour, she felt. More especially because it bridged the distance, through Aubrey's voice, to the time spent with Maynard About this hour it began to recur.

Thank you, Eden, Aubrey said. That will be all, I think. Let me see. Yes.

His chin drooped above his collar. Sometimes you felt, beyond the detachment of Aubrey, that there was some participation in the lives of other people, but not often, and not long. On the whole, the practice of detachment, like the cultivation of acute sympathy and understanding, puts you in a world of illusory proportions. Aubrey Silk, and probably at the other extremity, Connie Tiarks, she guessed, lived just as far removed from reality.

Good night, Aubrey, Eden said.

Even the voice in Aubrey's house acquired discreeter tones, dim, dove-grey, a little precious.

Walking from the house in Regent's Park, there was a rankness in February streets, a cold cluttering of newspapers that blew against the ankles, soon the glare from Tottenham Court Road. She took off her hat. She walked hatless, untidily. She walked this way every evening, there were the shops she knew, and the faces, the Italians and the Indians, that became part of this period of transit, of transformation, of growing foreign to herself, like the dark and just not rational Indian face above the tin of Bombay duck. She would never quite understand this, she felt. It was like a repulsion for a pair of hands. She was still surprised even by the printed MAYNARD above his bell.

He wanted her to go away with him, if only for a little, say for a weekend, so that he would have her completely to himself, he would be very grateful if she gave him this. Because in London, in the furtive hours they spent, you couldn't, couldn't *lose yourself*, he put it. Taking the words from her, unexpressed. To go away with Maynard, to lose yourself, or to find yourself. She found herself suddenly grasping at the possibility of what he said. It will be different, she said, I shall try, there will be no reserves of personal feeling. So she began to want it very much. The place was immaterial. She agreed when he suggested Dieppe.

I am going to Dieppe, Mother, she said, in a pause between stockings, that she glanced at, then rolled casually into their ball. Aubrey's given me till Tuesday.

Very casual the voice sometimes is, launched on the informative remark. Eden sensed this. It was too casual, transparent, the implication inside, like the hand behind the stocking web. The brushes made a little click.

But, Eden, dear, you didn't tell me, said Mrs Standish.

She stood in another morning, the recurrence of place was enough, to send back her mind on more than a geographical errand. In fact, Mrs Standish quailed. The long trailers of her sleeves settled helplessly.

There was nothing to tell, Eden said.

She resented the movement of criticism. This was one of the moments when you heard, beyond a person's critical silence, the noises in the street. She rejected busily her mother's face. Because it was too much. Hands clamped the brushes together again.

But it's, it's all right, Eden? said Mrs Standish.

She was not herself. Crises often made Mrs Standish lose the faith she had in herself. They tumbled her laborious façade. She became a face waking in the night, afraid of itself, the essential face, without the apologies of powder and rouge.

Why shouldn't it be? asked Eden.

I don't know, her mother said.

But it was there still, the implication, like the flashback in a play in which she doubled, and Willy's face that doubled also for a shadow.

Now I must go to bed, said Eden, I'll be up early. You needn't bother.

Then they were offering cheeks.

It will rain, said Mrs Standish. In Dieppe it always rains.

As if this were material, her voice offering a fatuous bleat, on which the door closed. Eden closing the door. They stood either side of a closed door.

Mrs Standish went to bed. Sometimes she counted when she was alone. She found it happening inside her head. Tonight she was counting it out aloud. It came more dispassionately than thought. Thirty-six, thirty-seven, counted Mrs Standish, before she stopped, listened. It would be too bad if, through a wall anyone had heard. After all Eden was old enough, she said. But this only made her miserable. She drifted in a glare of French woodwork and the flavour of macaroons.

Dieppe became, for Eden too, so many sensations, more this than forms, and the voice of Maynard that dissolved substance in its neighbourhood, its self-absorption did not take into account the independent existence. They took a room some-where near water. It was a backwater, or a river into which boats came, the small, hardy boats that penetrate and become landscape, their funnels and their sails. From the window, when he had gone down, when for a moment she was free, she watched the head of smoke upon a blackened funnel. From her window she tried to feel the special nature of their expedi-tion. She would force herself this time into the romantic atti-tude of two people taking trains. In the train he had held her hand. But little of the journey remained, stood the test of time. At the moment it was secondary, she knew, beside the *quin-caillerie* with the two men doing business, the man in the cap, its shiny peak, the man with the grey paper package. Voices hurtled over cobbles. There was also the door in the side of the Hôtel du Nord that opened on a square of lemon-coloured light, less northern than tropical, the wooden shutter swinging on the colour of a fever.

Maynard said that all his life he had longed to travel, but like most aims, this was squashed by his bad luck, whether the scholarship he missed, or the poverty of parsons' sons, or, afterwards, his wife's tastes. Her name, he said, was Edith. He had grown to hate her, certain things about her, habits, the way she licked the corner of an envelope and applied the stamp, or things she wore, like a string of artificial pearls, and the luminous dial of a wristwatch seen at night. Edith was also a symbol of gentility, of poverty. He was acutely ashamed of this, the second-best, the makeshifts at Cambridge, the calculations over meals and fares, the humiliation of summer weeks in English watering places. Edith preferred Bournemouth, it was less vulgar than Brighton, she said. After the break it would be different, he had felt. But he didn't bargain for his luck, the jobs just missed, the professional jealousies. This was something no one understood if they hadn't experienced it.

There was much like that. There was not much room for disagreement. Out of the monologue grew foreign sounds to which Eden tuned her ear, the collapsing phrase on the accordion, the Arab selling peanuts. She clung to these. She wanted not to criticize, not to destroy. So that she forced herself to accept, whether it was words or the sexual act. She became a kind of dog-like silence. There was much of the dog's attitude in the relationship of women with men, she decided. The acceptance, the waiting for the next move. For this reason you lay waiting on the beds of cheap hotels. You waited for a sign. You held the weight of an exhausted body stretched upon your own, with your hands you comforted the skin of a withdrawn and scarcely sentient being. This was the right attitude perhaps, that ignored personal distaste. Regrets were the footsteps that retreated down hotel corridors at night, but, there, recognizable.

She had to recognize the failure of Dieppe, that her mother also took for granted, with the glance that *understood*. She began to avoid her mother. In the evening she went to friends. There was a girl called Valerie Stevenson, whose sister she had known at school. Or she merely walked, or sat alone on benches, to escape the half-expressed solicitude. You're a distant creature, Maynard said. She failed to comment. Whether or not, she failed to know. To know yourself. That ludicrous presumption before entering the maze. Later on, events forced her to resume inquiry desperately enough.

Later on, it was in the spring, Maynard left for the United States. A job with commercial architects that took him to New York.

This is what I've waited for, he said. This is the beginning. This is a new life. I was meant to launch out. I was never insular. You don't understand, Eden. New York. And then there's California.

She tried to concentrate on something, some object, the butt of a dead cigarette, the worn heel of a shoe, to escape from the disgusting, the nauseating aspect of the human ego. But I asked for this, she said, knowing that it lacked consolation. Man was vulgar enough, as an individual, only in the mass there was a kind of abstract nobility. If this were not also illusion, the illusion induced by words, by books, by the sentimental dictatorship of heart and stomach in contact with the streets.

I'm glad, Maynard, she said.

Handing over the keys, so to speak. It was official. He made it so.

I knew you would be, he said. I'll write.

It struck coldly, not the parting, it was not a parting, it was the act of disposal.

You're pale, darling, Mother said.

It made you turn your face.

I need exercise, she said. I'll have to start walking some of the way in the morning.

She wanted to be left alone. Making events, they are your very own, also the consequence, whether the bitter abstraction of your own subsequent regrets, or the even more relentless concrete kind. Because Eden Standish found that she was pregnant.

It was one of those things that didn't, couldn't happen to yourself, she said, over against the evidence. Sitting at the window in Regent's Park or walking through the streets towards Victoria, her mind remained fixed to this, like the falling body to its parachute, though without the promise of ultimate salvation, there was no land. I've got to, I've got to, she said. After the first numbness she lived on half-formed, half-directed phrases. She sat holding her hands, she sat very close to the predominating misery. Sometimes she wished that her age, that recent events, would slip away from her in a moment of temporal dissolution, and that she could creep like a child under an eiderdown of sleep. But without this dispensation, she remained herself, avoiding eyes, the sudden footstep, or a voice, that intruded on her physical condition.

You shall take me to a concert, said Mrs Standish. I expect it will do you good.

As if, as if. It made you turn quickly.

Why? said Eden.

In front of your face you hung the defensive gauze of faintly irritable inquiry.

Because I think you're moping, said Mrs Standish, trying to look wise.

As if I should have a reason to mope, said Eden.

But her pulse went slower, relieved.

Alone or in crowds, you could hide, it was the half-way combination that made you start, wonder, the *tête-à-tête*, or the few friends. Listening to music Eden envied her mother, the immense satisfaction of the face, the half-closed eyes, whether this satisfaction were sincere, springing from the music itself, or merely from being in the right *milieu*. But her mother, bogus or not, sat in the firm protection of her own established envelope. Succinct, satisfied, proof against any physical or emotional disturbance, except perhaps disease or middle age.

They were playing Brahms. I am listening, I *must* listen to a Brahms concerto, Eden felt. She fastened on her hands, must give to music a structure, because this is the only way to listen, avoiding the backwaters of your own mind. It rose in waves, the Brahms concerto, blown beneath the carpet, the heavy, dusty waves, as if it were pinned down round the edges of the room, as if your hands could not stretch out to rescue a phrase from the heavy folds of its own just frustrated passion. More often than not, music moved like this. There was very little freedom. Except in the motion of a breast, Mother's, moving on its own wave of personal retrospect.

Elyot will be home, remembered Mrs Standish. Elyot, for good. For what? Her foot tapped. But home. She smiled. She must remind Julia to air the room. As if Julia never remembered such things herself. The foot tapped, swayed. There were moments in music when you couldn't believe in your own past doubts. These had been conjured away, were so much nothing, in the house, in the bedroom, in the nights lived and forgotten. Elyot stood on the stairs in a ragged, undergraduate moustache. I am going to work, Mother, he said. She hoped he would be a writer. If only one of her children were creative, her vanity would flourish like a tree, cover the dead branches of the bitter moments, the leaves as green, as soothing as the stroke of violins.

Opening her eyes Mrs Standish glanced on Eden. It gave her a little shock. This was more than the momentary effect of music. She closed her eyes again, not so much in retreat, she hoped, as to concentrate, yes, to concentrate on he problem of Eden, as if she knew much, well, *anything*, of her daughter's life, of her daughter's mind. Beyond the face was supposition. The growing pains of love. Something of this nature. And of course desperate. Love is desperate in the beginning and the end. Still far from the ultimate stage herself, she was sure, Mrs Standish could afford smugness.

The bland unison of 'cellos took possession. A long way beyond Eden. And without bearing. Her mother made her desperate. To touch, now, the eiderdown, she would have screamed, or broken down like a small child, cried into an eiderdown. Because the clarinet had lost control. It ricocheted among the strings. Her throat was as taut as strings. It was the pulse in drums, the big drum, that they screwed too, too *tight*.

She thought she was going to suffocate.

I – I'll wait, she heard herself. In the street. You'll –

Then she got up quickly, went in the rustling of programme sheets, that was also a protest, the sucked teeth. In the doorway the misery of violins fell upon her head. She groped her way down the concrete tunnel of the stairs in a long echoing of horns. Then there were stars, she saw, and the irrelevant spire. She was standing on the pavement, with the irrelevance of one anonymous star among many. After all, she said, one expected this.

Watching the calendar put a kind of lethargy on her. But she had to speak, somehow, somewhere. There was the girl, Valerie Stevenson. She worked for a publisher, fitfully, with long weekends in the country houses of relations, and the undefined weekends. Yes, felt Eden, it must be Valerie Stevenson. She had a sleek head, also a habit of sitting on the carpet towards midnight, and talking about life, less abstract by 2 a.m., by 2 a.m. life became more specifically men. Valerie Stevenson, Eden decided, would be this less personal confession, almost professional advice.

Darling, said Valerie Stevenson. You're so *young*.

It made you bite your lip. It made you feel you were standing in something that was not quite clean. Valerie Stevenson's mental eye visualizing events.

If only you'd come, but of course you didn't, that's silly of me, Valerie said. There are ways and means, if only. Now let me see. I'd forgotten about that man.

You went cold. It was impersonal enough, Valerie's voice. But attached to the other end of it, you couldn't deaden your own mortification.

She thought he was at 15 Dawson Street, Valerie said. Anyway, it was quite easy. It was just off Theobalds Road. There was a place that sold baths on the ground floor. The house looked sort of Morris-y. Red. With plaques and things. And the man, didn't it slay you, his name, his name was Jewel!

Against the iron railing that sprouted from the pavement, the afternoon was thin, the sky pale, the whole thin perspective of the street, in which was the voice of a woman selling violets. Finding the purpose in an errand, your feet still loitered, your eyes lingered on the shape of a bath. You found to the last detail, down to the last plaque, the Morris lily in its shabby red, the description given by Valerie, that was also a remembered dream, before the climax, that you avoided, resisted, that came up hot and panting to overwhelm.

Eden Standish rang a bell.

Now, she said, now. There were still violets. And the white violets that you brought home to arrange. You must have the china shoe, Mrs Macarthy said, if you are good, if you eat up your sago like a good girl, you shall pretend it is as white as violets. Elyot said he was asleep, the moon said, he was white upon his pillow. She shivered in the paler light of Theobalds Road, where the past sat oddly, extinct. It was better, she decided, not to think.

Yes? he asked.

He was reddish, both the skin and, over it, the pervading stubble. His mouth had that sewn-up look. Opening on words, it remained fastened in the corners, drawn together by unseen stitches. There was sleep in the corners of his eyes.

I've come – she said. It's – I heard – that perhaps you have the *Morning Post*?

Yes, he said, doubting her from top to toe.

But he opened up the door.

She walked, after many ages, down the passage, after footsteps that sounded through an always empty house. She heard her own feet fraying the carpet of downward steps. His sleeve was frayed, resting on a doorknob. She stood in a room, sickly with the light from areas and the naked bulb. Somewhere water dripped.

Sit down, he said.

The chair squeaked.

She was sitting, empty of any substance, of all emotion, she was a glass shell, but easily broken, beyond which the accumulation of disgust, of horror, was waiting to flood.

Now, he said, advancing. Let me see.

Now, she said, the face, this face, floated on a wave of nausea, jerked forward on the leaping nerve, and the hand that grew from a sleeve, to lift, to touch.

No, she said.

She heard her heels startling the chair.

Not – not now, she said. I didn't exactly realize. I didn't know. Perhaps a little longer, she said.

Perhaps. Perhaps. Her own feet, they went plap plap, she heard them plap plap, after her in the passage, moving in the now static dream. She could feel his face rooted there under the electric bulb. Then her nails were on the shut door.

Almost running, there were no faces, there was no sound, in the street, in her neighbourhood. Now it was mostly like this. As if one recent event had washed back everything else and left her standing with her own preoccupation. She could not help it. She was ashamed. But she could not help. There was only one purpose, ultimately one person, in spite of the selfless aspiration, which was hypocrisy, you were your own focus, you were your own mind, your own body. She paused, her hand on brick, trying with her hand to force back her own nausea.

When she got in, she knew by the trunk standing in the hall that somebody had come. It was Elyot, of course. He appeared from a doorway, the familiar and yet foreign face.

Hello, Eden, he said.

The moustache shaved, he seemed waiting diffidently for recognition. His eyes preoccupied with his own personal and quite insignificant change. It was natural, she supposed. But younger than Elyot, she now felt older. The last year had made her so.

Hello, she said.

She tried to make herself mention the absence of the moustache, and failed. She was a mingling of her own hungriness and nausea. She held her coat with her hands in front.

You look sort of green, don't you? he said.

It made her tingle with sudden fright, wonder if a glance.

I'm feeling a bit off, she said. Something I ate at lunch.

An elaborate banality of the voice that she hoped was sufficiently and not too casual.

What are you going to do with yourself? she asked.

How?

I mean, now that you're down for good. What are you going to do?

That made him retreat. She could feel it, also a certain pleasure in achieving her own defence.

God knows, he said. Wait and see.

She made him uncomfortable. She was darker, remoter than he remembered, the Eden as a child, which was then just a discrepancy in ages, now a distance that came perhaps from experience. Eden had fitted herself into a fresh pattern. It made him feel gauche. Watching her as she went on up the stairs, casually out of the corner of his eye, there was self-possession, an indifference in the trailing coat. His superior years fell away from him. She implied that he didn't know, and he didn't, he was hesitating at the bottom of a staircase, he was waiting to see, still with no purpose in the general pattern.

Reaching the landing, Eden remained conscious of his eyes. If only he would stop. Elyot withered her away with his eyes, still. Almost, but not quite. She was uncomfortably conscious of the remaining core, he did not wither this, the shame, that he continued watching.

I think I'll lie down, she said. Don't tell Mother. She'll only fuss.

In many fussy, external ways, while remaining separate. They were three people in the same house, each in a distinctive box, there was little intercourse between these. Now she was glad of her box. Closing her eyes, she lay, drooped, in her own blessed, separate darkness.

But this release no longer happened often. She was a continual waking to a more uncompromising consciousness. She sat in a perpetual white light. You could touch the oppressively important minutes, the way time, under pressure, becomes more concrete. And her body, she was conscious of this too, tied to it in a subtle way that was new and horrifying, in sleep she stood outside it like a pale shadow beside stone.

It was Valerie Stevenson who heard, somewhere, she was a source of relevant information, heard there was a place, of course, my dear, it's bound to be rather round-the-corner, but still, but still, it's a possibility, she said. Listening to the voice of Valerie, its frankness, for Valerie there were no surprises, she was born all shell, Eden felt her returning disgust, even through her gratitude. The place was at Ealing, Valerie said. She had written down the address. Then there was the money question. It was bound to be in the neighbourhood of forty, perhaps as much as fifty, she said.

Eden looked at a slip of paper. This was a commercial transaction. She was about to do business with a Mrs Moya Angelotti.

If I could help, but I can't, Valerie said.

Yes, said Eden, vaguely. Of course.

Already her mind dealt with a possibility, that was to-morrow morning, that was sitting by a window, the little ridges that the mower made on grass, silver with light at ten o'clock. Aubrey, she must say, I wonder.

Aubrey, she said, and never had grass looked more tranquil, or the pale, disinfectant pink of geraniums in an urn. Aubrey, I want to ask you to do me a favour.

She was afraid listening to her own voice, and asking Aubrey, it was like speaking into thin glass, waiting for this to shiver into pieces.

And what's that? Aubrey said.

He stirred coffee. He wore a dressing-gown of grey silk. To ask Aubrey now, it was ironical, to ask him to step down from his silky cloud, even if unconsciously, to bring him into contact with Mrs Moya Angelotti. It made her hold her breath.

I wonder, she said, if you'd let me have a week, or ten days. Or perhaps just a week. Because I feel – I want –

Yes, yes, he said. Certainly.

As if he didn't want to be touched by the breath of any explanation. As if explanations were dangerous.

And Aubrey, she said, this is something more difficult. If you'd lend me fifty pounds. It's a lot. But it's only a matter of time, and you'll have it back.

Then she looked at him, he made her, for the first time, there was no suggestion of evasion in the attitude of Aubrey Silk.

Yes, he said. Fifty pounds.

Thank you, she said.

Whether he knew or not, she was grateful for his silence, which did not quite cover his eyes.

And Mother, to Mother I'm staying with Valerie Stevenson, I shall come here every day. Do you understand? she said. You see, Aubrey, Mother's sometimes difficult. Sometimes I feel I've got to get away. Even if only for a week.

She could feel the sweat on her forehead.

Don't let your coffee get cold, she said.

The villa in Ealing was no different from those on either side, except that its blankness was arrested by the drooping of an eyelid over the right eye, the pale membrane of a half-drawn blind, either negligent or intentional. Otherwise No. 2 St Georges Villas was expressionless, uninformative, no plate even to announce the face, the plump white pouchiness, the straying hair, that became on acquaintance Mrs Moya Angelotti.

Mrs Angelotti billowed through her house, overflowed with a kind of Irish expressiveness that left no room for other inmates, swallowed these, existing or not. Sometimes there were sounds, a far murmur under the full orchestration of Mrs Angelotti's brogue. There was also a face, the face of a Miss Teece, who assisted, Mrs Angelotti said, or who dusted and swept, who ran at Mrs Angelotti's voice, her Teece, Teece, slip an' make a cup of tea, Mrs Stevens likes her cup of tea, an' sure I'll take one with her if you don't mind.

Yes, Mrs Stevens, said Mrs Angelotti. It's many that's in a like position. I wouldn't be for prying into your private affairs. Don't think for a minute, dear. But.

She picked a dead frond from a fern. With plump fingers she prodded at the mould.

Your own business is your own, Mrs Angelotti said.

What? Oh yes, said Mrs Stevens.

She was tired. The sheet that she pulled up, its harsh, foreign texture, sawed roughly under her chin. Mrs Angelotti waited, her breath held pigeonwise, she seemed to swell over her almost white apron, to encroach, to increase. Mrs Stevens closed her eyes. Soon it will be over, she said.

In a couple of shakes, said Mrs Angelotti. Now dear, open your eyes. Just a minute. To swallow this down. It'll be like one long Saturday night. Mrs *Stevens! Dear!*

Eden Standish opened her eyes. She was a different person, she was the Mrs Stevens chosen in the bus. She swallowed down a draught, and it was a different throat. A thick, yellow sunlight flowed beneath the pale blind, or at night the lamp, the greenish lamplight. She measured time, this otherwise unbroken week, by the ebb and flow of light. It gave her some bearing in the flat fly-buzz, the fly that followed a frieze of fruit, or was it pumpkins, anyway, pink, that drooped down into her head, or not the head, the stupor, that alternated with the pain. Into this, into the arid white days, pushed the face of Mrs Angelotti, or the hand of Miss Teece that became a sponge. Then she closed her eyes again. She wanted to be left.

Mrs Angelotti sat upon a chair. You heard the planting of her thighs, and the crackle of a not quite clean starched collar that she wore to salve professional convention.

I like to think I do what I do for a *definite reason*, said Mrs Angelotti. An' you shall see the letters, the very nice letters, that I have from those as appreciate. You wouldn't believe. There's actresses, there's names. It's many a hole I've got the theatre out of.

Mrs Angelotti's voice drifted like a skein of ether through a state of almost consciousness.

Yes, she said. It's the connexion I have. It's Angelotti. *Was*, that is. That brings the theatre near. He was trapezes, Angelotti. Then he went an' missed the net. Oh yes, she said.

Her collar creaked.

Alone, Eden began to take notice. At first it was things. There were the half-dozen daffodils in the silver-plated trumpet vase. Her relief fastened on things. It is over, she said. She was even grateful for the pain, for the heavy, tumid legs. Because this meant release, even if bitter to admit, and it was, the perpetual clutching after freedom. This is a new life, said Maynard. She disposed of what she didn't want to remember. Lying on her back, she began to look outward, out of a trance of more than physical pain, into Mrs Angelotti's room. She realized now for the first time that she should have had a child. Instead she was free. She lay on her back looking at the six pallid daffodils, late and spindly, that stirred in a suburban breeze. There was no sign of the abortion that had been done, the child they had taken away, and which she had only just begun to consider as a child. Only now, afterwards, it had ceased to have connexion with herself and Maynard, the shoddiness, it had begun to have a significance of its own. Round her face, her hair felt heavy and oppressive. She was at a loss, had lost, there was after all an emptiness, she told herself there should have been a child.

The week dwindled. It was not time, she decided, but an insertion of painfully intense sensation. She stepped back into her own waiting footprints, on the dust in Mrs Angelotti's hall. She stood there while Mrs Angelotti's voice hovered between the technical and abstract generalities.

Good-bye, dear, she said. It's been nice. Even so. Yes, she sighed heavily. I shan't say happy returns. And remember, dear, not for the next six weeks.

Eden Standish went home. It began to be evening in the streets. She caught the train. She caught on diffidently enough to the slackened thread, but there was no reason for diffidence, she saw, it tightened logically enough. There was the fruiterer polishing his apples outside Victoria. There were the pink and placid sausage skins, and varnished pies, in the cold-food shop. She walked homeward through the heavy evening light, too warm, she felt, perhaps the time of year, her strange new feet tasting the pavement, entering a fresh phase.

There you are, her mother said, glancing over a book.

Mrs Standish was annoyed. She would hide her annoyance in indifference. She burnt with an intense dislike for that Valerie Stevenson. No better than a magpie, she said to herself. She was pleased with that.

Eden went on up the stairs. The carpet had worn, the dress tarnished that her mother wore, the refurbished gold gown that she liked to put on in the evening, she sat there in a pool of gold, of light, liquescent in the Louis XV *bergère*, and not quite real. Altogether there was an air of unreality about this house, of remoteness in chance unity. In the sitting-room her mother's thoughts touched on some cloudy shore of their own. She put up the book in front of her face. In a minute she would say the dinner was getting cold. And on the upper landing underneath the roof, Elyot would be sitting, equally remote. Eden went into her own small box, closed it on herself, on her experience.

On the upper landing, underneath the roof, he heard the closing of the door. It was Eden slipping in, after a week's withdrawal, slipping into his own thoughts, the renewal of disturbing influence. Elyot leant out of the upper window. In the warm evening he had taken off his coat. He hung out facing the dusk, across the street the window of light where two girls in a kitchenette fussed and giggled preparing dinner, exchanging anecdotes. A taxi floated, dimensionless, its roof, passed dissolving in the street. She asked him what he would do with himself now that he had come down. It hung interrogatively in the evening street, tingeing his skin with sweat beneath the shirt. Because your own inadequacies suddenly faced you, hanging formless, but definitely implied in the approaching night landscape.

Light fell on the opposite façade, from a light released below, from Mrs Standish turning on the light. She felt bitter, bad-tempered. It was not like her. She looked in the glass at her face, which was like her, and yet unlike. One is very unlike one's face, she felt. She put up her hand, touched it. How awful, she said, when this suddenly crumbles away, leaving, leaving – It horrified her, this. She heard Eden walking overhead. Nervously she went in to Julia, the swish of her skirts gave her some courage, she went in to ask why, why the dinner was late.

A preparing of dishes, a washing, as before. Eden dried her hands on the towel she found for her in her room, not waiting, but probably put there after she left. Searching for her nose in the half-light, she applied powder. All these actions, gestures, the bowing of the body before habit. Out of these and the numb mind, she would grow again, she felt, not so much herself, this was immaterial, but what she would do. The transient pain in her body, the little whimper for the lost and finally regretted child, waking in her some emotional theme that she wanted to express, she lost herself in the darkness. She put her hands to where her face had been. She listened for some word in the darkness, that you listen for, listen, of reassurance.

He listened. Sometimes he could almost hear her listening to his thoughts. Or insinuating herself into his thoughts, critical. Eden was the dark street. He retreated quietly into the room. To do something. That shiver on the skin. Soon it would be dinner, the voices call to a roast, and family conversation. You will have £400 a year, she said. It had an accent of certainty as opposed to the night sounds. Inside the room it was also safer, even if smug, among the sheaves of notes, the stuffy hours from museums and libraries, the Cambridge lectures that became a kind of automatic writing, but something to hold between you and doubt. There were the notes on Büchner. My son is going to write a book on, well, anyway a book, she said. Pulling off his shoes, he put on slippers. These were easy to the feet.

Part Two

8

Mrs Standish asked everyone if they would have some soup, in a tone of voice that expected the offer to be refused. It was the consequence of many years spent ignoring the second-best. The material second-best, of course. Spiritually, she liked to believe, she managed to keep to the heights. A precious country, it was also cheaply reached.

Will *you* have some soup, Elyot?

The voice glanced. It was not the glance of diffidence. It definitely implied a disparagement of soup. Looking at her as she sat amongst them, at the dining-room table, in the lap of a flat Sunday. Elyot decided that his mother could never lay claim to the quality of diffidence. Doling soup, her hand, obviously disclaiming the significance of its own gesture, turned it to an act of magnificent charity. This she distributed impartially to those about her, to Eden, to Connie Tiarks, to himself, delivered through the medium of Julia. She sat there indolently in the remnants of her beauty, fondant, with a head of spun caramel, her hand resting with distaste upon a ladle.

The tureen in front of her had suffered too. Originally perfect, glimpses of this perfection still defied chips and rivets. Elyot felt the touch of nostalgia in the green and gold of the soup tureen, as it drifted out of the conversation, into a sudden focus. There was a horrid attraction in the little gilded pineapple on the lid, that now covered what remained of the soup. Ignoring words, that were irrelevant, he could not keep his eyes off the little pineapple. It stood out like a boss on the face of the last ten years, a tangible reminder of escaped time.

Because it was almost exactly ten years since the tureen made its appearance, that evening, he remembered, his mother telling him what she couldn't afford, but did, the evening that was somehow significant without an explanation, the noises in neighbouring rooms, and Eden coming in, she had been away. Just down from Cambridge, you hung about, you hung out of windows, you waited for strangers to value your unique and sensible qualities. To unpack this from under the weight and cynicism of ten years was painful. It was also midday Sunday. They were eating soup.

Connie said that she burnt, she burnt for the People of Spain. She talked about Oppressors, almost as if she were repeating the correspondence in *The Times*.

Eden snorted.

And what are you going to do? she asked.

Do? repeated Connie vaguely.

Yes, said Eden.

She waited.

Well, said Connie, one can – only hope –

Hope, said Eden, is one of the incurable diseases of this day and age.

Elyot went on drinking his soup. Cynicism in other people, especially cynicism in Eden, shocked him. It had a hard, meretricious glint that was altogether absent from cynicism in yourself. It is after all a little difficult to catch the reflexion in your own armour. Adopted as a defence, this becomes a habit. Like the intellectual puzzle as a substitute for living, which you chose deliberately, in the small hours of the morning, in a Cambridge college, drunk on bad Chablis and talk of Beethoven and the universe. Contact with the living moment, that you watched in your shirt-sleeves from an upper window, the vague, formless moments in the street, made you recoil inside your shirt, too conscious of your own confused flesh. At dinner, he remembered, it was the gilded pineapple, it was that evening, there was the scene with Eden. Out of his own diffidence and doubt, very smug inside his own bright cynical armour, he had remarked that sex, like illness, was purely a state of mind. He had heard this, somewhere, a midnight *tour d'esprit* in a Cambridge college. Unprepared for Eden's attack, for a show of passion, for the slammed door, he had sat there smugly rewarded for what, in his own estimation, was an increase in wit.

Now swallowing soup, Elyot Standish shuddered for his adolescence. At least one was ten years younger, he consoled himself.

Connie Tiarks was dabbing her eyes over the political state of Spain.

Why is it possible, asked Mrs Standish, to be completely unconscious of political states? Because, Connie, you make me ashamed. This morning I went for a walk in Kensington Gardens. I have never seen so many boats. I must say I was delighted. If only I could paint a landscape, I said. Beçause I've never had so much pleasure, just from a pondful of boats. Then you talk of political states. Perhaps I'm superficial, she said.

Half waiting for someone to contradict her; nobody did. Mrs Standish lapsed into an inner contemplation of her own pleasure, of many states of pleasure, though at the same time a little perturbed, she was ignored, she felt that time had won.

I'm very silly, said Connie, blowing her nose.

She listened to the clink of Eden's spoon. It made no comment. Or Eden raised her head, to look, not at Connie, but beyond windows, into some distant country where there were answers.

Julia came to take away the soup. The tureen gone, the conscience remained.

Elyot retreated from the eyes of Connie Tiarks. He concentrated on bread. In a minute, he feared, she would ask him about his work, the trustful, over-interested voice of Connie, that upset him in the way her letter had. In the way you can be upset for the ingenuousness of the persistently ingenuous. You are suddenly appalled by the perpetual danger into which they run, you hold yourself helplessly responsible for this danger, both future and past. So Elyot Standish contemplated bread.

He impressed Connie, he knew with some embarrassment. To reach that stage at which you did not quail before the people you impressed was to achieve a state of felicity. To have the confidence in yourself, to be the person that impressed. It was like living, he imagined, in a world of bright illusion, of discarded honesty, in which you became a synthetic entity from the minds of reviewers for the Sunday papers. Because this, *au fond*, was what you were for Connie and the people you impressed. You ceased to be the dumb self sitting on the edge of other people's conversations, stammering on the telephone, avoiding familiar faces in the street. To be the creature of your work, which anyway was a highly detached, synthetic product, to which you were related as an instrument. But for Connie this would be contentment. For Connie it was not a question of personal integrity. She only wanted to accept what she wanted to accept.

Tell me, Elyot, she said, are you working now?

He warded it off.

One doesn't work, Connie. It happens or it doesn't.

Feeling gauche, she blushed. He made her feel obtuse.

She made him feel a prig. It was the inevitable action of Connie Tiarks. And perhaps he was a prig. Recognizing this, there was still no remedy. Telling yourself you have a harelip still does not make it whole. But Connie Tiarks did attempt persistently to wrap him in the vestments of Art. She lowered her voice at lunch and talked about his work.

His work had evolved out of his innate diffidence, the withdrawing from a window at dusk, saying: I must do something, but what? Out of his bewilderment he had taken refuge behind what people told him was a scholarly mind. He hung on gratefully, after a month or two of uncertainty, to remarks made by tutors at Cambridge and the more wishful and hence more helpful remarks of his mother. So that he became before long, forgetting the process, a raker of dust, a rattler of bones.

There was the book on Büchner, which appeared very soon after Cambridge, out of the requisite notes. There were also Gérard de Nerval, Mörike, Mme du Deffand, and Kleist. Critics remarked on his taste, on his catholicity, on his clarity of style. So that except for those bleaker moments of personal inventory, Elyot Standish could experience satisfaction, review with pleasure the tasteful and intellectual milestones dividing the last ten years of his life. But now beneath the sympathetic eyes of Connie Tiarks, his hands made little piles of salt. This is one of the contradictions. The sympathy, the approval of Connie Tiarks made him more self-critical than any disparagement in the press. Irritated by his own hands, he watched them continue to play with salt. The little mounds that rose, only so far, that fell, dry, pure, and limited.

Connie sighed.

Mrs Standish looked at her, as if about to say something that she did not say. Once Mrs Standish had remarked, though not in the presence of Connie herself: Poor Connie, *elle est tellement vièrge* – her voice paused half-way between criticism and approval. There was always something of this in her attitude to Connie Tiarks, whose nose reacted shinily to the plight of Loyalist Spain.

Connie Tiarks lived in Kensington. She lived with an old lady, a Mrs Lassiter, who kept a canary in her ground floor window, front. She sat with Mrs Lassiter in a conservatory at the back, in a gloom of begonias and geraniums. Connie Tiarks was a companion. Sent out by her mother from the boarding-house in Cheltenham, she had been the companion of three such old ladies, continuing in the tradition of gas fires, crumpets, and maidenhair, that she had accepted in her youth in Cheltenham. She was passably content. She sat holding wool for Mrs Lassiter, letting her mind wander. It took quite strange shapes and turns in the green gloom of the begonias. Sometimes it made her blush. But she blushed most on having to commit herself, or to say openly, well, I'm a companion. She would never forget the day she had announced this to Eden.

But what was one to do? She lay awake at night, thinking of this, and her feet grew cold. She lay there on Mrs Lassiter's bed, on one side of which there were lumps, and regretted her lack of enterprise. But she was grateful, she was grateful even for the lumps in Mrs Lassiter's bed, she could always feel almost content when she pulled the blanket up to her nose.

Connie came sometimes to Ebury Street on Sunday, perhaps every third Sunday.

This is Connie's Sunday, said Mrs Standish.

But this only labelled the institution, was no pointer to behaviour, you embarked on what you had intended, this was always understood, even by Connie it was understood. Connie sat and talked of Kensington and Cheltenham. Or she looked at books. She was always a book-worm, Mrs Tiarks said. In fact, Connie had ruined her eyes by an excess of literary enthusiasm, by reading even in the bus, by reading the biographies she got from a library in Kensington High. Now she looked out, rounder-eyed than she should have been, through the thick-lensed, thick-rimmed spectacles which time had made a part of her face.

Even if it were only every third Sunday that Connie appeared in Ebury Street, Elyot connected Sunday with her, it spoke with her accent through the drawing-room door, flat and hopeful and uninterrupted, it wore the expression of her face, her slightly lumpy, shapeless face. It settled on him, whether Connie or Sunday, and he knew that all was up. Her gratitude, her anticipation of pleasure merely in his presence, went to meet him, you might say attacked him, just on his going into the room.

There was the Sunday, defeated by this, overcome by the incubus of Connie Tiarks, he had proposed a visit to the National Gallery. As if you could exorcize your own emotions by carrying them into public places, and of all public places the National Gallery, where the incubus of Sunday sits, breathing the breath of central heat, wearing the face of the English upper class, the expression of just sentient vacuity, of those who suffer acutely from Civil Service. He regretted this enormously. But he regretted also the reflexion of his own face, in Uccello, in Piero di Cosimo, in the Crucifixion of Raphael.

Connie began to gasp in front of Raphael. She made the little, round, gasping, female noses of a woman trying to identify herself with Art.

It's so, it's so *complete*, Connie said helplessly, her eyes already humid under thick glass.

He hoped she would leave it at that. The fervid desire of a certain type of feminine mind to identify itself with objects, with nature, with art, drained the dignity from these. They existed in a detachment of their own. He avoided the emotional commentary, especially when made by his own reflected face, the part of him that ventured through the glass into the Italian field, out of his own body, away from the environment it had taken, the habits it had formed. This was dangerous because it verged on the irrational. Twentieth-century London was eminently rational. He was glad of it. He frowned at his reflexion in the glass, at any recollection of the beech forests of Germany.

They were looking at pictures, he and Connie Tiarks, and Connie persisted in telling him how she felt, in front of Delacroix, Constable, and Turner. She clutched his arm. Her face glowed with a most unaesthetic emotion. There was a smell of damp macintosh. Because outside it was raining. They would return into the rain, were in fact already returning, the lions of Trafalgar Square were sleek from rain.

Well, said Connie, waiting for the bus. Thank you, Elyot, for the afternoon.

You would have said, afraid. You would have said it was her first and last.

We must do it again, he said.

However often you were touched by compassion for Connie Tiarks, you were appalled, on afterthought, by the sterility of the mood. Compassion for Connie that was also repulsion.

To be kind to Connie. Even if you wrote it up on the wall, it reminded only of the literal gesture.

Yes, we must do it, he said, in a scurry of wind, a flurry of bus, the touch of wet macintosh. If not next Sunday, very soon. Good-bye, Connie, he said. It's been nice.

Then it was gone, her gratitude against a bus window, that left him with the skin stretched tightly on his face.

This before they sat at the dining-room table, before Mrs Standish said:

Elyot, pass Connie the cream.

Connie said, oh no, she didn't, she really oughtn't, that last time she stood on the scales, but all the same, she thanked Elyot, she would.

He looked at Eden, or, not looked, felt his way mentally in her direction. Eden was as remote as Connie present, offering herself, her pleasures and preoccupations on a plate. Not that Eden could not move into the foreground, at times too forcibly. You might say that Eden flickered up, lapsed again into a state of burnt, spent passion.

Even then, if you weren't careful, as Adelaide Blenkinsop said, more by chance than insight – if you touched Eden you might get burnt.

Adelaide Blenkinsop was a friend of years. She was acquired the time that Eden had the breakdown and spent three weeks in the Engadine at the expense of Aubrey Silk. If it weren't for Aubrey, said Mrs Standish, not without complacency, almost expecting it as her due. It was also just at the time that Eden had begun behaving oddly, shutting herself in her room, going off to stay with the girl Valerie Stevenson, whom Mrs Standish instinctively disliked. Then the breakdown. For Mrs Standish, an alarming but interesting state of affairs. She talked about neuroses. She read several textbooks on psychology.

But for Eden it was three detached weeks with which she did not connect herself, she had ceased to exist as Eden Standish, either sitting at mahogany in the house of Aubrey Silk, or lying in a bed in an Ealing villa watching through pain a pale blind. In Switzerland she was now this sombre figure, to whom they brought tea beneath a palm, and the rich Swiss cakes, to which she helped herself with a little pair of plated tongs, in themselves a symbol of remoteness, those stupid little tongs, humorous, touching, part of the kindness of Aubrey Silk, but as a luxury, not indispensable. At the end of three weeks she would dispense with tongs, resuming her personal dimensions. At the time, though, she was dimensionless. She was leading the kind of life she would not ordinarily lead. She lay in bed till lunchtime and listened to the radiators of an expensive Swiss hotel. Beyond the window, the landscape, analogous to the hotel itself, the sumptuous, snowy mountains, the evergreens decorously laden with snow. None of this landscape ever quite escaped from the influence of the radiators. It suffocated, gently, slowly, luxuriously. You found yourself enjoying it, in spite of better judgement. This was momentarily shelved.

Eden Standish was resting. The manager of the hotel bent above her chair, his bald, alpine head, frosted at the ears, and asked her if she was enjoying her *Kur*. So that she acquired an aura of distinction, her pale face, her dark eyes, whether she liked or not, they forced it on her, they forced her apart from the healthy, mere animal-spirited horde that fell about the snow at winter sports. She did not resist. At the time she could not resist. Even if the corner of her mouth drooped in self-critical irony.

Adelaide Blenkinsop said – it was their first moment of conversation – that Switzerland was the only spot on the globe in which she could make her mind a blank.

Adelaide ignored the extent of her capacity, but at least it was an opening conversational gambit.

A large, white-skinned woman, Adelaide was also reminiscent in her forms of the Swiss landscape, that could alter in the night, that would drift up against the sides of houses, or melt, or melt. She was very white, soft. She had a kind of full and frilled elegance like the snow drooping from the eaves of houses. She settled on you like snow, or on her own chaise-longue, wrapped in shawls against the afternoon air, offering a soft hand.

Indifferent at first to Adelaide, Eden let herself be drawn in. Into the other's lack of prejudice. Because Adelaide was completely without prejudice of any sort, you discovered, eating chocolates with her in her bedroom, or driving with her in her sleigh. She wanted very definitely to impress this, that she was emancipated, open to ideas. She hung rather fearfully on your reply, afraid you might push her back beyond the fringe of her aspiration, where for Adelaide lived despair.

There was the spring I spent in Florence, Adelaide said. With the Berwicks. They're bores, of course, she apologized. But one can't always choose one's company. And I used to slip away. Florence is full of *profitable* people, if one knows.

Adelaide had many *entrées*, for which she perpetually apologized. She took Eden's hand as she spoke. They drove in the sleigh along the identical Swiss roads, in the cool, powdery spray of snow, of Adelaide's directionless conversation, purposeful only in that it begged, beseeched Eden to listen. She did. Even the warmth and cold, Adelaide's hand and the February air, had the temperature of unreality. And the figures that moved in Adelaide's landscape, her husband Gerald, the uncle who had the horses, the Spanish attaché, they walked with their faces averted from Eden Standish, the way the characters do, the characters you'll never meet, in somebody else's narrative.

But Adelaide persisted. You enjoyed her like a warm bath, the complete negation of ideas. You sat with her in the evening on the edge of a hotel orchestra. You became a familiar combination, not without its distinction too, Adelaide increased this, something that strangers and servants passed with deference, the manager hovered more frequently behind your chair.

Then you had found a friend, the manager said, in a tone that suggested he had reserved Adelaide for you alone.

Yes, you said. This Mrs Blenkinsop was very – very –

You searched for a label for Adelaide that was both ordinary and distinguished. You hesitated over interesting and decided on charming.

Lady Adelaide, suggested the manager, cooler, and with emphasis, was a great ornament to the *Haus*.

Eden received her gaffe stiffly. It was not so much the gaffe as the moral consequence of her discovery, the label attached to Adelaide, it was the change in herself, it was the change in Adelaide. It was the moment of consciousness in the sugar world of Switzerland. It would be nice to cherish this, she felt. But out of the distant playing of the orchestra, the sharp, aguish phrases of the saxophone began to prick.

Adelaide had been to fetch chocolates.

I hope you're not bored, she said, with a tremor that demanded contradiction. I should hate to bore you. I thought, I thought we might see something of each other in London. That is, if it doesn't.

Yes, Adelaide. By all means.

But Adelaide was not convinced.

She was afraid. She lived in perpetual fear, not of being bored, but of boredom in her friends. She could not be responsible for this. She rejected it, trembling. As compensation for her own stupidity, she frequently sacrificed her dignity by telephoning celebrities and asking them to lunch.

Of course, you're an intellectual, she said, sensing frigidity in Eden.

But Eden laughed. It made Adelaide tremble again.

If things were only as easy as that. Come and watch the moon with me, Adelaide. Then we'll go to bed.

The prejudice that Adelaide must not sense, standing by moonlight, on the terrace, in a tingling of fresh snow, was still there, you felt. One of the ineradicable absurdities. But you were coming alive. In three days, fully alive, you would pack, you would leave the lethal atmosphere of the Swiss landscape and of Adelaide Blenkinsop's conversation. Not that you hadn't bathed in this willingly enough, but not as yourself. You could feel a disconsolate Adelaide, her arm.

Adelaide had persisted, over many years. It was as much as anything an apology for what she was, Adelaide's policy of persistence.

Because you are so completely incomprehensible, my dear. You frighten me. Yes, out of my wits. You're so – so – yes, destructive. And uncomfortably destructive. Everyone with a *mind*, Adelaide said meaningfully, and in this category she tentatively lumped herself – everyone with a mind has communist tendencies. But one must draw the line. Otherwise think of the discomfort.

Recoiling and hopeful, Adelaide expected to be wounded. Whether she was or not, the anticipation was delicious, and asking Eden to lunch, and taking her to a matinée where, if you were lucky, you might meet some of your own friends. Because Eden had grown more haggard, interesting maybe, but used up, that thin line of a mouth that uttered the alarming things, or, if it didn't, there were still the eyes. Eden's eyes made Adelaide quail. She said so, in fact, to Elyot. I'm terrified of Eden's eyes.

Adelaide rang, said Mrs Standish, released from the ritual of Sunday lunch. She wants you and Elyot for dinner on Tuesday week.

Secretly, Mrs Standish enjoyed the patronage of Adelaide Blenkinsop. She used it as a backhander to the County. Ever since tea with her mother-in-law, she had wanted to aim a shot like this. And now that she was above it, oh yes, definitely above it, what was the peerage in the nineteen-thirties, she still took her pleasure secretly.

The drawing-room was dusted with Sunday light. Mrs Standish arranged herself in the Louis XV *bergère*. She watched Elyot absently picking a tooth, irritated first, then soothed by her recollection, a link with the Blenkinsops.

Yes, she said. On Tuesday. A party, it appears.

It was one of the invitations that Eden did not accept, though she kept this decision until later, out of respect for peace. It was good sometimes to sit, to feel the apathy creep into the soles of your feet, to admit a virtue in Sunday after lunch. Elyot sat looking at the floor. Elyot of course would accept the dinner at Adelaide's. Elyot said the right things, the slightly bookish things that Adelaide expected at her table. Because when she was not being deliciously upset, Adelaide enjoyed a passionless intellectual conversation. This was also approved by Gerald.

Mrs Standish looked at her daughter, decided that her face was haggard, it was working in that awful shop.

She looked, felt washed out. Thank God it was Sunday. To sit with your feet plumped flat on the carpet, the hands only just clasped between the knees. On Friday she had had the letter from Maynard, and the little snapshot of himself at Santa Barbara. Maynard had found fulfilment in California, so he told her, in his own idiom, at considerable length. The face of Mrs Moya Angelotti swam upon the carpet, dissolved in dusty particles. Not for six weeks, she said. This habit of sex that developed with Maynard sprang from a natural desire to please. That was what she liked to tell herself, to explain away, at the age of. Well. And hygiene, the books in Charing Cross Road. But she continued to give herself passionately.

There was a singular, feverish sense of waste running through Eden Standish's life. As if in her fear of an accusation of withholding, she was determined to give too much. It left her haggard, untidy. She was sometimes conscious herself of the untidiness of her life. Those grimly intimate moments walking home alone, by lamplight or in rain, where each dark perspective of a street opened in a queer subjective way into the more guarded places of the mind. Then she could be honest with herself, even derogatory, labelling as sensuality the impulse that prompted her relationships. It was easy at midnight to forget the little flickers of pity that might have exalted a transaction of the body. But by lamplight or in rain, it was difficult to ignore the carnal, not to see things in tones of the butcher's shop.

Mrs Lassiter never drinks coffee, said Connie. She's afraid it's bad for her heart. She's afraid she'll die.

Really, said Mrs Standish. Can't you make her, Connie? There are a great many people ought to die.

Oh, Mrs Standish!

Mrs Standish sipped her coffee, vacantly, beyond this evident vacancy a less evident contemplation of Gerald and Adelaide Blenkinsop. Not that she wanted, by any means, but she did not see why Adelaide could not ask her just once, so that she might refuse.

Julia handed coffee. She rumbled as she bent. Handing coffee, Julia became particularly impersonal. It surprised you when her apron gave a reminder of something you already knew. The life of Julia Fallon rounded out of scraps of accumulated dialogue, let fall in the kitchen or making beds, the life in Clerkenwell with Mrs Barnett and her cousin Joe. There were also the fragments of Julia's life that you had experienced yourself, clear and deliberate these. There are roughly speaking the deliberate lives, like the life of Julia Fallon, and the vague, less intentional lives, like the life of Adelaide Blenkinsop. Vague and digressive, Adelaide's, but Julia's as deliberate as a box. Eden had it, from memory, the sides of Julia's box. She could open it on its particular smell. She could walk into Mrs Barnett's kitchen, from description, to the smell of steaming cloths, into the shop that rang a bell, that fell among fruit-drops and peppermints. At the end of the street, against the Baptist chapel, the carpenter's shop where Joe Barnett worked, the shavings dragged to the edge of the pavement, the scent of pine that rose with a chapel bell. But most indelibly Julia had suggested the shape of Joe Barnett's face.

Mind, you'll spill it, Julia said.

Oh yes, the coffee, the coffee after lunch, that had tasted bad, she had never grown to like it. In the morning it was different, the slow nostalgia of the morning coffee before catching the bus. Drink it up, Mother said, as if you were a child still, as if it were your last cup, as Mother's sleeve trailed across the butter. The buses are stickier that move by early morning. You began to listen for the tone of buses, going to work on top of a bus. Buses moving into Bloomsbury on a sticky swell.

This is Eden Standish, you could hear Adelaide still. She's in that book shop, Adelaide said, the one in Bedford Street. For Adelaide one was always *in* a shop. One did not work in a shop. Only the lower classes did that. But the shop in Bedford Street had a kind of fascination. Left Wing literature, you know, Adelaide continued, for her more emancipated, her intellectual friends. She explained with an air of uneasy exaltation, as if she were about to sacrifice her own throat. Because she liked to take things seriously, even other people's things. Irony pained her, particularly in Eden. When Eden said: Yes, Adelaide, I'm *in* a book shop, so many hours a day I stand prescribing for the moron, for the earnest, but more particularly the moron, Adelaide always replied, surprised: I thought you were a communist.

Mrs Standish was handing a box of small crystallized fruits.

Will you have one, Elyot? asked Connie Tiarks.

Her hand fumbled. She could have cried for her clumsiness, for the uncertainty of everything she did. She could feel the presence of Eden, the oppressive certainty of Eden. If one could act, without hesitation, like Eden Standish.

If one could push out from the grey fog of ideas, felt Eden Standish. Sometimes she felt that she was choking with unassimilated ideas. Then she clung desperately to her passion. She had this, the rightness of direction, in a scattering of cliché and terminology, at the meetings, in the Bedford Street book shop, or upstairs on the evenings when they held discussions. She had a belief in her passion. She looked at her hands and tried to ignore the voice of the Bloomsbury intellectual spilling statistics from Russia, from Spain. Her passion was something apart from economic equations. All her life she had been waiting to give expression to this, it was standing in her, somehow lamplike, waiting for her to lift the grey pall of words, giving it leave to shine. Instead you talked. You talked to the earnest uncommunicative faces. You exchanged the phrases that you used, there was no distinction between mouths. Except the aloof face, he remained a little aloof, unable to interpret, or the hands that did not know how to behave, folding and unfolding the cap. He had not been there before, he said. It was strange. It was a silence between you that you did not know how to break. You waited, hoping for some communicative language. Then you began to know. It was not so much from remarks. But you knew. You knew that this was a familiar presence. You heard the flow of Julia's voice lapping round the known face. And it was not all your discovery. It was also his. There was no need for names, the Joe Barnett and the Eden Standish. It was like pitching straight into what was already a common life. Julia Fallon had made it this. For a long time now, you had been interchangeable in her voice. But outside this discovery, people were still discussing political ideas. People stood in supposedly united groups. There would be a collection, someone said. Then you watched him handle money, the hand searching in the pocket, then the coins offered on the palm, very slowly, surprised, as if dealing in a foreign substance.

Mrs Standish helped herself to a crystallized tangerine. She took a little meditative bite. She held it up to the light, to admire its transparent prettiness.

Lovely, she said, half to herself. Such pretty stuff. Like – like Christmas.

Then she popped it into her mouth. She had eaten much too much. She began to feel melancholy, the melancholy of too many departed Christmases.

Elyot stirred.

It was easy to feel smug after Sunday lunch, at the same time not so easy to avoid a feeling of claustration. He would go, he would slip out, he would lose his conscience and Connie Tiarks, he would walk in the wind along the comforting paths of habit, as far as the pond in Kensington Gardens. Here the kites sailed above the signs of autumn, a clear kite in a cold sky, that appealed to his sense of proportion, his love of reason.

People walked below with their own submerged thoughts. But you avoided the submerged element, either in your own life or in the lives of other people, wherever this was possible.

I think, said Elyot, I shall go out for a little. You'll be here I suppose, Connie, when I get back?

Yes, she said. I suppose. That is, I expect.

Asking for help, she received none. She floundered in her own embarrassment.

I expect I'll be here till – I'm supposed to be back at Mrs Lassiter's at five.

Elyot trod softly. His footsteps on the carpet avoided his own guilt, that the voice of Connie Tiarks implied. Outside the door he breathed.

Mrs Standish stretched. She put up her arms and the sleeves fell back, over her arms that were still white, if now untouched, sometimes she stroked her arms and thought. Because it seemed that time had won. For Mrs Standish, life had become epistolary, sedentary, and dull. Sometimes a panic rushed at her down the windy stretches of the early morning. She waited for the light. In retrospect this was the hour of delightful, intimate conversations on the doorstep, sometimes a protest, sometimes a yielding. And the suppers, the days when she had pulled out all the stops of her personality, ranging from the swashbuckling air of supper at the Savoy, to the intellectual we're-in-the-know of the Café Royal, or her nobody-else-understands performance at Rule's. She was certainly at her best at Rule's. She sank with a sigh on to the plush and gave herself up to the exquisite pleasures of the exchanged confidence. No one could yearn like Mrs Standish over a late dish of bacon and eggs. But all this was long ago, before nature had her tiresome, if inevitable way, leaving her victim with the French belletrists and an overwhelming desire to prove nature wrong.

It was the sense of stagnation that appalled Mrs Standish, when mentally she still swirled, when she would still find in her mouth words from a conversation held only yesterday. She had great faith in herself, but the self that was a kind of

189

composite abstract of Kitty Goose and Catherine Standish, that
was a contradiction of time, and more especially the face that
yawned at her out of a Sunday mirror, with its elaboration of
emphatically copper curls and the tautness of an eyelid. The
hand of Mrs Standish played with a curl, or rather, with a
wisp of hair that had escaped from being curl, that was the
more essential present Mrs Standish, a bit bedraggled and grey-
ing at the roots. Her nails blanched against each other, fastened
against a strand of hair, almost as if she suspected lice. Or
perhaps not. Perhaps more probable that Mrs Standish was
bored, bored, B O R E D, though if she had expressed herself,
she would certainly have said: *J'ai des ennuis, mon cher*.

I expect, Connie, you have the makings of a saint, she said
rather irritably. That old woman! Holding wool for old
women. Though sometimes it's kinder to kill. One might consider it in that light. The saint who killed, as opposed to the
saint who continued to hold wool.

I beg your pardon? asked Connie Tiarks.

Beyond the field, the almost physical green, it was so painful, it was Raphael, his face withdrew on glass from the
remarks she made. If she listened she would hear the door.
Beyond this, the pavement that she would not hear. Except as
part of herself, the intimate misery, he was gone. Connie Tiarks
clenched her hands. She knew now why she lay with her face
in the pillow, her mouth rounded into an O, trying to express
the inexpressible misery. She could not say she loved him,
although it came bellowing back at her out of the room.

It doesn't matter, sighed Mrs Standish. It was something
quite irrelevant.

9

You walked out of the yard and down a couple of steps into
the kitchen. Here the predominating smell was one of damp

tea leaves and drying cloths. Out of these closely associated and first noticeable smells, objects formed gradually, the deal table and chairs, the painted tin canister, the bundle of coupons that stuck out behind the clock. With these Mrs Barnett hoped in time to get herself a fancy tea service, with real hand-painted flowers. At least, on the coupons it said that. Julia and Mrs Barnett sometimes sat and thought about the tea things they would get. They crooked their fingers thoughtfully in the steam of strong Indian tea, that they drank from less elegant cups, bought like the canisters at Woolworth's. The tea service even became a topic of conversation. One of the absorbing factual topics in which the Barnetts liked to indulge.

How many cups to go, Ma? asked Joe, washing his hands at the basin when he came in.

Cups, I dunno, but coupons, I do. There's eight, said Mrs Barnett.

She heard him splashing water in the basin, water on tin, and the noise he made dipping his face. He made a noise blowing through his fingers, like a plunger rising to the surface. She heard all this without seeing. Even if she turned, which she didn't, it was only Joe coming in from work, even if she turned she could not have seen, only his behind protruding from where the coats hung, her own with the piece of matted fox, Joe's greatcoat, and Julia's blue, if Julia happened to be there. It was all so much a part of custom, Joe washing his face after work, or on Sundays, only closer to tea, that Mrs Barnett went on talking to the pots that she moved mysteriously about the stove.

Yes, she said. Eighteen pieces. With pretty variegated flowers.

And who's the mug?

She heard him throw the water.

The mug? The mug? said Mrs Barnett. Who said anything about a mug?

Somebody's going to be the mug.

She heard him talking through the towel. It was meant to be

funny, she knew, he knew, and funny it was though you didn't let on. This was part of the Barnett technique. Privately, Mrs Barnett was given to thinking that Joe was a one.

Go on, Joe! said Mrs Barnett. You're always ready to believe the worst.

He came out looking rather solemn, still mottled by the cold water, but pleased with his contributed repartee. Actually Mrs Barnett was wrong. Though this was also part of the technique. For Joe was frequently sold a pup, and once he was sold a literal one, the liver spaniel that became a hound, and went off finally in a fit. Joe Barnett liked to believe. He was born with a faith in faith. He liked to believe in people. He liked to smile at a face in the bus, if he liked the look of that face, but often enough he was deceived, by more than an appearance in a bus. Finding himself deceived, that simplicity didn't pay, he continued all the same to put his faith in simplicity. He moved slowly. He moved in a world of images and facts, propelled by his own conviction that, even if something had gone wrong, man in himself was right enough.

Julia said Joe was a bit too soft. He was full of fancy notions. But secretly she admired him. Not that she would have let on. With Mrs Barnett she was agreed on that.

Hello, Auntie, hello, Joe, Julia called when she came in. Sundays found them sitting in the kitchen, or when she came in late of an evening, she called out through the banisters.

Julia Fallon and the Barnetts enjoyed each other's company, best of all on a Sunday, when Julia arrived after lunch, when the steam in Mrs Barnett's kitchen rose to quite its highest pitch, and a bit of music on the wireless was in tune with the comfort of a cup. Julia sat with her legs apart, plump, and deliberate, and questioning. Julia Fallon liked to believe, but she couldn't. She couldn't believe what the wireless, what the paper said. There was no fact in which she could believe that had not touched on her own life. She shook her head, amazingly, over earthquakes in Japan. Did you ever! said Julia Fallon. Even so, with suspicion in her voice.

She was suspicious of people, she was suspicious of things, most emphatically she was suspicious of her own emotions, that none the less tied her mysteriously to Clerkenwell and Ebury Street. Through her mind moved the people there, intermingling and yet distinct, protected by her own peculiar insight into the suspicious motives of the world. Respectful of the people she defended in their absence, she was somewhat contemptuous of them in their presence. As if they were her own making, as if she were responsible. But Julia was mostly very content surveying her own works of art.

You're always making excuses for folks, said Joe.

Folks is folks, Julia said.

When they're not considered as cattle. By the folks as do decide these things.

If you're working up political, Joe Barnett, you'll hear me sick out loud.

Joe said Julia was a capitalist.

Julia said Joe was an awful clown.

It made her breathe rather hard. Because she had no time for this, whether it was Joe Barnett or – Julia's mind slid abruptly over the alternative.

It appears we don't all agree, said Joe.

Yes, said Julia. It appears.

The air was heavy with warnings. Joe had spoilt her afternoon. Change and the unforeseen, the shifted furniture and the cracked cup, were the only things that threatened her composure.

In his more thoughtful and expansive moments, Joe Barnett started out for most extravagant utopias. Not that he was personally discontented. He took a great pleasure in his work. He was a cabinetmaker by trade. He worked in the workshop of Mr Crick at the corner of the street. He got up early in the morning, in winter when he had to blow on his hands and sound was vague and flannelly outside, in summer when his limbs were still slack and his feet trod through the pale pools of early-morning light. He took a pleasure in familiar things, the clean grain of wood planed in the workshop, the steel of a chisel that was very cool as he laid it in calculation against his cheek. Evenings, he read, or stood in a pub in the next street, silent, unless approached, above a pint of mild.

But behind all this, the habit, the substantial detail, there was much that he hadn't accounted for. You still had to reckon with a kind of shapeless force. It made you wonder. It was a force of opposition that showed itself in moments of pain, injustice, and hunger. You resented the dictatorship of something that you didn't understand, even if it hadn't yet touched you personally, even if it only showed itself round the corner in the next street. So that Joe Barnett in his more thoughtful, selfless moments considered a possible existence free from this abstract dictatorship. He could not formulate the details of his desired utopia. But he was conscious, inside him, of a strange, peaceable, physical sensation that persuaded him a state of rightness must exist, that rightness must predominate.

Less satisfactory were the meetings. The toffs speaking in halls. He sat embarrassed and looked at his cap. It became a talking for the sake of talking. He did not know what it was about. Things happening in Russia were remote.

He said that once and Eden agreed with him.

At the first meeting in the hall, she had made him feel all right. He had waited to go to the shop. He had waited so many days, then made up his mind. He had marched in to find her standing in a glare of books, and the people looking at books, talking in quiet voices as if they were afraid. She was surprised. He was a bit surprised himself. But she made him feel all right. She came one afternoon to Crick's workshop. She trod through the shavings and he heard her asking for Joe Barnett to his back. Well, he said, I'll be blowed. Yes, she said. She laughed. But she kept turning round, as if she wished she hadn't come, and it was a mistake after all. But he was glad. They talked a bit. They talked about nothing much. She called him Joe. Her name, she said, looking round, looking at her feet, her name was Eden. It was a name meant to be used.

Eden Standish, he said sometimes. He wondered at the name.

The tales that Julia told were not the same, or the same Eden Standish, that you had heard for a very long time, it just went on in Julia's talk, the things that a name did. It was not the Eden Standish standing in the shavings at Crick's. She's all right, Julia, he said. That got Julia narked. You could see that. It's none of Miss Eden's business, she said, to come nosin' round here. Her face was red. It made you laugh. Because Julia had ideas about the Upper Classes. Julia closed up like a winkle. She was going to speak to Eden, she said. As if she was a kid, you said. Sometimes you wondered, said Julia, indeed you wondered.

Joe Barnett wondered also, about a lot of things, with which Eden Standish became connected, she was always walking in, if not to Crick's, into Joe Barnett's mind. We must meet sometimes, she said. Yes, he said, doubtfully. It was Julia's voice. He was a bit uncertain. He waited for her to take the lead, because, because she was Miss Eden Standish. She was this above the girl he liked, that he liked to talk to. Which was wrong. Eden Standish, the girl he liked, was connected with the right side of things, the moments inside you that made you know rightness must predominate. It was a state where there was no fencing off of things. You didn't listen to Julia's voice. You listened to your own conviction.

Under the low roof at Crick's, in the smell of glue, of shavings, in a spell between working, Joe Barnett felt a decision must be made. It would not be Julia's decision. He knew that. He looked at the little bubble in the spirit-level that he held in his hands. The bubble was very steady. Like the decision in Joe's mind. Because he couldn't leave off thinking of Eden Standish, as more than a name in Julia's talk. He thought about Eden, as she was when sitting near her, when standing by her. She had a thin mouth. She was altogether pretty thin. She had a used-up look. But it got you. He felt the little pulse in his throat, that was less steady than the bubble in his hands.

Wotcha, Joe! said Mo, the young Jewish kid who was a second hand at Crick's. Wot's made the clock stop, Joe? asked Mo.

We're regulatin' a bit, said Joe.

He took the plane. He took great sweeps out of the surface of a plank, till his shoulders ached, but it felt good, the sudden crack in the muscles of his shoulders, that told him he was alive.

Julia came in, evenings, said she felt tired. She would sit in Auntie Hetty's kitchen, lumped in the coat she wore in the street, sitting up against the raked fire.

What's up, Julia? asked Auntie Hetty. You look that glum.

Nothing, said Julia. I feel tired.

The Barnetts were not communicative people, emotionally that is, except Mrs Barnett perhaps, and even then it was not Mrs Barnett's own emotions. What Mrs Barnett expressed emotionally was part of a mass emotional effort, like at the meetings in the chocolate-coloured Baptist chapel at the end of the street, or an expression of national disaster with the other women in the neighbourhood. Mrs Barnett was a public wailer. A pale, dank woman, she had a belief in disaster and death. She liked to talk to the undertaker, Mr Coghill, who lived two doors up. It was beautiful, the plaster flowers, the paper lace, the varnished coffins that Mr Coghill made. Nothing she liked better than to close the door of her little sweet shop, and slip up to Mr Coghill's, to stand in the odour of sanctity and death. Then Mrs Barnett would frequently brim with tears of pleasure. But that was one thing. She did not obtrude on Julia's preoccupation, even though she sensed something of this. She kept it behind her spectacles.

They says a slop basin, murmured Mrs Barnett, reverting to the concrete topic of the tea service painted with variegated flowers. I suppose, decided Mrs Barnett, you can always use a slop basin when the sugar's gone an' broke.

Very often in Ebury Street, Julia stood by a window looking out. She was in a muddle, she told herself, which meant that her values had been confused, and by someone else; never would Julia Fallon have allowed such confusion to settle on herself. To say to Someone. There she stopped. She listened to her angry duster, flicking where there was no longer any dust. To Julia Fallon there had been a contradiction of nature. It was as if oil and water had mixed.

Julia's a thoughtless girl, said Mrs Standish on one occasion. I've a good mind to tell her she can leave.

She had contemplated this at least twice a week ever since Julia came to her.

Julia! Julia! called Mrs Standish, pulling fretfully at drawers, that broke her nails, that stuck, or else came galloping out to hit her in the stomach.

It happened on Julia's afternoon off. It would. Mrs Standish's headache, one of her regulars, that made her regret her sensibility, clamoured for one of those little French cachets, it was the chemist in the Rue St Honoré, the little French cachets soothed her as no English aspirin ever could. Before Julia hid the cachets out of stupidity or spite.

Elyot! called Mrs Standish from the landing. Are you working, Elyot? she called.

He opened the door on a scent of eau-de-Cologne, a warning gust from the floor below, it transported him to a different climate, in which the nerves already fluttered in a kind of tropical exasperation.

I wonder, Elyot, his mother said, her voice entirely tentative. I wonder if you could go perhaps – the hesitation, the doubt wrung a pathos of words – if you could go to Julia's and ask, not if you're busy of course, but I thought, not so very long on the bus, and ask what she's done with those cachets, you see, my head, they're the little ones from the Rue St Hon –

The voice quivered out of eau-de-Cologne. He could have crushed it, the sprig of white geranium on a staircase window-sill.

Yes, he said.

It went, flatly, ironical. *Yes, Mother*. The bleat of a white word.

Thank you, dear, she said. The blow on the bus will do you good.

He went downstairs. He reached the more temperate region of the hall. There was an impotence in irritation divided from its origin. Sideways he caught his face in the window of what had once been Mme Adorée's, which was now antiques. The bits of bric-à-brac, reminiscent of his mother, reminded him that technically, to the detached observer, he was all filial affection. He kicked his foot against some ironwork and nearly fell.

The journey to Clerkenwell was at least, as Mrs Standish put it, a blow. The wind made his eyes water, and the openings to streets on which he looked, farther on for the first time, all this made him narrow his eyes, made him remember much time spent with books. He remembered also occasions in a country lane walking against the sky. Houses, the façades of shops, and then the little pinched villas with their cataract of dull lace, slid between the lane, the sky, and his own face. There was a mystery of juxtaposition abroad which Elyot Standish had forgotten to suspect. He had begun to arrange his life in numbered pages. He had rejected the irrational aspect of the cramped houses, the possibility of looking inward and finding a dark room. Just as he had forgotten how he lay on the sand at Ard's Bay, feeling a blaze of sun in his dissolving bones.

In the street where Julia lived with Mrs Barnett, he trod suspiciously, excited, through the shreds of newspaper that blew against his feet. The chocolate chapel, a kind of Victorian Italianate, stood remote and closed between two pendent wings of houses. A little twinge of passion started in him, somewhere, remotely, it was part of this mingling of the past with the present, the known with the unknown, Julia holding her face to be kissed before darkness, and the present taken-for-granted Julia, who lived beneath the green sky, against the dead, chocolate-coloured chapel. Later on you forgot how to talk to servants, he felt.

His ringing at the door, at the closed, bleary shop, brought a neighbourly head in curlpapers from an upper window in the next house.

Mrs Barnett and Julia was gone to the pictures, the head said.

When would they be back? he asked.

The head was doubtful.

Was it anything she could do? she said. Or there was Mrs Barnett's boy, Joe, who worked at Crick's along on the corner.

He started again, expectantly, walking down the pavement, through the net of strange sensation that the street spread. The sky grew paler. Voices called across the backyards.

In Crick's workshop it was still light enough to see, you sensed an air of anticipation, the whistling of the boy Mo, the sawdust in his hair, his eye fixed on some future pleasure, the girls who stood in groups outside the fish-shop door. The mouth of the boy Mo frequently got pensive over a bowl of jellied eels, as he stirred the money in his pocket and thought of girls. Now in the half-light they drifted in their giggly groups, their tight buttocks and sleek calves, up against the planks of three-ply and the pieces of unfinished furniture. You could hear old Crick on the telephone. You could see his shadow in the little office, under the electric light, the quiff of hair that was standing out, and the belly of his nose. The boy Mo whistled. It would soon be knocking off.

Is it true what they say about Dixie? sang the boy Mo.

Joe Barnett's hands engaged on the tenon of a dovetail. She would come, she said, to Crick's, at a quarter past six. He heard her voice darkly down the funnel of a telephone. He went over each little detail of phrase, in what had become a mist, his mind was a mist in which things jostled unexpectedly. She had left him with the receiver in his hands. He looked at these. They were blunt, reddish. They returned a receiver carefully, because unaccustomed to the act, the shape. But he could see her thin mouth, working, shaping on words in the funnel of a telephone. Talking in the telephone was like having your mouth up against another person's mouth. It made him gulp down words, like water running down the sink.

Old Crick drowned in the darkness of the office after switching off the light. He went off grumbling to his tea. He walked cautiously, did old Crick, holding his right hand to a rupture inside the trouser pocket.

A quarter of an hour an' who's for the briny? said the boy Mo.

At a quarter past six, she said.

Even the chisel in your hand had a kind of funny look, that was like a chisel for the first time, and your hands. You began to be ashamed of your hands.

I'm goin' to finish this off, said Joe.

It made you sort of guilty at your own words. As if the kid might perhaps get wind.

O.K., said Mo. It's your coffin. It's eels for Mo up at old Ma Seeley's.

He began to brush the sawdust off his ears.

Life's a bugger, but there's always eels, sang Mo.

That was when the toff came in, you could see by his coat, that was not the cloth as Uncle Herbie used, who had a business Hoxton way.

Mr Barnett? said Mo. Why, yes. That is Mr Barnett over there. Mr Barnett, I'll be sayin' so long.

The figure stood in the almost dark of Crick's workshop. There was a great distance in the floor, in the light that separated two figures, held there now without initiative, it was as if this motive force had slipped, leaving them fixed in a permanent still.

Yes? said Joe, finally.

It was a releasing cue.

I'm Elyot Standish, said the strange voice. I've come. But please don't let me interrupt, he said.

Explaining an errand was less important than resuming a lost thread. Elyot sat down quietly on a trestle that happened at his side. The broken thread of Julia's voice mended in the form of

Joe Barnett. It was all so familiar. It was no more than resumption. You were no longer surprised at yourself after the logical entrance through a familiar doorway.

So you're Elyot Standish, said Joe Barnett.

The hands dealing with wood did not hesitate or wait for confirmation. The voice itself was confirmation, telling itself just for its private satisfaction.

Elyot Standish realized that he felt tired. He touched a cold sweat-band inside his hat. He listened to the chisel and the knocking of a mallet. He felt still the irrelevance of his errand beside the pure satisfaction of sitting silent in Crick's workshop.

I've come to ask Julia where she's put some medicine of my mother's. They tell me she's out at the pictures, he said.

Yes, said Joe. She'll be back soon.

Of course. There was no move that was not logical, assured in Joe Barnett's voice. In the dusk he was a steady zone of reassurance.

In the light that he switched on, they leapt up at each other, their faces, smiling at each other to discover perhaps an unexpected feature. Joe Barnett and Elyot Standish faced each other across the shavings. Their glances were approving, if exploratory. It was natural enough, accepting each other for so long.

Well, well, said Joe. It's sort of funny.

It was, Elyot agreed.

It was funny, it was satisfying. Like arriving from abroad after a long time. Everything was all right then, you felt, looking at Joe Barnett, you approved the short, cropped hair and, rising from the shirt, the solid tower of an uncovered neck. There was no hurry. Soon you would begin to say the many things that waited. But you liked to enjoy the waiting, to taste a presence.

I'm a little bit late, Joe, said Eden.

She waited in the doorway, in the first glance that accepted only Joe Barnett. The whole of Eden Standish concentrated in that glance. Beyond the arc of this, Elyot, the objects in the room did not exist, were excluded from the moment that she made for Joe Barnett and herself.

Oh, she said, quickly.

It had broken in on her consciousness. It was like flashing a torch on the face of someone in the dark. Her face was still moving with the emotions she had hoped secret. She could not forgive Elyot, any explanation that he might give, after the confession of her unguarded face. So he made no offer. He accepted the full pressure of her hatred.

10

Adelaide Blenkinsop drifted in her dining-room. On evenings that were less acute, with people one might be expected to know, or even minor royalty, she left it to Varcoe with an easy conscience. But on the evenings when, in Gerald's words, Adelaide cut her throat in an interesting way, she brought her own mind, in a series of uneasy little hints and queries, and offered it up on the Empire table half an hour at least before the actual operation. This, to Adelaide, was the most delightful and excruciating moment. Because, for one thing, her mind was a blur. All the clever remarks she hoped, but knew she wouldn't make in the course of the evening, all the little tags that she had dutifully prepared, were dispersed in this blur that was her mind, or table, the swooning of glass and silver, the reflected, artificial-looking roses, still fresh from an artificial dew. So Adelaide floated in despair. In and out of words she went, they were the words of Varcoe, that ought to and ordinarily did console. The words of butlers, Adelaide often felt, have a firm, if respectful hold on life that nobody else achieves. There is a security in the form of butlers, black and caparisoned. She remembered days driving with her grandmother. She remembered the black, smooth rump of a horse, a suggestion of brass, the ease and security of these, outside and yet part of the security of a brougham.

But on the difficult evenings, the ease and security of retrospect, like the bland advice of butlers, did not help. You were adrift in your own flimsy personality, on a sea that was not yet candlelight. The details of the room stuck out like rocks emphasized by electricity.

Perhaps – I'm sure, said Adelaide, that Mrs Mounsey will expect to eat peculiar things.

That is her peculiarity, not ours, milady, said the reassuring voice.

Adelaide could have put out her hand and patted Varcoe, like the black, sleek coat of her grandmother's horse. Instead she touched the back of a chair. Her hand rested on one of the gilded eagles that always jutted into the kidneys, that made conversation at the Blenkinsops' table a physical experience. But it was solid, the blessed eagle, it had a reassurance, like the life you have already lived, like the portrait of Adelaide's mother by Sargent, for which Adelaide always apologized while secretly admiring.

Somehow or other her mother's portrait reminded her, if only by its incongruity, of Eden Standish, who had refused. Adelaide clouded over. The roses drooped. Because Eden despised her instinctively, she felt. Eden made her quiver for her own ineptitude. From the door she glanced back to lose the thread of her discomfort in the table as a whole.

Yes, Varcoe, she said. The roses are splendid. Quite splendid.

Though why, when roses happened as a matter of course, when roses were safe, she did not know. Going across the hall, the discreet black and white of its marble chessboard, she was struck by the full force of her own banality. In the circumstances, Eden Standish would – Adelaide hurried to regain her confidence on the stairs. She was at her best on stairs, at her full, white, transitory best. Her clothes, her jewels told her this, in motion on her skin. Putting her hand over the topaz necklace, she tasted a sharp little triumph that was connected also with the evening, the clever people she would soon command in theory, the evening also the painter brought to her box, exalted her above Wagner, the Thursday, he said, if the light, it made her admit what she had always suspected, the dreariness of *Tristan*. She had paid. She had paid two hundred guineas. She had caught a cold in a Chelsea draught. But it had remained a kind of topaz triumph, that she resurrected, rather than any occasion of ruby or of diamond, as a concession to interesting people, like Mrs Mounsey, and Muriel Raphael, and Elyot Standish. Touching topaz she was sure of herself. She began to enjoy her own appearance. She was smart, but not too smart, in spite of Molyneux, in white satin. She melted, flowed in white satin, she froze at the shoulders in little sprays of crystalline flowers, she swept across the stair-head in a blaze of somewhat glacial light, contradicted by the hair, the head. Adelaide's head recalled the remark overheard at Aix in the casino: *Cette tête d'Anglaise reconnaît la tendresse que son corps n'a pas connue.*

Gerald, said Adelaide, reaching the dressing-room. Don't forget Muriel Raphael.

Muriel Raphael? Why? What?

Gerald Blenkinsop swallowed his words in the physical discomfort of managing studs.

The Jews, breathed Adelaide.

Any more danger zones?

'I don't know, said Adelaide, I'm not sure, but I *think* Mrs Mounsey *may* be a Catholic.

Add to Mrs Mounsey, Juan and General Franco. Very ticklish, Gerald said.

The roses are splendid, said Adelaide.

She went out of Gerald's room with sherry on her mind. She had made the kind of remark she made to Gerald. Their life together was full of these, the preparatory remarks. Or they called to each other from neighbouring rooms, holding a post-mortem before bed.

If the roses were splendid, and they damn well ought to be,

considering the expense, so was Gerald Blenkinsop, even before the hairbrush, the final stroke of brilliantine. His face, smooth, pale, turned to eye if possible its own profile, had the formalism of a nineteenth-century silhouette. Emphatically nineteenth century, said his friends. Which was as it ought to be. The implication aesthetic of course, unless it was remembered, and most had forgotten, that Gerald's grandfather made bricks. Married to the daughter of a peer, Gerald had liquidated Blenkinsop's Bricks. But the fortune remained, as substantial as red Victorian bricks, as the proud, plump, forgetful neck of Gerald Blenkinsop.

Adelaide liked to think she was democratic. The absurd, shabby people she sometimes patronized. As the daughter of a peer, she could afford to. But when you were trade once removed, then it was a different matter. You sat tight. You thought twice. You lived with your tongue in your cheek. It was more desirable, especially for a Government M.P., to be coldly, amusingly flippant. To avoid seriousness of purpose, just as you destroyed a stepping-stone in brick. Seriousness of purpose, anyway, was in itself of bad taste, besides getting you into holes, making you answerable. Gerald's was a mind of excellent taste. He was proficient in the right names. He read *The Times* with his breakfast, he sprinted with a possible hare by glancing through the *New Statesman* at his club, he knew how much money to put on Somerset Maugham. But above all Gerald was admirable in dealing with his fellowmen. It was not that the wrong people were quite impossible, even they might be dealt with at the right time. Some people said it was hard work being a snob. This was not so to Gerald. But Gerald, of course, had genius. He was a Wellington in the tactics of snobbery.

Weekends at his father-in-law's gave the greatest scope to Gerald's genius. Stroking his hair heavily under an electric bulb, the eyelids heavy too in the face of a reflexion, in the rich, male scent of the brilliantine from Jermyn Street, he returned to the first weekend, the nervousness and satisfaction. Six weeks before his proposal to Adelaide, Gerald knew all the excitement of the nonentity expanding – in the large, full house, in the knowledgeable conversation, leaning against fireplaces, or strolling over lawns. In the house of Adelaide's father, the air was full of statesmanship, the atmosphere ambassadorial. There was a diplomatic dealing in souls between luncheon and dinner. That roused, definitely impressed, inspired a certain emulation. Almost ankle deep in lawn, you heard history being made. You watched the magenta women strolling beneath cedars. You were definitely *inside*, as opposed to *outside*, beyond the iron railings, the iron gates, where the road ran, where sweaty faces peered above bicycles and the people ate their sandwiches. Oh yes, definitely outside.

Gerald Blenkinsop stroked the shoulders of his coat, almost as if he were loving himself. He would go down. He would find Adelaide in the drawing-room, gathering together the first brittle fragments of conversation made by nervous guests.

It was such fun, Desmond Harcourt was saying, as he warmed his hands, a cold but moist ball, at the drawing-room fire.

What was fun? Gerald asked.

Oh, Ge-Gerald, don't make me *jump*! quaked Mr Harcourt. I was telling Adelaide about the pictures at Lizzi Maurer's amusing show.

Adelaide began to laugh, perhaps at something foregone in the interrupted narrative, or perhaps it was part of her showmanship, she was showing Mr Harcourt off.

She had pictures? Gerald said.

Oh yes, pictures too. And then, you'd die, quite ravishing clowns and things. Real clowns. She wanted a seal. A real seal. But I said: No, Lizzi, *dear*, we know you're nuts, *dear*, but not seals, they're *wet*!

Desmond Harcourt giggled.

Ravishing clowns, he murmured.

It came up like a faint asthmatic echo out of the regions of his shirt.

Living for things that matter, he was in fact music critic on one of the advanced weeklies. He could also turn his hand at a pinch to painting or to literature. He could discuss the proletarian novel. But almost the only points at which the proletariat was allowed to leave the abstract for human dimensions, these were at the Marble Arch and Chatham. Desmond occasionally dined at Adelaide's. No, not Tuesday, I'm dining with Adelaide Blenkinsop, he told his friends across the telephone. His life was one long ravishment, his conversation a series of *arpeggios* which, when settled down, became a recitative of reported speech.

Adelaide swam forward. They began to arrive. Adelaide wove backward and forward, the interweaving of the white satin, and the little flat white phrases that she caught and dexterously fastened together, just as they left the mouths of the members of her still unconsolidated party.

Elyot, she said, this is *so* nice.

It was specially for him, she meant it, and her hand.

You know Desmond, she said. Elyot Standish, Mrs Mounsey, Miss Raphael.

Standing on the edge of so many deliberate, hostile smiles, it was difficult to choose one, they swam, the smiles and the voices, the brilliant aquatic form of Adelaide in satin. In the comparatively twilit depths faces announced a wall, the faces of portraits, and the formations of furniture, like baroque grottoes, offering no shelter from the conversation. But it was splendid, this, like the roses, and equally forced, that Adelaide fanned with her hand, with her whole attentive body. It was altogether splendid. He had chosen it. To plunge, head forward, into the aquarium.

Mrs Mounsey screamed with laughter. Somewhere a shivering of glass.

Literature pay! shouted Mrs Mounsey. Literature's a pain. Literature's a disease, a smoker's cough, a husband's curse, the jirniny-piminies. Anything you like. Does literature pay!

Mrs Mounsey went off again, right into one of the colder smiles on Gerald Blenkinsop's face. Flashing, dashing, Irish, Mrs Mounsey took the opportunities given her by birth. Irish, then make use of it, was Mrs Mounsey's attitude. Especially in a house like this. Still, the dinner was free.

The dinner was served. They went down, they tossed back the skein of colour on the stairs, the clown colours that trickled into colder black and white, the shrill to the bass tones. Elyot Standish, in silence, knew that he was being dull, would be the stone round somebody's neck, the Jewess, perhaps, with the mauve eyelids that looked as if a mauve snail had made a desultory pattern there. They were going down, down. A ladder of words. Silent, you missed the rungs, fell. In the hall from which coats and hats had disappeared. The hall was a model of discreet bleakness, of rich nonentity, that was a comment also on the lives of Gerald and Adelaide, the lives they partly lived in their town house. The house was suggestive of long weekends, flowers up from the country, dust sheets after the season. There was condescension, you felt, about the town houses of the rich, they sighed after Cowes, they waited for September.

The dining-room had dwindled to candlelight and reflexions, divided up into the little particles of light, only partly substantial. Except the chairs, the eagles on the backs of the chairs; these dealt you a kidney blow and waited.

She had the most, the most *dove*-coloured face, quavered Desmond Harcourt.

It began to tinkle, glass or silver, or Mrs Mounsey's beads. There began to be food, that arms let down into appropriate places. The mind fished for an opening.

Surely, said Muriel Raphael, I've met your mother?

She touched the soup tentatively with her spoon, as if she had seen soup for the very first time, or as if she meant it not to encroach on her effort to establish Mrs Standish, met in the gallery, was it, or somebody's room, anyway, the burst seams, the reddish hair, was the mother of silence on the left, she wasn't exactly partial to either. The face of Muriel Raphael hung above soup. The orange cheek-bones, touched into a life of their own, had no connexion with the rest of the face.

It must have been the gallery, she said.

The daughter of Raphael, of Raphael and Kiev, she was decorative, she had learnt to choose positions, from standing on a soft carpet by many pictures. She knew what to say about Picasso and Matisse. You got out into the street and found you had been sold a Rouault by Muriel Raphael. Elyot found her repulsive. Her voice cut. She was reduced to voice, and the steely texture of her dress, that moved with her body, metal-plated. He could see the nipples when she turned to him.

Mrs Mounsey had begun to talk, it was her privilege, about herself.

I'm at least honest, Mr Blenkinsop, she said. I'm a sensualist. When I was a child, I liked to take off my shoes and paddle in the mud. I liked the feel of mud. I like to feel it coming through my toes.

Am I to expect metaphors? asked Gerald.

Good God, no! cried Mrs Mounsey. When I say mud, I mean mud.

When she talked, her ear-rings, two pendulous semi-precious stones, swung and hit the sides of her face. You watched them, at least Gerald did, the collision, the rebound off Mrs Mounsey's cheeks. He contemplated not so much her muddy youth, as her inky middle age in Maida Vale. Outside, definitely outside, in spite of the clever, bitter novels that had let him in for an evening of her company. The intelligentsia. Rootling down the mountainside, making perpetually for some sort of fancy revolution. It was satisfying to know that at least they were always the first to go. Mrs Mounsey's head separated from her beads.

Mrs Mounsey's head pursued its *vie de sensualiste*.

And what about bacon fat? asked Gerald.

Whether Gerald's behaviour was rudely polite or politely rude was a question that often puzzled those who knew him well.

Bacon fat gives me very little pleasure, said Mrs Mounsey. I can't stomach the unctuous.

Then she helped herself to sole, her own and half of someone else's. She hoped it *was* Someone Else's. Let her see, let her see, it *was*. Mrs Mounsey returned with relish to the pleasures of conversation.

It began to go, it began to flower, to open out, it blossomed on a mouth, it branched. There was a fine confusion of wine and words. Gradually out of all this, a purpose formed, or just some vague *raison d'être*; you creaked no longer as you turned to make a remark, no longer the remarks of shirts, these softened by the warmth of claret. Even the steeliness, the Muriel Raphael, flowed, the little patches of molten steel or quicksilver in the glass of claret.

There was the church, said Muriel Raphael. The one up in the hills. Goudron, was it? Anyway, it doesn't matter. They had a Velasquez. And a Murillo, one of the melon-faced madonnas.

The voice of Muriel Raphael went directly to the point. She clipped and trimmed her words to the bare skeleton of words, because it was amusing, she had found, she knew the places where to pause, collect her laugh. It was quite as transparent as, well, the volatile mesh of steel that no longer hid, you knew by heart the contour of a molten breast. And you laughed. Because it was expected. Before she allowed herself to go on.

You know, she said. The yellow Spanish melons.

Because she enjoyed, you knew; it was too good to let escape, the Murillo madonna, without further embroidery. Laughing, her mouth opened up. It was wide and thin. It was not, felt Elyot, particularly humorous.

Adelaide would have switched, if she could, by a sign, by some desperately conveyed expression of disapproval, manoeuvred Muriel's voice on to another track. Herself as a child, gloved, in the smell of prayerbooks, and prick of horsehair through a hassock, felt a twinge for Muriel's madonna. Muriel

Murilla, started Adelaide. And a Jewess. And Juan, half in the defence of General Franco, rising to bite at Muriel's Murillo.

Yes, Juan, said Adelaide. One admits, I suppose, the atrocities, but –

Her mind gave out vaguely in the shallows. If she could shift to anything, say, Bach. Spaniards sometimes frightened her, their eyes. Juan or Eden Standish, in opposite camps. Yes, they were frightening, the convictions of other people for the things you did not understand. She preferred Juan as the attaché, was it ten years earlier, those elegant little lunches at the Ritz. Something in vine leaves. It shrivelled up in a voice.

The true Spain, said the voice, the destructive rabble, the red, the red.

Only the touch of glass was cool. Adelaide looked at Elyot Standish. Gerald approved of Elyot. But not the mother, said Gerald, she smells. Oh, Gerald, said Adelaide. He made her feel bohemian.

Elyot and Muriel were silent. He bored her, or not altogether, she was not sure, perhaps she would find out, later, but not now. She was very conscious of her arm, naked, and a pale, faded brown lying on the darker table-top.

Her nakedness, because the steel-plating was no remedy for this, reached him through the envelope of claret. The arm, the brown arm with the darkish hairs, the thin arm of Muriel Raphael. She cast very little shadow. She could stand, you felt, shadowless, under a full light, the burnt, flinty flesh, the orange clay modelled too abruptly, too formally into cheeks. He found himself suppressing the laugh that began to saunter down his nose. If you could fasten your teeth in the naked arm of Muriel Raphael, to shatter the reflexions in the glass and wood, to cut the tangle of remarks that strayed without point or purpose, except when camouflaged with claret, out of the surrounding mouths. Or if there were a point, it lay in a clever arrangement of words and refined sensation, the point of glass and wine and peaches. Not to forget the flickering of candles. These just failed to go out.

The evening followed the worn path of other evenings in Gerald and Adelaide's house.

In the drawing-room was a Poussin that Adelaide had inherited from an uncle, the pediments of stone, the deep Mediterranean sky that no wind moved across. Remote in its solidity, it was remote and present too. It was like the evening you had sat before dusk on a carpenter's trestle in Clerkenwell. This started to form again in the less substantial debris of the conversation. So that Adelaide's head began to dissolve cloudily against the Mediterranean sky, and Gerald, the solid, material slabs of Gerald's life, the hands held talon-wise in the manicurist's bowl, lunches at the House, all less significant than Clerkenwell and Poussin. Adelaide talked about her husband. My husband, Adelaide said, to reassure, to wrap a kind of mystical aura round the fish skin of Gerald Blenkinsop, his official kisses. But did it? So you're Elyot Standish, said the voice of Joe Barnett. It took for granted. The Italianate chapel was a chocolate tower that did not melt. You waited calmly for the bells. Poussin's two old men walking to draw water, moved and did not move, they had time and all time, the certainty of time in which to step from stone into the dark grove of Mediterranean trees. Nearer, and in a different convention, three people stood in the naked light, or the two and Eden's face, it was not more than this, that you dared not think of, that returned, the expression on Eden's face. Certainty exists, taken for granted. There is also evidence in the knowledge of Poussin, but not the personal evidence. Then Eden's face. This was very personal. It remained with him, the unguarded expression, the intensity of an expression divided even from a face.

What is it you find in Poussin? asked Muriel Raphael.

Her presence insinuated itself. Elyot closed the door very quickly on the more private, personal moments. Even then, Muriel's smile. He had to defend himself.

I enjoy his conviction. His detachment. Particularly his detachment.

I'm sorry, she said, her drawn mouth.

She found, she regretted, that he interested her. To reach out and touch something she wasn't sure it was possible to touch.

The air moved with little convolutions of smoke, the spirals, the baroque scrolls, in deference or not to the furniture, there was too much premeditated pattern. There was too much Mrs Mounsey. And in the corner the Wild Boar, Adelaide's guardee cousin who collected pictures, listened to Desmond Harcourt lay the law. You waited for the ultimate gasp of smoke. You waited for Desmond Harcourt to take flight in nothing. But you wooed, in the meantime, you seduced with words, the guardee or the Jewess. This was social intercourse. The rape of the ear.

Mrs Mounsey started to go. A puce retreat to Maida Vale and sensualism.

Yes, it was time, it was time, the voices remembering discretion. There is always a certainty about departures that is quite absent from arrivals. There is not the doubt of destination. It is sleep, or sex, or cold pickings in the larder. You are back on your own track.

Good-bye, Elyot Standish. We also have a Poussin, said Muriel Raphael.

Her smile remained a symbol of emotion, not emotion. You accepted it, the hieroglyph. It was like Adelaide reading off the success of her party, knowing by the right reactions. This consoled Adelaide, just the equation. But Elyot Standish, watching what became back, buttocks, the splintering of steel, regretted the dimensionless. Even the hand of Muriel Raphael and all it offered. The sloping belly, the dress where it shaped the thighs. The whole physical Muriel, which was still the hieroglyph.

Elyot, said Gerald, his voice already light with relief. We must ring each other up. We must dine one night at the House.

The word *dine* in Gerald's voice implied all sorts of confidences. Those dinners with Gerald *tête-à-tête*, the cold narrative of a very private life. Eden had once said apropos of something you forgot, and anyway immaterial: Elyot and Gerald Blenkinsop. Because for Eden, there were the Elyots and the Geralds, the linked, the passionless. His mind settled in a fury on Muriel Raphael, to contradict, but encountered the deliberate equation.

Outside in the street a few dim electric flowers blossomed in a yellow fog. There was also the Spaniard. They walked a little, their unnatural voices, their unnatural warmth against the damp of a pavement the other side of the shoes.

England is very puzzling to me, the Spaniard said. I go into the houses of the rich, the houses of the Blenkinsops, I eat their food, I speak their language. It is like an unpleasant dream. The dream language, hinting at things. Sometimes I think, not hinting. It is an elaborate charade that meant something once, a long time ago. When the figures, the gestures were related to enthusiasms.

Yes, Elyot Standish wanted to say, the Elyot Standish who sat upon the edge watching the charade, would have spoken, without the warning of the shadow that participated. Instead, he switched flippantly.

At least the dinners are sometimes good, he laughed. Even in England.

He hated his own voice in the fog, an echo of Gerald Blenkinsop. They were drifting apart in the fog, saying good-bye, it was doubtful if they would meet again. You were always dismissing people. It was seldom you came any closer. You dug the ferrule of your umbrella in the pavement with a cold metallic hatred, walking homeward, as if you wanted also to deny the cold, answering sensuality of Muriel Raphael. In his fury he wanted to possess something, make it answerable, because it was so far distant from the other, the faces of Eden and Joe Barnett discovering a reality, finding a substance for which the symbols stood.

11

The bus toppled into Bond Street taking Mrs Standish on her errand. Shabby to the inquiring eye, grotesque in her effort to appear interesting, the flaming hair, the crumbling face reinforced by rouge and a muscular determination, she could still stare a stranger into believing on second thought she was impressive. At least she had a figure. She sat sideways in the bus, the sideways seat, her arm resting on the window frame, with the assurance, with the smile of one who has a faith in the body. The hour, it was after lunch, together with the motion of the bus, lulled her into an indulgent frame of mind. She smiled to herself. She was contented. She took in the detail of the figures in the street. It was all fresh, invigorating, she let it play on her mind, sensuously, the accumulation of incident.

Mrs Standish was on her way to look at pictures. It was a duty to look at pictures, just as it was a duty to sit through a new and cacophonous piece of music, while her imagination wandered to the renovation of an old dress, the duty was still fulfilled by her presence in the concert hall. Very seldom her devotion and determination failed her. Only sometimes she was faced with her own spuriousness, but that, after all, was a *chef-d'œuvre*, her one and only, so much more elaborate than a child, so many more years of gestation, endless, endless. So that she was not altogether taken aback. It might certainly have been easier if one had been an out-and-out intellectual. But one hadn't the gift, or was it only the time? Her mind fastened on poor Connie Tiarks, who had ruined her eyes by reading in the bus. Time, time, or a gift, meandered Mrs Standish on her way down Bond Street, a gift from Aspreys in the days when there were gifts, those little superfluous objects in tortoiseshell and brilliants that made one feel so delightfully, safely feminine. But she jolted herself with an effort out of reach of the material. The tortoiseshell at Aspreys was not to be the stuff of regret. She had come on a pilgrimage that was purely spiritual, namely to look at pictures in a Bond Street gallery.

Leaving the bus, which her indulgent frame of mind had made a pleasant and familiar object, and turning into Raphael and Kiev's, Mrs Standish was uplifted by the thought that soon, in that atmosphere of dusty damask and Turkish cigarette smoke, she would once more make the attempt to look at more than pictures, to lose herself, and even if she failed again, she would still know the moral satisfaction of having tried.

In the gallery there were all the usual things, the faces you could not quite connect with places and events, the face of the Jewess talking to a young man who tied himself into knots in the corner. Mrs Standish looked hopefully at canvas, inhaled the smell of pictures, that was also a nostalgia, afternoons in the studio, with tea she made in the brown teapot, and all the canvases that Willy wasted, the lumpy, muddy, nude girls, and arrangements of fruit in the *art nouveau* dish. You began to feel sentimental, a little bit out of it, in a world of Picasso and Contemporary Movements. As a girl Mrs Standish had never realized she was contemporary with her period. She suspected that contemporaneity was an invention of the thirties, a term coined by your children to keep you out. It made her raise her chin sharply at the dissolving guitar on Raphael and Kiev's red damask. And the Movements. By middle age, these had become either incomprehensible or irrelevant – Communism, Surrealism, the Oxford Group – but at the same time still a source of irritation, of knowing you were caught in the backwash, were fixed there irrevocably, that the unattainable was a dissolving guitar.

Why have I come here? said Mrs Standish.

She is quite ridiculous, pretentious, the red-haired mother of Elyot Standish, said Muriel Raphael. And why should she materialize at just this moment, too apposite, a reminder?

Then she added, audibly, to the young man who expected a reply:

We're a gallery, not a forcing house.

She sounded, she was sharp. She resented the liberties people took, the demands made. She recoiled as a matter of course from a face about to ask a question. As if she might lose one little bit of Muriel Raphael. Her admiration for herself made it necessary to remain intact.

Nosing round, she said, narrowing her eyes resentfully at Mrs Standish. Finding out for herself.

Because the admiration of Muriel for Muriel inclined her to jump to a conclusion. She resented also her own preoccupation since, when was it, her hand on the telephone, her almost failure to restrain. In her more controlled moments she smiled to herself and said: This is nothing, a few words exchanged at a dinner party, also perhaps the sexual impulse. Muriel recognized physical necessity. She ran her life along these lines. Any sign of unruliness annoyed her. It pleased her when the disappointed told her she had a masculine mind. All the better to eat you with, was the attitude of Muriel Raphael.

Mrs Standish, also narrowing her eyes, at a face, at the Jewess, passed within reach, but without recognition. Fusing in the abstract compositions on the wall, the Jewess became with the guitar, *Le Journal*, and the segment of a clown, Mrs Standish's regret. Sideways she was conscious of a voice pointing to a firmer body. The contempt of the bodies of assured younger women.

That's final, said Muriel Raphael. It's absurd, she said, discussing with a soon-to-be dismissed young man, who stood holding his awkward elbow, some development that Mrs Standish had failed to tap at its source.

People came and went. Women smelling ot gardenias. Young men in camel-hair coats. People flushed by long lunches.

Mrs Standish had not heard, because she wasn't anxious, she wasn't intent on words. Out of her eyes she criticized the broad shoulders, the narrow hips of the Jewess, with a terrible regret, like a lost traveller in some spiritual Basutoland.

This is all wrong, she felt, remembering the easy, plugging motion of the bus. To concentrate. This was difficult. Her mind had always been something of a double exposure. She rested with relief on the comparative naturalism of Matisse. She invested a grove of trees with a little story, in which she herself when younger, it was unavoidable, moved up a clay-coloured path towards an unspecified but obvious goal.

Muriel Raphael shook her shoulders, as if to rid them of annoyance. She threw back her head and blew out a trumpet of smoke, a figure in an Assyrian frieze, her clothes, her Bond Street *milieu* were of secondary importance. The woman with the red hair, the mother, was there as a warning that you disregarded. Underneath the skin was a suspicion that you were no longer making the plans.

Mrs Standish? said Muriel.

She had moved in the silence of a thick carpet. Her voice was reduced for a stranger to the tones of struck copper. Mrs Standish rose to the encounter. The personal element always put her on top of her form.

The Jewess was talking of a meeting, or it was Elyot, the meeting of Elyot and a Jewess, the daughter of Raphael, Muriel Raphael. Mrs Standish smiled. Because it was the next move. Mrs Standish would have smiled if Muriel Raphael had produced a bucket of water and poured it out on the carpet.

At Adelaide's? she said. Adelaide does *gather* people. Such energy, she said, implying Adelaide's lack of discrimination.

People dribbled in and out, through a scent of gardenias. Somebody coughed in the curdled air, a reminder that a silence, that the eyes flickered to reject.

A pretty Matisse, said Mrs Standish, with much *savoir-faire*. Yes, she said, largely. Quite a pretty bit.

We can show you some others, said Muriel Raphael. If, she added, thoughtfully, if you *like* Derain.

That the breath drew out just a shade too far, then left isolated in the air. Mrs Standish listened to her own shame. She felt a hotness in her veins. Her voice was singing a song that belonged to phonographs before the War. But brazen, it was brazen, there was no way out.

It's a question of *if I have the time*, she said.

She looked at an imaginary clock, she looked at the face of the Jewess, at a sympathetic smile.

If I have the time in this day and age, said Mrs Standish. Because there's so much. But he ought to keep, your Monsieur *Derain*. And if he won't, it's too bad. Look, Miss Raphael, I'd like immensely, and Elyot, I'm always at home on Thursdays at five. I shall tell Elyot. Now remember. I shall be most disappointed if it isn't Thursday next.

To smile it out, to retreat, the smile brazen on the mouth, like the song from a pre-War phonograph, emphatically superannuated. On the stairs Mrs Standish went back lamentably, detail by detail, over the played scene. Now, she said, this is absurd. But it rankled, the teeth of the Jewess biting on an understanding smile, that made you want to receive her on your own ground. On Thursday, said Mrs Standish, with a mingling of hope and horror.

Thursdays in Ebury Street, in spite of Mrs Standish's admiration for the French belletrists, her enthusiasm for the salon, herself a kind of letterless Sévigné, remained an affair of watercress sandwiches and orange pekoe. Sun in her room tarnished the many little objects, the photographs, the books. A place where the stringy background of the carpet had appeared was covered by the little footstool that everyone inevitably kicked. But optimism and perhaps an unconfessed weariness got Mrs Standish past the shortcomings of her room. Then there were the lilies, fresh for Thursdays, there was also Mrs Standish's voice, sailing through, resting on things, persuading herself and sometimes other people that elegance was at a premium.

Miss Raphael is coming, Elyot, said Mrs Standish, her voice taking stock of its own effect.

She looked at him. She had the sudden hopeless sinking that comes from not knowing someone you ought to know well. The voices of Muriel Raphael, of many Muriel Raphaels, of many strangers, united the other side of the wall.

That will be nice for someone, said Elyot.

He swallowed his words. Because it was all too obvious the trend that things were taking, it was like the voice of Muriel Raphael, we also have a Poussin. You took it or left it. There was toast for breakfast.

You might look in and see her, said Mrs Standish.

Revive the physical Muriel, who was all this, as obvious as your hand.

After all, she's your friend, his mother said.

She hoped she didn't sound preoccupied, behind lilies, her voice.

Well, he said, *you* know.

It was a conspiracy he half wanted to take part in, or had already, it was like a fortune-teller in Brompton Road. A dark lady, dear, morals is none of my business, only facts. Only you always resented your own knowledge when it got there ahead of yourself.

Elyot Standish went upstairs to work. Under the skylight there was a hard, clear gloss on the table spread with papers, the operating table on which you dissected other people's minds. To lay bare their faults, the little manias, the unsuspected vices. To behave in the convention of a clever age that encouraged corrosiveness, destruction. This was also necessary, you liked to think, afraid to stand looking at yourself, afraid your own turn had come with the forces of destruction. He sat down. In self-defence he began to arrange the papers. There was the monograph he was doing on Mme de Warens. In the searching light of afternoon it seemed sadly irrelevant, one more word from Elyot Standish, its opposition to the solid fact of Mme de Warens, a case of lives and the shadows of lives. There was a warmth and fullness about the life of a Mme de Warens, that a Standish, even a Rousseau didn't destroy.

There came back vividly, if unattached to any context, the sunlight on bare arms, the frosted road that the feet trod beneath spring trees, somewhere, he felt, the sea. Like recovering the innocent eye to look back through a window in time. He pulled up his socks. He held in one hand the smooth red and mauve pebbles that still smelt of the sea.

Downstairs the door-bell went.

He held in his hand a sheaf of papers, a combination of words. He was the commentator, on more than the life of Mme de Warens. And Muriel Raphael adding her voice to the same cerebral commentary, moving her body in the same gestures, that you deduced, from the behaviour of other people, was the behaviour of certain situations, of living, of loving perhaps. He faced what was more than probability now, a relationship with Muriel Raphael. It appeared logical enough. The conjunction of two consciously sentient bodies in moments of sensuality. There appeared no alternative for the Muriel Raphaels and Elyot Standishes. You had chosen the dictatorship of the mind.

Downstairs Mrs Standish had risen to the occasion of visitors in her drawing-room. A guarded enthusiasm of women's voices. Mrs Standish's own voice rose above the others, flattering them, warming them, flirting them into a belief that suspicions might partly rest. Mrs Standish enjoyed this mental flirtation with her own sex. She enjoyed the strange undercurrent of affinity that drew together in the same women as different as Adelaide, Connie, Muriel, and herself, the something other than tastes and enthusiasms in common that amounted to a kind of physical and mental well-being in unconfessed feminine conspiracy. It even clothed the sharper moments, took away some of their sting, just this sense of freemasonry.

It's so nice for you, Muriel, I shall call you Muriel, it's so nice for you, said Mrs Standish, to be able to wear amusing things.

It was, in fact, an amusing kind of white lacquered boater, that made you feel like a Tissot picture, its intention, it also made you annoyed to hear the effect translated into Mrs Standish's voice. Muriel Raphael sat straight and lacquered, lacquered all over like her hat, altogether brittle. Her face set in a lacquer smile. It was the smile set to receive a telling remark, that you could not deny, like finding a spot on your face. No doubt Mrs Standish would also discover many spots on the faces of her friends. No doubt she would also make it known in the same clear tones of sympathy and surprise. Muriel waited. She could wait a long time. She settled in behind the barricade of platitude, the statements her voice made on the outer edge, fulfilling anything that was expected of her. The door opening, she would stand, or sit, she could not decide, her head inclined against furs, would say. She cleared her throat in anticipation.

Eden scatters herself in little bits. For other people to pick up, said Mrs Standish, hoping she had made a *mot*.

Eden doesn't come near me any more, Adelaide complained.

Nothing can be so galling as the superior economic position. Adelaide constantly felt this. She made excuses for herself, she made concessions to other people, like putting on slightly shabby clothes to come to Ebury Street. She was the interloper, a delicious tingle of discomfort and regret.

When Adelaide said that in a couple of weeks they were going to Cannes, she felt bound to reduce what might be taken for enthusiasm. Of course it was a bore, she said, but Gerald –

Yes, said Mrs Standish, accepting the modification, though impressed. I don't regret my lack of independence one bit. I never learned to *absorb* till I was forced to sit in a room. Connie, tea? I mean, one loses contact, one loses contact *with the substance of things*.

Shaping phrases, pouring tea, it made her want to flourish the pot, it made her look at Adelaide, as much as to say: Adelaide, there, if you don't ask me to your dinners, the loss is yours. Essentially superior, benevolent, even *spirituelle*, Mrs Standish handed tea. Also the watercress sandwiches. She handed them as if she were doing a favour, as if they were a material element of the ritual by which the favoured made communion with her mind.

No, thank you, Mrs Standish, said Connie Tiarks.

It was her throat, refusing food, the pulse that must be visible, at least to the eye of Muriel Raphael. Often when scared or miserable Connie Tiarks was ashamed for the palpitation of her flesh. It was time she threw in a word to Muriel Raphael, the friend of Elyot's, Mrs Standish said. The hands of Elyot's friend had the cool, well-defined look of the hands of women who do expensive things. Bracelets jostled in metallic impact when she moved. Now, said Connie, now, I shall say some, some, what. She sat there feeling herself overflow, her stupidity, dumbness, into the room. Evenings, she hung her stockings to dry in front of the gas fire. It came to her now, always in a full room, a frantic nostalgia for the unalarming acts, the tangible things, the smell of yellow soap as she washed her hands in a scullery, the mud that grated from her shoes on to an iron mat.

Sometimes Connie Tiarks felt she could only talk about the films.

Have you seen –? she began, dreading her own quaver, it was like a party dress, and awkward moments at country dances, you held Garbo between yourself and silence.

What was that?

Elyot's friend jerked, an awareness of bracelets, and was it violets, swept in a wave of terror on to Connie Tiarks.

Elyot will come down soon, said Connie.

It came keeling over with the wave, anything, anything, she was leading her own rescue party.

He works in the afternoon, she said. I always wonder how one does, I mean, not exactly work, I mean, turn it on. Inspiration can't just happen like a tap.

Can't it just! said Muriel Raphael.

She laughed. She opened up, her mouth, the little cavern of her furs from which her neck sprang, and the too concentrated smell of violets. Any suggestion of mirth finished, if it had begun, with the closing of the magenta mouth.

However, Muriel said, by compulsion I'm a Philistine.

You watched the picking of a finger-nail, its passage down a seam, the head bent beneath a lacquer hat. All too clearly. As if Muriel Raphael were isolated in a magnifying bottle, or sitting for inspection under cellophane.

Now I expect I've shocked you, she said.

No, said Connie quickly, too quickly. Elyot said –

You watched a finger marking time.

Yes?

Elyot said you were stimulating, breathed Connie Tiarks.

It hung between them now in a glance.

I know Elyot very slightly, Muriel smiled.

It flashed out quickly to destroy the lumpy, asking face. Muriel Raphael resented the presence of intuition in other people. She also regretted obsessions in herself. So she smiled in defence at Connie Tiarks. Her mouth was thin, and defensive, and bitter.

We were children together, said Connie.

Not consciously exalting herself in relationship to Elyot, but equally defensive, against what she suspected in a glance, only this, she would have said. To Connie Tiarks, the safe, the admissible, was the past. You could not aspire to a future. She clung even to the incident of the mulberry tree, because it was safely accomplished, it was incontestably hers. When she cried into her pillow, it was more for physical comfort than anything else. There was no actual hopelessness attached to anything you could never have achieved.

Dear me, decided Mrs Standish, how stupid of me, Connie is in love with Elyot, well, well, that Colonel Tiarks, the knickerbockers and the roast beef. She raised her eyebrows. There were many little incidents to check. There was also her child, Elyot as a child, very close, physical; she felt him through the thin nightdress against her body. Mrs Standish frowned. And then these two women, the absurdity of women in love, the way they raised superior claims.

Then he came in, as diffidently, as distastefully as Elyot always did.

There you are, Elyot, said Mrs Standish. We've been waiting.

She got up, she had to, it was true, to kiss him in a rush of passion that she feared, knew, would return coldly to her mouth. But to touch him in front of these women, to reject her own spasm of vanity that had made this moment in the drawing-room, Elyot, and Connie, and Muriel Raphael. She was a little frightened of her own doing. She was frightened of afternoons alone and pianos in the street. She was frightened of her own body still desiring to give what nobody would take.

Thought I'd drop in. Just for a minute, he was saying, as if he had to explain, modify, anything so strange in motive as his intrusion into this room.

Connie noticed that he looked pale.

His hand was hot, decided Mrs Standish. She tried not to look, looked towards Muriel Raphael. Now with all your superiority, your knowledge of yourself and other things, you are exposing yourself in front of me like anyone else, was Mrs Standish's attitude. Pleasure made headway against regret. She looked at Muriel, as much as to say: You see. It was some consolation in her helplessness.

Hello, Elyot, said Muriel.

She allowed her words to take the initiative, lead her body into a state of affected indifference as she sat.

We've been discussing the artist's mind, she said. Inspiration *v.* the Tap.

He could see his hands touching sandwiches, taking advantage of tea. Muriel's presence reduced him to a process of behaviour.

And needless to say, you plumped for the Tap?

To be honest, she said, yes.

Looking at the face, the mouth, the small erection of white lacquer, a garlanding of ineffectual net, he experienced an awful sense of complicity. It made him start talking of the things you talked about in drawing-rooms, making a screen of words to offer to other faces.

Connie Tiarks stifled, her face perpetually intercepting glances. Soon I must go, she said. She tried again to make a virtue of familiarity. The face that Elyot did not notice, accepted, furniture or conscience. She hoped. She waited to receive confirmation of this across his shoulder.

A parting of the ways, only just visible in fur, gave up a scent of violets. It was the strange, ridiculous convention, Elyot felt, that your mind and eyes were able to make obvious comment on the physical fact, this was accepted, though under cover of irrelevant words. The breasts of Muriel Raphael were quite irrelevant to words. Her smile, her eyes, under the shadow of lids and the Tissot hat, openly acknowledged this.

Mrs Standish listening to a chime, heard six o'clock, heard Elyot asking Muriel Raphael for dinner, no, for supper, as if one hadn't the key to this code, for supper the following week.

12

Sometimes it seemed to Connie Tiarks her life was spent writing letters. It was a series of letters in which very little was said, the transcription of other people's lives, rain, wind, heat, the set piece on daffodils that appeared the right time of the year. At the back of the house, in the conservatory, an auburn *toupet*, the head of Mrs Lassiter, crested a horsehair wave, that also had a history, that was the chair in which the Bishop of London sat the day he came to tea. At the front of the house, in the dining-room, the little bird chirped and pecked at his seed, in a smell of seed and watered sand. There were also the houses, the damp pale faces of other houses that peered unnaturally through trees, the wall on which someone had written something about the fascists. But the wall had this singularity, looked back to its moment of importance. She found herself growing to hate the wall. She found herself tearing up envelopes half addressed. To Mrs Tiarks, 6 Brunswick Crescent, Chel— And outside, the wall that had its moment of writing, the quick moment of passion in the dark, the droppings of white paint upon the pavement.

She realized, with disapproval, that she had passed from her state of gratitude, that state which is designed expressly for a Connie Tiarks, like a standing cup of Bengers. You were brought up on thankfulness, on the warmth of practised gratitude, it became a comfort greater than religion. Without it, the water grew tepid in the bath, the nose obtrusively catarrhal. And taking stock of herself, Connie Tiarks had to admit that this had happened. She could no longer make the best of the worst. She had to take out on someone her resentment at other people's writing on other walls. Even the brighter mornings were gritty on the face, her stomach a little sick in Kensington High, she counted the days to renewed humiliation in Mrs Standish's drawing-room.

Harry Allgood told her she was moody.

She told Harry not to be tiresome, it was his choice seeing her, anyway, there was no reason to phone. Then she relented. Because she was taking it out on Harry Allgood. Even while taking it out she was sometimes ashamed, she found, gladly, it was a sign that she had not suffered a complete moral, yes, moral collapse. Because Connie took herself seriously. She had to find moral reasons for things.

I'm sorry, Harry, she said, catching sight of his red knuckles, the knuckles always made it worse.

Harry Allgood was a born recipient of other people's spleen. He took it as a matter of course. He waited. He was very good at waiting. He could sit on a chair waiting in a hall, and somehow the clock-beat remained the right side of his skin, he sat there smelling of stale tobacco and tweed. In her remaining grateful moments Connie accepted the smell of Harry Allgood's coat, its nearness, the chance contact with tweed, for this was never deliberate. It was not a deliberate relationship, anyway on Connie's side, forming out of the letters of aunts, the meeting outside Swan and Edgar's, the risotto in a Soho restaurant. Harry Allgood sat looking at his hands, or more intently into her face, that did not return from another situation. He told her about the hospital. The anecdotes of Harry Allgood anaesthetized the mind, its foreground released it on an errand of calculation and retrospect. Then she felt, through Harry's voice, I have never said anything to Elyot, never, never, nothing that matters. Her conversation with Elyot became, in its turn, a cloud of anecdote that anaesthetized, she could see it in Elyot's face. So that when, on successive occasions, Harry suggested a second cup of coffee, she was irritated, she frowned, she said: No, thank you, Harry, coffee always keeps me awake. As if she wanted to fall asleep there and then, over the bread-sticks in a Soho restaurant.

But Harry Allgood continued. He was the voice composing suggestions over telephones. There was the Sunday they went hiking on the Weald, the friends of Harry Allgood, the equally tweedy, more boisterous after beer, till songs came in the train, the German songs in a suburban Sunday twilight, you were touching tweed, and the one in shorts, the one who made the joke about the wagger-pagger, was the one that altogether officially made the jokes. Walking against the wall, they were alone again, she and Harry Allgood, in a flat and breathless Kensington, you could almost touch the yellow light that fell from lamps at the end of the street, in the tactile summer evening. There was the sound of Harry's pipe, the suck suck, that she mostly wanted to stop, or listening, hoped would miss a beat. The ppuh-ppuh, ppuh-ppuh. Waiting, his voice broke out. It was a proposal from Harry Allgood. It was Harry totting up reasons. When he was in a practice, he said. It was now particularly that Connie Tiarks regretted her lost capacity for gratitude. She was shocked by her own irritation, by her wanting to say: But, Harry, this is absurd. And it was, or essential at least to the hurting of Harry Allgood, that had to happen, it had accumulated over too many Sundays in Mrs Standish's drawing-room, it had to fall on Harry Allgood in the side street in Kensington. But Harry continued to sit in halls. She made him wait while she mended a holeless glove. Because sometimes she could not face him, not at once, the stream of hospital anecdotes that took no account of her ingratitude, that passed undiverted across her unreceptive face. Harry Allgood apparently was all bone. Glancing at his knuckles, at his cheeks, she was sure of this.

So Connie continued to write letters. Sometimes she slipped out alone, she went to the cinema. Pictures about cripples, pictures with Irene Dunne, always made her cry. All the things she had never said, swelled and almost formed, became a dark gulp in that too encouraging atmosphere.

She went also, less subterranean, on errands for Mrs Lassiter. There was the afternoon she took the books, the Hugh Walpole and the Warwick Deeping, to Miss Lumley-Johnson in Wellington Square, because, said Mrs Lassiter, I know bronchitis, and these will be something to occupy the mind, or else to dull it, there's nothing like a book for this, poor Ethel is so alive. So you went. You were glad. You were glad of buses. You were glad of silver paper in the King's Road.

In a way it was a special afternoon, without a reason. It was the white sky. Gulls flew over Chelsea Hospital no paler than the sky, the whiteness, as if your blood had drained back, hands no longer belonged. Connie Tiarks experienced a numb pleasure in her own detachment, the remoteness of things, the tinsel shops, was even able to take out a name. Elyot Standish, the shape and taste of this, throbbed in confusion through the cheese and fruit and the bright faces of the fruiterers. Love in the King's Road had a definite shape, unlike the abstract desolation that consumed in cinemas, but an expression, almost a hopefulness. Connie Tiarks made a decision. She wanted to give some something, to express by some proxy for words, that failed her always, became a blush. She wanted to give a shape to, and perhaps exorcize as well, her miserable abstraction. Without the excuse of a birthday or a Christmas, she had to do this for herself, for Elyot Standish.

Miss Chilberry, it was Netta Chilberry on the cards, had the shop that coincided with Connie Tiarks's decision. Miss Chilberry herself, peering through the coloured forest of her Bristol glass, the face sprouting from a vase, was the colour of fallen leaves. Very dry, her breath rattled through the bell of an announcing door. She was going to look, Connie said, she did not know what, but she was going to look. She held her breath for fear of glass, and the humming birds on wires. Miss Chilberry wheezed. She rubbed her rings, the rather dirty garnets that she wore.

Buying a present it did not seem altogether material what. There was purpose enough in the present itself, whether the paper-weight, or the little cloudy box with the faded stars. Because this whatever would say what mattered, sent, no, taken, and put in Elyot's hands. Her own on a Bristol cloud, her voice decided.

I shall take this, said Connie Tiarks. It's a present.

It's a dainty gift, Miss Chilberry emphasized, the words rubbing over garnets, they were encrusted with her voice.

Perhaps you would send it? Connie said.

Because, after all, to put in anyone's hands your own visible shame.

Miss Chilberry's face swung. Her neck was wired. She quivered like her own humming birds.

Ordinarily we don't, she said. Except the lady, the lady that fancied marbles. Then she died.

You listened to the whistling of bone or breath. It was Miss Chilberry picking up her pen.

What is the name, dear? she said. There's a boy we get. It's cold. You don't notice, of course. You're covered. What did you say, dear, the name?

It began on the little parcel, the name, the street, that was more the perspective of a street under Miss Chilberry's pen. Connie felt she was sinking in a lift, or the more essential Connie Tiarks, leaving a visible surplus behind. But definitely the slow, slow sinking of the lift.

There, said Miss Chilberry. A crow flew across my path this morning as I was leaving my house. Yes, she said, it was marbles. Some of them are very pretty, as you see.

Her great, swollen, leaf-coloured nose hung above the tree of humming birds, like a larger and more ominous bird itself. The mouth lolled on its words. The flanges of the nose twitched. In the wire boughs you almost heard the whirring of glass wings.

I think, Connie, I think that I may take the box. On second thought. Thank you, she said. It's very kind, but –

Her eyes wouldn't retreat out of Miss Chilberry's face. But she must take the box, she knew, so much that was chance, or more than chance, hung there in Miss Chilberry's voice.

As you like, the voice said.

It pinged in the last bell. Connie felt for the firmness of the pavement, to become a face in the King's Road, to brush against a reassuring basket, to hit the thick, safe air that flowed out of a sixpenny store. This became her elation. The bus sang. She would take a bus. She would leave the box. Just long enough to say. Or not to say. She would leave.

Connie Tiarks stopped to buy oranges in the King's Road. There was Mrs Lassiter's orange juice, that became the rumble at bezique, dear me, said Mrs Lassiter, excuse Connie the tum-tum, is that a Queen I see. Connie Tiarks excused. She was all excuse. She was all admiration for the gaudy oranges, for the whole face of the King's Road. She felt she had paid cheaply for her moment of elation. Sitting on the bus she found she could think without tremor of a face, as if a face had crystal-lized, and all she had been wanting to say to a face. Her whole life moved forward with the bus, the ease of its pneumatic tyres. Because the box.

Turning into Pimlico Road her mind reached out with a jerk, then more sickly, step by step, to what had been the box. Somewhere in the King's Road, the fruit shop perhaps, Connie Tiarks had left the box. Her whole life ended in the King's Road. It popped with the finality of the gas fire in the top bedroom back at Mrs Lassiter's. The bus was carrying her somewhere, it did not much matter, too firmly, stickily, with the firm pneumatic irony of buses.

Back in the King's Road the stream lapped very quickly over the personal moment of Connie Tiarks. The beige women staring at prospective joints, the hymnal voice beyond the kerb, the corduroy brigade, many moments in themselves, refused to deal in past time. It is always this way with the gaudy streets, Edgware, Whitechapel, Chelsea, these are perpetually present tense. There is no time for nuance. Pig-coloured, pored like oranges, their voice is a barrel organ, their breath the hot gust from the sixpenny store. Pause in the back streets and the tone is reminiscent, the frozen lace, and the static portico, a gentle wash of past time crumbling step and column. But out in full stream, the vulgar, sucking present, there is no hope for a Connie Tiarks, her effort is a small circle on the mobile surface of the King's Road. It takes the un-provoked, the all-of-a-piece, the smooth, the rubbery, the unconditionally resilient, it takes a Wally Collins to make the current of the gaudy streets.

Things could bore the pants off Wally Collins, dames, and rent, and broken contracts, but there remained a sense of well-being in the gaudy streets, a kind of mental oxygen absorbed. Just to walk down a pavement under neon, his hat, the brim curled like a leaf, stuck at the back of his head, the elbows cocked, swaying at the hips. Just to walk down the King's Road on a certain afternoon, away from the unmade bed, the cute, oppressive, all-in-luxury box at Godiva Mansions, this was renewal, just to feel the hustling of the air, it was a kind of blank content.

Wally Collins stopped, sucked his toothpick thoughtfully at oranges, the big, glossy, golden globes that settled easily as an image, he began to fasten his mouth in a pleased smile. It sat there, with the desire to talk. He wanted, he would, to someone. Because he felt good. He would buy, he would buy some oranges.

Half a dozen of the big ones, Steve, said Wally. Gee, they're a temptation to the hand.

Then it began to dawn, the little package that was half hidden, it got his attention, he had to cover with his hand. Not that Wally Collins was dishonest, it was finding something, just that, it didn't happen every day, Wally Collins felt in his hand the firm shape in the little package. So what did he want with oranges, what the hell oranges.

O.K., Steve, Wally said, the shilling tossed carelessly. Take 'em home to the wife. A present from a friend. See? We has our flush moments. Or you can call it nuts.

Strolling down the pavement, anywhere, Wally Collins tried with his hand the shape enclosed in the little package. Achievement started to twist his conscience. He was straight. It was the finding, Wally Collins said. He bit the wooden toothpick through. Rewards in police stations, the faces on placards, got him down. No one could say he wasn't honest, had a placard face. He spat the wooden toothpick out.

Gee, no, he said, drawing the mucus up through his nose.

Reading an address, it lay in his hand, at a street corner, Wally experienced a wave of virtue.

Mr Elyot Standish, he read. *89*. The purple ink. *89 Ebury Street*.

Virtue gave Wally Collins a kick. His code was the code of the grey-haired mother, Deanna Durbin, and the Queen of England. The boys said Wally was O.K. He wasn't mean. He'd stand the drinks, Leicester Square or West 52nd, he'd bring the money right out of his pocket, which was more than could be said of some. So that what with virtue inherent and implied, it began coming over Wally now, and feeling good, and time on his hands, it began to seem as it wasn't so far, just a step in fact, to a hint dropped by purple ink.

Guess I'm the dope, said Wally. But what the hell.

Wally Collins sauntered. He had all time. He began to whistle a number, more than whistle, mentally transcribe into terms of the saxophone. And that got him, that and all, there was nothing like the deep bass notes of the sax, or the higher, climbing, shining ones for burning up the guts. This nightly burning of the guts was the *raison d'être* of Wally Collins, a brief, orgasmic almost death under the glare of chromium, more important this than sex, though appreciated too, the pursuit of skin through lingerie. But nightly the bowels rose in a sad surge of saxophones, the skin eroded by a white light, the mouth grown round and moist on a persistent note. He could feel his whole body shaped by a chord in music. His whole body writhed to burst its casing of black tailor's cloth. It drained the sockets of his eyes. By 2 a.m. these were bone-dry.

Wally Collins was at home in crowds, the slick and gaudy places where you lived high, round about Leicester Square and Piccadilly, the Metropole at Brighton, Broadway and 52nd, or Atlantic City. He got around. Because Wally Collins was a rootless one, an amoeba in the big green pool. His grips were always only half unpacked, the ties hanging out, and a crumpled shirt or two, the photo of a girl emerging from a cloud of tulle. There was no discomfort in any of this. There was no surprise. You got an eyeful of the orchids and mink. You also saw the chairs piled afterwards, sleep sticky in the waiters' eyes, the dirty ball of tablecloth kicked into the shadow of a palm. It was all natural and above-board, like waking with a mouth that felt like sawdust, like taking a swig from the bottle of gin. The racket was O.K. while it lasted, the drink, and the saxophone, and the faces of girls, tongued and moistened by the neon signs.

Wally stuck his hands into his pockets. He nursed the package against his thigh. Sloane Square, that waste of concrete, grey and gritty in the afternoon, invaded his mind's vacancy. The discomfort of a wrong environment, the forms of class fixed in a definite mould, upset his natural indifference. It was too far distant to the big green pool, that home of an instinctive and at least theoretically classless splashing. Sloane Square reminded Wally Collins that perhaps he lived on sufferance.

Some way back in time lay the street in Bethnal Green, the dip in the road between the yellow houses where the big red bus appeared from Holborn, out of the high world of plate glass and leisurely women. You took that for granted, as something the bus suggested. Saturday nights, the barrows flared in Bethnal Green. There were the aniseed balls and the stiff bloaters. Or you pushed your face against the fish-shop window, in a rich haze of anticipation, already feeling the grease on your mouth and the intruding strain of vinegar. All this had its origin and place, Saturday night in Bethnal Green. Rooted in the back streets, you got to envy, then to hate the rootless. A saxophone in a back room made its own emotional comment out of a crackle of cooking fat. Later, the loosening of the roots, the slow tugging of circumstance, the sensation that you were floating yourself, even if in a sixpenny *palais* crammed with sweaty, hopeful tarts cancelled out the bitterness. Wally Collins was seldom bitter. Sometimes over girls, but more often not. There were more dames than could go round.

Rootless by achievement, Wally chose also the different skin. It came to him easily enough, the tight, slick suitings that snoosed along his hips, the hat forgotten on the back of his head. He paused at corners, Shaftesbury Avenue or Times Square, pleased with his own effect in glass. This was as much his own achievement as the idiom he used. He had an ear for the quick phrases, the phrases that showed you got around. His voice had acquired, over its native insolence, the more noticeable Manhattan veneer. That bloody Yank, Collins, they said. It made him grin. Sez you, he smiled. It tickled him to remember the back street in Bethnal Green, it made him stick out his chest like a barrel, over the buttocks the cloth almost bursting as he walked. Because all this, the disguise, whether Yankee ways or the flashy line, was symptomatic of emancipation. Wally had bought this, cheaply in fact, dearly in many private, under-the-skin ways. He had bought it in the clubs, on the sidewalks of Manhattan. Somewhere on Ninth Avenue, in a small five-dollar room, he had peeled off another, a more authentic Collins.

Out of Sloane Square, Wally recovered confidence. It was a matter of association. He could adapt himself in time, even to the set formulas of the rooted rich, a tradition of stone, rather than that of the big green pool. The motion of his body, slipping through the cold air, made him feel he could aspire. Perhaps it was just side. Or a sense of his own virtue, the little package he held against his thigh. Anyway, he didn't give a damn. He even made a private noise into the face of Eaton Square.

Gentleman by the name of Standish, Wally Collins rehearsed, before the bell in Ebury Street.

That bloody Yank, Collins, stuck back the hat farther on his head to emphasize his independence. Bethnal Green, more diffident, wrinkled the forehead, hand-on-chin. Waiting, it was a long time, ringing into silence. A composite Collins insisted, soothing to every element, that a guy was doing a good turn.

Yes? asked the voice, opening the door.

It was a dame, it was some dame sort of dolled up, she smelt good. Once over with the eye, she reassured. There were no corners. She was dolled up, and not so dolled up, she was like a comfortable pair of carpet slippers.

What do you want? Mrs Standish asked.

It was Julia's day off, and standing in the door was cold, the suit too tight, she saw, and the voice, the voice told you what attitude to take, firm but kindly, that put the vulgar at their ease.

Found it in the King's Road, he said. A fruiterer's. Guess it was left. Or lost. Mr Elyot Standish, it says.

Behind her stood the empty house that was less charitable than a voice. An American voice. It was perhaps not so ineradicably vulgar. It was perhaps just an American voice. The nostalgia of the exotic, the unforeseen, crept over Mrs Standish. It was also cold.

Isn't that odd! she said. Elyot Standish, that's my son. But a positive stroke of luck.

She smiled. She enjoyed the sensation. It had been an empty afternoon.

Call it fate, he smiled too. My happening to show along.

He began to feel pleased. The chance encounters of many movies stirred in the hinterland of Wally's mind. And a dame of some class. Back in Bethnal they played hoppy on the pavement, very far back. Now he felt sort of ripe, the sort of ripeness that comes from smoking a cigar on the *Aquitania*, that made you capable of saying a word that pleased to an A1 dame.

You never know, he smiled, what the wind'll bring in.

Exactly, she hesitated.

It was a moment of confusion, of indecision, but oh well, concluded Mrs Standish.

Perhaps you'd let the wind bring you in to drink a glass of sherry? she said. This doesn't happen every day. It's most unusual.

Not meaning to imply, she hoped he wouldn't take it, not that she meant he was strange, even if that suit.

I mean, your finding the little parcel, it's just as you say, fate, isn't it? she hurried.

She couldn't hurry enough, in words. But it was there also in her blood, that pumped away most foolishly.

I guess so, he said.

Of course. And you will?

That'd be fine.

Mrs Standish on her stairs persuaded herself she was being democratic. Eden should approve of this. If it touched one's children at all, one's own behaviour. She concentrated on sherry and the room, for which already she faltered, showing him into her drawing-room. Because this was something personal. It made her nervous. She was ashamed. Even if the tight suit were unaware of any significance in a room.

Takes your breath, he said. The stairs.

What! she said. At your age!

Mrs Standish could have run up the stairs. Her figure, she liked to tell herself, was the figure of a girl.

I guess I've been around too long, he sighed.

Americans live differently, of course, said Mrs Standish, as a help. Perhaps you're a victim of the Prohibition.

Yes, he said. Perhaps so.

It sat easily, the disguise. The bloody Yank, Collins, could feel himself expand against his belt.

Yes, she was swell. He sat with the little glass in his hand, swallowing the sherry that she brought, the sherry that he didn't much like, it brought the liver out. But he felt good, talking to a dame in a room with books and pictures. He looked around him at the furniture and curtains, it impressed in spite of shabbiness, or more perhaps because of this, it had the advantage of long standing, anyone could have the brand-new. Wally was always impressed by the antique, would lower his voice a tone in a Tudor cinema.

Pretty good set-up you've got, he said, swilling the sherry round in his mouth.

One has one's ups and downs, smiled Mrs Standish, sadly. Here you'll find it's mainly downs, Mr –?

Collins, he said. Wally Collins.

Mr Collins, said Mrs Standish.

The sherry made her sad and warm.

Here's to the ups, said Mr Collins.

Really he was kind. Her eyes marked time on his jaw, on what she liked to think was its firm, clean American look. Mrs Standish tried to look the way she imagined you looked drinking a toast with Wally Collins. She quirked up her mouth a little in a smile. She tossed the sherry quickly down, so quickly that a drop trickled out of her mouth, she dabbed in the corner with a handkerchief.

My son will be pleased, she said, to break a silence.

Or would he, you couldn't tell with Elyot, you had long ago given up trying to read a face. Secretly Mrs Standish cherished a conception of a world of which the main virtue was that she could understand the system by which it worked. Because she was tired, she was tired of groping after other people's motives, she was tired of having to disguise her own. But above all she regretted what had become the pursuit of the dissolving guitar, the abstract world that eluded, that eluded her, which for so many years had distracted her attention from the comfortable, sensual details among which she felt herself at home. Though even these, she admitted, looking at the jaw of Wally Collins, had been removed by the laws of nature to a point that was almost beyond her reach.

Yes, he said, returning to the room, to a vague and perhaps a shade uneasy commentary that did not touch her thought. Comfortable, he said. It's the odds and ends as makes a room. And books. I like a good read of a book. Not that there's time. There's not very often time, what with the rehearsals and things. We run through the new stuff most always of a morning or an afternoon.

Oh, she said quickly, drawing herself forward, so that she was present, so that he wouldn't be deceived by her eyes. Tell me about yourself, do, Mr – Mr Collins. When you say rehearsals now? she asked.

Across the space that lay between their two chairs, the scent of a hair oil had drifted, like in an advertisement, the advertisement in a bus, a young man stroking his hair, that was just too smooth, you could smell the sleekness, you could smell the cheap bottle that stood in the bathroom beside the shaving mirror. Wally Collins was sleek and scented. But she watched him carefully, in his mauve-flecked suit, it was Mrs Standish playing a part that she had played already many times, this unexpected revival that the evening had suddenly given her, the hands sank again into plush, sitting by supper-light, sitting forward to commiserate and understand.

Wally Collins shifted the shape of his throat. As if he were composing something, perhaps a justification of himself.

It's nothing much, Wally said. It's clubs. It's the Café Vendôme right now. You'll find me on the saxophone.

The fantastic nature of the situation, or was it sherry, began to go to Mrs Standish's head.

Now that is most, most entertaining, she said. You must tell me more. A saxophone!

It warmed him to hear, to watch a hand fiddle about with that rose she wore, the big, creamy, blowzy rose that was fixed just underneath the works. He liked to talk about himself. He liked to talk to women, though the sort of dames was mostly not, well, quite like this. She had class. The greeny, creamy rose fitted snugly where the hand pointed. A bit of a back number in the face, the sort that hadn't the courage even on an afternoon alone not to take a spit at the mascara, who put a dab here and there for old time's sake; she still got through nicely on the bust, had a bit of carriage to her name, you remembered you wasn't exactly addressing the wall.

It's mostly been the same, he said, leaning forward to talk at a rose. Yes, Mrs Standish. Clubs, and a touch of vaudeville. Not so hot, the vaudeville. One- and two-night Middle Western stands. But I guess I get a kick out of just being this. Couldn't lay in bed with something doing outside, and lights. I guess it's the lights. Take you out of yourself. And the music. Gee, it's kind of hard, Mrs Standish, to put.

He emphasized the difficulty by putting a hand on the pit of his stomach. She watched the hand, the little black hairs below the cuff. I should be repelled by this, felt Mrs Standish, and the common voice, by the whole crashing discordant note upsetting what one likes to think of as the harmony of a room. But in search, she found no displeasure, only a mild relief, to be able to follow up the cue, the many cues of her own superannuated play.

You mean it expresses something for you, she said. The music.

His face wrinkled above the jaw. She was dealing with a child. It says something for you, she explained gently, something that you have to say.

Yes, he said.

He gulped, as if he had just survived a difficult and dangerous operation. Nursing in his down moments a fear of his original shoddiness, he was suddenly full of gratitude. He wanted to, what she had said, *express*, while still failing, while realizing the difficulty of this, his gratitude. Normally you spent a bit on flowers or scent. It was a sure fire with women. And they liked your hands. They liked to be touched. It was plain sailing if a man could use his hands. But it wasn't like this. He'd been gone on several. But it wasn't any of these. He measured with his eyes the evidence of bust.

You put it the right way, he said rather hoarsely. A guy like me don't have the time for conversation. There's the boys, the orchestra. They're swell. But they don't converse. See? And it's conversation that a man misses. And books. I guess you read a lot of books.

He sat forward earnestly. He felt good. Somehow he felt he was talking like something never before, like something in a book.

Yes, sighed Mrs Standish. That is my chief and most indispensable vice.

She smiled, laughed a little wryly, got up and turned her back, shuffled something from here to there, intent on some of the business of behaving in a room. Or not so intent. Knowing he was behind her, she was pulled back. In ordinary circumstances the want of conversation would have led her to discuss books. But not now. She hated them. Mme de Sévigné, stomach-downward on a table. Across the other side of the room sat, she suspected, her own defeat. Her ear grappled with a not so foreign idiom, a whiff of harsh lavender made an unresisted assault, she wished she could sink down into the easy, satisfying coma of the flesh, for which the Catherine Standish, the Kitty Goose, her whole temporal being craved now, as always.

That's one way to look at it, he said, laughed, eased his collar. What's vice to the goose is good for the gander, eh?

She even accepted the banality of this. But she wished now that he would go.

In my line you get used to letting up in other ways, the voice trailed.

He was struggling out of his depth. There was not the rescue of touch. His breath came thick inside his shirt. Turned to him again, she was different, he saw, the face older, but it still got him sort of mixed up. He could have sat and told, not what he couldn't tell, but still had, if it wasn't for the bloody handicap of tied hands.

Someone came in just about then.

This is Mr Collins, Elyot, she was saying. Found a parcel. The King's Road.

She was explaining in a voice he didn't know, like the voice was dolled up again. He felt the incongruity of his own clothes.

He's from America, Mrs Standish still explained, making the excuse that was expected of her by another face. He plays a saxophone. Isn't that nice? In a band.

Her voice tumbled like a kitten. Some old kitten.

There's some call it an orchestra, said Wally Collins.

He would go from where he was not wanted by an inquiring face, he knew, even while looking at the carpet, could feel the cold, closed face of the rooted upper class. His diffidence returned, with the red bus looming out of Holborn, beyond the squat brown streets of Bethnal Green the world was a destination for buses.

Elyot Standish held in his hand the parcel, the warm, electric sensation of the crumpled paper, as if it had been smoothed by many hands, as if it had received from each of these a measure of its own fever and preoccupations.

Don't go, he said, trying to hide his interest in the parcel.

The man in the mauve suit looked uneasy inside his clothes. He was not taken in by the convention of a voice.

I got to go, Mrs Standish. It's been swell, he said. If ever you come to the Cafe – he pronounced it to rhyme with chafe – if ever you come to the Cafe, you'll find me on the saxophone.

Some last expression of regret, in the eyes, in the relaxed rouge, the way her face settled back again, and she seemed to understand with her face, made him add glancingly:

Ask for Wally Collins.

Elyot Standish, only just hearing his mother on the stairs, was not concerned with any departure, the man who became a banging of the front door. The man was a man who found the parcel. His significance was attached to this. As a man, the What's-his-name, the Collins was too remote to reckon with. But out of a suspicion of its origin, the parcel lay, a warm-cold excitement, in the palm of the hand.

Mrs Standish had returned.

I had to ask him in, she explained. Bringing the parcel, it was only right.

Because she thought she read the criticism in Elyot's face. It rose to reproach, with the resurrected form of Wally Collins, filling the whole room.

Yes, said Elyot vaguely. Yes.

He was unwrapping the parcel.

But he was nice, protested Mrs Standish. A simple creature. And I enjoy, well, getting other people's angles, she said.

Her charity was forced. She despised it. Back turned, she closed her eyes, and Elyot anyway was non-existent, she was making excuses to the air, she was denying herself to the room, in the face of her own contempt. She was denying her own mind, that was still preoccupied, not so much with Wally Collins, the saxophonist in the mauve suit, as with her own intimate desires, for warmth, for the long-drawn note of contentment that her own body could become.

Elyot held in his hand a glass box, only just opaque, its milkiness, with a worn constellation of golden stars.

Beyond his attention, his mother was saying things, the things his mother said. This had no bearing on a box, which connected very quickly with what was in his mind. The box lay in his hand. It had a white, cold, inherent sensuality. So many glances crystallized almost too quickly, and the just opaque remarks that her mouth attached. The head, the object of Muriel Raphael was obvious enough without the intrusion of a box. But Muriel had bought, lost the box, that still returned to be a warning, a pointer on the mantelpiece. He would touch it. He would know in anticipation this relationship with Muriel, self-contained like a glass box, not indispensable, but somehow inevitable. Somehow it was like this, and Elyot Standish, the days spent in his room.

13

Men is all fools, Julia often said, but she continued to lavish a disinterested concern on those she came in contact with. This she did so casually, under her brand of scepticism, that no one ever noticed it. Julia Fallon was taken for granted. But the necessity remained, she had to hold herself responsible for the material welfare of her world. The postman's cough haunted her, the woollen scarf he didn't wear. The postman's cough became her own. Julia was inclined, in a crisis, to hover with cups of tea. Because these were within her reach. You heard her breathing outside the door, you heard the rattle of a cup. Tea made you sweat, and that was a comfort, Julia said. She stood and watched you drink the tea, as if hoping for a visible sweat, you could see the conflict of hope and doubt played in the theatre of her face. For Julia still had doubts. She picked up the coal that the fire spat out, she picked it up when cool enough, because coal that rattled when shaken meant a coffin, Julia said. She wanted badly to believe, even the prophecies of coal. Her scepticism was a millstone that she much regretted having to wear.

Born this way, she accepted it. And the physical Julia was no contradiction, was the image of her own life. Whether as the young girl, the Flemish primitive that held the baby in her lap, or as the older woman, a comfortable Vermeer. The woman with the red arms that shone like onion skins, that light splashed, and cold mottled, and heat warmed to a bursting red. Julia belonged in an interior. Objects that she used absorbed her. These were the instruments of that material well-being. No different plane was to be desired. Things that she could not understand disturbed her.

It was this that puzzled her now, the behaviour of other people, that made her lie awake at night, an angry turning in a hot bed. She could not breathe for darkness and the pressure of her own problem. Sometimes she got up and opened the window. She stood on the lino, on her flat feet, and felt the cold swill against her legs. She was both hot and cold, angry and desolate at once. I dunno, Julia said. She didn't. If she could speak her mind. She moved about the dark room, brushed against the handles on the chest of drawers, heard the board creak beneath her feet. She would say, Joe, she would say, now, Joe, I mean to talk straight. She would unravel it beautifully, like a bunch of knots from a piece of string that she afterwards put away in a drawer. If she could speak her mind. But something had occurred that was beyond the things she knew. She drifted helplessly. Her mind was a flickering of pictures, most real and objective, which in fact was the cause of her despair. She could not reduce the pictures according to her own satisfaction. They remained detached and provocative. Eden in her pram by water, Joe brushing his best suit with a would-be careless hand. It was like this. It was like the past and present, and a coming together of past and present, that Julia Fallon couldn't accept. Apart from the distance between Ebury Street and Clerkenwell, she could not forget Eden in her pram, connect her figure with the brushed coat.

I dunno, Julia sighed.

She was tormented by the night. The bed groaned. She pushed back her heavy hair.

But mornings also were without their clarity. Only the body touched the familiar outline, only the eye accepted the evidence of clocks. The afternoons were like lying in a sick-bed, the great stretch of time that meals would come to punctuate. Or bells.

Julia's natural curiosity always rose to meet a bell.

Hello, Julia Fallon, he said.

She looked out stupidly, scenting the next phase in her perverse collapse of reason. She looked out sullenly to say:

And what may you be doin' here?

Coming to pay a decent call on a relative who don't appreciate it.

Joe Barnett smiled at Julia, at her disapproval, undisturbed. This was a day, an outing, the days you came up West, in the thump and rumble of Crick's van, to deliver or to fix. The job itself didn't much matter. It was not a job. All of this gave way to the unfamiliar streets, the day no longer round, it lay in broken pieces, you kicked the pieces carelessly, and knocked off in your own time, like any private individual.

Well, said Julia. Seeing as you're here.

Her face opened grudgingly. It was Julia Fallon making the best.

If it's sufferance only, it isn't me.

Don't be a clown, Joe Barnett, she said.

At least there was a cup of tea. To sit with a cup of tea. Tea filled in the silences, softened the reproach. If only you could pour out words with the ease and warmth of cups of tea.

He sat in the kitchen and watched her. He held the cup awkwardly. Though why, he didn't know. He looked round the kitchen to assert himself, and began slowly to expand. He laughed pleasantly in Julia's face, which always made her turn away. It was the way he tossed his head. It was the little apologetic line that came in one corner of the mouth. So Julia turned away. She picked at a head of celery.

It's no use, Julia, he said. I put your back up like.

She traced a grain of celery.

Why, she said, why, Joe, whatever is it makes you think that?

Through the pungent scent of celery, the wounded flesh, the crushed leaves.

Things, he said, comfortably.

She heard him gulping down his tea.

Go on, she said. You know you ought to be ashamed.

Why?

It came very cool, the tea hot, she felt the steam upon her face, she felt the menace of a cool word.

I'm not a fool. No, Joe, you can't fool me. Talking in half-meanings, she said. Making out as. No. Oh, go on, Joe, you do, you make me mad.

She planked it down. It rattled on the sugar bowl.

That's honest at least, Julia.

He sat watching a pool of tea.

There's some as respects honesty, she said.

Yes, he sighed. There's still a little in the world.

Head down, she knew he smiled. She could feel it moving in his words, the mouth shaping in a smile. Then he began to whistle.

All alone, Julia? he asked.

That's no business of yours.

She could not ill-treat enough the handle of a cup.

I was makin' conversation, he said.

We know.

Now, Julia.

On her arm his hand, that she knew too well, it was the hand the time the saw cut, does it hurt, she said, wait a bit and I'll do it up, felt her own teeth bite her lip in an imitation of pain. It returned now with a scar. Almost physical pain.

Oh, lay off, Joe, she said quickly. You know it's no good. What you're up to. It don't lead to nothink at all.

It led, at least, to silence, and on her arm a thoughtful hand.

What? he said slowly. Her?

Yes.

She's all right, he said.

He began to whistle again.

She was all right. He listened for her, wondered, in the empty house. He whistled the clipped, tight tune. For a moment closing his eye on the path across the common, he knew that it was all right, Eden Standish or the world, he was walking, he was born with some purpose, he was on the side of right, there wasn't any longer any doubt. He seemed to listen to his own tune. The face drooped. No longer any doubts, except the understandable ones, the ones that Julia liked to put up, that were real enough and shouldn't be. Walking with Eden across the common, there were still the moments of difference, there would always be the moments of difference, man-made, that you stumbled over.

It's time I went upstairs, said Julia. It's time I took Mr Elyot his tea.

She emphasized the *Mr* Elyot. Joe looked at her slowly. He began to assemble her remark. The evening at Crick's took shape, Elyot Standish sitting on a trestle, the moment also of understanding. Elyot Standish sat upstairs. Julia had begun to take him tea. Elyot Standish was a closed door. The real, the man-made doubts rose in Joe Barnett with the closing of a door.

Upstairs Elyot sat. He was forcing shape into the shapelessness of notes. It was a deliberate process, which the mind at the same time struggled to resist, the crust of old ideas, followed the live sounds, the flowers in the street, voices rising from the house. You held your fists against your ears. But there still remained the problem of the eyes, the fragmentary blur of sky through glass, the milky object on the mantelpiece. Added to the room, the box had immediately belonged, to the room itself, to the details of behaviour in Elyot's room. His fists against his ears, he sat with all the visible aspects of his own existence, quite static, self-contained. Only on a distant shore, on which the hands pressed, the wave of sound swept, the voices that he wanted to trace, to walk out, to follow some thread of sound in the street on which no one could impose a limit.

Julia was bringing tea, he saw, Julia angry in the face.

Visitors? he asked.

Yes, an' no, Julia said.

She could not toss her head enough. Her whole body protested, to the floor, the furniture.

Visitors if you like, she said.

Who?

It was unimportant. It was the kind of remark you made to the people you had known too long, too well.

It's not what you might call a proper visit. It's our Joe, Julia said.

Now she was anxious to go, to protect, as if from some indiscretion. There was always someone for Julia to protect.

It's nothing as concerns you, she said.

And why ever not?

Because, because it's like that.

Ask him to come up, Julia, he said.

He wanted, was afraid to rediscover in this room, if only as a contradiction to the finite statement of Muriel Raphael, the different moment on a distant shore. He remembered the darkness melting a chocolate tower, the evening in Clerkenwell. If possible, he wanted to experience once more the antithesis of Muriel.

Julia slammed the door.

Waiting, the noises in the street were sharp, each thread a nerve that the ear picked out.

Hello, Joe Barnett, he said.

It sounded forced, came out too apropos, like a spring wound up, for the purpose of release at a given sign. This was at the entry of Joe Barnett. The hand that knocked was foreign to the custom of knocking, the feet to carpet. He stood, looking strangely isolated in his working clothes, in the smell of carpenter's glue and sawn wood.

So this is where you live, he said, looking round him doubtfully.

He moved uneasily from foot to foot, the little tentative movements, his whole attitude was one of isolation. The fresh smell of glue reached out. They began to exchange words. There was not very much to say. In the absence of words an uneasiness. It was an occasion of words or embarrassment. There was no alternative. As if there ever was, felt Elyot. Or else there was something in Eden's reach that was beyond his own. There were the two countries, the countries of different moons, the different languages, intuitive and reasoned. He touched the lid of the glass box. It had become a symbol. It was like the words, the symbols you exchanged, Elyot Standish and Muriel Raphael, the symbols of finite knowledge. The moment in Crick's workshop was, after all, no verge of discovery, of passing from one world to the other. Joe Barnett denied this, clumsily, with his closed hands.

Joe Barnett stood by the window.

You're high up here, he said. Funny living at the top of a house.

He watched the distorted bodies in the street, tilted on their various errands.

Well, he said. I'll be leavin' you. You won't be wantin' to be disturbed.

You wanted to say, no, you wanted to say, there is something, Joe Barnett, that it is possible for us to communicate, as two people, standing at this moment on a common pitch, if only this, the universality of two people, surely, Joe Barnett, it is possible to learn.

It'll be late, said Elyot, by the time you get to Clerkenwell.

He heard his voice. This was the way it would close, as always, in a closing of words, of doors. He watched the back of Joe Barnett, anxiously making for the passage.

Julia was wiping her hands in the kitchen. She folded them over each other, over and over again, unnecessarily in the towel.

I hope that did someone some good, she said.

Yes, said Joe. There's nothing wrong in two people passing the time of day. He's all right, he said.

You'll be tellin' me I don't know him next.

She resented that. Because Julia knew Elyot intimately, whatever difficulty others had. She knew how to alter her voice according to the shape of his back. This was her approach. She could sense very keenly through the shape of things.

Feet were on the stairs now.

Yes, Elyot Standish is all right, said Joe.

Only, he said, only a couple of people can be like a couple of fools at times, it was the room perhaps, the strangeness of a room, that became a strangeness in Elyot Standish. You were warm now, as if your circulation had returned. Listening to feet on stairs, it was a kind of physical warmth. It moved upward with the feet. They approached as if they had a single purpose.

Seems to be someone else, he said.

He was satisfied. He might have exhausted himself in walking or eaten a large meal. Julia yanked the towel on its roller. She longed to manoeuvre people, to restore order in the house.

You'll be gettin' off home to your supper. You'll be off in double quick time. If you ask me when, when the stairs is empty, she said.

Obedience was a natural reaction to Julia's voice. It was the natural reaction of Eden Standish, her pause outside the door, her silence on the landing. Even now, there was something oracular for Eden in Julia's voice, in Julia herself, her presence in the kitchen, she was rooted firmly in the past, out of her the past still flowed, through her many branches of activity, she was still a face above the bed at dusk, a hand offering a slice of cake, or a soft scent of baking that soothed the more jagged grievances in a kitchen corner. So that you accepted the warning now.

Eden Standish would go upstairs. She was tired. The evening released her, the full bus, with its smell and crackle of evening papers. Evenings she sat in the bus. She no longer resented her own exhaustion. This, and occasionally the voice of Julia, was a grievance from the past. Joe Barnett is in here, the voice of Julia warned. Joe Barnett, and more than Joe Barnett, the visible Joe Barnett to other people, there were also many other aspects, moments, the private ones, the meetings at corners under lamplight, the hand encountered by chance, the path across the common, cutting the grey face of Saturday afternoon. The extraneous disappeared. Geography was indeterminate, the grey streak of common, with gasworks ballooning out of fog, the two greyhounds in a little wind, a flashing of their pink, stretched thighs as they snapped and whined for imaginary game. The relevant details in an otherwise insignificant landscape were Eden Standish and Joe Barnett. There was no actual point in time. Because Saturday was a release from time, from all the preoccupations of behaviour.

On the Saturday common, Joe was talking politics. She heard his voice under the movement of their feet, as feet slurred through the dead grass. Joe discussing revolution in the winter-coloured landscape. She felt very tranquil inside his words.

I might as well save breath, he said. I'm talkin' to someone that isn't here.

No, she said, smiled, touching her own warmth, a hand.

She took his hand. They walked across the common in their own silence, in more than words.

There's something you'll never understand, Eden. Either you or yours.

What? she asked.

Drastic measures. You wrap your good intentions in blankets. It ain't your fault. You're born to blankets.

And Joe Barnett to revolution!

He was putting her at a distance. It came often enough without deliberate effort, she knew. When she wanted, in her own exaggerated eagerness, to strip away any remnant of superfluous prejudice. But this returned in the warning of his voice. The voice alone turned her in a moment to a snobbish schoolgirl, sitting at the end of a dormitory, discussing the habits of servants. This made her bite her lip. Because there was more than this, there was the mere warmth of being, of being with Joe Barnett, in the shape and texture of a hand. She clung desperately to a hand.

Sometimes, she said, you mean to underline the difference.

The wind was too cold to hot eyes, the horizon a burning sepia.

It's a good job as some of us are realists, Eden Standish. In more than politics.

Politics! she said. I'm sick to death of politics!

Because now that she had let this fall, out of a full conscience, it was true. So much dead grass that the feet slurred through. There was a big drumming and throbbing that became her ears. The two brooding gasometers that her eyes distorted, these were waiting to burst.

I guessed that, he said. I guessed that right from the first moments. Some folks take to crossword puzzles.

The whole horizon tipped up, with its fringe of little jagged houses. It was whirling. It was wheeling. Her stomach clung to the small of her back, for want of intermediary substance. But out of this physical collapse, she had to rescue the truth, which was more than a small personal truth, she had her positive conviction, she had played the game of words, she had sat in many halls on the cold, collapsible chairs to the limits of self-persuasion, but underneath the act remained a certainty.

Yes, she said. Sick. Sick. Of politics. The political lie.

Her voice reeled. She could feel her own cold sweat. She was becoming something of which she was afraid.

I believe, Joe, but not in the parties of politics, the exchange of one party for another, which isn't any exchange at all. Oh, I can believe, as sure as I can breathe, feel, in the necessity for change. But it's a change from wrong to right, which is nothing to do with category. I can believe in right as passionately as I have it in me to live. This is what I have to express, with you, anyone, with everyone who has the same conviction. But passionately, Joe. We were not born to indifference. Indifference denies all the evidence of life. This is what I want to believe. I want to unite those who have the capacity for living, in any circumstance, and make it the one circumstance. I want to oppose them to the destroyers, to the dealers in words, to the diseased, to the most fatally diseased – the indifferent. That can be the only order. Without ideological labels. Labels set a limit at once. And there is no limit to man.

She fell back into the exhaustion that follows extreme effort. They were walking, she knew. Somewhere houses built a skyward pattern. At the foot of the gasometers a lamp, just lit, flashed across a rockery built round the steel roots, the little, spiky, sturdy leaves of ice-plant struggling in a smell of gas. Soon it would be quite dark. The legs ached.

Joe Barnett was silent. He carried her hand, that she let him carry, after the quick spasm of passion that came with her words, it lay dead. But he felt warm touching her hand. There was a rightness in this. There was a little zone of peace and rightness through which they trod in the shadow of the gasworks. It was outside him and part of him, in a way he did not trouble to explain. It sat on the relaxed face. He could feel it in the stomach. It was asking to be acknowledged, shared.

In the shadow of the gasworks, mouth on mouth, a tired but certain shudder ran along the line of wall. Somewhere a cold dog yelping in the silence. Becoming her mouth, he was in possession of the universe. He could not hold her too firmly, her body, confused by more than the sense of touch. They were in agreement. There was an essential unity, in their bodies, in the almost darkened world, over which the shapes of the gasometers brooded still.

Joe Barnett, standing in Julia Fallon's kitchen, felt beyond the door the moment of silence. It was like a continued reassurance.

254

Soon she would go upstairs. Soon he would walk along the street homeward. He looked at Julia. He could have kissed her. There was nothing he could do with his hands to express this great contentment. It was part of him, and all around him, as he listened to the answering silence on the stairs.

14

You went down out of the street through a glass tunnel. Your head, your body, so many identical heads on so many identical bodies blossomed in recurrent bouquets, around, above. The faces wore an expression of surprise, even the habitual faces, there was always this about the glass faces that descended with the tunnel into the Café Vendôme. Rejected by glass, grouped in the little silver foyer with its smaller bar, the faces resented their transitory surprise. After all, it was chic, and the Vendôme, and the emotion of surprise was not chic, it presupposed the unexpected, there was nothing unexpected in the foyer at the Vendôme. The man who gnawed his fingers at the cloaks, smelt the kippers he had eaten at six. It was usual to eat kippers at six. It was usual to glance through the TO LET and PERSONAL columns before taking the bus to the Vendôme. By supper-time, which was the supper-time of clients, outside the peelings of their overcoats, the kippers had lapsed, except the smell, which was also usual, like the faces you bowed in. The man at the cloaks yawned. Ice jostled vaguely on the fringes of his mind. He knew, without turning, enough about the movements of glass, or the tight, crouching behinds that topped a row of stools. People gathered in the foyer with an air of pretending they were not gathering at all. The hand on tie. The cold, composed, women's voices rising from behind the strands of pearls. They knew all the answers, the women's voices. These, like their handbags, could meet any emergency.

Farther in, the balcony contained the light, that was also

music, the light interpreted the music, tuned with a cunning consistence, you looked down from the comparative darkness of the balcony into the saucer of light that contained also the sluggish figures of the dance, arbitrary in detail, but singularly similar in purpose. You pressed your belly, you felt the retaliating pressure of the thighs. Somewhere in the bones the music flowed, turgid, only just liquid, seeped along the slack muscles, flowed in a warm wave over the naked back. Towards midnight the dance at the Vendôme only just repudiated the erotic act, only momentarily, in a forest of almost visible harmonies. Through these the dancers moved. The voice glanced along the cheek. The debutantes surrendered their bodies with a willing shudder into the arms of the Wild Boars, sensed the approach of a moustache. And the music pressed, pressed, the sad and gummy tendrils of the saxophones a rattle of sultry thunder in the drums, great clusters of orchidaceous light stirred in the tonal undergrowth that rustled round the legs, that struck an answering note from sequin or from tulle, or the taut black cloth covering the expectant calves.

This was like living again, felt Mrs Standish.

It's quite like old times, Aubrey, she said aloud.

Quickly she banished her own anachronism in raising her champagne. She wanted to feel that pricking in the nose. The smoke, the smoke from Aubrey's cigar, hung between them, softening a face. She was soft, soft, her body. It was either champagne or retrospect. Even if Aubrey, wry-faced, tried to squeeze a drop of shame out of her hilarity.

Good, Catherine, Aubrey said. Thanks for the discovery.

She had always been enthusiastic. He remembered the little sallies of the hand, of furs, in the intimate smell of hansoms. Now he looked at her indulgently, because indulgence to Aubrey Silk was an easy, almost the only emotion. His feet lay cold inside his pumps. His hands, through habit, knew the texture of the things he had about him. He looked down at his blue veins. Time had mapped his hands with a fatal geographic scheme.

Yes, Aubrey, she said. We're inclined to withdraw. Too soon. I refuse to be forced, by my children, by my friends, against my own conviction. Other people make such plans for one's development. I detest making plans.

Which was true. Except an inspiration on the telephone. Aubrey, you must take me one night, quietly, you must take me to supper at the Vendôme. And this was hardly a plan, a glance forward into a region where possibility crystallized. Because, she said, it will be like old times, Aubrey. Aware of her own shortcomings, she had brought her voice closer on the telephone. She could make it close and warm. Her lovers had resented its timbre, but afterwards. Not the voice on the telephone. She brought this right forward, tried to chafe a second voice to the pitch of her own enthusiasm.

Catherine Standish had charm. It was the way she leant forward. Aubrey Silk could feel it, theoretically, all the little moves too well known, then forgotten. The other side of his dead skin he knew what was going on. As it was, there was very little to say. When you had ceased to participate.

Have some more champagne, Aubrey said.

The small duties still remained.

Aubrey, she said, you're a dear.

She put her hand over the congestion of blue veins. She touched a coldness that frightened, it frightened almost as much as many present emotions in herself that she had tried to hide, just as she covered up the basic skin, making an illusion at her dressing-table which could ease her mind. Then Aubrey's hand. It settled down coldly over the warmth she had induced by drinking so many glasses of champagne.

The music shot out. It made a great funnel of sound. It reproduced the funnel of the saxophone.

Presumably, *hot* music, said a tentative Mrs Standish. It has a quality that excites, but is it something that one understands?

She knew that her voice was stilted, precious, her neck rigid that would turn, turned, she would see if, just a glance, the

257

first since reassuring on arrival, she would pick out a head to which she had given its importance, and her glance resting on a saxophone.

He swayed. He moved from a pivot on his seat. Out of this grew the purpose of his being, the nightly blossoming of Wally Collins. Governed by the leader's hand, this set no definite limit to his own existence, as the music glugged out, he lifted his feet, only just, in a sweet, sticky fluid, the drawn-out, sticky strings of music elongated from his fingers and the stops. He was a little drunk without wine, sexually satisfied without sex, he had that warm throbbing in the belly, in his genitals a kind of numb urgency. This made him sit forward on his chair. His mouth was round, moist. The veins in relief upon his neck, the fixed eyes, could not give too much in concentration to some supreme, orgasmic moment in the music. He floated, like the lavender he used, like the images on movie screens, all these that were the dissolved components of a Wally Collins, and the unmade bed at Godiva Mansions, and evenings in Manhattan taxi-cabs, the hand beneath a skirt.

Mrs Standish tried to focus this head. It blurred. Its distance, its unconsciousness, brought it closer in her own mind to her own uneasiness. Because it would remain distant, with all those dim, unformulated desires, which one never did succeed in focusing. She returned quickly to Aubrey Silk. Awful if Aubrey were to guess.

Disgusting really, she said.

What?

It came with an effort, back to the present, in a puff of smoke.

Why, all this, said Mrs Standish. The caricature of – of *oneself*.

She was safe again behind the language she had learnt to speak on her afternoons.

If one knew, Aubrey said. But I've never made up my mind, Catherine, which of your turns is not a turn.

My dear, don't! You make me feel like a seal.

Beating the little cymbals, she had seen in a circus, or wearing the little bonnet, anything but itself, the essential seal. Still, she was safe, safe, from her own conscience, or from Aubrey Silk, she could look sideways again, it was time, casually enough, to focus a head.

In this operation Mrs Standish encountered Elyot on the distant stairs. She looked at her son with a chilly feeling of annoyance. She shook her bare shoulders, as if someone would try to spoil, the way one's children could spoil, with too direct a remark or glance. She looked at Elyot descending into light, discreetly black, he was made for black, and with him Muriel Raphael.

Muriel has a handsome figure, said Mrs Standish, in a tone of voice that suggested she was just about to take back what she had given. If only, she added, someone would teach her where it begins.

Muriel moved in the oblivion of a woman getting to her table, of the chic woman, in a non-existent situation, in an almost non-existent room. Browner against her dress, she had she knew, that *amusing* cachet, she had paid for it at Schiaparelli's, she was ready for the commentary of eyes. But prepared, she also failed to notice, she might have worn sackcloth, not the scarlet nipple embroidered on her left breast, not the little dagger at her waist made of glass and shells. Shells were also in her hair, almost an encrusted bowler hat. She sat and began to arrange her face, holding a small mirror in which to preen a great macaw, smoothing the mauve lids, grooming the plumage with a scarlet claw. Other people, and her mirror, often disparaged this face, but you wondered sometimes if Muriel chose to give them deliberate cause.

A waiter stood, a slab of shadow, half-way between sound and silence, light and darkness. He was a headache, and possibly fallen arches.

Food, said Elyot.

This at least was a concrete detail. Gave you time to find yourself. The menu in a night club is as reassuring as the wall you touch in a disturbed sleep.

Mm? Muriel said, as she snapped her bag. Something not too – not too – you know.

Her great purpose was enigma, but a shared enigma, her voice slid, bringing you in on it too. She even admitted the waiter if he cared. She looked up and initiated him with a smile.

I want something, she said, something I probably wouldn't think of at any other time.

The unsurprised waiter was suggesting quail. But remote now from food, as if she had never given it a thought, her mouth snapped open in a smile. She was recognizing friends, or the people with forgotten names. For these, the flash and snap of a metallic smile.

Quail, Muriel? Elyot asked.

Oh yes, she said, remotely. Quail.

Elyot remembered that he hadn't thanked, the way the days slipped, for the present of a box, would discuss, but not now, there was a time and place. The proximity of other people had given her the cloudiness of white Bristol. She had left him to his own isolation. This was frequent in public places. In your own time, in your own silence, you could count the stones of the public desert places. Once at a dance, as a boy, standing between palms, he had realized suddenly he would die, which was not the sensation in the Macarthys' attic, the shapeless child-fear, but a calm, indifferent acceptance. Shorn of any of the material ties, he had stood and watched the unconscious faces of those who had not shared his revelation.

You asked me out to supper, she said.

He looked at the orange, the winged cheeks of Muriel Raphael. Certainly. It had been arranged the week before. There was complete understanding. Understanding also of the hand that now connected with the back of his. There was no excitement in the contact of flesh.

Come on, he said. We'll dance.

Not without malice aimed at his own indifference. He had to find somewhere, in motion, in closer collaboration with a body, an answer to the secret that was already no secret. There

260

were no secrets with Muriel. Her body became his under the excuse of the dance. It was just the additional invitation of the music that the mouth had never offered. Noticing his mother, who had not seen him, he half closed his eyes. His mother would make him Muriel's lover for the benefit of Aubrey Silk, his mother would make it official in words. A contract was being made between two sentient bodies.

Elyot is, was, always, oblivious, decided Mrs Standish. Standing on a garden path, among the spikes of dew, his face had closed up sullenly, his legs were reddened by the frost. He chose distance even as a child. He has never wanted to see me, she felt. She began to pity herself, in what almost became a belch. The comebacks, Maudie Westmacott used to say. And now this Muriel Raphael, she would become the lover, the lover of the still sullen child, it was too obvious even to suggest to Aubrey across a crumpled tablecloth.

Aubrey had closed his eyes. A little drawing by Constantin Guys that he had somewhere in an album, the greyish paper, was lost, he had lost his eyes, he was looking for them somewhere, somewhere on the grey belt of sand along the Norman coast. The wind rocked his boater, the salt rattled in his thin moustache, but the wave was distant, or close, or distant, now and then, it was his blood, it was a cold ticking in his veins.

It was a hammer hammer on the glass box the music made, before it shivered into glass, it became the swift rubber strips that struggled with incipient draughts, out of all this the sequin swooned, she said it was worth at least the mink, because she was large-hearted, she was large-hearted as the Albert Hall. A saxophone held up its face for kisses. She had the deep voice of saxophones. She had a scarlet nipple. Oh where, oh where can my little dog be, it was still the same party, the same ices, the same kissings, it was holding up the same arch for oranges and lemons. Only the faces drifted out of reach with time, the bodies losing their old line, the air now floated between the interstices, desire nosed and fingered at the cracks. There was the emerald protecting her cancer with a smile. You heard the calculations of the pansy with the crucified voice. Some day the floor would sweep clean of pattern, a trumpet of light blowing a last judgement.

They were beginning to sit down. The floor was washed with bluish light. You were waiting. You were waiting for the singer. It was none other than Ruby May, as Stella Maris remarked in her Friday column. The singer began to sing. She could do things with her voice. She knew all the tricks the audience knew, guying them, or not quite, it was this that never pricked the bubble of appreciation, that made of Ruby May something authentically *mar-vellous*, she was the amusing insect in black and magenta you went round to see afterwards.

Ruby May lifted up her elegant boy's head and sang. It was a great joke to sing. It occurred to Mrs Standish, under her bare skin, she was sitting on the edge of a joke. However. She made herself receptive for other people's jokes.

> *No more love,* [sang Ruby May]
> *It isn't for want of trying,*
> *No more love,*
> *I've lost the art of crying.*
> *Do you remember*
> *How, in September,*
> *You took my heart and squeezed it?*
> *I can remember*
> *How, in November,*
> *You ran away and cheesed it.*
> *No more love,*
> *No more memoree.*
> *The cabbage in his patch*
> *Is just the kinda match*
> *For meee – –*

The voice gargled with the lusher words that were close to the skin and at the same time quite *mar-vellous fun*. Mrs Standish put up her hand against what had become her own private agitation. She would not, would not give in to riddles, would escape from the dried mummy of her self. You put things the right way, he said, the mauve shirt, with the little pleats she had seen before behind Shaftesbury Avenue glass. Vulgarity was something you drowned in a glass. Not the other, there was no escape from the abject dictatorship of the body, no persuasion could make her believe or, anyway, accept the cabbage in its patch. No more love, gargled a sleek voice. The throat burnt dry. It was for Mrs Standish the burning white of the saxophone.

Shoulder to shoulder, Elyot and Muriel sat over cold quail. The voice drew itself out in a long, aching ribbon of banality, that was still a comment on its own doing.

> No more love,
> It happens to be the fashun,
> No more love,
> I've shot my bolt on pashun.
> Burn up the roses,
> Blo–how the noses,
> Look in the ice-box, baby.
> No one supposes
> That fella Moses
> Was such a bulrush, baby.
> No more love,
> No more memoree.
> So take a chance on gin,
> A substitute for sin,
> With meee – –

The singer's words translated themselves into the breathing, the occasional laughter of Muriel Raphael. Sideways, at close quarters, the withdrawn light had stripped her face to the bones against which he sat. And Muriel's laughter stripping the song to its last layer of banality. It was the knowingness that began to appal. You began to long for the opaque condition of what Muriel would call the moron, the steamy atmosphere of the high teas at Lyons, banter among the cabbages, the fumbling rather than the direct approach. To feel bewildered without knowing why. But Muriel knew, her eyes paraded in a world of implied knowledge, quite apart from, behind the words she used.

She was whispering something now, he heard, something about *Ersatz* love that he inclined his ear to receive. No doubt funny. You laughed without effort, without bothering to piece a fragmentary remark. The purpose of the Café Vendôme was not verbal lucidity, but the contracted thigh. Under the table Muriel's leg lay along his own. His hand brushed the little scabbard of glass and shells.

Shall we stay or go, Muriel? he asked, in the silence after songs.

You could feel her hesitate, deliberate some refinement in attack.

Look, she said, there's Brenda Askew. Everything but the girdle of chastity.

Switched like this in words, her body still gave him the ultimate attention.

Wally Collins felt dry. Upstairs, the bar reflected the foreheads that almost touched in early morning intimacy, as the voices launched after old sorrows, as the mind raked the muck for another sally. The bar reflected Wally upside down, his hand tipping an inverted glass, and the black, inverted tulip of a torso with its protruding pistil of a head. Jesus, but it felt good, the shock of liquor on the dry throat. And the second. You began to settle into things. You put a hand upon a shoulder. A foreign eye swam up and promised friendship. Wally Collins could make friends. There was nothing he wouldn't promise in the name of friendship, in a world of friends. Wally, they said, was a good chap, or a swell egg, according to where he was. Do you remember how, in September, Wally hummed. His jaw shone like an afternoon shave. The eyes of women from the LADIES undressed politely in so many glances, passed, leaving him to pick up the clothes. He was very light on the balls of his feet. He felt all rib and muscle. In the dough, he could have gone out and bought up something for someone, something in a velvet case.

Make it another double, Wally said.

There was no one could say he wasn't generous. Enjoy yourselves, Wally said. He liked to come in with his arms full of things from the delicatessen. Afterwards, the radio and the sofa, and the sort of soft things you said, they ate it up like chicken sandwiches, you called them baby, and all that. But sometimes they went home. You sat looking at the empty cartons. It was a corny business on the whole. Sometimes you put out your arm and there was nothing there.

Mr Collins. Wally! she said. How are you? I fancied I saw. But you don't remember?

Remember the face that got between the Scotch, your face is just a memoree, look in the ice-box, baby, and no baby at that. What you called a fine old tawny, matured in the – Jesus!

Sure, Mrs Standish! Sure I remember!

He took her hand. She felt he remembered, was pleased. Wally was always pleased on shaking hands. The face that shone with pleasure and exertion.

Sure, he said. What'll you have?

He brought himself close. She was glad, her hand that he held, if only it would not tremble.

What? she said. Oh, anything. Gin. Gin and. Gin and.

Tonic, he said.

Yes, she said. Yes.

Well, now, this is swell, Mrs Standish.

Somewhere a pulse made it almost too much, if beating just a little closer, she would not control. She did things with a chiffon handkerchief. She waved it desperately, a desperate chiffon flag, asking for immediate rescue, now that she had floated out to sea.

I've wondered about you. And your band – orchestra, she said. You see, I remember. Our talk.

Here's how, Mrs Standish.

Here's – how, she said.

It put them on an equal footing. The levelling influence of drink.

I came here with a friend. Friends can be dull, she said.

You're tellin' me. Can friends be dull!

It made it all rather confidential.

Yes, she sighed, uncertain with gin.

To talk to a dame, to a confidential dame, he could have gone out and bought that something in a velvet case. The boys said he was nuts. But some dames understood. And a high-class dame that read books, and carriage to her, you could skip the face, but an understanding face, it made you feel kind of warm. Wally Collins, talking to Mrs Standish, might have been listening to the Wurlitzer. Roses on a trellis and the *vox humana*.

You an' me'll have to get together and talk things over, Wally said.

Though out of respect, he dressed it up as take it or not.

That's an idea, she said, smiled, making him believe he had thought of it himself, I tell you what, Wally, we must lunch together one of these days.

It was all so simple, and the gin, she was all glass, the whole future so transparent that she mustn't, she mustn't begin to laugh. She would have shattered in one gust of laughter, already smoothing her gloves for lunch.

I shall take you to lunch, she said, she felt, gaily.

It was going to be one of those occasions. He liked her for it.

She would take him to some little place, she didn't quite know, except that as a snob, but no, it was practical, and Wally Collins, if the shirt were mauve. There were too many questions. There were too many eyes. There were the eyes of.

Mrs Standish turned her back to avoid Elyot and Muriel Raphael. She sank for the moment on her own raft. But she would rise again. Oh yes. Afterwards. She would float upon a sea of immense relief. But she waited to sense the retreat of the little silver shells, these were the rock bottom, that carried their own reflexion in gummed glass.

Taxis move on a spiral at night, round many corners, there is no end to the sweep and collusion of corners. Anxious or not, he was thrown against a thigh, and an encrusted scabbard. He heard the conversation, the works of art, the people met, which proceeded still in spite of the circumstances, there was no visible hesitation in the rise and fall of the scarlet nipple, that lamplight touched, the rattle of light in shutters, or the intermediate greyness, it filtered through the cab, half-way between moon and darkness, with a scent not reminiscent of flowers, the synthetic scent exuded by silver shells.

Here we are, Muriel said.

She broke a thread, opening the door. It was premeditated and final. Like the gesture of the hand that touched light in her house. She went deliberately to things, to lay her furs, to smooth a flower, the big, drooping, feather flowers that borrowed a little of the same scent. She was glossier than any bird, with the inquisitive, detached mind of a jackdaw. The way she frowned at a displacement, emptied ash. He was not there for Muriel until she chose to return. She was busy among her possessions. He had become one of these possessions, inanimate on a field of black glass with banks of white kid upholstery.

I promised to show you a Poussin, she said, still turned.

Must one see a Poussin at three o'clock in the morning?

He began to warm with pleasure to the ritual of words. The cock-bird doing his stuff. He strutted at the entrance to the female's bower, warming his coat tail.

No. Not necessarily. But one has a conscience, she laughed.

It's easier not to, he said.

Yes. Much easier. Because. Because there also isn't a Poussin.

She offered him her face. It had drained right to the bone. Her body moved against him with a little flicker. He could possess the whole of Muriel with his hands, that had held the glass box, she was like this. Inside the limited convention, he was the dictator of her sensuality, he could enjoy this power such as it was, but like the power of a dictatorship, such as it was.

In a second room, their two bodies took the shapes of passion. In a darkness that he felt unnecessary. It was still the same object, the same room, in spite of the illusion that forced itself, the illusion of change, and loss, and discovery, in spite of the little secret cries, it was a bitter mouth. Somewhere at the end of this dark perspective there was the light that removed itself, just out of reach, the face remembered from a dream. It began to sicken him. The sweat of his own body. The shape of his ribs. He lay passive, withdrawn, the whole core remote. He touched her and she was remote too, as impersonal as an accomplished act.

There, she said, in the light. You can give me a cigarette.

Muriel Raphael lay on the bed, making no secret of her body. The brown skin was almost without shadows. It was time he went, they both agreed, in silence. She had slipped back amongst her own possessions.

Give me a ring, Elyot, she said, as if she were establishing a prerogative.

Out of his own distaste returned the probability that he would. Because there was this understanding, the common ground of rational sensuality. The skin that he touched in leaving acknowledged this. It was without surprise or comment. Ash had fallen between her breasts.

Outside, an early wind came up through railings and hit him in the stomach. The empty pavilion in Berkeley Square was emptier in silence, it led the unconvincing life of the early morning shapes, the abandoned houses, the black streets. He began to move along these streets. He was his own shadow, the surfeited cat pushing through the area railing. It was some other person, some other time, in the German street, the white oxen in the vegetable carts, some other sky touching a renaissance gable. Unfair to resurrect this now, but it came in the face of a February wind, the promise against the fulfilment. Getting up early in the lowing of white oxen, his hands trembled for a something, for a mystery behind the wall, that was still untouched. The days were full of objects that hinted at a correspondence. You held your breath a minute before opening a door. The drop shuddered on the geranium leaf. Now he was sick of his bones, and the stubble on bones that he touched, he half suspected two hollows in his skull.

A sight for a sore conscience, he thought, and the woman in the striped dress, was it, her no more passion, no more memoree, only the touch of sheets in a shallow present, the little saucer in the brown thigh. No more love, he sang, softened to his own vicinity and his own annoyance, because what was love, and a song, if not an equation for a voice and two bodies? He wanted it out of his head. Because it was both facile and abstruse. Eden, he had forgotten, how she looked, to remember feature by feature Eden's face, Eden's life, that went on still behind closed doors, with sudden indications in a glance. Eden, he said. There was a sickness, a sadness in the distance, in his own bones. Or how did Mother, humming a tune, know, with Aubrey Silk, each in a sort of champagne desperation, each in their own way, fulfil the stinking moral of a little song. Feet passed, the ragged feet, the face without questions. Burn up the roses. He hated that song. He hated it because it was both meaningless and pointed. Like the thin sky that began to bind the roofs of houses. It stretched there almost transparent, thin, with some withdrawn purpose, lighting the thin, withdrawn face of the beggar on ragged feet. He wanted to put up his hands, to split the thin membrane of the sky, supposing, supposing there were some clue.

A door banged in Grosvenor Gardens. The sound shook the wet trees.

Muriel Raphael. His memory rattled like a dice box. He had forgotten to speak, to thank her for the glass box.

15

They were finishing the bread and cheese slowly, after walking. She watched him gather up the crumbs on the ends of his fingers, the fingers pressed together, stamping on the crumbs, very matter-of-fact. Outside this, the clang of the fruit machine, the collision of silver balls on the pin-game table. All the activity of the saloon bar lapped them round. Peppermint and rum stood beyond the haze, the woman in the *toupet* drawing an endless, thoughtful towel out of the pint glass. All their Saturday afternoons were like this. They were part of them, and yet not. Just as you were part of a relationship you made, the many little contacts, and the phrases of conversation, without penetrating really beyond the outer skins of the personality. She looked at Joe. She was as far distant again as the sound of the pin-balls from her own conscious ear.

Outside, fog had released the building from any dependence on the land. It floated foundationless in the sea mist, where birds cried, and the sudden apparition of a gull skimmed the vestige of a mudbank. You took the evidence of a finite world on trust, from newspapers read in public houses, the apparent fact of Spain or China. Fog and the floating banks of mud denied such evidence. And the woman at the bar, unwinding her thoughtful skein of mist out of the pint glass.

Joe Barnett cleared his throat.

He could put out his hand and touch just so much certainty, the intimate, personal world they made. He loved Eden Standish, not in so many words, he never stopped to formulate this, it was sure enough, like meeting again, you expected this, Saturday afternoon and Sunday, you couldn't cut out the end of the week. He believed in rightness, she said, giving him this, she had given it to him with her own voice, he believed in the living as opposed to the dead. This was also what made him ache sometimes in the pit of his stomach. He read the newspapers and felt sick. The certainty of your own life, the day to day in Crick's workshop, the Saturdays with Eden, were no guarantee against the sick feeling in the pit of your stomach. This became the sad, sick, stinking world. He was responsible in a way. But his hands were helpless, could not cope.

He finished up the last of a scattering of crumbs. On the face of the table the newspaper map, with the names you couldn't pronounce, the Spanish names. This was a dagos' war, they said, the voices in bars, disclaiming any responsibility before the next bitter. The pin-balls scurried for shelter in the familiar warren. But there was no getting round the queer, drawn-out Spanish names and the black line that was no river.

Let's get out of this, he said.

His hand produced a few cold pennies that turned hot in his hand.

Here's a contribution, she said, making it casual, very casual, as if she had picked up a half-crown from the floor, anybody's half-crown.

He often felt this, Eden trying to ignore a situation.

The fog'll lift perhaps, said the woman at the bar.

It expected no answer, addressed to no one in the room.

Yes, she sighed. It's terrible.

They went outside to where frost had stiffened the mud holes on the sea wall. The coast was a wavering edge of frost, above the mud, above the saltmarshes. And the voice was too clear, too stiff with frost and purpose. Eden's voice attempting a conventional gaiety to gloss over a difficult situation. Just because a half-crown had pushed her back on an island of privilege and prejudice.

I hate that half-crown, she said, with a kind of light grimness. It's going to make me bourgeois for the rest of the afternoon.

He laughed and touched her face with his hand.

You're all right that way, he laughed.

But he settled back, she could feel, whether it was the incident or not, into a shell of resistance. She listened to their feet. She listened to a cold bird. The physical fact of their being on the sea wall, the common warmth of their bodies, on her cheek still the roughness of his fingers, these were a source of tranquillity that let her close her eyes in safety. But the worlds that stood apart, the less material worlds, infinitely separate, these were what frightened her, these were what she wanted to possess.

I'd like to get lost, she said.

In all this frost?

Oh, we might find something, she said. A house.

With H. and C. in the bedroom. You're that sort of an escapist, Eden Standish.

She laughed. Perhaps. But to escape with Joe Barnett to some remote acre, to remove anything that might account for the apartness of those infinitely separate worlds. Oh Lord, she sighed, but I am happy, is there no virtue in pure happiness, always this desire to over-reach it?

Oh, look out, Joe, she said. How, how disgusting!

It was the body of a dog that his foot kicked as they came along the path, a little, indeterminate terrier bitch, who had staked herself in the marshes. The guts hung out through the belly fur. The nose was wrinkled in a last shudder of pain. His foot made a dull thumping noise on the frozen body of the dog. He stood there prodding it with his foot.

Don't, said Eden.

She's done for all right, he said.

Eden began to go on.

Leave her, Joe, she called.

Done for. The festoon of helpless guts torn out like the last existing privacy. The dog disgusted him, but he had to look, as if it had a bearing on himself, the sickness in his own stomach. He made himself look. But he spat on the ground. His mother went to chapel. She expected death. To lie on the ground with your guts hanging out. Man was born to this, no other dignity, announced the map of Spain, or the voice of his mother retailing a laying out. But there was a dignity he was jealous of, his own body, his privacy of thought. This was what made him tremble when he read of the killings in Spain or saw the body of the dead dog.

Eden was calling. He went on.

Nice little bitch, he said.

I'm beginning to think you're morbid.

Only a scientific interest. Used to be a bit of a fancier myself.

But his voice couldn't get used to the words.

The fog shifted on the miles they walked, it split open like a paper bag, spilling a powdered field, a hillside with an oast house, the little feathery branches of a Japanese orchard. But near the sea the land continued sour, the saltmarshes with a crust of ice that lifted sometimes round the roots of reeds, a lid of silver opened on the black mud. They came to a house, a thin, pale house, like the last slice of a house left standing in a field. The house was called Mon Repos. There was a Hovis sign, and a plaster pixie in the parlour window.

It seems the obvious thing to go in, said Eden.

That's for you to decide, he shrugged.

He turned his back on Mon Repos. She sensed the recurrence of a theme, the inevitable half-crown.

Then I think we shall, she said, touching his arm. There's no denying the bourgeois appetite.

They sat in the neat horsehair parlour, that smelt of horsehair and mahogany, it had the surprised expression of many family groups, and the hushed air of a vault. Because it was less a room than a repository, for the valued, the inherited, like the plaster pixie, the dome full of coloured sand and the view of Shanklin, the certificate for bell pulling, and the cut-glass cruet in which the salt had caked. At first you talked in a lower voice in deference to the parlour.

I think I'll take off my boots, whispered Joe.

Yes, she said, doubtfully, looking at the door, the hearth.

So he sat with his feet smoking in the hearth. She filled her mouth with bread and jam. And then the lid was off. It was all up with the parlour.

Why? she said, her voice positively shouted, and full of bread and butter. Why is it never Hovis? she said.

Why should it be Hovis?

But the sign outside. And there never is.

Do you mind? he asked.

No. But I like to know. If a sign.

I expect they just don't keep it, he said.

That's one explanation, she said. But it isn't satisfying.

She looked at him. She could have swallowed him up in one gulp of the bread that wasn't Hovis. His face was brick-red by firelight, above the paler throat. Her relationship with Joe Barnett gave her life a form, a substance, she could touch it, touch herself, in a way that she never could with Maynard or any of the others, she could not have said this is Eden Standish with any degree of certainty. Of all the faces in the street, how many are there which are not directionless? she wondered. Firelight, and a knowledge of the sterile years, made her compassionate. She walked down Theobalds Road to find a shop with baths. She steadied herself against a railing. Or she lay on her back at Mrs Angelotti's, watching the pale trumpet of a daffodil stir in a suburban breeze. It was all logical enough, and Mrs Angelotti's room, part of her own abortive efforts at living, that the sterile years threw back, with the dead child.

She went and sat beside him, to be closer. She sat on the floor against his legs.

Presently the woman came to clear away the things. She began to talk. She had a long, horselike face, discreet and polished as her own parlour furniture. It was very lonely, she said. Her husband was a carrier. There was only the pictures in Rochester, that was six miles, and few buses. You could hear the sea in stormy weather. It boomed against the sea wall, and she wasn't half afraid, she was from Surrey, she was used to brighter country. Then she gave a last suck to her teeth, and went away.

I want to stay here, Eden said. If she'll let us.

What? he said. All night?

Yes. All night.

She could feel his hand moving in her hair.

Because, Joe, she said, for once I want to feel we've been left behind. I want to feel we're outside everything, the people we know, the things that are happening. Sometimes I'm afraid circumstances are going to be too much for us. So I want to take this. Just this moment.

She was touching a raw spot, the belly of the dead dog, it came back, the guts lying on the frost. Circumstances, the things that are happening might be too much, she said. But this was certainty, good, to sleep with your girl, to hear the sea the other side of the wall. His hand moved over her scalp. You forgot what was happening outside, outside what you could touch, as the voice suggested over beer. Tonight he would put aside his conscience, she said, he was the world, and all was right and knowable inside this world. He stretched back his arms so that the chair cracked. He bit the mouthpiece of his pipe.

Yes, he smiled, looking down at her. You're right.

The woman was doubtful. Her mournful horse face scented immorality. She would ask her husband, she said. You heard the footsteps, the words, the silence in the kitchen. It wasn't usual, she said, but for once, and a cold night, and a long walk, well, she would make the bed.

So it happened that way. Their teeth chattered in the colder room, the brass bedstead shaking with cold, and the wash-basin on the rickety stand. And he wanted to touch her. He could not touch her enough. There were too many phrases of tenderness that he wanted to express, could only be expressed by the touching of hands. And darkness. Her face was for a moment clarified and transparent as she put it up to the lamp glass to blow. Then the darkness, that became their bodies, out of the first contact in the cold bed. He smoothed away with his hands, with his arms, in great sweeps. He was like a swimmer surmounting infinite waves, there was no end to the extent of his achievement, he had broken the last bar to possibility.

There was a silence of frost in the room. Beyond it a dull motion of the sea. She lay and listened to it some time, through his exhausted breathing, he was asleep now, she knew, she could feel his body lie heavy against her. Eden Standish closed her eyes. She could not, did not want to sleep. She was too febrile, discomposed, this throbbing of tenderness that she had become, and to which there was no end. She had repudiated anything of her that remained in memory. She was content to be this creature the moment had made, to live in a world of immediate sensation. Out of the darkness, out of his breathing came the dull answer of the sea. But in undertone. As if she had flooded the world with her own importance, with her own love. To flood the world, she sighed, her face against his warm skin, to draw back warmth into the body of the world, to chafe its limbs with love. Oh dear, she sighed sleepily, I am impotent, quite impotent, but in love, in love, this has happened, and this, and this, then why not. She drifted in a bell-tone that came from seaward. Then there was just the sound of frost.

Somebody rattled on the door with a can of water.

It was a long way back, a long way into the now white room, it was the light off frost, or snow. She pushed sleep back from her face, found she was there still. She watched a sleeping face. It was very close. In sleep it allowed itself to be possessed, a no longer separate world that she touched in thought, protected with her own solicitude. Outside their own immediate warmth it was cold. She got out of bed into the cold of the room, still naked, felt it on her skin without recoiling, she was a pillar of warmth from which the cold receded, and the landscape, the stretch of barren marsh on which a little snow had fallen, and the black line of a canal, these trembled through the window frame in a glow of Eden Standish, in the face of her pervasive, irrepressible warmth.

From the bed he asked her what she was doing.

Nothing, she said. Looking. And most probably catching cold.

She came back into the bed so that he could touch her again. She wanted to communicate her own contentment and warmth.

Waking into morning Joe Barnett blinked his eyes. It was the glare off snow. It was also surprise at a lapse in habit.

Going downstairs now, he would have made a cup of tea in his shirtsleeves, bought and looked at the Sunday paper, caught on to the thread of things. Sleeping with Eden Standish had broken this. He loved her. Did he sleep with his girl, asked the boy Mo, not in so many words, but insinuating like, because what were girls if not. The boy Mo made him feel inexperienced, uneasy. The darkness was filled with a hot panting, laughter stifled against walls. A puzzling business altogether. So he didn't encourage the boy Mo, said it was none of his business, or something like that. But sleeping with Eden Standish, it happened natural enough, like meeting again. Sunday lay becalmed in a pool of frozen light. She had done this. She had smoothed out any ripple with her hand. To lie like this, the mouth on mouth. To bring yourself closer. Outside this there was no business that was any business of yours.

Outside a gull blew, flapping coldly, its sea cry. It brought you back out of a half-doze.

We ought to get up, he said.

There's no ought, she sighed.

A gull, blown inland over the marshes, cried against the window. It seemed close.

Sunday morning you went out and bought the paper. You returned to things. Suddenly he didn't want to touch her. He wanted to be left alone. There was no longer anything mutual, there was Eden Standish and Joe Barnett. There was no real change had happened over night, except the lapse of conscience, of habit. There was still a sick world mewing at the windowpane, lying with its guts frozen on the sea wall.

Yes, he said, jumping out of bed and putting on his trousers. Can't let everything slip.

She watched him shake his shoulders. He had receded in so many gestures. His eyes were dark.

Why? she said. Surely this is our day?

Yes, he said. But. I wonder if she'll have a paper, old Horse Face down there.

She watched his darkened eyes, that did not admit her into a separate world, she had never been there perhaps, except on some night journey into imagined territory. Accept this, she said, accept, there is nothing to be done. And there are always the crumbs of affection, the few glances, the few words. But her throat stifled.

He came and sat on the bed, dressed. He put his hand on her throat.

You can't tell in this place, he said, what people are about.

He stroked her throat. She could feel a kind of absent tenderness in the hand. He could feel her softer skin, that was like a lapse of conscience. I love Eden, he said, but what can this do for the world, the sick, stinking world that sits in the stomach like a conscience? He was helpless. He was always helpless, unless it was something he could do with his two hands. He could love with his hands, he could shape things out of wood, but the wind slipped through his fingers, the dark, disturbing wind of abstract forces and ideas, the things you sensed and could not deal with. You sat and stared at your hands, that could give no answer but their own emptiness.

No, he said softly, more to himself.

He looked down at her and found she was crying. It made him a bit afraid. He did not know her very well, the other Eden, what she was really like.

16

When her hand shook as she did her hair, when the clock had apparently stopped, when she found on her tongue a fragment of Swinburne dredged from some half-silted and long-forgotten emotional well, Mrs Standish supposed she was in love. Even though her rational moments roused her fastidiousness and told her that Wally was normally a sleek and nauseating young man, she was still uneasily prepared for all the furies of love to set upon her and tear her to pieces. Just this once, she said. It made it seem not quite so bad, her own ridiculousness, as she sat facing her reflexion in the glass, as she sat waiting for Wally Collins in the restaurants where no one else would come. Wally was usually late. People are mostly unpunctual, Mrs Standish decided. She had spent her whole life walking round the block and waiting at tables for people who didn't come. She sat at tables and assessed her own weakness. It was this, above all, that made unpunctuality a crime. It reduced the character of Mrs Standish to so many little pellets of bread.

The unpunctuality of Wally Collins, and it seemed to increase, the number of pellets, the number of glances at the door, gave her the opportunity to remind herself: My lover is a saxophonist. It was both terrifying and comic. It sounded like a popular song, one of the *numbers* that Wally hummed into the chromium shaving mirror at Godiva Mansions. My lover is a saxophonist. She tried it on her tongue, then before some invisible jury, to explain to the attentive faces that waited, when there were no explanations forthcoming, that is, nothing so rational as the arguments to which juries respond. She could only offer her own unsatisfied face. She could suggest her horror of an empty room, of the nights in empty rooms, counting the clocks across the square. Quite apart from the physical aspect, I must have something to think about, she said, even a saxophone. This is recompense enough for a collapse in dignity, for the defection of the interesting Mrs Catherine Standish, who was always more or less a lay figure, so many acquired conventional poses that people labelled Dignity.

In a way she now felt freer. She told herself this, crumbling the bread in a Soho restaurant. You rested when and where you chose in the world in which she now drifted. When she went home, the house was no longer personal. She looked inside her drawing-room, at the snug if somewhat shabby cocoon, which no longer belonged, or she no longer belonged. She belonged only to the clothes she stood in. Reality was the particular current emotion that disturbed or eased her mind. It is better like this, she told herself doubtfully, it is also something of a triumph at my age to live, well, passionately.

Mrs Standish looked up from a chequered Soho tablecloth and watched the approach of a fawn hat. Pushed like a halo, it left the forehead bare to glisten.

Hiya, toots, Wally said.

She gathered herself for a blow, his words, his smile, all of them unconscious and benevolent. But Wally frequently made her wince. Habit, she said angrily, I am a fool and a snob. My lover is a saxophonist. But her mouth remained wry, she had to probe a little deeper at her own wound.

Late, eh? Gee, that's too bad, he said.

Late? she said, surprised. I hadn't noticed. Or, oh well, just a few minutes. But I've only just arrived myself. Really, Wally, she said.

This was part of a ritual. And you couldn't afford a scene. She had reached the age where you put your money on diplomacy. It was necessary, if sometimes a strain, the muscle that never dared relax. But she appeared easy-going. Wally said she was a good sort.

He began to tell her about a pal, his name was Tiny Martin, he was in the fur trade, Wally said, he was also in a hole, there was a girl, a blonde, one of the cheap, brassy bits that Tiny liked, well, she had him on a string, that dame, and there was a guy, a guy called Gallagher who was sort of messed up in it too, a bookie or something, anyway, to cut the story short, the blonde said a girl had to live, and it's only natural if Gallagher, not that she wasn't fond of Tiny, but it was like that.

Yes, said Mrs Standish. And now shall we eat?

Wally's conversation was largely anecdotal. It was refreshing, she told herself at times, the significance of fact. More often she plunged beneath it, into the waters of her own preoccupation, let the current of narrative pass overhead. Still, she could register a surface interest, her eyebrows raised, her mouth fixed in a receptive smile.

Do you know why I like you, Kate? he said. Because you always understand.

Now, Wally, she laughed. You'll make me feel like an oracle.

A what?

Oh dear, she sighed mentally. It was sometimes exhausting. A Greek priestess who knew all the answers, she said.

Oh.

Greek priestess or not, she knew the hell of a lot. It often made him afraid. It was not like the tootsies you laid once and talked about the movies afterwards. That old bit of Wally's, the boys said. It made him ashamed, trying to explain. She knows the hell of a lot, he said. *I'll* say, it was an easy crack, so she oughta, at her age. He could have lammed out at someone. It made him sore.

Wally Collins himself wondered a bit, in his private moments, how it happened, him and Kate. Because it happened without your knowing, but easy enough, it might have been arranged. Sitting on the sofa, there was the radio, and an early highball after lunch. She wasn't in the habit of drinking, she said, but there, what have you, you couldn't go on sitting around. And then he began to tell her about himself. The radio was playing the 'Chanson Hindoue'. It was sort of sad. I'm glad, she said, we met, it's sometimes meant for two people to meet. She was that sincere, moved, the way her bust, that you put out a hand. Sometimes it made him sweat, just how it happened, and a dame of her class.

A dame of her class. She looked at a pair of hands and knew that she would dwindle to anything that Wally made her. She lay exhausted on a rumpled bed. She lay with her eyes closed, the hair moist, the skin still tingling. Out of the radio the steady wash of music that drenched the limbs, as lethal as the erotic act. But somewhere, some time, out of all this she would grope towards her self, just not lost, pick it up with the discarded clothes. To lose yourself. This was the ultimate but ineffectual aim. You opened your eyes on the furniture. You thought about catching the bus home.

Now they sat eating minestrone in a cheap Italian restaurant.

Does you good to get some good hot food inside of you, Wally said.

Satisfaction announced itself in his whole body, through the smacking of the lips, in the drawn-out string of parmesan swinging from the mouth. Mrs Standish tried to eat with bravado, in the way expected of her, eating with Wally Collins, the women he must have known.

Yes, she said, sweeping with her spoon. Lovely hot soup.

It sounded ineffably silly, she knew, but without a quiver now, the remarks she made, she was humouring a child. Besides, she tried to persuade herself, we waste so much time on what we like to think subtleties of conversation. To attack anything that remained of an intellectual past lessened the shortcomings of the present. This was the attitude of Mrs Standish. It had to be.

But you're not eating, he said.

I'm taking my time.

Sick? he asked.

No, she said. Why? I like to enjoy things slowly.

She looked straight at him, making it very meaningful. Then she gave him an intimate smile, that came out rather broody, transferred itself to the opposite face, and satisfied.

Sure, he said. Every man in his own way.

He looked at her thoughtfully. Because she was awful deep. Sometimes he wondered what she saw, tagging round with a bum like Collins, there was no telling, and a woman in love, sometimes he would have said crazy, he couldn't hold her, and calling out. She excited him. Looking at her in the restaurant his mouth drooped open. All the things he'd never had, and wanted, seemed to put themselves in reach in the body of Catherine Standish. He could not possess her too quickly, in case they removed themselves again.

I've got the afternoon, he said. What about going back, eh?

She listened with a disturbed fascination to a proposition.

Well, she said, diffidently, there *were* one or two things –

Because there was still some show to be made.

Go on, he said. You don't sound certain.

Perhaps for a little, she said. Perhaps for an hour or so.

Negotiated, she began to tremble, hoped that she didn't show, uncertain, he said, when she could have screamed out: I have sat here half the morning, waiting, waiting, I have built so much on this moment of release.

In the taxi he took her hand and began to talk to her out of his limited vocabulary.

You're swell, Kate, he said.

Inside the glove her hand burned. She had seldom experienced nerves in playing a part. The language, the pantomime of love had come to her easily, adapting itself to suit her men. Except now. The vulgarity, the cockiness did not cancel out the goodness, the kindness, the touching stupidity of Wally Collins. This made her feel her imposture.

Swell? she said, knowing that in self-defence she would turn on the self-pity. For the moment. It's always easy to discover virtues, not so easy to remain interested in them, she said.

Here now! he protested.

Yes, she said, looking away. One doesn't last for ever, Wally. And I'm not as young as I was.

She waited anxiously for him to contradict. Playing her card, she regretted it. Putting ideas in his head. Sincerity often lodged perilously close to stupidity.

You might call it mature, she heard him say thoughtfully. Yes, he said. Mature.

As if he liked the sound. *Une femme mûre.* She had helped him stick the label on. This was the price of a conscience in love, when you couldn't afford, when there was one capricious gust of passion between you and what amounted to ultimate extinction.

She began to laugh. She tried to make it mysterious, remote.

What's the matter? he asked.

Nothing, she laughed, looked, only just offered him her mouth, so that she felt his lips.

She knew, with a spasm of relief, that she was still desirable. Gently, imperceptibly, she returned the pressure of his thigh.

I don't always get you, he said.

No? she laughed. Anyway, we're here.

Here was Wally's inevitable choice in dwellings, the large brick grid with its encrustations of neon, extinct now, but still functional enough to announce GODIVA MANSIONS in bleary tubes. The whole situation was a little bleary, the rockeries in the court with their deliberately coaxed alpine plants, the trickle of a fountain that stained a basin brown. Mrs Standish made an extra effort to insulate her sensibilities on these regular visits to Godiva Mansions. Difficult at first, it began to come easily. She walked in like someone you read about in the picture papers, a minor scandal, either bigamy or champagne parties in the nude. She could feel her joints loosen in the lift. *Bravura*, murmured Mrs Standish. It was a word of which she was most uncertain, but it had a requisite brassy swagger that fitted the situation like skin. She swayed softly in the lift and hummed a tune.

Wally's key turned in a thin and not very private door.

Got to have heat, he said.

You noticed this at once, the little airless box that took your breath away, if it hadn't gone already in anticipation; there was a smell of airlessness, of dust, a dry rubbing on the skin. Doors stood open, it was all open doors, and the unmade bed beyond, the bed in Wally's flat seemed never to get made. She no longer shuddered. She put down the remnant of her furs. She prowled.

Some day I'll turn the place out, she said, very practically, as if she meant it, as if she knew where to begin.

Too much exercise, sugar, Wally said.

Her feet jostled empty milk-bottles on the floor of the kitchenette, just so many accents on an accepted squalor. She could even accept it herself, when it was a means to escape, the bottles only just fringing the conscious, what there remained of this after the voluptuous release.

Quit nosin' around, he said.

He came up and took her from behind, his hands upon her breasts. She closed her eyes. Her face sagged. He was leading her, anywhere, she let him, all she desired was a complete surrender of the will.

When she looked at him, his face younger, washed bare of any thought by its sensuality, she could not bear it. Even in achievement, she was writhing on a bed of uncertainty. Supposing a face withdrew.

Wally, she said, harshly. You won't.

Won't what?

He couldn't soothe her enough with his hands.

You won't, you won't. You love me, Wally? she said.

What do you know!

She didn't know, know what. Only that you couldn't quite destroy uncertainty. This was what maddened her, made her fasten her mouth on his. She moaned against his mouth, the little moans of half-realized pleasure.

In between, the hours and days when she resumed her own life, these were an ashy colour. Her head gaped open at eleven o'clock. She felt pains in her body. If only, she said, the telephone, but anyway, he said five.

It's the doctor you want, Julia said.

Julia watching from doorways made you turn away, as if Julia's eye.

Go away, Julia, you said.

You couldn't cope with the watchful eye.

I tell you what, said Julia. I'll make you a cup of tea.

But you wanted to be left alone, not Julia insisting on bodily ills, as if these were more than a symptom. Julia's face was your own conscience, pointing towards a more orderly past, scrubbed, and tangible, and clean. And it was too much, the effort of justification, of self-defence.

I shall have to cultivate patience, said Mrs Standish. This decision translated itself to her face in an expression that was too sweet, quite unreal, because deliberately chosen. Like some twentieth-century martyr waiting hopefully for a stake. She sat with her expression, she sat in the afternoon, often in the deserted balcony of the Café Vendôme, only half listened to the numbers they were running through, her mind picked at the gluey debris left by the saxophones. Faces glanced. But she did not respond. It was understood, her relationship to the Boys, without the elaborations of introduction. They looked at her. They accepted. She was as explicit as a bit of private life can be. Wally's bit. Wally's old girl.

So she continued to sit on the edge. She sat at one of the little bare tables that no tablecloth disguised, the chipped gilt, the stains. Night receded from the Café Vendôme leaving a rime of nostalgic desolation. Waiters brushed past, or the shadows of waiters, their dirty singlets, their pale skins. There was no flourish to the gestures of the daylight waiters. It made you feel cast up, together with the pale waiters, the empty tables, a flotsam of dead sensation from the night before. Or from many nights, or days and nights, the Catherine Standish of the Louis XV *bergère*, the Kitty Goose of the imitation furs. Willy, they said, was dead. Willy and Wally. It was like a vaudeville act. If she had been drinking, she might have laughed. But not by day, by the ash-coloured light of the Vendôme. Thought had a grey tinge. It was the face of the mother-in-law, and the Gothic smile, that confirmed its first judgement out of a tomb. Old Mrs Standish, Willy, the frightfulness of death, had made her shudder when younger. Her hands hesitated in opening the letters that might announce a death. There was something terrifying about involuntary extinction. Before you realized that destruction self-imposed and chosen, in the ash-coloured afternoons at the Vendôme, on the unmade bed at Godiva Mansions, was the ultimate negation.

Mrs Standish burnt her fingers on what remained of her cigarette.

You look kind of down, Wally said.

The notes were extinguished. The music dispersed on its several ways.

You can buy me a drink, she said.

She was grateful for his presence, the mere animal presence. She was relieved by the suggestion of physical habit that the presence of Wally Collins implied. To cling to this was essential, to avoid the shadowy ways of introspection.

It's the light, she said, shaking off a mood.

She squeezed his hand. For the moment she was genuine in gratitude.

Wally, like Julia, diagnosed in physical terms.

We'll take a weekend, he said. We'll go down to Brighton.

Her stomach quailed, her eyes dazzled already by the brassy comet of Wally's Brighton.

Yes, she said. If it weren't for the business of getting there.

What? he said. Sitting in the train? You got to snap out of yourself.

So it was Wally's Brighton, the Sunday glaze along the Front, with the reality of a picture postcard over the breakfast table. To breathe the air, it was good, they said, you must do this, as if it were justification for being in Brighton. They stepped out along the asphalt through the satin Jewesses. They walked on asphalt, or the thick carpet smelling of old cigars. In the bedroom, opened by the page, she met the smell of someone else's powder, someone who had been there before her. It was disgusting, she would have said normally, her face half wrinkled to speak, with Wally behind her prodding the bed, only now the intention lapsed, the comment on other people's powder, the comment on someone who was not there, because this was the condition of Catherine Standish. Lapsed somewhere, the gestures continued from habit and convention.

Want to go bye-bye? asked Wally. You look done up.

No, she said. Let's do something. Go somewhere. After all, it's Brighton.

With an attempt at raucous gaiety which went with the brass bedposts, and what Wally expected. She could not be this enough. The goodness, the kindness of Wally Collins surged forward in heavy waves, the hopeful glance, the hand arranging the collar of her coat. It was still in the convention that the mechanism of Catherine Standish should play its part.

They sat in the bar. They sat among the blondes, these were either ripe or acidulated, and their smooth, glossy men in tweeds.

I came here, said Mrs Standish, I came here before the War. Before Elyot was born.

Or long before that, in some prehistoric age, to which spiritually she still belonged, and her clothes, which she had liked to think timeless, an expression of herself, that now drew the sideways glance.

That's Harry Simmons, said Wally.

Out of the present, he fidgeted. Or anyway, in the shapeless stream of someone else's past.

Who? she asked, as a matter of course.

As if a dark face could make much headway against yesterday afternoon, the soft, withdrawn, pregnant body sitting by an open window, listening to the compliments of Aubrey Silk.

Harry Simmons. Orchestra, he said. There's a leader for you. Harry's going places, or I'm not Collins.

She took a sip of whisky in reply, coughed through her cigarette. She sat, indifferent, in the just interested glances of neighbouring blondes. She had stopped making excuses for herself.

Wally began to tell the history of Harry Simmons, to which she listened theoretically, but sitting in a cloud, the perpetual cloud that had begun to follow her about. My lover is a saxophonist, she said. But this again, theoretically. She began to feel, in the haze of drink, of narrative, that her body had dissolved, the physical passion, except in theory, those little twinges of jealousy for a glance that rested too long on a neighbouring blonde. To possess in theory, in retrospect, perhaps this would be the ultimate solution. But she wasn't sure she wanted this, to renounce the discomfort of self-assertion.

We might go and eat, she said, shaking an inertia off her shoulders.

She looked at him affectionately enough. She was fond of the source of her reassurance. Some women, she supposed, would keep a dog. Then she began to hate herself.

I'm looking forward to my dinner, she said, out of a full conscience. You shall order me something. Something for an occasion.

What sort of an occasion?

Just an occasion, she said. I like to make occasions.

She was a queer one, Kate, but a good sort. His eye rested thoughtfully on a trail of blondes. Yes, he said, a queer one. Sitting there sometimes as if she wasn't there. Talking about the War. His eye rested on the cleavage in a blonde bust that blossomed from the contours of an armchair. It was an uneasy journey to the dining-room.

She said yes, lobster, lobster, thermidor, because it reminded her.

O.K., he said, if it was going to be like that.

The decorations made him affluent, the trellises with gold grapes, and the pink shades. Here he liked to show off what he had made himself, out of the side street in Bethnal Green. He liked to touch the heavy hotel cutlery. He anticipated the rich flavour of the standard hotel foods. Whether she liked it or not, he was her equal now. Sometimes he felt the pressure of her disapproval, just enough to throw him out of his stride. But he looked across at her possessively, and beyond her at the room, which became an illusion of his own importance. Not as young as she was, she said, which was true, but a good sort. He could afford to be generous. And there remained in Wally Collins the sentimental streak, the roses and moonlight streaming from the saxophone.

A face advanced, nodded, across the room.

That's that Harry Simmons, he said.

What? she said. Again!

She began unaccountably to feel annoyed. A cold current passing.

Yes, he said. He's at liberty, you know. And the girl, I guess he's tied up with that girl, the little, cute, dark piece. He's putting her across. Croons. Alice Delaware, Wally said.

Mrs Standish looked at Miss Alice Delaware, sized up her assurance and the crimson nails. The nails dug into bread. A moist, crimson smile drifted on a face.

I should think he is, said Mrs Standish.

You think he's what?

Tied up with Alice Delaware.

Knives rattled on a plate.

Gee, he said. You're out to bitch somebody.

Only a contribution to the conversation, she said.

She couldn't pay too much attention to that lobster thermidor.

Alice's swell, said Wally. She's a New Jersey girl. Went to high school with a pal of mine.

It began to happen across the room, the suggestion of *rapprochement*, a friction of the senses. Obliquely, Mrs Standish was conscious of Alice Delaware's salient features, which were difficult to ignore, they were public property. More especially the property of Wally Collins, his eyes, the moist stare that betrayed in Wally a concentration on the physical.

There was music somewhere, the spun caramel of violins, a drawn-out Massenet.

Farther in, Wally had begun to sup his soup. She was trying to get him down. You could feel her laying on the silence. Wally's bit, they said. But it was sometimes too much, and a man had a right to look around, to pick up an easy smile rather than a sour puss. Sometimes you felt you had stuck around too long, and what was the game anyway, the game you didn't understand, the words, the meanings. He began to feel free. He mounted under golden grapes on the trellis of a smile. He could have put out his hand and touched a moist, swelling grape.

Afterwards, he lit a cigar, one of the expensive ones he couldn't quite afford. Benevolence returned with so many shillings' worth of smoke. You couldn't throw off what had grown a habit. Or respect, for that matter. You couldn't help respecting Kate.

Sometimes you take me up, he said.

She had begun to ease back into the safety zone. Out in the lounge she felt the soft give of the ash-trodden carpet, she felt the pressure of his arm.

Yes, she sighed. Sometimes.

She looked nowhere in particular, into a marble wasteland.

I got to leave you. Nature, he explained. Then we'll go for a bit of a stroll.

Mrs Standish stood in the marble wasteland, waiting not here, not anywhere, she had lost her bearings, was without a map. You will wait here, he said. The easing of tension had left the ticking of an eye. Told to behave in such and such a way, she could still hope, she supposed, for further directions. But she could not move on any intuition of her own in the marble forest, lit with the glittering of foreign smiles, filled with the idioms of foreign voices. A traveller who had chosen to lose her way, she could not regret this, or the last moments of lucidity. She stood in the marble clearing awaiting the pleasure, the condescension of her guide.

Somewhere there was still a music, a terrible jauntiness of violins playing the dances from *Henry V.III.*

17

The meetings with Muriel happened regularly enough. Her telephone voice suggested the Ritz Bar, or a walk across the Park, or a string quartet in Wigmore Street. Muriel Raphael's voice was too rational to make a practice of enthusiasm. Taught to react in the right way, it had caught an even steeliness. Because uniformity was desirable. She had discovered this very early. As a child in pigtails, a smudgy Jewess, just a little different, she had suffered from hot palms, the sudden spasms of passion that came from looking at pictures or listening to music. She could not pour it out quickly enough, communicate her passion. But people made it difficult, the surprised and embarrassed English faces that translated Muriel Raphael into an uncomfortable fourteen. She began to be conscious of her race. Resenting, she also envied the aloof voice, the discreet face, that were free from shame, the hot, darting Jewishness. She began to be secretive. Because she had to form herself, and there is always a secretiveness to mask the process of conscious evolution. Muriel Raphael was deliberately making a second Muriel Raphael that overlaid the first, so many layers of habit, opinion, so many mannerisms, each tested already by convention. Only sometimes the recollection of an adolescent ecstasy, Mozart in a sticky twilight, the greenish-yellow light through limes, and the braided shoulders of an officer, or whirling in her father's gallery, her own skirt caught in the stiff chalkiness of Degas, her own shoulders taking the curtain bow, these pursued her sometimes with a just recognizable nostalgia that she was anxious to disown. She had realized, tested, why, she had proved the superiority of the objective, the intellectual approach. Mozart had become a neat mathematical pattern that stimulated without disturbing. She sat, just a little inclined, and traced a figure in sound right to its neat conclusion. There was no looseness. There was nothing unexplained. A Mozart symphony left Muriel clear-eyed, satisfied. It was, she felt, a triumph of accomplished intellect.

To know what you wanted, and to achieve it, this was desirable, just as to desire the unattainable was not to be encouraged. In the morning Muriel Raphael stood in front of the open window and breathed in a certain way. She drank the juice of crushed carrots. Alone, she ate mostly vegetables. She had prescribed this for herself. She took great pleasure in realizing the rightness of her behaviour, the behaviour of a rational being. She glowed with this rightness, walking in the street, breathing at the window, eating her raw salads. Beyond the circle of this right existence other people moved in a maze of unco-ordinated instinct, lost in the tangle of their self-encouraged loves and hates.

For Muriel Raphael, a personal relationship was a practical arrangement. She took just as much as she needed. She did not choose to give very much of herself, perhaps remembering a door closed in her face, locking herself in the bathroom to cry as a child. But achieving self-sufficiency, she kept emotion at a distance. She controlled the voices on the telephone, her own and those that answered her. She could reduce these to the tempo of her own, listen to their echo, it made her smile, a thin, satisfied motion of the lips that almost brushed the listening ear.

Like an echo, was what you felt. Elyot Standish hung up a smile. He had become the echo of Muriel Raphael. Or more tangibly, a possession. Out of indifference, you didn't object, except in moments of exasperation, when you had hoped to penetrate a little deeper, to discover a suspected core, you found that you were touching glass. The just opaque Bristol box remained on the mantelpiece, a constant reminder of Muriel. This both irritated and roused, to take it in the hands. It was, of course, absurd. Muriel made no promise that she didn't carry out. But sometimes, in frustration, he could have broken more than the passive elegance of glass, he wanted to press with his hands, rouse an element of fear or surprise, some sign of the spontaneous. Then it became too easy to counter this with a confession: This is what I have chosen, this is what I have encouraged.

This was Elyot Standish at thirty. But his face didn't betray him. The kind of people who say rashly, oh yes, Elyot Standish, we know him well, without stopping to think what this means, accepted the face as beginning and end. It was also perhaps more comfortable. Second glances are thin ice. It was safer, easier, to make the kind of general conversation that you make at parties, and this Elyot could make very well when he liked, pleasant, and cultivated, and forgotten with the dry martinis. Elyot Standish could be an asset to a party. Except when he grew silent. This happened. He found himself standing alone in the corner of the room.

There's a point where you freeze people off, Muriel said.

It was the moment after people had gone, when the room had not yet recovered, there were glasses and broken sausage sticks. He watched her calculating hand. As if she were testing on a bracelet just how much she could say, one two three, and then no farther. She was as calculating as a cat.

There's a point, he said, where there's no more virtue in words. The only alternative is silence. But silence, of course, is immoral. A kind of private vice.

The room contracted in a yawn. He watched the arc her arms made. He was too well acquainted, he decided, with all Muriel's gestures. She bored him, not that this rankled, not half as much as to realize he bored her in return.

Quite, she said. But we mustn't indulge our vices in public. A hand reached out to patronize.

Don't think for a moment, she sighed – it came as a reassuring afterthought, perched on the tail of a yawn – don't think I don't understand, Elyot, because of course, darling, I do.

She opened her eyes in emphasis. He could feel the thin bones of her hand, claiming an intimacy of mind and body that no doubt existed, even down to the last flicker of boredom experienced by two people that habit kept united.

But to the general public, she said, silence can be opaque.

She smiled the smile of someone who has said something both apposite and final. Even if this were possibly a waste. He bored her a little, but not enough. She got up to rearrange her room, to juggle with the ornaments in jade and glass. Elyot would stay. She would take him up, in time, in her own time. She moved about the room, content with her arrangement of the details of her life.

He smiled the indifferent smile of someone accepting a situation. No more than a situation that circumstance had arranged, in so many episodes, through so many instruments. Adelaide

Blenkinsop, his mother, the saxophonist Wally Collins, who had found and delivered the Bristol box.

By the way, he said. So many weeks, and I don't believe I've thanked you for the box.

The box? she said.

Her turned face was cloudy with surprise, asking for some kind of explanation.

The Bristol box, he said. I thought.

She began to be remotely interested.

I thought, he said, that you sent a box.

I'm sorry somebody thought of it first. This delicate attention.

She laughed off what might have been an edge of sarcasm. She smiled to anoint a wound. This was part of Muriel's technique. But she scarcely touched him. He was preoccupied with the box, which he held again in retrospect, inquiring and deducing wrongly from the crumpled and electric paper. Muriel's voice shrivelled a whole series of events that had developed out of the Bristol box. It almost destroyed Muriel herself. It was like discarding an illusion, he felt, as she stood waiting. It was recovering part of yourself.

You'll stay to dinner, she said.

She sensed somehow the partial collapse of her authority. Interest revived in a too compelling rush. She had to put out a feeler, to reinforce.

No, he said. No, Muriel, not tonight.

She had to collect herself.

Then Friday. There's the Queen's Hall.

Perhaps, he said. I'll ring. We'll talk it over. But now I'll be late.

He took his hat. His face revived under the touch of air. He could not walk fast enough, or think. You had to accept the evening as you found it, the shapes and sounds that started up, narcissus from the Scillys, and the blue policeman, and the tapping of the blind man's stick. Now Muriel Raphael, and all that she implied, was dead. She was an error in deduction. She was little more than a lingering disgust.

When he got in, his mother said flatly, one of her domestic remarks, that she stamped with her distaste:

Connie is here, Elyot. I asked her to stay to dinner.

Not that Mrs Standish actively deplored Connie Tiarks. Connie was too negative for that. She was one of the unavoidable details, like ordering the meals, or buying a toothbrush. So you accepted Connie. She had kept on happening for such a long time.

Connie Tiarks was more acceptable to Elyot, tonight, and going into the drawing-room, and seeing Connie peering at a book. She looked at it very closely, because she had strained her eyes. She could not look at it closely enough, and this was not altogether eyes, it was also the eagerness of Connie Tiarks, her fear of waste, of wasting time, of not absorbing just another drop of knowledge. Connie Tiarks glanced up. He received the lumpiness of a face. This was in some way a resumption of many things.

Hello, Connie, he said. You can't see. You'll strain your eyes.

It was the sort of thing you said to Connie.

Oh no, she said rather breathlessly, and felt red. No, I can see perfectly. Really I can. And I was just glancing, she said. These prints.

She could not excuse herself enough. As if she were caught in a shameful act. She could feel the hot flushing of her face.

I *love* prints, she said.

But it sounded the desperate invention of a moment, to throw out something, she was climbing up the endless ladder of her own embarrassment.

Let's have a drink, Connie, he said.

He poured out the sherry he didn't really want.

Sherry always makes me feel funny, she said. Do you think, do you think perhaps I ought?

Definitely, Connie.

She couldn't contain so much pent-up gratitude. Her hand slopped some of the sherry over the edge of the glass.

But Connie Tiarks's gratitude was not without its vein of regret, that persistent nostalgia that rises out of impossible things. It lay around her all the evening. It spoke in her glance. It lay in the neighbourhood of Elyot, almost perpetually. All the things I have never done, Connie sometimes said. There was a tinge of failure to almost every enterprise. There was the glass box she had lost in the King's Road. If I were anyone else, she said, I would have the courage to say, well, something, there are the people who always manage to convey intentions, even if no more than this, an intention. And the box had a certain value as an intention. If I were this kind of person, Connie felt.

Julia says lettuces have gone up twopence, Mrs Standish announced.

She did not know why she said this. A seeding, of lettuce, or the intellect, it was easy enough, and the things he said were tootsy, in a mauve shirt. She had listened to many anecdotes. She had listened to the prices of things. This was now conversation. But she could also hear, almost, the ticking of an eyelid. A moist mouth flowered in her sleep, the moist words of crooners, dissolving the emotions in a shower of words. There was still the pressure of his arm. Under the harsh bulbs along the Front at Brighton, she could feel the pressure of an acquired affection.

Connie said she supposed the frost

The what? asked Mrs Standish.

The lettuces, said Connie. I suppose it's all due to the frost.

In a moment, sighed Mrs Standish inwardly, I shall say it is colder for this time of year, we must condemn the lettuce and the frost, quite firmly and finally.

They were eating dinner, in a silence, in the shreds of insignificant conversation that fell plateward. Elyot was glad of this banality of conversation, just as there are moments for the carpet slippers and an easy chair. Now particularly. To relax after the glassy tension of intimacy with Muriel. So you allowed the rub of unimportant words that polished the undistinguished table, which was one of those timeless pieces his mother collected indiscriminately, or these became timeless in the jumble of a house, whether French rococo or amorphous Morris. How much these depended on his mother herself, he did not know. He looked at the offering of a face across the table, or the little that this disclosed, the cardboard face on which somebody had chalked with a flamboyant hand. It had undergone several metamorphoses. He could space the periods of his mother's face, right down to the present, and his own guilt, because it made him guilty, looking at a face, to find it suddenly lodged in the foreground on the lifting of his own indifference. People were so dependent on what you made them, lapsing through lack of attention into a state that was almost non-existence. Out of such a state, with a shock, he received a chalky, cardboard face. It was quite dead, and the words dead that fell from the dry lips, these fluttered in a chalky dust. He noticed the bluish veins in the eyeballs. She put up a hand from habit to touch her hair, that was glued round the forehead in little whorls. The curls made him sense a degree of effort he had never suspected in his mother's life.

A meeting I went to, Connie was saying. A meeting about Spain.

This passion the English have for sitting in halls, said Mrs Standish.

Because she was uneasy, under Elyot's eyes, inquiring too far, asking answers to questions that she couldn't give.

Connie looked too bright, too upright, bristling with cudgels for other people.

We have our sense of responsibility, she said.

When it suits us. Mrs Standish tapped. When it suits us to martyrize ourselves in draughty halls. Then we go to bed with a cold, and feel we've contributed something towards a cause.

It was unjust, as intentionally unjust as Mrs Standish could make a remark, that brought a smart to the eyes. Connie Tiarks held her tongue. She was very good at doing this. Circumstances had taught her it was best. She sat smoothing her woollen costume, a costume of an uncomplaining beige.

Elyot laughed. But it was not the laughter of concentration, of approval, he could not concentrate on his mother's words, these pointed nowhere, he laughed because it was the place to laugh. His mouth closed on this dubious contribution. In repose she looked like an old and rather scurvy clown, that she half recognized herself, in his eyes, they were playing out a scene between them in front of the unconscious audience of Connie Tiarks. You have seen too much, and for the first time, Mrs Standish seemed to say. The train of a gold dress surged in a molten wave across an upper landing. Or she stooped in the garden to pick off the withered heads of flowers, and the bronze skirt opened on the frozen spikes of flowers that gave it the shape and tension of part of an umbrella. Yes, you can look, said Mrs Standish, there is no longer the time, the necessity for deception. There was no longer the glitter, the early morning excitement of frost. The curtains in the dining-room had faded, leaving on a pale background a pattern of small salient sprigs.

Connie sat outside the playing of this scene. She sat and nursed the cause of Loyalist Spain. The universal problem was far distant from the personal, he felt. There was an accusing selflessness in the motion of the stumpy hands.

Mrs Standish coughed. She frowned. She swallowed down a trace of phlegm that had risen into her mouth.

We'll go into the drawing-room, she said.

Meekly enough, Connie got up and followed, the resentment clamped down, not only the resentment of an evening, but of many, but right down to childhood, her shame that spread hot and moist on Mrs Macarthy's plush couch. I am weak and despicable, she said, only the weak and despicable would return for fresh humiliation, either from Elyot or Mrs Standish, each stands in a different way for a refinement in the art of humiliating. Mrs Standish touched a switch. She transformed firelight into the familiar outline of a room. You wanted to invent an excuse, a headache or Mrs Lassiter, against the onrush of electric light. Instead you would sit, you would wait for the next twist, or to gather up an unconscious smile that he dropped for anyone to take.

There is a consuming importance about the tenderness you haven't been asked to give. It becomes the all-important. Try to reduce it to the abstract, a mere state of disinterestedness in the presence of its object, and at once it takes a shape, it becomes a string of words, the things you have formed but never said, the gesture of a hand that could illustrate, if allowed, touch a face into awareness of what it so foolishly, carelessly rejects. My dearest, my darling Elyot, wrote Connie Tiarks mentally, the many letters that mentally she tore up. Or she looked at him. It was not possible not to know, sitting within reach, that an emotional explosion might very easily take place. But looking at him she did know it was just as possible. If the Himalayas stretched between, the distance could not be greater. This brought it on again, with greater intensity, the spasm of obsession. She wondered it didn't destroy the room, bring it about their heads in a rain of fractured glass and wood.

Mrs Standish sat without composure in the Louis XV *bergère*. It was like sitting at the end of a telescope. She watched the two intensified figures of Elyot and Connie Tiarks. It was so clear, the activity of other people, right at the end of the telescope. But was it possible, seeing, to reach out and arrange? She thought not, even if she herself hadn't reached a state of preoccupation and passivity. On the edge of this the clock ticked. You watched the spidery, possessive hands.

When it was time for Connie to go, for her customary announcement, she slid forward awkwardly on her chair, she said she had enjoyed herself, it was kind, it was all pure Connie Tiarks, or what she had been taught to offer of herself. Then she went to put on her hat. It was a kind of beige tam o' shanter hat, with an apologetic, droopy bow, put there, it seemed, by accident, the whole undeniably found in a sale. You wondered sometimes, or Elyot wondered, how much a Connie Tiarks was conscious of the things she wore. Probably not. A Connie Tiarks with her selfless indignation for the lost causes. You could not imagine a Connie Tiarks dwelling on the personal detail, whether a subjective passion or just a hat. Connie's hat made him shudder. It was such an outspoken comment on her own life.

But it also drew you closer, your hand beneath her arm as you walked downstairs.

You mustn't mind Mother, he said, in an effort to console.

No, she said vaguely. Of course. After all, we know each other so well.

But still as if his voice, its intention, had touched only on the distant fringes of her mind. She was stiff with terror of his hand that provoked a trembling in her body. She was afraid of what she would do, say next. If some uncontrolled instinct would take possession, if she could provide a clue to the box she had bought and lost, then take cover in the darkness with her face and her admission.

I'm glad you have your convictions, Connie, he said.

They're not always comfortable.

Or the cold that was also your own body through the door he opened.

They were standing on a dark step. He tried to find her in the darkness, interpret through the face what he couldn't gauge by a voice. Because this seemed to be hinting at a personal life in Connie Tiarks.

Goodnight, Elyot, she said quickly. You'll catch cold.

There was no longer any shadow in her voice. It implied at once the lemon drinks she brewed for old bronchitic ladies, or a cup of Bengers by a boarding-house fire.

This after all, he said, was Connie Tiarks, and the indignation for a lost cause that she couldn't quite express. But the conviction was there, the hands twisted in the lap to a desperate yellow-white. Upstairs, taking off his clothes, he became suspended, isolated, in the lit box of his own room. It contained the whole of Elyot Standish. All the emotion, the frustration you had experienced at any time, spilled nightly into this receptacle, no farther, just as there was no intrusion from the outer darkness, none of that wash of distant events that instinctively affected Connie Tiarks. Connie overflowed, dissolved, became part of a mass emotion, that was too abstract, impersonal, you couldn't identify yourself with this. Just as you hung back on the edge of crowds. You remained intact. You could not speak the language of their emotions, share the mass sympathies and fears. You had no relationship with these.

Sleep met him half-way, or the allegory of waking, it was the Greco she had seen, the centurion in Spain, he was walking in the field which was where he lost, beyond the white cocoon, when others asked a priest, or went to Spain, there were many roads out of the field of sleep, the difficulty was to choose, there were many roads the feet took without faces, these were directionless, he was walking in a white sleep, there were the priests as white as aspirin, there was the saxophonist talking to the old ladies, the old clown, and the sleeping figures, your own, lay in the white cocoon, it was a personal Spain, it was a destruction of the superfluous, either the priest or the glass box, it could not write, write too fast, it could not write the papers black from white, this was sweat, the necessity, if I do not do this you said, if not the singing priest the no more love, the wilted brown nipples that were bitter on the mouth, and losing the face, it was the face of Joe, they had lopped the tree, it lay in blood, you could not touch, because the eyes, your eyes, became the mirror that moved too clearly to, that saw too clearly right down to the heart, and the blood moving in a cone of glass, it was the clearness that revolted, that you didn't want to see, you put up a hand to hide your own bones and a transparent, fruitless egg.

Mornings he read the paper over coffee. He shut himself in his room and worked. Outside were the house sounds, the flap of the duster, the rumble of a cistern, the creaking basket that delivered the groceries. These were no longer irritating, not like the times he ground his fists against his ears to make for himself a layer of silence against the outer world. Either you began to accept the insignificance of your own activities inside a larger pattern, or it was just plain indifference. Or not this. Indifference implied an end, and this was a period of waiting. You could feel the waiting. For a cataclysm perhaps. All round you there was pointed evidence of your own anachronistic activity. But of temporary anachronism. Like the lived moments that were gathered together again in sleep, into one vast anachronism of behaviour. It was also, in a way, a summing up, but without the finality of this. There is always the prospect of morning.

Elyot Standish failed to make much headway against a spring morning. It was the presence of a sky for the first time in months. And the sounds that you heard, or a sudden awareness of sound, of circulation renewed in the street. Against all this, the muted existence of the house. It struck a dead note that belonged to the sequence of your own perplexities, that you wanted to ignore, or the dead chalkiness of a face looming for the first time. He went downstairs. The other side of a door a cough, raucous from too many cigarettes, suggested what he would find, the ash, the tea stains on the sheet. Indifference implied an end, implied a face, which he realized for the first time was his mother's face, or what remained of it under the custom of powder and rouge. But midday made no bow to custom, became the suggestion of a face through smoke, the eyes half-doze, half-flicker, that wondered if the telephone.

He walked softly past a door.

Julia, he called. Don't wait lunch.

From the kitchen an answering of pans.

Julia? he said.

The door stood open in a steam from pans.

I probably shan't want – he said.

Julia, prodding into a pan, was the sullen, closed face that reflects the more secret events in the lives of servants. The life of Julia lay open, it had for years, it had become part of the composite life lived under the same roof. But there were also the secrecies. Her face was swollen red with them. It made you respect, without comment, whatever you weren't meant to see.

Yes, she said, not looking. All right, she said. I heard.

She could not concentrate enough on the contents of a pan looking for some answer perhaps, a steamy kitchen oracle.

He went outside. There were the streets he took, past water, chimney and water, and the little pools of mist that still lay in Battersea, close to earth or water. The world was partly soluble. There were still the faces of Julia and his mother, when the morning hinted at a structure, a form, the great chimneys pointing to their own solid importance, and the gardeners in their shiny gumboots bedding out plants in full bloom. Water wound about the paths. Close to his face a dampness of leaves. A mauve skirt reflected in water had the tone of a remembered voice, the tightly waisted tweed, he plays in a band, she said, isn't that nice? On a spring morning your own conscience was too brittle. So much was going on that was perhaps pertinent to yourself, as to other people, it was the same striving, the same desire, that linked Joe Barnett and the saxophonist in the night club voice. No more love, she sang. It settled like the mist on water. It became the unconscious comment of a conscience. It ran in syncopated undertone, behind the personal aspiration, beneath the unrelated events in evening papers, slaughter in Guernica, or the clerk hanging by his braces from a peg. And under a spring sky, the chimneys pointed at an illusion of their own solidity and greatness, gardeners pressed the earth round the roots of flowers, as if you could transform with so many heads of bloom what was a sour, sick earth.

Beyond the park were streets of houses. He preferred these to the decorated corpse, rather the closed, unseeing eyes of houses. There was a smell of cooking, of cabbage, of midday activity in the close streets. A huddle of identical houses. Like their tenants, these chose the uniform in which to ignore discrepancy.

The women ladling cabbage in their kitchens were almost interchangeable, behind the skin the identical wishes, the pale hopes, the thin desires, spoke from the closed eyes of houses. On a level both different and similar lived Muriel Raphael. He shuddered over this, or more especially the part of himself identified in Muriel. He had to recognize his effigy. Mrs Mounsey is so *aware*, said Adelaide Blenkinsop. It was one of the expressions with which she seasoned what intellectual conversation she had acquired. But Adelaide herself was singularly unaware, spoke with the mouth of death. Conversation with the Spaniard returned to him, the evening in the street after the party at Adelaide's, and his own retreat from what had been too pertinent. As if the Spaniard were presenting the choice of the two ways, of the living or the dead. You wanted instinctively to close the eyes, like Adelaide and Gerald, like Muriel, or the ranks of red suburban houses, smothered in a plush complacency. Because the alternative, to recognize the pulse beyond the membrane, the sick heartbeat, or the gangrenous growth, this was too much, even at the risk of sacrificing awareness, and the other moments, the drunken, disorderly passions of existence, that created but at the same time consumed.

This morning it was as clear as glass, if the choice no less bewildering. To recognize the sickness and accept the ecstasy. He could not walk far enough, hold the miles between himself and what he saw. Standing still, the muscles quivered, not altogether with the distance.

At home it was a sober afternoon to which the key returned him. Except that the voices, the voices he heard from the kitchen, rose, then stopped, waited. He found himself waiting outside on the landing, knew there was something that had to be faced. Now, he said. He was tired, almost indifferent.

Julia came out, her face still red, but open. He could see now, there was no denial, that Julia had been crying.

It's Joe, she said.

It might have moved at the back of his mind, her saying. Joe Barnett pitched forward, with sudden relevance, either to a dream dreamt but unremembered, or to the whole conscious morning, Joe Barnett as undertone.

He wants to see you, said Julia. He's come.

Her voice snapped.

Yes, he said. All right, Julia.

Beyond her Joe Barnett in the kitchen dressed unfamiliarly in Sunday clothes.

Come on, Joe, he said. We'll go in here.

It was almost as if all this had been expected, and you found your hand on the nearest door, the drawing-room door, by appointment. Either it was this, the prearranged, or else you were tired. It was the indifference of physical exhaustion. But he thought not.

Joe Barnett sat on an awkward chair, one of the gilt chairs that groaned, or the cloth of the Sunday suit, stretched tight, firmly, across his thighs. Joe Barnett sat holding his cap between his legs, like some peace offering for intrusion. The hands offered this before words. You could watch a rallying of words beyond the face, before they had quite assembled. But on this afternoon, unlike the other afternoon, in the room upstairs, which perhaps was why you had chosen the drawing-room now, there was no specific barrier, the tight inner constriction that comes with the wrong moment. Because there are the moments when there is no channel of communication. Nothing will open this. You are faced with the shuttered eyes, the closed skull. But not now, you felt. In repose, in silence, it was only a matter of time, and silence itself soothed, both Elyot Standish and Joe Barnett. They were closely united. The distance of the carpet was cancelled out.

I'm goin' away, Elyot, said Joe.

For the first time the name, that you did not question, it seemed natural enough. In the present state there was nothing that was not direct, expected. Unless a suspicion, the way a fear starts up, that you wanted to delay. Elyot Standish resented an intimacy that proposed at once to destroy itself.

I been thinkin'. I got to go.

The voice was heavy, as if still in the process of decision, but unguarded, it offered itself quite humbly in its process of still deliberating thought.

I'm goin' abroad, he said. To Spain.

Somewhere on a white plain, it was the Greco, it was sleep, there was the choice of paths. You remembered, just, sitting across from Joe Barnett in a more conscious present. And you waited, tensed, because something was also happening in yourself, a stirring, had been going on all day, beyond the mist that was Battersea. It was a painful emotion, the acceptance of emotion, the sickness and the ecstasy at once.

There was a time, said Joe, when I could read the papers and keep things in their place. That's where they belonged, in the papers. It was other people's business. It was foreign names. Then it got to being part of yourself. You couldn't keep out your feelings no more. It got mixed up with what you did. I can't think clear. I got to go, you see? There's no use, Julia says, there'll be time enough, and troubles of your own, without fighting other people's wars. As if you can keep it parcelled out. Because it's right here, Elyot, sure as ever there's right and wrong.

Joe Barnett smoothed a situation with his hands, helping out the inadequacy of words. He wanted to take the words with his hands, shape them the way they ought to go. Deeper than these lay the conviction that she had given him, their feet moved still over the grey grass of the common, she planted a conviction with her mouth in the shadow of the gasworks where they stood. It became the right, the wrong, that she said. It became a sickness in the stomach watching the frozen body of a dog.

I see, Joe, Elyot said.

He would speak now, say or not, when there was nothing to be said, when everything had been said or sensed.

There's a chap name of Halloran, said Joe. Used to see him at meetings. Comes from out our way. He's in Barcelona now. I got a letter from Halloran, tellin' me as what I ought to do.

He's an Irishman, but he's all right. I got to be off to catch my train. Halloran says as there's a couple of others. We're going to get together, I expect. Halloran's given me their names.

He touched his pocket, what apparently was a piece of paper, the letter from the Irish Halloran. Joe Barnett, setting off across Europe with a piece of paper, in his Sunday clothes. Already the train rocked, the light flickered, but there was no moving the intention in a face.

There's something, Elyot, the face said, something I want. There's something I thought perhaps. It's not so easy, he said.

It had gone on hammering, the nights, the not-said, the nights you lay and thought that now. Joe Barnett folded his hands. These were resigned to the impossible. He couldn't say that he loved Eden. He couldn't say what was too much. It was something that you knew. It was your own bones.

I haven't said nothing, he said. You might see her. Soon. You might say. You might say as it's all right. It'll always be all right by me. And she'll understand. There isn't nothing I'm surer of. It's just like that. But I got to, he said. It's one of these things. She'll know, because – because Eden knows.

So it boiled down to this, the folded hands, the ultimate simplicity in the silence of a room.

I got to go, said Joe. I got to catch my train.

This was no leave-taking. They might have just met. Time plays no part in intimacy. Elyot recognized Joe Barnett in a moment, in the fumbled word, and more than Joe, the many inarticulate moments of many faces, not excluding his own. A world of Joe Barnetts laid itself bare. You forgot the individual in the presence of this. After the groping behind the dry symbols of words, you experienced a sudden revelation in a shabby, insignificant room.

They sat a minute longer by agreement. They sat in silence. Then Elyot Standish was offering advice, the advice to people going abroad, the Channel and the trains. Joe Barnett fiddled with his cap. He was awkward now. He was conscious of the flow of unusual events. But his attitude was surprised, as if this were happening to someone else. At home, on coming in from work, he bent above the tin basin and washed his face. He couldn't connect himself with the other, this suspension of what he knew.

Good-bye, Joe, Elyot said.

Forms translated themselves into the more acute statement of sound. There were the voices, the doors that closed and opened, the resignation of feet, Julia in slippers returning up the stairs, the plump plump, the protest of loosely fitting slippers. All this went on beyond the room. He has gone now, Elyot said, I am standing here, why, trying to recapture what? It began to be dark. A confusion of shadow in the room. But there is still Eden, he realized. To do this. He experienced a return of exhaustion that was not entirely physical.

He had, he knew, to reach Eden on the telephone. This was imperative. There was something complacent, cynical, in the expression of the little white disc. His purpose there, what he had to say, revolved in the blurred mind, a white enamel circle.

My dear, such shoulders, she said. And the kind of red moustache, the standing-up ginger whiskers that look as if – Hello? That look as if they're just about to bite.

Two languid female voices soaped at space somewhere on a crossed line.

Thursday, he said, she said. He said a girl. Hello? We're crossed, Evelyn. Of course it's *safe, darling,* and they'll take us shopping *afterwards.*

Hello, he said. Is that –? Hello? Eden? he said.

Pitched out into the darkness, he grasped at what was no more than a fluttering, her still impersonal inquiry, fencing with the intervening voices.

Hello, said Eden. Who?

His hands began to sweat in his failure to reach a destination.

Hello, *Evelyn,* said a voice. Are you there? Of course if you'd rather a *cheque.* Somebody's in on this bloody line. I'll make it clear that a cheque. A lovely, minky cheque. One of them's Rumanian.

Then it snapped. You heard the ping ping, the glurg. You could pitch your voice, your whole soul, into the cone of darkness, to have it bandied about, a ball of ineffectual down.

Hello?

It came, Eden's voice, suddenly close inside his ear.

Eden? he said. It's Elyot. Something's happened. I've got to see –

Already defensive, he could sense, gathering, before making her reply.

I'm going out to dinner, she said.

Yes, but something. I've got to see. Just for a minute, he asked.

He waited for a silence to break.

All right. For a minute. If you think.

As if she wanted to postpone. He knew. He could see the tightening of Eden's mouth.

I'll come straight over, he said.

She was putting on her hat in a room at the back, through the shop, a small cupboard of a room, filled with the bills, the invoices, the slick publishing circulars, and a typewriter's dominating hulk. She was pulling on one of the rather shapeless, shabby, unfashionable felt hats that occasionally she chose to wear. Looking in the glass, the mouth, against its own inclination, was making this an occasion. He noticed that her mouth was red. She held her face away from him, which the glass returned in spite, the drawn, defensive expression of Eden. More than this he seldom saw, apart from the unguarded moments, the evening for instance in Crick's workshop, when Eden smouldered into a revealed existence of her own. Now the skin was haggard on her cheek, the ash of many dead emotions that he hadn't seen.

They walked out into the street. The crowd pushed her against his shoulder, associating their bodies, making a relationship. Otherwise this didn't exist. They were two unacquainted entities walking on the edge of Bloomsbury in the neighbourhood of Tottenham Court Road.

We must find somewhere, she said, somewhere for the messenger to do his stuff.

The unrelated faces of a crowd were more personal than Eden's voice. The face of a woman billowed, its pale paper bag, and the mouth greasy from fried fish. You could almost smell the scarlet neon, a hot smell of the synthetic oil, with the gusts of violet from an amusement arcade.

It was always the messenger, she said, who had the best bit of the play.

She turned, thoughtful, to face what she couldn't avoid.

Where do you want? she asked.

Let's go somewhere quiet, he said.

They stood in a draught of buses. Their feet planted, they were the one static, deliberating point in an otherwise volatile neighbourhood. If you excepted thought. Her mind, beyond the eyes, he saw, floated with surmise.

Is it that kind of a message? she asked.

Well, he said, played for time. It's not what you –

Then we'll go in here, she said quickly. At least we shall find noise.

Which was not so much perversity as Eden taking cover. He followed her, drawn in beyond the door, into the white glare, the aching marble planes of the Tottenham Court Lyons. She walked very straight to the table that she picked out. The orchestra was playing Grieg as if it had never stopped, from the last time, and the time before, this was as permanent as marble, 'Anitra's Dance' in Lyons.

Coffee, she said. Two coffees. Oh, she said. White? Yes. White.

But this was of secondary importance, beside the convention of coffee. Coffee was the price of confession, of confidence, of imparted knowledge. The undrunk, cooling coffee on the tables at Lyons, this poured in torrents down the ages, he felt, generously overwhelming the exchanged remarks.

Now, she said, looking, trying to read in the pale contents of a cup. Now you can fire away.

His fingers moved by strings. A rheumaticky *pizzicato* that was Grieg.

Joe came to see me, he said in a breath.

Sugar for a moment disturbed her cup. She sat and watched it disappear.

He wanted me to tell you he was leaving for Spain. He dropped in on his way. He wanted me to tell –

It rose at her in a surge, out of the milky pretence of coffee, the paralysing wave of violins. A train went rocketing across a marble field, over the darkened plain of France. It racked her body, the sharp physical spasm she could feel. As if at first the memory of the physical were the most difficult to bear, the body looming again in the shadow of the gasworks, or the white light of frost on a sleeping shoulder. She wanted to protest. Because this must not be taken away. She wanted to resist with her hands. When there was no tangible object to which you could protest, except the dull slabs of distant marble. Falling asleep at night in trains, she felt the world crumble. There was very little substance in the world. A cold star, flat as the star on a Christmas tree. At night the trains whistled into air, and the face jolting southward, under the skin the suspended blood. Walking over dead grass, she talked about right and wrong, glibly, as abstract concepts. But this was the expression of rightness, the southward face, the beginning in an end, rather than the end of a beginning. If you could accept the personal end. She had to, had to cultivate acceptance. There is no Eden Standish, just as there is no Joe Barnett, you said. There is more than this, there is the stock of positive acts and convictions that two people infuse into the dying body of the world, their more than blood. Then she closed her eyes. She could not accept the blood, the torn face of Guernica. Because I am in love, she would have said, I shall die if this is taken away.

Elyot, she said.

She was asking him to take control. Without touching, she gave him her hand.

I was going out to dinner, she said. I'd rather, I think I'd rather we went home.

18

Wally phoned her. He'd been running around. Irons in the fire, he said, you couldn't afford, and after the Vendôme, it was a racket where you had to think quick, and Harry Simmons, a contract, he hoped that she wasn't mad.

No, she said. No.

She gave him back a monosyllable from which all trace of expression had been carefully extracted. The body spread without symmetry in the bed, drooped, the breasts, at eleven o'clock, the body had not yet taken on a shape. Out of the sheets a scent of sleep still drifted to overpower the senses. Mrs Standish was grateful for her bed. She had let it take possession of her. Its form was easy, yielding, if second-best, she preferred its passivity as she did her own. Only the bell rang in her ear, and this stirred, disturbed, raked up the emotions she had hoped dead. Under the taut shape of a monosyllabic reply, the throat tightened. Her complacency had drained right to the bottom of the bed.

No, she said. Why? You're your own master.

He missed this. It was too close.

Listen, he said, ignoring. There's a party Sunday night. A couple of girls I know up in Maida Vale. They'd be glad if you could come.

Mentally, a row of glossy mouths offered an unwilling invitation. Mrs Standish closed her eyes.

Eh? he asked, waiting. Kate? Are you there? What do you say?

If she could have rung off, to assist the lapse of will. Because there are moments when it's no good, the better judgment.

Yes, she said. If you'd like. If it'd give you pleasure, she said.

Now, he said, you're mad. I been busy. Honest, Kate. A man's got to go places, get around.

She could see him scratching his forehead, the hat pushed back, somewhere in a booth, the coin had dropped. She could not argue at eleven o'clock. She thought she would never argue again.

Yes, she said. It'd be fine, Wally.

Just as he had taught her. She heard the record grinding out. O.K., Kate. That's swell. Sunday night at ten o'clock.

Goodbye, Wally, she said.

Standing in the booth, he breathed freer, the kind of free breathing that comes with a sense of duty satisfied. His chin was still black that he scratched, a stubble from the night before. But he felt good. It was the morning sounds. It was the slick scurrying of legs he eyed, the silk stretched tightly over calves. Wally Collins began to stroll. He had a kind of glow when satisfied. A door opened in his mind, her hand, come in, she said, why, Mr Collins, for goodness sakes, in all this time, no I haven't forgotten the Metropole, Harry's out at the moment, if you'll stick around. In those pyjamas with initials on the doings, the A D embroidered on the skin, sort of Chinese and spidery and black. She spoke about her work out of a chocolate nougat, and a highball if he liked, and she didn't mind, no she didn't mind, but he had to fix it with plenty of ice. London was sort of funny, she said. Quaint. She was nuts on anything old. And quaint. Only once before, and not professionally, she said, to Poland with her mother, her family was Polish, and the name. He listened to a Polish explosion in chocolate nougat. That was before Harry changed it into Delaware, of course. That was before a silence. A D on oyster satin moved with his own breathing. Chocolate glistened on a wet mouth.

Wally Collins began to whistle. He turned down Shaftesbury Avenue. He loitered by the Monico. And then the afternoon she let him put his hand. No, she said, you're fresh, you boys are all the same. Go on, Alice, he said. She did. Wally Collins expanded in the morning just outside the Monico.

A man was only human, he said. He did no harm to Anyone, calling on the phone, and flowers, and the party Sunday night. The Boys said: Here comes Collins, stepping out on the Old Girl, hiya, Wally, how's the clover? That got to making him sore. It made you sort of foolish. It made him turn up his collar in the street. Because he was still fond, you had to respect the Old Girl, what she stood for and all that, she had the class the others hadn't, she had the answers you didn't understand, that was education, books, but, gee, it sometimes got you down, and sometimes sudden on the bed, well, there was a place for everything, and an A D on satin near where it showed through. Wally Collins had to sigh. As if he had something on his mind, as if he heard the morning burst, its bright, skyward balloon. What price the Old Girl? the Boys said. If anyone figured he was letting her down, well, and so what, and a man was human. Wally Collins moved from his corner, could not step too carefully, not to hurt of course, but to move, out of reach of a sagging face.

Mrs Standish reached out from the bed and picked up a mirror, the silver mirror, dimpled now with many dents, more than its pattern of irises, that Willy gave. She was looking at her face in a mirror, or the past, the succession of aspects that became the final article. Outwardly it is quite awful, she said, *but*. Pinning your faith to a conjunction, it was still small comfort, the excuse of some inner distinction, if this existed at all, she doubted. She rootled about in her mind to find some consolation, among the cabbage stalks a handful of withered epigrams. At the farm, it was '16, and Rémy, the droop-eared sow rootled after cabbage stalks. What's-his-name talking about Love, something neatly waiting on a plate, spoke from a small, nervous moustache, or evening, the book of sonnets. In your nose the sharp, sour smell of pig's dung from a French farm. You reached down and dredged up the pale cabbage stalks, which were what remained, and it had never been convincing, the distinction of the mind, something that a girl in an upper room in Norwich copied before supper into a book. Inclination was to live outwardly, like a face. There were the people who lived outwardly, altogether, without a backward glance. There were the girls, the parties in Maida Vale. These could make you touch rock bottom, sink a face right to the bottom of a mirror.

Because you couldn't yet accept, though it was still early morning, you said, the volcanic skin, the grease that lay in the valleys of the nose, that you had to own, the tousled accusation of a face, it was almost sub-human, or else an accentuation of the human, it was this perhaps that hurt. It was this more than Wally Collins. There was no longer any Wally Collins. There was the composite regret that rose up to confront the too concentrated human mess, to which time had reduced a face. It made you stiffen under the blankets. Because there was still the question of hiding, Sunday he said, the regret that pointed to defeat.

Sunday rang gong-like through the week.

This will be decisive, said Mrs Standish.

She could not do too much. She could never do too much before parties. Even after death, felt Mrs Standish, I shall overdo the preparations for a party, both emotional and otherwise. A party is an orgy of anticipation. And this, this will be the archetype of parties. Something apart from Maida Vale, because, after all, a party is not a matter of environment, it is something that happens in yourself, it is a supreme statement of your capacity for power.

Yes, said Mrs Standish. There was no need to hurry. There was time to feel, to taste, the first contact of the skin with silk, of the old dress with the older body, that somehow became the first time. She wore the red dress, or not altogether red, a kind of rose, anyhow reddish. There were times when she had regretted this dress. It was a jangle, a mistake. But she had to wear the rose, the reddish dress. She had to wear it for Maida Vale, her own discordancy, and the weight of gold, too heavy, sawing at her neck. The spilt powder made the eyes water.

Out of a rising cloud, the face. You worked on a face, deeply. You couldn't penetrate deep enough, the hand, force the colour into a mouth. You wanted to make and to destroy at once. The hair was brittle and expectant in its labyrinth of curls.

A jangle, said Mrs Standish.

It was not criticism. It was a pure objective statement offered to the glass. She felt better. She held herself tense and still under the weight of red and gold. She listened to the notes of her own discordancy.

Wally said she looked, looked, gee, she looked.

Thank you, Wally, she said, to help, her mouth driven by irony inside the warm smooth paste of rouge.

He began to make apologies. He began to repeat himself, the excuses on the telephone, he had been awful busy, Wally said.

We are going to a party, she said, adapting her body to the taxi.

Sure, he said. But –

Then why?

Telling him he ought to let it drop, he was still preoccupied. Because Kate. And getting herself up to kill. Already his eyes made excuses to people. He didn't want it too close, the accusing nearness of a thigh in the taxi.

She breathed with the excitement that comes before contact with fresh faces, even if Maida Vale, with the anticipation of unfamiliar sounds, and already the opening of a door. The taxi rattled. It had the smell of all taxis she had ever driven in.

Names are Kay and Molly, he was saying. Molly's a photographic model. Kay's a pianist. Broadcasts. Gets an occasional date with an orchestra. You'll like Kay, he said. And Molly, she's a hot number, but she's grand. A bit thin perhaps. Kay's mother's sick. She lives in Birmingham.

Irrelevant as Wally's conversation was in itself, it was also without relevance to Mrs Standish. She accepted the incongruous Kay, and the mother, a middle-aged woman with an enamel basin, wedged into a house, in a terrace, in the Midland

317

town. Rocked by the taxi, they spun, round them the night-time expressions on the shops near Marble Arch. You didn't move, they unwound, the details of a street, or of conversation, and it was all a kind of special benefit. A nickel urn blossomed in a doorway, in a steam of coffee, and flared out of sight.

Molly and Kay, they share this flat. Kay's got a guy, a racing motorist. He'll be the one with the broken nose. Name of Arthur Chance. You should see the cups and things he's got.

You should hear the, you should see yourself, you should see the face of Aubrey Silk. Mrs Standish sat up to resist the rocking of the taxi-cab. It went with a beat, the voice, the cab, that was not unlike the rhythm of the saxophone. And this, she knew now, was something that had always made her afraid, blowing from some country where she had never really been. She wondered also what she could say to Kay and Molly.

Then the meter jarred, she heard.

Wally began to whistle, as if he was nervous. He whistled thinly up the stairs, over the basic threads that were showing through the carpet nap. On the first floor a smell of canned tomato soup, above, on the second, the noises that the door just failed to contain.

This is it, said Wally, or his tie, it came out chinward, cannoned off an arranging hand.

You waited. You waited for a bell to connect. You searched for your lost personality.

Why, *Wally!* screamed the open door.

As if she was surprised. Or perhaps she would always be surprised. This was part of her policy.

Hello, Molly, I want you to meet, this is Mrs Standish, he said.

Mrs Standish put out a hand, touched a hand that was too cool.

Come and let's see, Molly said. They're all stinking, but you won't mind. They're –! Oh, pardon. Wally, whatever will your friend –?

Not that it mattered in so many eyes. Molly walked with assurance, inside the limitations of gin, threading a way, that dictatorial behind, and three white carnations that she wore on top of her head.

Oo-oo, Molly called. Here's Who's-This. You wouldn't *know!*

Shouted, it was only a small contribution to what the room already held, the walls groaning, you felt, flapped to the gramophone, faces formed with some ingenuity in smoke.

If it isn't that sucker Collins!

Hello, Kay. Hello, Arthur.

And you're Mrs Standish, she said.

More sultry than the white carnations, she was also more explorative. Kay, of the sick mother, visualized a physical fact.

No, really, well, said Kay.

Wally's told me about you, she said. In between talking about himself.

Hey, wait on, Kay.

He tried to stop her mouth. She let him.

Mrs Standish stood on her own small island, realized that all activity had ceased, apart from the gramophone, its hiccuping over an endless scratch, all activity flowed just so far, up to her own shore. She was responsible for this. It was satisfying in a way, even if that way, as she gathered, was detrimental to herself. She listened to a blues hiccuping. She looked at the fingers that had clicked a time, frozen by her to an attitude, smiles still unaimed above a glass, waiting, waiting for release. They waited for something that she didn't know how to give, their secret sign that she hadn't learnt. Evenings she had spent at home returned, Mme de Sévigné and lime flower tea. There were the two shores. Then somehow she had fallen into midstream. Feebly, she watched, saw herself not even struggle, drift on the sweet smell of gin, the smell of fish paste under curled bread, the smell of powder over body. On the mantelpiece were a pair of inordinately ugly elephants.

Gin or whisky? Molly asked.

Gin, she said helplessly.

She lingered, she couldn't help it, there was a fascination in the elephants, their red and silver sides, and the howdahs stuffed with rubbish.

Those are for luck, Molly said. He left me three weeks afterwards.

Things began to happen again, perhaps a change in the gramophone, anyway, things took up where they left, you were sucked under, you perched yourself on the arm of a chair, visibly but not mentally, you revolved in the little eddies, the sticky stream, bubbles in your nose, it was the first smart of gin, or a laugh, which was a contribution to what you imagined was the Party Spirit, the man in the paper cap, he had lost his chin, the Funny Man, he bobbled the gold tassel on his cap and everybody laughed.

The springs on the sofa pinged.

Saw Alice, Kay said.

She watched. She was the slow, dark, watching type, soft and creamy, with sympathetic eyes. She watched Wally Collins with a slow, dark smile.

What about Alice? he asked.

Nothing. I just said. I'm at liberty to say I saw Alice.

You can skip Alice, he said.

He got going on the gin. He was a bit afraid, well, you couldn't expect, and someone like the Old Girl, though what the hell in that red dress, as if she had done it to shame you, and bringing her into a joint like this. Jesus Christ, I'm crackers, he breathed. But there was always gin.

I think she's swell, said Kay.

What?

This one. The red dress. What's her name? Kate. I'm going over to talk to Kate.

You know how to keep off the grass, Kay?

Listen, have I been around!

But you couldn't tell if a woman, if a sympathetic woman like Kay, oh hell, it was getting you down.

Help yourself to gin, Wally.

That's just what I was doing, he said.

He picked his way, to trip, almost. It was Arthur Chance's mechanic, who was almost fried. Lumped in his chair, he looked at Molly, or at one carnation waved above his face. He was small, and puny, with many moles.

One more mole and you'd fly, said Molly. Look, Collins, isn't he sweet? He's my baby. My real own baby. Isn't he playful?

She popped a carnation in an open mouth. He closed his eyes.

If my baby isn't a pain, she said. You ought to go and chase yourself.

Mrs Standish clung to her rock, her chair-arm, had tilted her head, her smile, as much as to say, now I am prepared, with the throat a sweet, harsh channel of gin swallowed too anxiously. She was very conscious of her glowing throat. It had solidity. All the rest had drifted away, sifted in a blue stream, except the two elephants, these were static, solid too.

I shall call you Kate, Kay said, smiled, the eyes closed up, then opened, too interested, too close. Now, Kate, what can I get you? A li-tle sandwidge? It was nice of you to come, Kate. I'm interested in people, of course. I've got to know about people. And that gives me such a lot. Ever had your horoscope done, Kate?

No, said Mrs Standish, much too gaily. I hate to know too much.

Then her mouth stuck in a smile, just so far and no farther, she couldn't get it back. She began to push into her mouth, to hide it, what she believed was a sandwich, but some pale, anonymous food that had lost its identity from lying about at a party.

Duckie, you'll never know too much.

The hand squeezed. And those sympathetic eyes. A woman's woman. But there was the broken nose, and the cups, that Wally said, said a racing motorist. My lover is a racing motorist. If you collected things, if you had an album, if there were still time. Oh dear. Mrs Standish returned remorsefully, gave two-thirds of her attention to a creamy face.

You ought to, Kay said.

Ought I? What?

You ought to have your horoscope. I should say you were a Venus subject. I'm a Venus subject. That's why I've had such a terrible time. And, now mother's sick, she said. That was in the stars. I'd go crazy if it wasn't for Arthur. And my work. Arthur makes me feel I'm not a plaything. That's the danger in a Venus subject. A victim of the passions. But Arthur. Mrs Standish, Kate, I love Arthur, body and soul.

You could have cried the gramophone it sank down and stroked the carpet it surged upward through the warm throat faces were bluish a gin bluish and the words the bubbles in gin the gold tassel the bobble bobble on a cap he had been waiting said to make your acquaintance without a chin to dance to push against a body she said a soul she said it was not a quiver of refusal you accepted a phrase you accepted anything after a point your own abject collapse.

What's that for? asked Mrs Standish.

She flicked the bobble on a cap.

That, he said, 's for girls to hit.

For the girls, the girls of Maida Vale. She was not quite one, and she had to show, she had to do something to show, to show she was all right. There was an old whore she had seen once, in a cellophane hat, who went to meet the late trains at Victoria.

I want another drink, she said.

Things were happening. There was Biddy, they said, tough, could stand on her head and drink two pints of beer.

Go on, Biddy, they said.

As the legs waved against the wall, all legs, and hair, suspended in the sea, the silence, which was breath held, over this the gurgle in a pewter pint, was Number One, and Number Two, it was tense waiting for the last sigh, that fell back with a last trickle into the empty pot. It released the noise, you clapped, felt the sting, of skin, of gin, a clapping in the ears.

Two bodies, interweaving on a sofa, traced a soft adagio in music. The carnations, which were now two, almost toppled from a head, that poised, swayed, searching for a climax in a mouth.

Praps I love you, Collins. Wouldn't that be awful? Molly said. You're lovely, you're lovable, she sang.

Only two china elephants on a mantelpiece stayed put. The rest flowed. Wally on the sofa with that girl, the tassel on a paper cap, the sympathetic horoscope. But you could focus on the elephants, their ugliness, they brought you up with a sudden shock.

Come into the kitchen, Kate, said Arthur Chance. Just you an' me. We'll have such a fish fry. Oh baby!

The white stove was a glare that the broken nose cut through and the bottle of vinegar or something that he knocked over, she watched it darkening over her dress. She looked down and laughed. Because it was not important.

Nice dress, he said.

The hand touched. She could hear the scrape of his hand on her dress, the rasping against silk, the callus on a hand.

Let's dance, he said. You an' me.

She sang. No more love, she sang. Then they fell against the table.

Kate, why haven't we? he said. Why haven't –?

He was on the floor, she saw, he lay there, the face bracketed by a nose, pained and at the same time content. She watched him inquisitively. Then she began to tiptoe, softly, softly, as if she must not wake.

Kate, he sighed.

Ssh, she said. You're asleep.

She couldn't tiptoe softly enough, as if the whole world were asleep on the kitchen floor. She tiptoed through her own sleep. Before the door made her head spin. She put up her hands, to hold with her hands what, she suspected, was spilling out. Her head split open on a door.

Somebody was laughing in another room. An elephant pointed with his trunk.

I am drunk, said Mrs Standish. This was once dreadful, is now unimportant, whether you peel off just another skin, or tip the table or, vinegar perhaps, it smelt the finger, H.P. or Worcester Sauce, Julia said she would run round the corner to the Internash, it was half an hour to lunch. Julia, Julia's eye, Julia said was drunk. Julia looked at a glass of gin. You want the doctor, she said. It hurt. But what was Julia, what was the will, it was the pamphlet said the Universal Will, or Cosmos Something, you only half understood. There was no will. There was no Julia really. Julia said: Wash your hands, you dirty boy. It was none of Julia's business, was never had been, anyway.

I've always hated ordering meals, Mrs Standish said.

Confided mostly to her glass, it came back in a bluish echo off its sides.

Boo-hoo, ber-boo-boo, sang Mrs Standish to her glass.

The Paper Cap was telling a dirty story to the girls. It was something about a motor bike.

Mrs Standish closed her eyes. If for a moment sleep. But I am doing this, she said, I I I, because I have chosen to do this, it is nobody's business that nobody cares. The song went what? It ran like that nerve that ticked underneath the face, till this was what you became, a last filament in a transparent bulb. Not Catherine Standish. Not this. Tear up the labels, throw them away, look in the ice-box, baby. That little thing, Ruby May, that they all went to see, the people in newspapers, round in a dressing-room afterwards. With their labels on. Because without the labels, they wouldn't perhaps recognize a face. If it were still recognizable, even to yourself, and beyond this, that you didn't want to see, the old droop-eared sow that rootled after cabbage stalks.

It frightened her back for a moment into a state of almost control. Over on the mantelpiece an elephant's trunk had begun to move.

If Elyot could see now, she felt. If Elyot. Because Elyot can see more, more than you like to feel, knowing, more than you like to admit.

Everybody laughed. It was the motor bike. Biddy told the one about the girl who lost her cami-knickers in the train.

Wally, said Mrs Standish.

She had to grope now, her words, his arm, her hand groping like a monkey's along his sleeve.

Yeah? he frowned. What's wrong?

Elyot mustn't know, she said. Elyot must never.

You're mopey, he frowned. Have another drink. Hey, Molly, give the Old Girl another gin.

Just when the party began to go, it made him mad, and nice and warm and matey, with a girl in hand, so many girls in so many hands, not that the Old Girl, gee, and a big blue bump on the side of her face.

Whatcha gone and done? he asked.

Nothing, she said. I don't care. If only Elyot.

Am I telling this story, or aren't I? Biddy asked.

I shall tell the story of my life, announced Mrs Standish.

We want new ones, Biddy groaned.

There is nothing new, said Mrs Standish. Or does that sound Chinese? Translated from the Chinese.

Listen, dear, Biddy said, I should just say plain Chinese.

You're the one who drank the beer? Well, I shall tell the story of my life without standing on my head. There are a great many stories, but this is the one story, the authentic version. Even if it's dull. Even if I'm drunk. Did, did you know, Wally, I'm drunk? You needn't tell me because I know. I know all the answers before they're made. Yes, even on the telephone. From sitting in a room. Have you ever sat in a room and heard your joints crack about five o'clock? Because that's the story of my life.

Psssss! Biddy said. Throw out the body, someone, do.

Say, she's sick, said Wally. Don't take no notice. She ain't well.

I've never been more lucid, said Mrs Standish.

Though she couldn't pick up her voice. It lay a long way off among the crumpled sandwiches. She was the frayed end of cigarette, the greenish-yellow olive stone, these were the remains of Catherine Standish, if only they would cremate these, she felt. More desperate was the voice, that she couldn't stop, it thrumped, it thrumped, the many stations passed by trains. And the sickness in her stomach.

I used to think, the voice groped – I used to think it would be un – unbearable to be lucid. Believe it? It was the men. They like the kind of things you say. They like to help you out. The number of hours I've spent listening wouldn't fit on that clock. Oh dear, no. That was before, before anything happened. See my face? I'll let you into a secret. That's post-dated, she said.

She nodded very wisely, a smear of mascara and a blaze of rouge.

But that isn't the worst, she said, the mouth taking control. It's happening inside. It all happens from the inside out. Now listen, you see I've thought about this. Whether it's an apple or a spinning top. It goes rrrrr. Bbpp! Take it from me. I know. Spinning and spinning and spin –

That the voice broke the thick gelatinous effort to talk or think it was the last shred the red put on for a purpose that was lost that was a purpose you looked to find on the carpet the big booming rose bury your face and hide bury the sick tick.

Take it easy, she heard.

It was not so far to the carpet, kneeward, to lay down a head, and the roaring funnel of a mouth.

Mrs Standish pitched forward, a red and golden meteor that was past directing, even if this had been desired. She wanted only to get on her knees and vomit. She had to throw up on the carpet the last fragments of her dignity. And lie. To find in the moving darkness some solid portion that did not quake. She fell where her body led her, the closed eyes. She lay on her side like a deck chair that the wind has overturned.

Somebody will have to take me home, she said quietly, without opening her eyes.

19

Outside the houses there was spring weather again. In the parks you were conscious of the change, the intent but diffident duck, floating brown and secretive in the lap of water, or moored in the shallows, her breast close against the mud. There was a pressure outward, earth and tree, of shoot and bud, a thawing of frost in the otherwise passive brick of the closed pavilion. It was expected and at the same time unexpected in its happening. It is always like this. It approaches you unawares. A soft, smooth wind venturing through boughs and along the cheek. You put up a hand to a cheek, wonder, the fingers just unable to grasp so subtle a situation.

For Elyot Standish this remained a distant, outer situation. The month on the calendar told him it was a period of change. It was also a regular event. You could leave it to take care of itself, the other side of your own preoccupation. But closer home, there was no such clockwork certainty. There was logical development in the progress of a season, but you could not say the same of human behaviour. Man deliberately shrouded himself, to hide his uncertainty perhaps, anyway, motive appeared obscurely the other side of the gauze, the faces of people you came in contact with, these if anything were most remote, the lives that touched on your own.

He went into his mother's room.

I've wasted so much time reading Saint-Simon, she said. I find he doesn't please me any more. Sometimes I wonder how much will remain at the end, how much positive time to chalk up against the waste. And does one regret the waste, or is it just a matter of indifference?

A book lay on the sheet. He listened to his mother's voice,

his mother talking like a book. She held out so many phrases in front of the expression on her face, that still spoke of the evening on the stairs. You hadn't mentioned this. But it remained implicit in the expression of a face, more so now that this had no assistance from the dressing-table. You have seen what you have seen, the face of Mrs Standish seemed to say, accept it as a fact, without asking for an explanation, explanations are tiring and involved. So that you hadn't spoken in so many words. It remained a garish incident. You remembered how the head lolled, she just wasn't well, he said, it was the saxophone, and on the stairs, the breath came out harshly, out of the smeared mouth.

This should be understandable, Elyot sometimes felt. If one had been aware. If one had not taken refuge in one's own private shell.

Now he watched a hand, listless on the cover of a book.

It is too tiring, too involved, implied the hand. Let us abandon this incident, if we can. There is a whole atticful of the sordid mistakes. Let us put it among these.

But he remembered, she remembered the evening on the stairs, how the head lolled, the eyes opened, watched the trailing of a red skirt, the arm brushing the carpet, as if it had no connexion, or at least sawdust-filled. The eyes had watched from a distance, dim in their own surprise. Now they deliberately created a distance, or hung a gauze over what they couldn't hide.

Mrs Standish had withdrawn since the evening in Maida Vale. She spent much time in bed. She lay there with a book, or just looking at the wall. She could lie there for hours, as if her moral collapse had exhausted physical initiative. Not that she didn't welcome a withdrawal into the hours of silence. You might say she wanted to come to a conclusion, was engaged in an elaborate and final summing up. At least the face suggested this, unmoved, withdrawn on the pillow, and the slow voice that spoke because expected. No longer painted, the face was no particular age. The bones of a face have in themselves a timelessness, a resignation.

If this could be the last stage, sighed Mrs Standish. Was it too much to ask for, to prolong the state of quiet withdrawal, or was there still another spasm of the body, before the final twitch? On the wall a pale sunlight had reproduced the window frame. She lay in her bed watching the patch of sunlight, its elongated, abstracted form, glass and wood that had turned to light and shadow. Or she moved in retrospect, not through the actual images of memory, this had undergone abstraction too, become the light and shadow, the sensation of an incident. If you could ask for the permanence of this, but you doubted, the fists suddenly defensive on the sheet. Or more, you knew. You remained tied to the body, to its final writhing, you felt the hand groping in the belly, the mouth gaped in an endless scream. There was no exaggeration in the engraving out of Dante that disturbed the childhood Sunday.

Eden had cried. Eden as a child. Now she came into the room. It is Sunday, Eden said, I shall take a train into the country. There were still compartments in time, there was other people's behaviour. But Eden has lived behind a closed door, right from the beginning, felt Mrs Standish. I shall catch a train, Eden said. You had just a glimpse through the voice, through the crack in the door.

Eden Standish walked quickly. There was great virtue in the anecdotal voice of the slow and easy Sunday trains, in the strip of sky and field outside that flapped across the window-pane. There was the old man with the joints, he had the rheumatism awful bad, he had a potato in his pocket, he wore a skein of scarlet silk. The knitting woman clucked her teeth. Beside her on the seat the pot of jam, with damson purpling the paper top. Her niece was expecting her seventh, she said. The teeth clucked. The needles clicked. You listened to the counterpoint of voices. You let them brush across the edge of the mind, soothing, this faint contact with the lives of other people that asked for no more than momentary attention, in the convention of train acquaintanceship. You were glad of this. Because you were still unprepared to give very much in return. But the train acquaintance made no demands, was as warm, and yet as passionless, as the wool played out and knitted up by the discursive hands.

Out of this, on a Sunday in spring, Eden Standish got down into a still countryside that the change in season emphasized. She heard her feet too clearly on the asphalt strip, the station-master's country voice calling from his toy official hutch. She walked up a hill, and the rim of the hill was too sharp, the ribbony song of larks too close that fluttered up, then lost itself in the pale, spring sky. She was walking with her hands empty in a world that was too full. Once, by the side of the road, the abandoned rags, the stamped earth of what had been a tinkers' camp caught her unawares. She had to hurry. As if someone had lived here too fully. She could sense it still. The throat tightened on recognition of what had once been her own. Farther, a hundred yards or so, she could look dis-passionately enough at the drops on brambles. But the uneasy moment experienced, remained. She closed her eyes, stood with her forehead resting on wet bark, listened to the muffled beating of tree or heart.

Out of this world you could feel a purpose forming. Just as she had seen, after refusing, a purpose that formed behind his eyes. It was not a malicious desire to annihilate that cancelled the personal relationship, that bound the earth in its harder seasons. The stripping of the bough was a sacrifice of detail to some ultimate and superior design. To dictate this to the heart, impress it on the mind, is necessary, she felt. Bark was cool on her forehead. I have to accept, to believe this, she said, because it is the only way, I must blot out all memory of touch, or the more intimate moments of silence.

On an afternoon in spring, Eden Standish came to this con-clusion. On the same afternoon, about dusk, when it was time to draw the curtains, her mother opened her eyes and said:

I think I am going to die, Julia.

Into the room came the scattering sound of curtain rings.

What a thing to say! Julia said, her voice shocked, because there were things you didn't joke about.

There was no answering Julia. You knew already that Julia had rejected what she wasn't willing to accept. As if by her rejection she would remove any possibility.

Let me shake up your pillow, Julia said.

But Mrs Standish knew now. It was more than an intuition. It was what she had suspected, dreaded most, this warning of what must follow the period of passive peace of mind. Out of an increasing pain flickered the engraving from the bookcase, the snakes she could remember, and the mouth prised open by an endless agony. She could feel the hair moist at her forehead. At night the darkness screamed a protest.

Elyot, she said. We must – I think I ought to have a doctor.

They shared for a moment what was too uncomfortable a state of intimacy. She did not look. She could sense. Somebody coming to a conclusion. Illness had peeled away the outer skin. She could watch things beating through a final membrane.

You ought to have said, he began weakly.

Yes, but I didn't. And Elyot, dear, don't let us talk, I am too tired. All my life I have done the things I oughtn't to. If I have done it once again, even if it's once too often, it's only logical. You must forgive me, dear.

He watched something immense, final, and at the same time too simple to be grasped, happening in his mother's face. Without the repetition of what she had said to Julia, he knew now, accepted the fact that she would die. It was, as she suggested, inevitable, logical. At least, this was what you had to cultivate, a belief in inevitability.

Elyot rang up the doctor, a Dr Leigh, who had appeared for years when necessary, a tall, stooping man, with dry, papery hands. It suddenly occurred to him now, waiting on the telephone, that Dr Leigh might have an existence of his own outside the periodical visits, was being dragged away perhaps from a boiled-muttony phase of that existence in his dark, mahogany dining-room. Dr Leigh would come, he said. You returned the receiver to its bracket, cut off a smell of caper sauce. You clung too willingly to a whiff, to an image, to a word, anything that the imagination offered in place of. Elyot Standish began to wait. The private existence of Dr Leigh flickered, was extinguished. Through a door you listened to a long sigh that was either pain or weariness.

Later you listened to the dry, papery rubbing of hands, to a voice searching for requisite words.

It was best to be prepared, said Dr Leigh, tossing a platitude, you felt, as a cushion on which to let fall the harder statement, to deaden the sound of this.

Elyot listened to a diagnosis. All this was happening to someone in the room above. It was his mother. A lamp, a book open on a table, made a corner of unreality in the drawing-room. The voice was slowly intensifying this, talking about disease, one of those cases, it said, of some standing, in which the pain was confined to the last few weeks. There would be a second opinion, of course, the voice concluded doubtfully. He was being told that his mother had a cancer. He was being told what he knew already, that his mother was going to die. But the corner of unreality persisted, the still life of a book, a lamp, the Louis XV *bergère*. The chair gave it a more personal tone that he wanted to avoid.

All one can do, I'm afraid, is to make her comfortable. I shall send a nurse, the doctor said.

A phrase that had been dealt out before, many times, to many people, depersonalized, anaesthetized. Mrs Standish become *the patient*. Seeing a doctor to the door, Elyot was suddenly horrified. It was not so much the prospect of death, the end of physical existence, it was this sudden draining of the personality which events, people, conspired to bring about. You couldn't allow it. Then you were standing on the darkened doorstep, listening to the steps of Dr Leigh return to another phase of his own personal existence, the mutton, the mahogany, out of the zone he had just depersonalized.

Elyot went upstairs.

He was left with death in the house. It was something that happened to other people, that you couldn't associate, except at moments of acutest intuition, with yourself or people round you. The idea of death, of his mother's death, was something he still had to carry round in his mind, constantly referring to it, before he could convince himself that this was more than idea, an actual and pressing fact. In and out of the process of persuasion wove the incidents, the images, all those moments with which she was connected, and it seemed now there were few with which she was not. She had taken possession in the way the dying possess the living.

He went and sat for a little in her room.

The doctor's sending a nurse, he said.

A nurse, she said, is always either too aggressive or else too apologetic. It's always a case of extremes.

But this was offered to no particular ear, the voice a little stiff, you would have said waiting for something to happen. I am waiting to die, Mrs Standish seemed to say, we are not sure what this is, but soon we shall know, as much as we are allowed to know, there is very little we have seen except dimly.

A nurse came to the house. She was known as Sister Chadwick. She had cold, mottled, adept hands. She had come, said Julia, who found a comfort in narrative, she had come from nursing a theatrical manager, there had been champagne for supper, and a bracelet. There was a friend of Miss Chadwick's, Julia said, had a minx coat from a patient, and a suite at the Savoy. Remembering, beyond her narrative, Julia plodded past the door in sagging satin slippers, the slippers that Mrs Standish had never dared to speak about. Without its envelope of narrative, Julia's mind got panicky. She sat in the kitchen with a cup of tea. She drank the strong, bitter tea, and resented the arrival of the white Miss Chadwick to sterilize a needle.

We'll take this bowl, Julia, said Miss Chadwick. Thank you, yes. And now some water if it's on the boil. *Thet's* it! Just a teeny drop more.

Julia objected to Miss Chadwick, who bounced like a rubber ball, and her superiority, that at the same time attracted, her store of knowledge, her knowledge of illness and death. For Julia, death was a varnished coffin and a pair of white marble hands, but for Miss Chadwick a colourless, airy something that opened quickly, suddenly in a room. Sometimes Julia cried. She cried for the things she began to remember, there was no end to the things she remembered now, her own life seemed to be attached to someone who was about to die.

It's awful, Julia murmured, plodding in perpetual satin slippers.

There was more than ever a coming and going of people on the stairs, the doctors, their spongy, rubber soles, the stiff swish of Miss Chadwick's cap, as well as the step of the dispossessed, Elyot and Eden, these had grown insubstantial under the pressure of events. The relations of the dying emerge again only after the actual death. But you welcomed the forced withdrawal, almost an anaesthesia of the conscious, thinking life. There will be time enough, you felt. Meanwhile you sat numbly evenings, almost physically bruised, you sat, and if you thought at all, it was tomorrow's meal or a bill still unpaid. Elyot watched Eden knitting. She had suddenly taken to knitting, caught from somebody watched in a train. Her hands moved like the hands of the blind, but with determination, afraid of stopping.

On the windowsill, the bulbs that Julia had put there began to flower. For Mrs Standish the suggestion of a crocus, its little golden phallus pressing at the air.

This belonged to a world of physical things, already a far distant mosaic that the memory made. The windowsill was yesterday. Somewhere Willy Standish, the tilted hat, punted down the green scent of water, his arm where the white began, that startled her to see, the whiteness above brown, and hard, it was as hard as blankets pressing down, she could not lift, she could not lift the weight that moistened the forehead, that girl standing on her head who gurgled into pewter, or the red dress she must say to Julia was H.P. or vinegar. Too poignant or too irrelevant the physical world, reduced, like the golden blur on the windowsill. Mrs Standish opened her eyes. Her body drifted in the stream that was not herself, gentle and inevitable. Or it moved in jerks of pain, this was too close, too much the self, as if you were answerable for the act of living, the answer was the racked body. People came and went through this. Sometimes the face passed through, sometimes remained unbearably stereoscopic. And you talked about the things, the flowers that people brought, but already different, confused. The cap above the needle smelt but did not feel of starch. Time became a closing and opening of curtains, a closing and opening of eyes, a closing and a closing, a closing time.

It frightened Julia. The house had dwindled to a single room. You waited for the walls to burst.

It won't be long, Miss Chadwick said.

You would have thought Miss Chadwick was waiting for the bus.

In shadow Eden's hands had grown thinner, as she played out the skein of grey wool. Sound become the grey sigh of wool, the slight protest of bone.

Elyot? said Mrs Standish.

The eyes stared now, focusing out of the distance some intention, or point, of very great importance.

Yes? he said. Yes, Mother?

The silk was wet, she held too tight, the banging of a door against his head.

I wonder, she said, is my hair tidy? It ought – on Friday – There are no pins.

Twenty-four hours later Mrs Standish died.

Now, said Miss Chadwick briskly, you should go and get some rest.

Morning was a broom on the stairs, death the relaxed face, no longer mapped with thought or passion. Elyot looked at a face by morning light. It had the simplicity that was still impossible to grasp, the immensity or simplicity, it was all one, in front of which man wavered, did not completely understand. Soon people would begin to say the kind of things they say about death, to wallow in their own sympathy, or shudder at their own repulsion. But death was a silence best left intact. Dying and death, he said. Dying. It did not fit the mouth. In the street a milk delivery rattled on its way. There were things to see to, details to be arranged.

There were the things, the people, the things, the people. Elyot moved stiffly through the unreal aftermath of death. It was a stiffness increased by the formula custom had already fixed, the line of behaviour laid down for relations of the dead. Sometimes you were glad of this, the set phrases, the rather fusty dignity of an undertaker's voice.

Then Connie Tiarks came. She knocked, and you opened the door. You noticed the gloved fingers dug too tightly into her bag.

Oh, Elyot! Connie said.

She would begin to whimper, it had begun already on her face, the moving forms, the blurred eyes beneath the thick glass. He did not want what Connie was about to give.

To Connie Tiarks the death of Mrs Standish left her without protection, one degree closer to a frightfulness, and all this in spite of the bitter things that Mrs Standish had sometimes said, the things that whipped your cheeks with shame and left you sitting on the chair's edge. The death of Mrs Standish, reported on the telephone, had plunged Connie into a well of temporary despair. She was moved, but lost, at the same time definitely lost. She stood again in her own childhood, the wind chapping her awkward legs, the twigs stinging as she fell through the leaves of the mulberry tree. Poor, poor Mrs Standish, and the awfulness, the pain, said Connie Tiarks. But she shuddered also for herself. She experienced unconsciously the winter nights in buses, and the leery, sideways looks of the old men in buses, the feet that followed down a dark street. Death, the deaths of people she knew, left her isolated. There were noises the other side of the wall. So that pity in Connie Tiarks now had a two-fold significance. It became a very personal matter, her own fear translated into the sympathy she felt for others.

Friday? No, Harry, she said to Harry Allgood. Friday I can't come. Because. Well, you know how I feel. Mrs Standish was a very old friend. It upsets me to think. And besides, there might be something I could do. For Elyot and Eden, I mean.

She heard the pp-pp pp-pp of his pipe, the contained but angry fizz of spittle making contact with the hot bowl. There was something stolid, comforting in the presence of Harry Allgood for which she might have been grateful. But the fizz of the angry spittle was too much. It made her boil. She recognized what was almost perpetual, a desire to take out on Harry any bitterness she felt.

After all, I was practically brought up with them, she said. All my life we've –

The pp-pp of a pipe cut in.

I didn't contradict, he said, sideways, slowly, out of the corner of his mouth.

Silence was more potent than contradiction. Harry had discovered this. He waited. He was seldom moved by exasperation for the waywardness of other people. This exhausted itself in time. You could break it by waiting, as the rock broke the sea, the unimpressionable rocky forms of face and shoulder throwing back a shower of ineffectual passion in the direction from which it came. Walking down the street beside her, this often stirred the helplessness in Connie. She hated, or respected, she did not know, the tweed jacket with its leather elbows, the firm, necessary remarks he passed, which were aimed either to humiliate or to save. But either way, she had to take it out on Harry.

There was the practice in Lichfield, he said.

Oh, she answered, those Midland towns, smoke and dirt, and foreign people.

Harry Allgood offered rock against the spray of criticism.

He still wondered, he said, if she mightn't reconsider, when he had settled in, of course, his proposal; she could take her time.

Because he, it was implied, could take his. Time held no fears for Harry Allgood.

Really, Harry, she said, I've already answered, the difference in ages, for one thing, I've – you make it difficult, she said, I don't think I'll ever marry, I've decided in fact that I definitely shan't.

It was like throwing a bucket of water at a wall.

Tears came into Connie's eyes for her own perversity. The twists of the knife she gave, she knew, were aimed more especially at herself. She lay in bed at night and regretted her unalterable self into a hot pillow. The darkness was exquisitely painful with the little self-tortures that she practised. I am an old maid, she said. She fell asleep playing bezique with old ladies in terraces.

If only had begun to be written on Connie's lumpy face. It advertised its powers of sympathy, the powers that remained untried, because nobody ever called them out. If only the world had been made in a different way. If only the blind could see. It began to be like this. Before Mrs Standish died, frightening Connie, giving a sudden stir to the well of her unexpressed sympathies. There is nothing so violent, so desperate as a kind of unexpressed sympathy and unconfessed aloneness. It took possession of Connie Tiarks. Now is the moment, she felt, trembling at her own decision. Seeing what she hadn't yet done, knowing already her own failure, she couldn't get possession of her own will. She was acting quite outside herself.

The house in Ebury Street still had the atmosphere of death. Or her imagination, the nerve that shuddered with a bell, very quickly endowed it with this. But Connie, walking up the stairs, intent upon the living, hoped that something might have happened to a face, if only you might open the door on a change, out of contact with death the desired change, to walk in and say: You see, I have come, Elyot, I have waited all this time.

Now she waited in the doorway of his room. The fingers tensed, she could feel the things she had inside her bag. She felt inadequate, and clumsy, already fated.

It's nice of you to come just now, Connie.

He would have up tea perhaps for Connie Tiarks. She would sit about and talk of things that had happened. It was not unpleasant. The mind could close in Connie's presence, familiar as the furniture. If she would keep to the recognized routine, not uncover the corner of some hidden emotional life. You still wanted to keep to the substantial forms. You were grateful for the outline of a chair.

Connie was uneasy with intentions, with the things she couldn't say.

There are so many things, Elyot, she said, that I want to, and know I can't say.

She watched, anxious for encouragement.

Then why try to say them, Connie? he said.

Nervously, because it began to fill the room, the emotional surge of Connie's voice. Adelaide Blenkinsop had sent a sheaf of big white lilies from a shop in Berkeley Square. In sympathy. Now the voice of Connie Tiarks had the overpowering scent of lilies.

He had made her look at her hands.

But one likes to try, she said. There are so few people. There are so few occasions on which one can be of use.

Not intending self-pity, or to play a self-conscious part, she hoped she had not given this impression.

One doesn't like to feel oneself – quite one of the – useless ones, she fumbled rather desperately, caught in the tangle of her own pronouns.

No, he said, remotely. Quite. I expect you'd like some tea, Connie.

He threw in her face, what she suspected, her self-pity.

With the arrival of tea things, she launched more safely, she felt, on a biographical sketch of Mrs Standish. A little pointless perhaps, because already known, but he listened to her resurrect the dead, the driftwood incidents of life that did not altogether convince after the final scattering. He crumbled a piece of cake he did not want. Soon she will go, he said.

Soon I shall crumble, she felt, it is happening, there is an end to desperation, there is some word or incident finally responsible.

She listened to the clatter of a spoon on cup.

Whether to give up the house, he was saying.

But to give up all this? she protested. All the associations!

Her voice cheeped out, because Connie wanted to keep even the moments of frustration. She wanted to control, the new, the uncontrollable, time and her own emotions. So her voice swept round the walls, embracing the shape of a room. It beat and fluttered with her glance, as this rested on the mantelpiece, blankly, with surprise and horror. The box from Miss Chilberry's was a cold, white, passive square. It did not help the blood, the blink of stars, it sat calmly at the centre of a spinning universe.

Why, she said, the box! Then you did get the box!

Reminded of an incident, this was as cold as glass, as dead as Muriel Raphael.

Yes, he said. I supposed at first it was Muriel. Then when it wasn't, somehow one just didn't think to inquire.

She sat in a kind of horrified excitement.

I'm glad, Elyot. I thought I'd lost. I left it at a fruit shop. I wanted you to have the box.

She was glad, but doubtful, her voice, her face.

It was very thoughtful of you, Connie. Will you have more tea?

Behind the thick glass, she sat concentrated on some issue that seemed to be taking control of her. He wanted in defence to give her tea.

I would have spoken, she said, and then I thought – Well, after all, the box was lost. But I've wanted, Elyot, to speak about many things. I mean, Elyot, there's such a lot I might do. If only you'd ask me I'd do – do anything you asked.

Her breath fell quickly on the agitated cushion of her under-lip, before she turned, she had to, not exactly hide in a corner, but the face of shame. He noticed that the calves of her legs quivered, full, round, in the black stockings, agonized with shame.

It's always been like that. You wouldn't know, she said. But perhaps it might be different. Now. I don't ask for much. I'm not used to much.

He was fascinated by the calves, which continued to quiver through a situation, to intensify the daze and blur of its un-reality. Something sat on his stomach that he could not lift, or the voice to protest, against the heavy, possessive emotionalism of Connie Tiarks. Vaguely, but unconvincingly, he said: This is a moment for gratitude, this is the reaction that convention expects, and a quiet wedding, in *The Times*, on account of bereavement. Out of just how many similar situations, the moment of sticky, emotional sympathy, had developed quasi-solutions? He had to stop the trembling of the calves.

That's to undervalue yourself, he said.

She listened with her whole body.

Connie, I don't see why you shouldn't, shall we say, expect more.

Because somehow he had to withdraw from the quagmire of emotion in which the body quivered.

Elyot, you're so – so kind. But there's nothing I can – nothing I want to expect. Nothing any more.

Turning, she was over-lifesize. Her face had swollen with the tears that hadn't fallen. Intensity had stripped her. She was almost naked.

Elyot, if you'd understand, she panted. With your kindness. I could help. We're not meant to live in isolation. We're – I could love you, she gasped.

It became an advance, in space, the arms, he could feel the breasts of Connie Tiarks, her now unguarded desperation.

Impulse was to push away the eiderdown that stifled. But behind his resisting hands, he knew he had to speak.

Listen, Connie, he said. This isn't the way. This isn't the way for either of us. Though honestly, I don't know what is. Yet.

She became a restrained panting on his chest.

Then you don't think?

We can be of help to each other in many other ways.

That did not convince, or the too firm hands, you might have labelled it a final answer, which started her again, at the same time as a quivering retreat.

Backing, Connie had dwindled. She was a blotched face, the stooping, apologetic shoulders, she had almost reached her everyday state of humility.

Yes, she said. Perhaps.

Her breath curdled in a long whinge, as her awkward feet caught, it was the claw of the chair, she toppled, you watched, she toppled, she was sitting, lumped, heaped against the skirting board, her face turned outward without surprise.

My dear Connie! he said, bent.

No, she gasped. No. Elyot. Don't! I –

She sat there gasping, like a hen chased and exhausted in the heat.

I don't want, she said. I shall go in a minute.

She got up looking for her bag.

Please don't. I'll just go, she said.

The normal, tentative voice of Connie Tiarks died in the silence that she left.

The street was darker, out of it curved a cold avenue of lights. She walked without looking at faces, that might, she half expected, be aware of what she was hardly aware of herself. Immediately after exorcism, it is hard to believe in the flown passion. But distance soon revived a nagging of shame, and the irritation that became transferred, Harry's red and bony wrists, the way he always pestered her. Walking, she glanced at shops, rather than the faces passed, trying instinctively to make a secret of her thoughts, her face still hot and blotched. Elyot stood alone in his room. She walked alone in Ebury Street, soon would be sucked into the vortex of Victoria. Harry asked for what she couldn't give, just as she couldn't give what Elyot wouldn't take. Heads bent over evening papers, walking home. She was going in the opposite direction. Perpetually, it seemed. In isolation, she began, in the way it happens, she began to over-value the love that Elyot hadn't asked her to give. The sight of a mauve hyacinth suddenly made her snivel. Harry Allgood, in slippers, sat in the armchair in his digs, with his feet propped up on the mantelpiece, this always irritated her, even an image in Ebury Street, that she had to shrug away. But Elyot crumbling cake made her tremble with the immense weight of her Unrequited Love. It was like a film. She thought in the terms of the cinema, would have spoken now in the language of a film, since a moment in the room when her whole behaviour accused her of unreality. There remained the soft, wronged expression she had begun helplessly to wear. She was soft and indifferent, washed on the tide that sucked about Victoria.

Connie loitered in the station yard, to catch or not to catch a bus, she couldn't decide. The large, flat face of the clock marked the time for other people. She stood at the head of a channel, of flowing buses, of approaching forms, the red and black that fused and evened out, until there was no focus point, unless a pointing clock, the long perspective that it made, while offering no decision. At some future date she stood, appalled, on the same spot. She could not rely upon indifference. She began to walk quickly into the station to look for the row of telephone boxes. I shall do this quickly, she said, because it is wiser not to think, I shall simply say, Harry, I shall say. Two pennies fell a long way into the bosom of an iron box. Her nose rather shiny, she began to feel like a sacrifice. I suppose it happens like this very often, she said. She waited for a sign, the waiting that became a window opening on a Midland morning, the calm monotony of eggs and bacon, the morning paper, the morning kiss. Regretfully, she felt, at least this is

343

something tangible. Upstairs Mrs Standish was lying on a bed.

Oh, Harry, she said, pushing Button A. It isn't? Would you? Yes. Allgood. Yes.

Outside the box the night was less of a problem for Connie Tiarks.

Outside, the evening stream ignored individual stagnation. It is now some time since she left, said Elyot, and I am standing here, it is time to draw the curtains.

But Connie's face persisted, altered by a sudden storm, and Connie sitting crumpled by the skirting board. Intensity of passion in Connie Tiarks surprised more than it repelled. There was no end to the unsuspected. Connie was a different person. When you had made for yourself the abstract, selfless Connie, all neatly docketed out of your own intellectual conceit. Then the pressure of the eiderdown. He began to walk about the room. He noticed the box, so intimately connected with the two alternatives, Muriel Raphael or Connie Tiarks. Muriel's voice still rose from time to time out of the telephone, the direct, slaty voice, like a deliberate grey line scored across the black. Muriel offered suggestions, weighed, rational, water-tight. Muriel was not the kind of person to let a relationship lapse, even if its failure, she knew, was partly hers. She could still treat it sensibly, cynically enough. The cynicism was anti-septic, besides saving her face. Cynicism could imply the responsibility was someone else's. All that remained of a rela-tionship had been worked out in a neat geometrical pattern. He accepted this. It was not much less intimate than a more technically intimate Muriel. Because Muriel remained brittle glass, while Connie the possessive eiderdown. Emotional cosi-ness with Connie Tiarks. He looked reflectively at the box. A padding in slippers, in a snug box, surrounded by the many protective devices boosted in women's magazines.

But outside there was a cracking, a splitting of the darkness, that dismissed the two alternatives. He still failed to grasp, but beyond the rotting and the death there was some suggestion of growth. He waited for this in a state of expectation. He waited for something that would happen to him, that would happen in time, there was no going to meet it.

In the morning there would be the funeral.

20

It was Mrs Barnett who had the news. She could not see very well. She rummaged to find her spectacles, stuck behind the canister, the nickel frame of spectacles that now sat formally on her nose. The whole attitude of Mrs Barnett reading a letter, because it happened rarely enough, perhaps a line from a friend at Newcastle, or a cousin on holiday at Scarborough, was official, formal, the gestures that she didn't ordinarily use. She held it out in front of her now, not a letter, but a postcard, that someone had dropped in the mud. She studied, squinted at the information, out of her leathery face, the just deeper-toned skin of the lips moving with the words. The words, in pencil, she could only just see, were from the Irishman Halloran. She could not remember at first, but the pal of Joe's, the crazy bugger that sat spitting in the fire, and talked of the revolution as was coming. Well, and all, the man Halloran, and why, and why, said Mrs Barnett, why Halloran? It was plain enough, what she didn't want to see. She stayed looking at the signed name. Then.

Joe had been killed, said Halloran.

Mrs Barnett stood and held the postcard, the foreign stamp, on it the pretty colours, the foreign words. Outside what had happened was the dripping of a tap. Our Joe, said Mrs Barnett, remotely. She remembered the time he cut his knee, he would clart about with that knife, and the drops of blood in the backyard. He kept pigeons as a boy. There was always a smell of dung in the yard, and the silly, dozy, drooling sound the fantails made. Mrs Barnett began to feel she wanted to sit down. She sat on the upright chair, moving from foot to foot, exhausted and, in a way, resigned.

The poor, more often than not, are more detached in their attitude to death, as if a closeness to possible disaster prepares for the inevitable. And death, even as a personal blow, adds a kind of distinction. Mrs Barnett wiped at her eyes with the hard underside of her fingers. Sundays she sang in chapel, the fierce and saddening hymns that rocked across the yellow varnished wood. As a public mourner, and from conversation with the undertaker, she had appreciated already the dignity of death. This was something to be shared, exalted, not shut away with tears in a room. Mrs Barnett creaked from her chair. She swept back the dank hair from her face. She began to go out at the yard door, where a thin sun touched the cheek. Out of the scent of dung, the dead and distant fantails, as distant as the living Joe, Mrs Barnett went to get her share of pity, to share the dignity of sorrow.

Mrs Barnett's Joe, they said, the teapot frozen on the oil-cloth, the spoon halted in a midday stew. It began to go from house to house. A child, sucking his finger, wondered at the back door. It began to weave across the street, the conventional demonstration of a mass sorrow. They began to make a legend for the dead.

When Julia got in, it was her afternoon, the faces turned to communicate, the women who sat or stood. There was particularly old Mrs Viner, whose husband hit her with a kettle, and the thin young Mrs Cotty, standing stiffly with a belly underneath her apron. Mrs Cotty's mouth hung open. She stared still at the foreign stamp.

There was a stirring of bone, of breath, of silence, as waiting for an explanation. It was Mrs Barnett's privilege.

She sat in the nest of women. She faced Julia as upright as a chair.

It's our Joe, Mrs Barnett was saying. Who'd of thought that our Joe?

Who can ever tell? sighed Mrs Viner. Yes.

No, said Mrs Barnett. When it's done, it's done.

You never know as who, the women echoed.

Julia put down her case on the table. It made the cheap, cardboardy sound of an almost empty cheap case. Voices grated round about her.

But, said Julia Fallon. But –

It came on the postcard, said Mrs Cotty.

It lay in her thin, yellow hand. It had the distinction of a foreign stamp.

Julia's feet began to plod out of the too persistent stare, the shared emotion of the ring of women that she found herself unable to share. Because emotion in Julia was secret, almost indelicate. It was her own, her private business, that she did not care to offer abroad. Now it began to take her, the almost unbearable, pent physical spasm that rocked her on the stair, against the banister he'd always promised to mend but hadn't. She went upstairs. She wanted to get away to her room. What had happened was all bound up with the things she didn't understand, the voices on the wireless that spoke of Abyssinia and Japan, the Government, the paper talk, the politics that Joe. Outside one small box, your head, that was reliable and knowable, there was so much mystery. And death. Joe didn't ought, her breath said. She felt painfully clumsy sitting on the bed, the pain, the solid lump that hadn't yet begun to flow, because there was still the mystification, she couldn't quite see, grasp, either the washstand basin or his face.

Sitting on the bed Julia Fallon could only oppose to the mystery her own too solid flesh, the wheeze that rose from a corset, the thick chugging of the blood through her red and swollen hands. Then it began to move her. It hurt. She began to sway. She swayed with the great weight of what she would be unable to express, only the motion, and the wordless noises that the mouth made, so that the room collapsed, no longer contained a Julia Fallon, she had become a monument to sorrow. Downstairs the women sat. You heard the undertone, the descant of their voices, but little more than the chorus to a tragedy that dwindles round the central figure. This was Julia. She sat with her hands spread upon her knees. She forced her hands upon her knees. There was nothing left for them to do. The knees became a substitute for what you couldn't grasp.

If there was a meaning, there was the dust and the stairs, and then Joe slipping out, there was a Monday washing and the Sunday joint, as if the butcher wouldn't come, or Joe, but Joe, on a postcard come from Spain, she said, that Mrs Cotty with her belly, round and full like a bellyful of trouble, you might have swallowed the whole world, was a bitter taste of tears. Julia Fallon bent her head. She felt the weight at the nape of her neck, where the hair had straggled and kept it white. It was white above the elbows where his shirt turned, and where water ran, in the hollow of his neck, or blood, it will be a world to live in, he said, he said too much, you listened, you heard him say, sometimes like a kid, in the belly under her apron, his head rolled against your chest the time the fever, it hurts to die, Julia, he said, it's you, and that's right, Joe, it's me, as little more than a kid, and did it hurt too, the belly that you didn't, wouldn't have, Julia's got a boy, he said, it was that soft Ernie Flack, as if, if you was my boy, Joe, you said, I'd clout you one over the lug, you're a silly thing, a silly kid. Julia pressed her hands against her stomach. She began to feel empty, tired.

There remained the doing of things. There would always be this. Like a sense of responsibility. Julia held this between herself and the other. There was the bus from Clerkenwell in the sharp spring mornings. There was the morning after. The shops, the houses remained, though you wondered, the eyes gummy from sleep and a kind of sick bewilderment.

In Ebury Street she heard, through her own blunt footfall, the sharper scrubbing of a brush on area stone. Areas opened in the early sunlight. She looked down often to recognize a face. But the brush was a sharp hissing of what was still waiting to be told. Why do swans hiss, Julia? she asked. Come here, hinney, *Eden*, you said, you don't want a bite from a dirty swan, owning the place, the swans, contrary creatures swans. The warning neck of a swan stretched across a distant path. Julia walked dully. Leaving her mind empty, she hoped that something would fill it soon, would find what she had to do, done. Because already the house was there, her hand tightening on the handle of her case, tightening the hand upon the throat against what was going to return.

Light began with Julia every morning. She was the motion of the curtain rings.

She stood looking down. People you serve are most helpless on the pillow. Their unprotected eyes. Looking at Eden, her half-sleep, Julia again remembered swans.

Already? said Eden, her gathering voice.

Julia turned. She bent to pick up a pair of shoes. Action hid what she wanted to hide. Because she had wanted instinctively to take advantage of helplessness, the face upon the pillow only half opened, could have stood accusing in a corner, could have said, said. She's all right, he said. It went on twisting inside her, till the sweat was on her hands. Let the boy breathe, said Mrs Barnett, you're that jealous, Julia, my girl, why, to see you anyone'd think –

Oh dear, sighed Eden, or the last wave of sleep, as it curved, broke, became the bus she would soon take, the early morning coughs of the business men on buses, and cold, smooth pennies in the hand.

Julia did not speak. She was a sharp breathing in the corner, and a stooped behind. Day returned without compromise in Julia's form. Losing the softness of sleep, the face on the pillow hardened into bones, the skull of Eden Standish, in which the light revived a flickering of hopes, of fears. The body braced on the elbows, outside the fallen sheet, resisted what might possibly come. Because Julia, you could sense, an outward pressure of what, that Julia could never disguise, her emotions resisted the attempt, they escaped from the body and flowed round the room.

Julia's eyelids were a heavy red.

You'd better make haste, she said. You haven't the whole morning.

As if she wanted the wardrobe to hear.

Julia, Eden said.

Well?

She didn't want to turn, to find, under the thin nightdress the body that already knew too much. The clever ones, Julia said, there's the ones that don't know and the ones that give, but the ones that know and the ones that take, these are the clever ones. Her hand tightened on her skirt, feeling for her self-control.

I'll go and make your coffee, she said.

From the bed Eden, she felt white, frozen in the folds of sheet. Across the passage the clock had stopped. This was the morning she had been expecting.

No, she said. Julia!

Little remained in the room but their two stripped faces.

Well, said Julia, the thick voice. There's no other way but to know, she said.

To hurt or to protect. She stood above the bed, it was still the child, it was also that thin body, that you didn't want to look, because.

Yes, it's happened, she said, it tumbled. And somebody's had their way. Though what's the good, I'll never know. No one'll ever tell me that. To throw away what you've got. It's little enough, but to throw away. Of course, I don't understand. I'm the one as must take what I'm told. It's better that way, they say. I wouldn't understand. No, Eden, and I don't. I'll never understand why. What it's all about.

Thinned out, the voice stood still, like your own heart, your own fears. Outside the bed it was still cold. And the glass. To press your face against a window. A key down the back, they said. Eden held her face against the window, the line of roofs, the numb trees.

We had a postcard telling us. Just that he was killed, said Julia.

It was like the last line in an obituary. Now was the moment to add your own word for the dead. The letters of friends. But to have known too intimately turned the platitude to a shrinking of the body against glass. When the body has learnt its purpose at the hands of the dead, it fails to convince, becomes a fleshy shroud.

I'll go and make your coffee, Julia said.

While there was still time to call out: Wait, Julia, this is something that concerns us both, something we must both bear – the voice would not come. Julia implied that this was her own ground, on which no one must encroach. All the physical aspects of the dead, these would be stored in Julia's mind, the clothes sorted, the pipe left on the mantelpiece. Some stiff concrete image of the man, sitting in the kitchen perhaps, or a boy playing in the yard, would remain Julia's conception of the dead. Because the dead are what you make them, a personal matter, unshared.

Eden felt the cold begin to touch her body. She was alone now. The stockings hung waiting, sloughed and empty on the arm of the chair. The sense of aloneness, this is also a personal matter, she knew, this is no different from any morning, the sounds just restored to the house, except, except that somewhere, on a Spanish field or mountainside, twisted in the roots of the trees, in this same white light, there lies a little of myself. Drawing on her stockings, she began to shiver. She wanted not to think of the body, the kindness of the body, the many articulate ways it can have. It was easy to over-value these, and to set up the physical image as Julia did. But there were the other, the more pervasive moments that flower in the desert places of the mind or room.

Hatless, she went out later into the street. News was on the placards. Lorries made their early way, possessing the streets with a great, persistent chugging of their wheels. Feet marched along the scooped pavement, over the ploughed field. Place was of very little importance, or individual activity, except as part of a pattern of history or behaviour. She had left her face a blank. In time it would return, she supposed, some positive expression.

Time and habit began to knit across the tear. She did not reckon the so many weeks.

She sat across from Elyot, who tried to make suggestions, always now, that she might have resented once. His hands were nervous in the gesture that went with his voice, as if he were uncertain just how far. She watched the hands across the same table at which they had always sat.

Elyot spoke of selling the house.

Now that we're alone, he said.

Or was this a clumsiness, he wondered, the little shiver of a shocked glass that accompanied her agreement. His voice, it seemed to him, composed a perpetual monologue. Here and there, only rarely, she reached and broke it. But she wanted it like this, you felt, the lifeline of comment and suggestion. She wanted you to say: Now we shall do this or that. Remotely, inside her, something was still perfecting itself. Intent on this process of gestation, she let herself be led.

He said it was time to turn on the light. He said it was time for dinner. He said, if she put on her hat, they would go to a film.

They sat in the warm, plushy, accommodating cinema atmosphere. You adapted yourself as a matter of course, the relaxed body to plush and, more important, the relaxed mind to the play of predetermined incident. That was the virtue of the cinema. You knew on paying your two-and-six, you knew exactly what would happen. Outside your own uncertainty. On the screen, the moist and stereoscopic lips bent for the expected kiss. You could reach out almost and touch the lips. But returning to the elbow on the chair-arm, your own or Eden's, a matter of inches, here the unpredictable began, a common zone of uncertainty.

Eden stirred.

Two lovers and a tree faded into a perspective of the Boulevard Raspail. It began to be hot, a dissolving world of sepia and plush. Round about, the rapt women, heavy with mink and their own accepted uselessness. But dissolving irrelevant, the auditorium or screen. Already perhaps the body had begun to undergo its change, the soft, speechless faces of the worms pressing at the chest and loins. But this, you had decided, was unimportant, or only important as a state of becoming, of change. To throw away what is little enough, said Julia. As if it began and ended in the moment. As if it excluded the state of change.

A long way off, with a conviction that began to have a partial relevance, a man in a cap had begun to force a safe.

She sat with her hands held tightly in her lap. Soon it will be over, she said, I have been waiting for this, to know at last with certainty, to find out what is inside.

She came in about the time she usually came in from work. He continued with his paper, heard her moving to do something, to arrange flowers, he could hear the trimming of the stems, smell their sudden pungent smell.

I've decided, Elyot, I shall go to Spain, she said, in the casual way Eden dealt with moments of importance.

The voice did not ask for criticism or advice. This was a crisp statement. You heard the breaking of a stem.

When? he asked.

About ten days' time.

He sat looking at a sheet of news, what the Japanese, what Joe Barnett, a Council of War in Tokyo, or Eden taking trains, it wore the same face, was the same muddle, from which you woke at night to find tied sheets, go to sleep, said Julia, it's a dream, go to sleep like a good boy, here's a biscuit for under your pillow, it's a nightmare, she said, it's a tangle, that Eden's face struggled to unravel, very intently in the corner of a room, I shall be an airman, she said, even if I fall in the sea. Even if I fall in the sea, the voice repeated now, against the breaking of the stems. Eden's voice accepted the sea. You began to feel they had given you a sense too few, the sense of sacrifice. He felt smug sitting in slippers. Or what was sacrifice, a perpetual walking in the same tangle, Joe and Eden, saying soon we shall find it, soon, but where, it became a thin and timeless echo.

Oh, but I'm tired, she said.

He could hear her sitting down. Out of the silence now not even a breathing.

Well, he said.

What?

I should say something. This is the moment where one should.

He watched her sitting, the edges of her face, white round the protecting hands. She was tired, she said, but to protect a face.

No, she sighed.

Eden was as stubborn in an attitude, as unchanging as a picture on the wall, the surprised child or the sulky flapper, was the same Eden in a different frame.

No, she said. Don't let's argue.

But, Eden, the futility of this. And Joe.

That at once he wished unsaid.

Yes, she said. The futility of Joe, as Joe. Just another drop. But the many Joe Barnetts, Elyot. It's the drops that fill the bucket.

Her voice began to sound hollow from behind her hands.

It's the bucket that'll make the splash, she said.

The voice spoke from a distance. As if Eden had already undergone some process of physical destruction. She was convinced of the rightness of this, just as you were convinced there was some other way, not so very different perhaps, the means different, if not the end. You were aware of the same end. The arch-enemies were the stultifying, the living dead. The living chose to oppose these, either in Eden's way, by the protest of self-destruction, or by what, by what, if not an intenser form of living.

Out of the distance he watched her gather up the pieces of stalk she had broken off. He watched her twist them in a sheet of paper.

About ten days' time, she had said.

The people remembered from a voyage are the people met too late. We have been stupid, proud, insensitive, blind, you say, not that it helps, it is still too late. These are the regrets, standing on a wharf or waiting on a platform for different trains. You can only watch the moment recede down the perspective of the eyes, turn the back on the nostalgic smell of too possessive trains.

Julia snivelled at the last moment.

You ought to take food. It's a long journey. Though there's always the buffy, Julia said.

But for Julia, it was too painful, the tragedy of empty hands. Julia stood in a doorway watching goodbye.

Goodbye, goodbye, Eden called.

You watched the waving, wondering, the flutter of a strange black-gloved hand.

Come, we'll be late, Elyot said.

Upstairs a curtain waved outward from an open window. Waiting, watching from the street, he felt cold. In the pit of his stomach a fluttering that was like the desperation of a curtain waving in the wind.

Eden said there was plenty of time.

She was calm, could afford to be calm, with so much decided. It was only a matter of walking out of the house. But your things, Julia said. Yes, she said, my things, but I shan't want much, Julia. Looking into a drawer these were just things, altogether superfluous, like many discarded events of your past life. She had listened without a twinge to the closing of a drawer. A door.

They were walking down the street.

Look at the time, Elyot said.

No, she said again. We have plenty of time.

Which was true. Because in a minute, standing on a station platform, you could relive a whole existence. In the station there was a creaking, a groaning, a hissing, an outline in black to the parting faces, and the less defined shapes from the past.

They stood in the black smell of trains. Waiting. A basket of unnaturally complexioned apples shone near by on a stall shelf, till distance shrivelled, you smelt the atticful of summer, or under trees the grass played against the legs, the cedar pencils sharpened at eleven, spilled out into the station grime. Eden's mouth, you looked, was a flicker of recognition. Outside the sighing of an anxious piston, there was still the bay, smooth, almost circular, the glistening of red and periwinkle stones. You went down alone. This was a secret expedition. To lie on the back, the sun glistened on the teeth, a hot sinking of the bones. Eden turned to say, say, the bay, you would have said, remember, as if it were possible that Eden, except at this moment. There are the moments, the moments on railway platforms, when there are no barriers to recognition.

A crying Jewess held a crumpled handkerchief to her face. You listened to the anxious piston, the last words. Eden was removed now. She dealt in solid, detached words. The little Jewess turned her back.

I expect Julia will have gone, said Eden. But I told her to leave some bread and cheese. You'll find it in the kitchen. Some bread and cheese.

You suspected she was trying to insist on fact. She had to plank down the cheese. One lived, after all, in a world of substance, of fact.

Then it was time, he knew, he was watching the flutter of a gloved hand fail where the darkness swam against the greenish light. He was turning his back on nothing. There was very little indication now that he would ever see Eden again.

21

Already he was drifting in a half-resentful, half-reassured lethargy with the many themes that the house offered, only muted on his first opening the door. The house was a receptacle.

They were two receptacles, he felt, the one containing the material possessions of those who had lingered in its rooms, the other the aspirations of those he had come in contact with. Even that emotional life he had not experienced himself, but sensed, seemed somehow to have grown explicit. It was as if this emanated from the walls to find interpretation and shelter in his mind. So that the two receptacles were clearly united now. They were like two Chinese boxes, one inside the other, leading to an infinity of other boxes, to an infinity of purpose. Alone, he was yet not alone, uniting as he did the themes of so many other lives.

He had sat how long, since the station, in the empty house? A queasy drunk still sidled uneasily along the carpet's edge. You accepted him now. It got to being part of yourself, said Joe, like the disappearing glove, like the face that crumbled under rouge, like Onkel Rudi's gramophone, as if you can keep it parcelled out, because it's right here, Elyot, sure as ever there's right and wrong. Or not so particularly confined, it flowed, it overflowed, a gritty protest of the walls that opened out, rain that passed across the mouth, the wheeze of mortar falling, and of powdered brick. All this has served its purpose, you felt.

Again he walked downstairs. He began again to walk along the street, guided by no intention, taking the direction offered. The house, the shell of the house, pitched its last comment through an open window. The curtain jerked at its rings. It still blew outward in the wind. It moved. It made the landscape move. There was no fixed point, either the long and shiny ribbon of the pavement, or the fiery hub that became Victoria.

The labels on buses expected a choice. He watched the coming and going of the buses, the meeting and flowing. He watched with a disbelief in the final destination of buses, Islington, Homerton, Camberwell. But there was the Chinese box, the infinity of boxes. The toffee-coloured terraces of Islington moved into place beside the frozen derricks of Rotherhithe. The buses became significant enough, the red threads that moved across the darkness, joining its component parts. There was no end to darkness, but there was no end also to its unity, watching the movement of the buses.

Faces peered from behind glass, gone before they had established their expressions, would be shuttled out in all directions, pale and unprotesting. But the faces in the night buses were potentially communicative. They huddled, face on hand. They swayed in the protective atmosphere of herded bodies, the peppermint drop with the steaming macintosh, the mingling of heliotrope and sweat. They touched in a haze from the last pint that merged these ordinarily hostile smells and made them for the moment compatible. But soberly, by daylight, you lived a life of segregation, recovered the instinctive defences, the compartment of a face.

A bus received Elyot Standish. It was any bus. He was bound nowhere in particular. There were no reservations of time or place, no longer even the tyranny of a personal routine. It was enough to feel a darkness, a distance unfurling. There was no end to this in the bus, trundling down its dark tunnel, in which the faces smiled gravely out of sleep, the mouths almost spoke. If only to touch these almost sentient faces into life, to reach across the wastes of sleep and touch into recognition with your hand, to listen to the voices, like the voices of people who wake and find they have come to the end of a journey, saying: Then we are here, we have slept, but we have really got here at last.

He yawned. He felt like someone who had been asleep, and had only just woken.

FOR THE BEST IN PAPERBACKS, LOOK FOR THE

In every corner of the world, on every subject under the sun, Penguin represents quality and variety – the very best in publishing today.

For complete information about books available from Penguin – including Puffins, Penguin Classics and Arkana – and how to order them, write to us at the appropriate address below. Please note that for copyright reasons the selection of books varies from country to country.

In the United Kingdom: Please write to *Dept E.P., Penguin Books Ltd, Harmondsworth, Middlesex, UB7 0DA.*

If you have any difficulty in obtaining a title, please send your order with the correct money, plus ten per cent for postage and packaging, to *PO Box No 11, West Drayton, Middlesex*

In the United States: Please write to *Dept BA, Penguin, 299 Murray Hill Parkway, East Rutherford, New Jersey 07073*

In Canada: Please write to *Penguin Books Canada Ltd, 2801 John Street, Markham, Ontario L3R 1B4*

In Australia: Please write to the *Marketing Department, Penguin Books Australia Ltd, P.O. Box 257, Ringwood, Victoria 3134*

In New Zealand: Please write to the *Marketing Department, Penguin Books (NZ) Ltd, Private Bag, Takapuna, Auckland 9*

In India: Please write to *Penguin Overseas Ltd, 706 Eros Apartments, 56 Nehru Place, New Delhi, 110019*

In the Netherlands: Please write to *Penguin Books Netherlands B.V., Postbus 3507, 1001 AH, Amsterdam*

In West Germany: Please write to *Penguin Books Ltd, Friedrichstrasse 10–12, D–6000 Frankfurt/Main 1*

In Spain: Please write to *Alhambra Longman S.A., Fernandez de la Hoz 9, E–28010 Madrid*

In Italy: Please write to *Penguin Italia s.r.l., Via Como 4, 1-20096 Pioltello (Milano)*

In France: Please write to *Penguin Books Ltd, 39 Rue de Montmorency, F-75003 Paris*

In Japan: Please write to *Longman Penguin Japan Co Ltd, Yamaguchi Building, 2–12–9 Kanda Jimbocho, Chiyoda-Ku, Tokyo 101*

The Outsider   Albert Camus

Meursault leads an apparently unremarkable bachelor life in Algiers, until his involvement in a violent incident calls into question the fundamental values of society. 'The protagonist of *The Outsider* is undoubtedly the best achieved of all the central figures of the existential novel' – *Listener*

Another Country   James Baldwin

'Let our novelists read Mr Baldwin and tremble. There is a whirlwind loose in the land' – *Sunday Times*. *Another Country* draws us deep into New York's Bohemian underworld of writers and artists as they betray, love and test each other – men and women, men and men, black and white – to the limit

I'm Dying Laughing   Christina Stead

A dazzling novel set in the 1930s and 1940s when fashionable Hollywood Marxism was under threat from the savage repression of McCarthyism. 'The Cassandra of the modern novel in English' – Angela Carter

Christ Stopped at Eboli   Carlo Levi

Exiled to a barren corner of southern Italy for his opposition to Mussolini, Carlo Levi entered a world cut off from history, hedged in by custom and sorrow, without comfort or solace, where, eternally patient, the peasants lived in an age-old stillness, and in the presence of death – for Christ did stop at Eboli.

The Expelled and Other Novellas   Samuel Beckett

Rich in verbal and situational humour, these four stories offer the reader a fascinating insight into Beckett's preoccupation with the helpless individual consciousness.

Chance Acquaintances and Julie de Carneilhan   Colette

Two contrasting works in one volume. Colette's last full-length novel, *Julie de Carneilhan* was 'as close a reckoning with the elements of her second marriage as she ever allowed herself'. In *Chance Acquaintances*, Colette visits a health resort, accompanied only by her cat.

BY THE SAME AUTHOR

Riders in the Chariot

In *The Tree of Man* Patrick White re-created the Garden of Eden in Australia; *Riders in the Chariot*, his story of four outcast mystics, powerfully re-enacts the story of the crucifixion in a like setting.

'Stands out among contemporary novels like a cathedral surrounded by booths. Its forms, its impulse and its dedication to what is eternal all excite a comparison with religious architecture. Mr White's characters . . . have the symbolism of statues and spires' – Maurice Edelman in the *Sunday Times*

'This is a book which really defies review: for its analysable qualities are overwhelmed by those imponderables which make a work "great" in the untouchable sense. It must be read because, like Everest, "it is there"' – Jeremy Brooks in the *Guardian*

The Solid Mandala

This is the story of two people living one life. Arthur and Waldo Brown were born twins and destined never to grow away from each other.

They spent their childhood together. Their youth together. Middle-age together. Retirement together. They even shared the same girl.

They shared everything – except their views of things.

Waldo, with his intelligence, saw everything and understood little. Arthur was the fool who didn't bother to look. He understood.

BY THE SAME AUTHOR

The Tree of Man

'A monumental, moving epic' – *The Times*

This great novel could fittingly claim to stand as the Australian Book of Genesis. A young man, at the turn of the century, takes a wife and carves out a home in the wilderness near one of the growing cities of Australia. Stan Parker becomes a small farmer: he accepts life as he finds it. To him Amy bears children and time brings a procession of ordinary events – achievements, disappointments, sorrows, dramas, dreams. There is the daily intercourse with neighbours of their kind and at the end death walks in the garden.

Voss

The plot of this novel is of epic simplicity: in 1845 Voss sets out with a small band to cross the Australian continent for the first time. The tragic story of their terrible journey and its inevitable end is told with imaginative understanding.

The figure of Voss takes on superhuman proportions, until he appears to those around him as both deliverer and destroyer. His relationship with Laura Trevelyan is the central personal theme of the story.

The true record of Ludwig Leichardt, who died in the Australian desert in 1848, suggested *Voss* to the author.

BY THE SAME AUTHOR

The Twyborn Affair

Eddie Twyborn is bisexual and beautiful, the son of a judge and a drunken mother. With this androgynous hero – Eudoxia/Eddie/Eadith Twyborn – and through his search for identity, for self-affirmation and love in its many forms, Patrick White takes us on a journey into the ambiguous landscapes, sexual, psychological and spiritual, of the human condition.

'It challenges comparison with some of the world's most bizarre masterpieces' – Isobel Murray in the *Financial Times*

The Burnt Ones

Eleven stories to which Patrick White brings his immense understanding of the urges which lie just beneath the façade of ordinary human relationships, especially those between men and women . . .

A girl, beset by her mother's influence, who marries her father's friend . . . A young man strangely moved into marriage with a girl like the mother who never understood him . . . A pretty market researcher who learns the ultimate details of love with a difference . . . The collector of bird calls who unwittingly records the call of a very human nature.

Flaws in the Glass

A Self-Portrait

With force, candour and emotion, Patrick White writes of his youth in Australia, his English boarding school, his life at Cambridge and trips to Germany, London during the Blitz, RAF wartime intelligence in the Middle East and his first meeting with the man who was to become the central focus of his life.

'A singularly penetrating act of self-scrutiny, a cold, calculating stare into the mirror of the artist's life' – David Lodge in the *Sunday Times*

BY THE SAME AUTHOR

A Fringe of Leaves

With *A Fringe of Leaves* Patrick White has richly justified his Nobel Prize. Set in Australia in the 1840s, this novel combines dramatic action with a finely distilled moral vision. It is a masterpiece.

Returning home to England from Van Dieman's Land, the *Bristol Maid* is shipwrecked on the Queensland coast and Mrs Roxburgh is taken prisoner by a tribe of aborigines, along with the rest of the passengers and crew. In the course of her escape, she is torn by conflicting loyalties – to her dead husband, to her rescuer, to her own and to her adoptive class.

The Cockatoos

These six short novels and stories achieve the majesty and power of the best of Patrick White's great novels. They probe beneath the confused and meretricious surface, exposing the true nature of things with chiselled, polished images.

'To read Patrick White . . . is to touch a source of power, to move through areas made new and fresh, to see men and women with a sharpened gaze' – Elizabeth Berridge in the *Daily Telegraph*

'It is good to be reminded, by a masterly new collection of short stories, *The Cockatoos*, how brilliant Mr White can be' – Francis King in the *Sunday Telegraph*

Also published

Memoirs of Many in One
The Aunt's Story
The Eye of the Storm